The hinges creaked as she pushed on the ancient wood door. It was surprisingly heavy. Having opened it enough to stick her head through, she peered into the alleyway and was surprised to see it full of potted plants. Further down it appeared to open up into a lovely garden between the tall stone buildings. At the end of the alley, she thought she could see eyes peering out at her from the bushes.

She'd already pushed the door fully open and put one foot inside when her brain finally kicked in.

She stopped.

Despite the seeming innocence of the alleyway, something felt off. Lily finally realized it was the plants. They seemed greener, more…intense. As if more fully real than reality itself. Not only that, but they also appeared wild. Unkempt. Untamed. The garden in front of her didn't look at all like the carefully tended and trimmed courtyards and quadrangles that appeared all over Oxford.

Taking a step back, she stood in the doorway, thinking. It was then that the silver fox, perhaps in response to her hesitation, poked its head out of the bush. It examined her, then emerged fully and sat in the middle of the alley, head cocked to the side as if asking why she was taking so long.

Now that was most definitely not right. No matter how curious she was, she knew better than to wander into strange gardens alone with creatures that acted abnormally friendly. That was Wizarding 101. But she couldn't just leave. The alley had appeared for a reason, and it might be important.

Also by Lydia Sherrer:

THE LILY SINGER ADVENTURES SERIES

Love, Lies, and Hocus Pocus Book 1: *Beginnings*
Love, Lies, and Hocus Pocus Book 2: *Revelations*
Love, Lies, and Hocus Pocus Book 3: *Allies*
Love, Lies, and Hocus Pocus Book 4: *Legends*
(books 5-6 coming in 2019!)

The Lily Singer Adventures Novellas:
Love, Lies, and Hocus Pocus: *A Study In Mischief*
Love, Lies, and Hocus Pocus: *Cat Magic (coming soon!)*

Dark Roads Trilogy (Sebastian's Origin)
Book 1: *Accidental Witch*

OTHER WORKS

When the Gods Laughed: Part 1

Hope: A Short Story

1046091

LOVE, LIES &
HOCUS POCUS
⊶ LEGENDS ⊷

The Lily Singer Adventures
Book 4

LYDIA SHERRER

Chenoweth Press

LOVE, LIES, AND HOCUS POCUS
The Lily Singer Adventures Book 4: Legends

ISBN 13: 978-0-9973391-7-8 (paperback)
ISBN: 978-0-9973391-8-5 (ebook)

Published by Chenoweth Press 2017
Louisville, KY, USA

Cover design by Molly Phipps: wegotyoucoveredbookdesign.com

Chapter illustrations by Serena Thomas

To my super fans, who care more than they should, thank God

Acknowledgments

Many overflowing thanks to the people who made this book happen. There were my faithful beta readers who met ridiculous deadlines, not to mention my ever-loyal super fans who give me motivation to keep writing with their unabashed enthusiasm. Then there's my wonderful editor, Lori Brown Patrick, who still seems to think I'm worth her time. Much thanks to my exceptionally skilled and patient cover artist, Tony Warne, and illustrator, Serena Thomas. Both of them have to put up with my picky perfectionism and, believe me, I'm fortunate they haven't kicked me to the curb yet. Huge, huge thanks to the vibrant and positive writing groups I'm a part of on Facebook who share so much advice, aid, and encouragement. I've grown exponentially in the midst of such amazing fellow authors. I'm also indebted to Pat and Cindy Tinney, Stephen Logsdon, Tony and Kae Thompson, David and Jun Mcinteer, and Ted and Beth Thomas whose generosity helped make this book happen. Most special thanks to my wonderful parents, who brag on me shamelessly, and sisters, who only roll their eyes a little bit when I start talking about books. And lastly, to my beloved husband, my best friend in the world and the most faithful and hard-working partner I could ever ask for.

Contents

Episode 8
The Good Fight

Cast of Characters

Main:

Lily Singer - introverted wizard, library archivist in Atlanta, GA

Sebastian Blackwell - ne'er-do-well "professional" witch, Lily's best friend

Sir Edgar Allan Kipling - talking cat, Lily's closest companion, Lily is "his" human

Madam Ethel Barrington - wizard, Lily's mentor/teacher, Sebastian's great-great-aunt

John Faust LeFay - wizard, Lily's father, plots to revive wizard race and rule mundanes

Lily's Family:

Allen LeFay - wizard, John Faust's younger brother, Lily's uncle

Trista - mundane, John Faust's daughter, Lily's half sister, skilled fighter

Caden - wizard, John Faust's son, Lily's half brother

Freda Singer - wizard, Lily's mother, formerly Freda LeFay

Jamie Singer - wizard (untrained), Lily's half brother by her mundane stepfather

Sebastian's Family:

George Dee - wizard, Sebastian's great-grandfather, lives in England

Day Barrington Dee - mundane, George's wife, Madam Barrington's sister, deceased

Elizabeth Dee Blackwell - mundane, George's daughter, Sebastian's grandmother

Stephen Blackwell - wizard, Elizabeth's husband, mysteriously disappeared

Thomas Blackwell - wizard, Sebastian's father, deceased

Alison Blackwell - mundane, Sebastian's mother, deceased

Frederick Blackwell - wizard (untrained), Sebastian's brother

ENGLISH CAST:

Nigel Hawkins - mundane, George's manservant, lent to Lily and Sebastian

Helen Pemberton - wizard, Bodleian library system administrator at Oxford University

Cyril Hawtrey - wizard, history professor at Oxford University

Emmaline Nichols - mundane, designer and seamstress for her family business

Mary Falconer - mundane, friendly local

FAE:

Kaliar/Kaliel - fae king and queen, the dualities of growth

Thiriar/Thiriel - fae king and queen, the dualities of decay

Urdiar - high fae, a duality of earth/soil

Shariel - high fae, a duality of plants

Yuki - a duality of the aspect of fox, loves to annoy Sir Kipling

Pip - low fae of the aspect of plants, specifically flowers, loves rum

Grimmold - low fae of the aspect of decay, specifically mold, loves aged pizza

Episode 7

The Calm
Before the Storm

Chapter 1
A HOP ACROSS THE POND

LILY SOMETIMES WONDERED WHY HEALTH INSURANCE DIDN'T COVER THE COST of cat ownership. It really ought to, since cats were one of the leading contributors to stress reduction and overall happiness in households across the nation. They were one hundred percent natural and had no harmful side effects—well, if you ignored the hair. She supposed, to be fair, it should cover dog ownership as well. But dogs didn't purr, so they were at a distinct disadvantage in the stress-reduction department.

At the very least, she thought she should get some sort of premium discount, since Sir Edgar Allan Kipling—her snarky, obstreperous, talking cat—was solely responsible for preventing a variety of health complications over the past twenty-four hours. Heart attack. Anxiety attack. If-you-do-that-one-more-time-I'm-going-to-kill-you attack. The therapeutic effect of burying one's face in a fuzzy cat tummy knew no bounds.

Not having a heart attack was a good thing, since the fate of wizardkind currently rested on her shoulders. Being a socially awkward introvert didn't help, and she'd long ago admitted she needed all the friends and allies she could get. Which brought her back to the heart attack. It was an understandable concern, considering that her most powerful ally lay near death, afflicted by an unknown curse.

Madam Ethel Barrington was Lily's friend, mentor, and instructor in the wizarding arts. Though the woman was more than a hundred years old by Lily's best guess—wizards aged well, she didn't look a day over seventy—she'd always been a pillar of wisdom and stability in Lily's life. Now she lay cold and ashen as the grave, and Lily was trying very hard not to panic.

Lily sat by her mentor's sickbed in her uncle Allen LeFay's townhouse situated in the heart of historic Savannah, Georgia. Though one of the more modest of Savannah's historic homes, it was nonetheless an impressive example of antebellum architecture with its high ceilings, wood-paneled floors, and plaster walls complete with crown molding. Madam Barrington's room was clean and well lit by sunlight streaming in from four tall windows, two each on the east and north walls. Privacy was preserved thanks to a handy spell that made it appear from the outside as if the curtains were drawn. Allen didn't like mundanes nosing about, and there were plenty in this city full of curious tourists.

Despite the sunlight, however, and copious layers of warm blankets, Madam Barrington's hand was still deathly cold as Lily gripped it between both of hers, keeping silent vigil beside the bed. Her heart felt as cold as the hand she clutched, and just as immune to the sunlight. Back aching, limbs stiff, and eyes stinging with weariness, Lily tried not to think too much as she watched the slow, almost imperceptible rise and fall of her mentor's chest. But with nothing else to occupy her thoughts, like iron to a magnet they inevitably gravitated back toward the cause of this whole mess: her father, John Faust LeFay.

It had been less than twenty-four hours since their…confrontation. Though to call it a confrontation was a bit of an understatement. If you asked her best friend, Sebastian Blackwell, he would have described it as an epic battle between good and evil. Which was why she rarely let him explain things: he liked to exaggerate. She supposed he deserved a break in this instance, however, since he *had* gotten his butt soundly kicked by her half sister Trista. The young mundane was a veritable expert in armed and unarmed combat and had unfortunately been brainwashed by their father to help him in his grand plan to "save" the wizard race and bring about an age of "benevolent" wizard rule. So from Sebastian's perspective she supposed it had been an epic battle. He'd had to use every bit of his fae magic—acquired in a trade, as was the witches' way—along with his own natural wiles to eventually run her off.

And that was the other reason Lily preferred to think of it as a "confrontation." They hadn't won. Oh, they'd rescued Allen and freed the other wizard children John Faust had been raising as his brainwashed minions. And John Faust had fled, along with Trista and her wizard half brother, Caden. But they hadn't won. Madam Barrington had been almost killed by one of John Faust's curses, and their adversaries had escaped with knowledge of Morgan le Fay's location. Morgan was one of the most powerful wizards from the past two millennia—and Lily's ancestor. There was no telling what kind of power John Faust might obtain from her, whether she was still alive or not.

What with John Faust getting a head start, her mentor being fatally ill, and knowing she had to go to England and fix it all, alone, it was a testament to the power of Sir Kipling's purr that she hadn't lost it already. Alright, so, not quite alone. Sir Kipling would be coming, and then there was Sebastian.

"How's she doing?"

The soft voice behind her made her jump, and she turned to make shushing motions at Sebastian's bright-eyed, boyish face as it poked around the door into Madam Barrington's sickroom. Turning back to the bed, she gently released the ice-cold hand she'd been holding and laid it on the covers, trying not to think how like a corpse her mentor looked. It was the blue lips and grey skin that did it, and the fact that her breathing was so shallow it seemed nonexistent. To make Madam Barrington more comfortable, Lily had taken down her strict bun and combed out the grey hair to cascade over her shoulders. It was the first time Lily had ever seen the older woman's hair down. It made her look more vulnerable. More human.

With a sigh she moved away, pausing to pet Sir Kipling, currently stationed in a catloaf on the older woman's chest, where his warmth and purring would do the most good. Then she slipped out of the bedroom—the last room at the end of the hall—giving Sebastian a weary shrug as she quietly answered his question. "I can't see any change yet. Allen seems sure his antidote will at least get her conscious, but I can't help worrying. What if she doesn't wake up? I can't bear the thought of leaving before we know she'll be okay."

Though she fought to hold it back, moistness formed in the corners of her eyes and threatened to spill down over her cheeks.

"Hey, hey. It's gonna be fine." Sebastian assured her, giving her shoulder a comforting squeeze, then leaving his hand there. While its warmth was not unwelcome, what she really wanted was to wrap her arms around him and bury her face in his collar. That was out of the question, of course, so she compromised by leaning forward slightly to rest her forehead on his chest and taking deep, slow breaths to calm her emotions.

While she was eternally grateful for his friendship and knew she couldn't have gotten this far without him, he did create his own set of problems, though not exactly the ones you'd expect. The fact that he was a witch was a non-issue, even though witches and wizards were traditionally rivals. Being born with magic, wizards tended to distrust and look down on witches for their wheeling and dealing to acquire magic for themselves. But Lily and Sebastian had long since decided to ignore the traditions of their elders. The fact that he was a ne'er-do-well who considered rules to be more like guidelines was, surprisingly, not a major problem, either. He had a good heart and always meant well, even if he drove her crazy.

No, the biggest problem was that she had finally, sort of, almost admitted that she loved him. She hadn't spoken about it openly, but the fact that she had progressed from denial to semi-acceptance was a huge step for an awkward, controlling, up-tight introvert like herself. Of course, the most sensible thing to do would be to ignore her feelings and get on with the task ahead. The problem was, she didn't know if she wanted to be sensible anymore.

Staring at the polished wood under her feet, she felt Sebastian's chest rise and fall in a sigh of his own, making her uncomfortably aware of how close they were. Raising her head and stepping back, she turned to stare out the hall window that looked over the busy street below, giving absent, one-word answers to Sebastian's concerned queries.

The whole relationship issue was made more complicated by this life-threatening adventure they'd been sucked into, clouding her judgment with worry and fear. Everything depended on her. With Allen recovering from his own injuries while simultaneously nursing Madam Barrington, Lily was the only wizard with the necessary knowledge to track down Morgan le Fay before John Faust. They might already be too late. Who knew how long it would take them to puzzle out her location from their copy of the ancient journal Morgan had left behind? John Faust, on the other hand, had already discovered her resting place, using a location spell he'd devised. A spell he'd channeled through her Uncle Allen, almost killing him.

They'd "confronted" John Faust too late to stop him using the spell, but at least they'd survived the encounter intact and had deprived her father of his base of operations. The old mental ward he'd been using as a magical laboratory was now an FBI crime scene where Agent Richard Grant—their contact in the agency—was busy leading the investigation against his illegal activities. Not that the FBI knew anything about John Faust's larger plans. They thought he was just some crazy cultist wacko. Lily wished it were that simple.

The worst part was, she agreed with her father. Not with his methods, of course. They were deplorable. But his goal to repopulate the wizard race was a noble one, especially since most wizards were in denial about their slow decline and eventual extinction. Even her father's vision of ruling mundane society, putting an end to their petty wars while using magic to make people's lives better, was a laudable goal. Supremacist, racist, arrogant, and wildly idealistic, but still, laudable. If her father hadn't been such a miserable excuse for a human being, she might have been tempted to join him. But having already been held captive by him and experimented on herself, she'd thoroughly and irrevocably burned those bridges. Her father was wrong. The ends did *not* justify the means, and no amount of future good could justify present immorality.

Lost in her own dark thoughts, she became aware of Sebastian again only when he gripped her by the shoulders and gave her a gentle shake. "Hey. Hey! Are you hearing me, Lil? You're gonna be fine. You know why? Because I'm going to help you. And so is Kip, and Allen, and your mom, and everyone else. You're not alone. We'll figure this out together, okay?"

Lily took a deep breath and nodded. She opened her mouth to say something bracing that she didn't feel when she heard a weak, halting voice from inside the bedroom.

"Hello…Mr. Kipling. I do not suppose…you could… fetch some water…could you?"

Whirling, Lily rushed back into the room with Sebastian close behind. Madam Barrington lay as motionless as ever but her eyes were half open. Even this simple task seemed to take great effort, but despite her weakness, a ghost of a smile came to her lips as Lily and Sebastian entered her field of vision. Lily gently took her mentor's hand and gripped it tightly. It was still ice cold.

"You're awake. How are you feeling?" Lily asked as Sebastian took a cup of water from the bedside table and ever so carefully helped his aunt take a few sips.

"As weak…as a newborn foal. Allen? Is he…alright?"

"Quite a bit better than, well, yourself, I expect. Ahem, Madam." Allen's wry, reedy voice came from the doorway, and Lily and Sebastian moved back to allow him room to examine his patient.

He poked and prodded, muttering things under his breath like "good, good, good," and "what's this now…interesting." Finally he straightened, looking grave. "It appears that, hmm, the coma was, as I feared, a p—precipitate of trauma rather than, er, a concomitant of the c—curse's parameters. While consciousness is a p—positive development, I fear it does little to illuminate the lexical c—composition of the curse."

Lily's face fell, and she shot a worried look at Madam Barrington, who had closed her eyes, saving what strength she had.

"Okay, could someone translate for the witch in the room?" Sebastian asked, looking back and forth between them.

Lily almost smiled, but her cheek muscles felt heavy and stiff. "He said that Madam Barrington's coma was a reaction to her physical trauma, like when you get a concussion, rather than magically caused by the curse. So, it's good that she's awake, but it doesn't help us figure out the specific wording of John Faust's spell, which is what we'd need to reverse it. We can treat her physical symptoms, but until we get an idea of how the curse was cast we'll have little chance of breaking it, much less reversing it."

"Oh," Sebastian said, subdued.

There was a long silence in which only Sir Kipling's purring was audible.

"So, what do we do now?" Sebastian finally asked.

"I sh—shall do my best to keep her, well, strength up while I investigate a c—cure."

Lily bit her lip, hesitant to appear rude, but absolutely certain Allen would make a terrible nursemaid. "Um, Uncle. I know you'll be terribly busy experimenting and researching, so wouldn't it be helpful to have someone around to care for Madam Barrington?"

"What? No, no, not at all. My, er, constructs are p—perfectly capable of…um, well, you know…" he trailed off, looking suddenly uncertain.

"I think what Lily meant was, wouldn't it be good to have someone around to keep Aunt B. company? A female someone perhaps?" Sebastian offered, wiggling his eyebrows significantly.

"Oh, yes! Yes, yes, of course. But, well, I'm afraid I d—don't exactly—that is I'm not acquainted with—"

"There's no need," Lily rushed to say, extremely grateful for Sebastian's diplomatic wording. "I'm sure my mother would be happy to help nurse Madam Barrington. Let me call her."

"If she can be here by tonight, we can get going tomorrow morning," Sebastian supplied.

"Yes…I, suppose," Lily said. The words caused a lump to form in her throat. As desperate as the situation was, she was in no hurry to leave. Here, it was safe. Here, she wasn't expected to fix everything. Yet…she'd always dreamed of going to England. Perhaps it wouldn't be that bad. After all, who said you couldn't enjoy a few rounds of tea and biscuits in the process of saving the world?

The conversation with her mother was brief as Lily gave her the condensed version of recent events. Her mother's support was unhesitating. Of course she would come. Anything for dear Ethel. Sally—Lily's oldest stepsister—was perfectly capable of looking after the household while she was gone.

Lily gave her mother Allen's address and Freda promised she would leave within the hour.

Once she hung up, Lily let out a sigh of relief, feeling a

weight lift from her shoulders. She knew her beloved mentor would be well taken care of while they were gone to England.

With that task out of the way, there were still many things to arrange. She had already called her boss, the library director, and explained how Madam Barrington had fallen ill and that she needed a few personal days to help look after her. That would get her through the weekend. But how was she going to explain needing a multi-week vacation, especially considering she'd already used most of her vacation time? With September already halfway through, the fall term was in full swing and the library needed all of its staff. Could she couch it as a research trip? Perhaps ask for a leave of absence for professional development?

Then there was the tiny problem of what to do once they got to England. She'd been avoiding thinking about it, hoping vaguely the whole mess would go away. But, of course, it wouldn't. And the longer she delayed, the more time John Faust had to find Morgan.

Her first task was to get the names of Madam Barrington's acquaintances at Oxford University. A week ago—had it only been a week? It felt like months—they'd come to Allen's house to find and study Morgan le Fay's journal, and Madam Barrington had wanted to run John Faust's questionable translation of it past some experts at Oxford. Lily was nervous at the thought of introducing herself to a whole slew of strange wizards, and British ones no less. What would they think of her? But there was nothing for it. She couldn't let her mentor down.

Though she hated to bother her, Lily ducked into Madam Barrington's room and gently shook her awake. Except for a brief break to relieve himself, Sir Kipling hadn't left the old wizard's chest since they'd arrived at Allen's house. So he took this opportunity to slip out and stretch his legs while Lily was there to keep his charge company.

"Hold her hand while I'm gone," the feline instructed her. "Your body heat helps."

Lily gladly did as asked, cradling her mentor's ice-cold hand in her own as they exchanged quiet words.

"Sorry to wake you, Ms. B., I just wanted to let you know Freda is coming. She'll take care of you while we're gone. I thought she'd make a better nursemaid than Allen." Lily forced a smile for Madam Barrington's sake, hoping to lift her spirits.

"A relief...I'm sure," Madam Barrington breathed, smiling back feebly.

Lily patted her mentor's hand and continued. "I have a few questions about, well, our mission. Since you won't be..." she paused, swallowing. There was a heavy ache in her chest, as if a hand were squeezing her heart to bits, but she forged onward. "Since you'll be busy getting better, I need to know...well everything," she finished in a rush, trying not to sound desperate. "What am I supposed to do, Ms. B.? How am I going to get along in England without you? Where do I start? How do I find Morgan?"

"Slow...slow down, dear." Madam Barrington coughed. "You'll be...just fine. Use what...I have taught you. You are...the best student...I ever had...you know."

Lily gave a nervous laugh. "Don't be silly. You don't have to lie to make me feel better."

"Not a lie...good work ethic...intense focus...quick learner. You are an...accomplished wizard...Lily. Especially for...having started...so late."

Now she had to choke back tears, scrubbing furiously at her eyes with one hand as she responded, refusing to break down. "Nonsense. I'm sure Allen could have run circles around me by the time he was seven years into his studies.

But let's not argue, you need to save your strength. You said you had contacts at Oxford. I suppose it would be best to go there first? My problem is that I'm not sure how to get several weeks off from the library. I've already used most of my vacation. What will I tell the director?"

"Helen   Pemberton…colleague…wizard…used   to be…Bodleian   librarian…now…library   administration." Madam Barrington's sentences were becoming more fractured as she struggled to speak, pausing between phrases to catch her breath. The older woman attempted to raise her head as if looking for something to write on, but Lily pushed her back.

"I'll look her up," she promised, scribbling down the name on a piece of paper.

Madam Barrington gave a long sigh. "Explain…ask for temporary…position or…internship…perhaps. Good friend… she will…aid you."

"Alright. Is there anyone else at Oxford I should contact? Any other wizards?" She felt a bit better now that she was taking notes and making plans.

"Dr. Cyril…Hawtrey…took over…Dr. Grootenboer retired…"

Lily's ears pricked at the latter name. It sounded familiar. Then she remembered. Her father had mentioned Dr. Grootenboer back when he told her about his own studies at Oxford. For a moment her blood ran cold, imagining she would have to meet with old friends of her father's. But then she forced herself to think rationally. Madam Barrington would never send her to seek aid from someone she knew would favor John Faust.

"Those two…will know others…guide you…" her mentor continued, voice becoming weaker as she coughed. Lily put down her pencil to help Madam Barrington sip some water.

Once she'd drunk her fill, Lily helped her lean back. "I'm afraid I've tired you out, dear Ethel," she said, using her mentor's first name in a moment of tenderness. "Get some rest. Mother will be here soon and she makes the best chicken soup you've ever had. You'll be back on your feet in no time."

As she tried to rise, however, Madam Barrington clutched her hand, eyes opening very wide as she stared up at her. "One last…" she coughed, then took a deep breath, gathering her strength. "One last thing…Lily. You must contact…my sister's husband…George Dee. He is a very powerful…and influential wizard. After I married Arthur…I was struck from…the family records and…left England. But I kept contact…with my sister, Day. George will…hear you out. No friend of…LeFay's. Explain…the situation. We may need…his support…in the coming days. If I…if I do not…recover…go to him…for protection. Take Sebastian…his great-grandfather…after all…will do it for…my sister's sake…loved her dearly." Her strength finally running out, she sank back onto her pillow, eyes closed and breathing labored.

Lily fought to keep her voice from shaking as she plumped the pillow and tucked her mentor snugly in. "Don't talk such nonsense. Of course you'll recover. I'll tell Mr. Dee you'll come thank him in person as soon as you're feeling up to it." Lily chattered on, filling the air with noise as if that would hold back the fear trying to latch its claws into her.

By the time she'd finished and straightened, Madam Barrington had fallen back asleep. Sir Kipling appeared, jumping up on the bedcovers and examining them both before curling back up on the old woman's chest.

"I hope you got the information you needed, because she won't wake again for a while. She's barely holding on as it is, and needs to save her strength." He sounded disapproving, as if Lily had been bothering his charge with trivialities.

"Oh shush, pussycat," Lily said, using Madam Barrington's name for him. "We all want her to get better. It's not like I asked her to dance a jig."

"That's good," Sir Kipling purred, eyes already half-lidded in either scornful disdain or feline contentment—they were often one and the same. "Jigs are a horrid excuse for something as ancient and noble as dancing. You'd never catch a cat flailing about in such an undignified manner."

An image of Sir Kipling doing the Irish jig popped unbidden into Lily's head. She snorted, failing spectacularly to suppress her mirth as her face split into a wide, genuine smile for the first time in days.

Sir Kipling sniffed, nose in the air.

Deciding to let things stand as they were, Lily left her cat to look after his patient while she went in search of a landline from which to make an international call, still chuckling as she made her way down the hall.

Though it was embarrassing to admit, Lily had never been to an airport before, much less flown on a plane. She'd never needed to. While she'd dreamed of traveling the world, it was done from the comfort and safety of her living room sofa with a nice cup of tea close at hand. As tempting as all those exciting new experiences were, they had the misfortune of being exciting, new, and experiences. All the things Lily tried to avoid. She didn't have anything against excitement or new things, just as long as they kept their distance. She was a creature of habit, and excitement was generally disruptive to her routine. There was a fiery adventurer buried down deep inside of her somewhere, she was sure, but as of yet she hadn't found it.

Thus it was with great trepidation and not a little bit of stress that she followed Sebastian through the doors of the largest and busiest airport in the world—Atlanta International. Behind her she pulled a gigantic suitcase packed with every item she might possibly need—and quite a few she wouldn't but wanted with her just in case. In the other hand she hefted a cat carrier containing one extremely unhappy feline.

Sir Kipling had complained long and loudly at the idea of being separated from his mistress and trapped in a small crate for over nine hours. After all, he'd been able to slip in and out of no-pets-allowed areas before. Why couldn't he simply sneak onto the plane? Lily didn't even bother arguing. She was taking no chances, not when it involved hurtling through the air in a metal tube thousands of feet above a vast ocean.

Now, as she struggled to get her oversized suitcase up to the check-in desk, she tried not to think about how many things could possibly go wrong with said metal tube hurtling through the air thousands of feet above a vast ocean. The fact that—statistically—it was much deadlier to drive a car than to fly on a plane didn't comfort her in the least.

They'd had to get up before the crack of dawn to drive back to Atlanta and pack the necessary items from both their houses before heading over to the airport. Plus, they'd had to allow for an extra hour to fill out all the paperwork associated with shipping a pet internationally. To Lily's great relief, there were no special hoops to jump through as long as her pet was microchipped, which of course he was. She had rigorously followed all the various vaccination and checkup schedules recommended by her vet in the hope that it would balance out her cat's tendency to do what, and go where, he pleased.

Unsurprisingly, Lily looked around at her fellow travelers with bleary eyes and a frown of general discontent, brain frazzled from too little sleep and too much worry. The fact that Sebastian was bright-eyed and bushy-tailed, bouncing on the balls of his feet in excitement, did not improve her mood.

"You are disgusting," she grumbled, giving her friend's cheery look a sideways glare.

"Come, now, Lily. Where's your sense of adventure?"

"At home. In bed. Asleep."

Sebastian chuckled, drawing odd looks from those around them who, like Lily, knew it was impolite to be happy this early in the morning.

"Why are you so chipper, anyway?" she asked. "You hate getting up early and usually do your best impression of a zombie until at least eleven o'clock."

Sebastian shrugged, giving her a silly grin. "Just excited, I suppose. I mean, come on, we're having an adventure. Anything could happen! Daring escapes from dastardly villains, life-and-death struggles with monstrous creatures, intrepid explorations of wild landscapes never before seen by the eyes of men—"

"You do realize we're going to *England*, right?" Lily asked dryly, smiling in spite of herself. "England, where the biggest native animal is a deer, and the average mountain is so short they're technically considered hills? This isn't Africa we're talking about, Dr. Jones."

"Shush, you're ruining it." He flapped a hand at her, eyes closed as if to keep his adventure fantasy fixed in his mind. "Just because you're a stick-in-the-mud doesn't mean we all have to be."

Lily was interrupted from replying by the line moving ahead, and she took a moment to wrestle her suitcase a few more feet forward.

"Just remember your manners, alright? *Please*," she implored him. "The British are a very reserved and proper people. They won't look kindly on your usual mucking about."

Sebastian grinned a very wide, very impudent grin. "I know. I'm counting on it."

Lily groaned but was unable to admonish him further because her turn had come up at the ticket counter. With no computer at Allen's house and everything being so rushed, Lily hadn't managed to call ahead to reserve tickets. She simply hoped there was a flight available that morning.

"How can I help you, miss?" the attendant asked.

"We need two tickets for the first flight to London. Is there anything available this morning?"

There was a moment of silence as the attendant checked. "Yes," he said slowly, "but the only seats left are first class. Will that be alright?"

Lily's heart sank. Her bank account could cover an economy ticket, but there was no way she could swing first class. "Um…could you check when the next available flight is that has open economy seating, please?"

"Of course, ma'am." The attendant typed into his terminal and seemed to take a depressingly long time to find what he was looking for. "It looks like things are quite busy today, ma'am. The next flight with economy available is tomorrow around noon. Will that work?"

Her heart sank even further as she desperately searched for a solution. Could they afford to wait another day?

"We'll take the first-class seats, thanks." Sebastian had shouldered his way between the line to stand beside her and now held out a card to the attendant. It had that dirty, sticky look of having been in a wallet for a very long time, yet the edges weren't worn, as if it had never been used.

"Of course, sir. May I please have your passports?"

Sebastian dug his out—thankfully they'd both already had passports, Lily having gotten hers in a fit of optimism when she started college.

"Ma'am? Your passport?" the attendant repeated.

Lily shook herself, realizing she'd been staring, openmouthed, at Sebastian while the attendant looked at her expectantly. Closing her mouth with a snap, she hurriedly handed over the requested document while glaring at her friend.

"You have some explaining to do," she muttered out of the side of her mouth, resisting the urge to demand then and there where he'd gotten so much money.

"Later," he shot back, his chipper look now tinged with discomfort as he smiled politely at the attendant.

The check-in procedure went as smoothly as could be expected with all the paperwork they had to navigate regarding Sir Kipling. Once their tickets were issued they had to go to a special desk to get it taken care of. Before she handed over her cat's carrier, she crouched down to stick her fingers through the door and mutter some parting words.

"Just be good, alright? And for heaven's sake don't leave your crate."

He gave her a baleful stare.

"Yes, I know you can get out if you want, but that's not the point. You know how much trouble we could get in if you're caught. Just...please. For me. Okay?" She wiggled her fingers invitingly. After a moment of disgruntled glaring, he gave in and pressed up against the door of the carrier, accepting her affectionate rub behind the ears with reserved dignity.

"Fine. But I'd better get some of this famous clotted cream you keep going on about."

Lily grinned. "I promise, you will. Now, be good and stay safe. I'll see you in nine hours."

With a pang, she watched as they carried her companion away. Despite her best effort, the long list of things she was trying, and failing, not to worry about had just gotten longer.

They got through security without a hitch, though there was a bit of a fuss over a large, silver coin Sebastian forgot to take out of his pocket. Lily recognized it as the one he liked to play with, rolling it over his fingers. He'd been taking it out less and less these days. In fact, she hadn't seen him messing with it since she'd noticed, and pointed out, that it was covered with dimmu runes. It was probably some heirloom from his family and she was beginning to suspect it did something magical, but had no idea what since he wouldn't let her examine it.

So many secrets. He was full of them, and every day that passed she discovered more. Speaking of secrets…

"*Now* would you mind explaining what that was back there?" Lily asked with barely suppressed impatience as they chose seats in the waiting area for their gate. "I kept my mouth shut when we paid Anton that ridiculous sum to get in touch with Tina, but this is too much. I won't be part of anything illegal." She tried to keep the huff out of her voice, aware that her usual reaction to his rule-bending—outraged indignation—was not as mature as it had once seemed.

"What makes you think I'm doing anything illegal?" he responded coolly. Lily couldn't tell if he was upset or simply trying to deflect her question.

"Weelll, you live in a junk-heap apartment in a sleazy part of town and drive a car that belongs in the scrap yard. I honestly don't know how you get by. For you to suddenly have thousands of dollars in spare change seems…well… suspicious." She looked away, embarrassed and hoping he wasn't insulted by her words. It *was* a valid question.

There was a long silence in which she didn't dare look at him. When she did finally glance up, she was surprised to see an expression of weary sadness. Far from glaring at her in outrage, his eyes were distant, as if focused on faded memory.

"Um, Sebastian?" She touched him lightly on the back of his hand, worried.

At her touch he visibly shook himself, eyes returning to the present, though he didn't meet her gaze. "I get by on my own blood and sweat. Being a professional witch isn't lucrative, but it pays the bills, and that's all I need. All I want. I don't take anything I haven't earned." His tone was defiant, yet his words conveyed vulnerability, not his usual brash confidence.

Lily gulped, unsure what to say. This was a Sebastian she'd rarely seen. Charming, teasing, roguish Sebastian she knew how to deal with. But this?

Hesitating, she laid her hand on his, jumping a little when he twitched, perhaps in surprise at her boldness. Ignoring the blush this caused, she said quietly, "I believe you," and left it at that. She wanted to say more, to demand answers. But she didn't. Hopefully he would volunteer them on his own.

Sebastian sighed into the silence between them, the soft noise barely audible over the bustle of the Atlanta airport, even this early in the morning. "When our parents died, they left Freddie and me rather, um, large sums of money. Mr. Perfect used his almost right away to invest and start a business before he even finished college. He's done quite well with it, of course." A flash of something, perhaps envy, or disgust, accompanied his words. "Mine got put in a trust. I haven't touched it since."

"Until recently?" Lily prodded gently.

"Well…yeah."

Silence again. Lily was fine with that, since her head was too full of thoughts to sort them out into words anyway. She'd always assumed Sebastian's parents had been relatively middle-class, at least for a wizard family, and that Madam Barrington's fortunes were unrelated, since she'd come directly from old English stock. She'd never before known the particulars of her mentor's relationship to her friend, beyond, of course, that she was his aunt of several generations. But now, knowing he was George Dee's great-grandson…she'd done a bit of research last night on the name, and, while he was no noble, his list of accolades was so long you could have cut it up and sewn it into a suit. Much of it was decades old, of course. She'd noticed that once wizards passed the normal, mundane age of retirement, they did their best to fade into the background and not make a fuss about the fact that they appeared distinctly impervious to age. But of all the people who mattered, she was sure there were still many quiet, unspoken connections that lasted long after the public limelight had faded.

Though it had made her squirm inwardly, she'd also done some research on the Barringtons. She'd resisted before now out of respect for her mentor's privacy. But if she was going to travel abroad and attempt to make allies out of foreign wizards, she'd better know the lay of the land.

Surprisingly, or perhaps not, she could find no information about an Ethel Barrington. This would make sense if she had, indeed, been disowned after her marriage to a commoner, and a mundane, no less. Lily had more luck with the sister's name, Day Barrington, at the time of her death, Day Dee. Day was the only recorded daughter of Miles Reginald Barrington, 10th Viscount Barrington of Aylesborough—one of the many variations of the city name Aylesbury. Though Lily had no idea if Day had been a wizard, she suspected the marriage between her and George Dee had been more about magical lineage than titles and property. If George Dee was as powerful as Madam Barrington had implied, even a wizard of great property and title would be anxious to ally with him despite his lack of noble peerage. Because of English peerage laws, upon Miles's death the title of Viscount had gone to his closest male relative—a cousin—rather than pass on to Day. But still, her inheritance would have been substantial.

Lily hadn't been able to learn any more than that in the brief time she'd had. So she was eager, if rather nervous, about meeting George Dee and getting the full story. She wondered if Sebastian had ever met his great-grandfather, or even knew who he was. With his father's anti-magic attitude, it seemed unlikely they would have maintained strong ties with the wizard side of the family.

"I couldn't use it."

Lily almost missed the words, they were so quiet. Distracted, trying to corral her wandering thoughts, she gave Sebastian's hand an absent-minded pat to show, well, something. Solidarity perhaps? Only then did she realize her hand was still there, resting on his. She thought about withdrawing it, purpose achieved. But before she could decide, Sebastian turned his own hand over and laced his fingers through hers. After that she didn't have the heart to pull away.

"I…it would be like admitting they were gone. Like I would rather have the money than have them back. It's ridiculous, I know…"

"No, it's not." Lily still didn't know what to say, so just said whatever came to her. It was a thrilling, and terrifying, experience. "Even though they left the money to you, it still feels like theirs. And if you use the money, it becomes yours, and that would erase their memory from it. Sort of like that watch you showed me once, the one your Dad gave to you. You never wear it, right? Maybe because, if you wore it, it wouldn't feel like your Dad's watch anymore and you'd lose that small part of him, one of the few you have left…" She trailed off, hoping she'd said the right thing. Judging from how tightly Sebastian gripped her hand, she thought she had. Her next question was hesitant, since she wasn't sure if it was prying too deep, but at least it might get them off the topic of his dead parents.

"So, why did you finally decide to use it?"

"Because you needed me."

Lily sat, stunned, not sure how to take that answer.

"It was for you, not me, and…Mom and Dad would have liked that." He finally looked up at her, face full of pain, but eyes softened by a hesitant hopefulness.

No words came to her, and obviously her brain had stopped working a while ago. So instead she just smiled and squeezed back. It was enough.

They did not, in fact, see Sir Kipling nine hours later. Unbeknownst to them, it took several hours to process animals shipped internationally, so they had quite a bit of downtime before they could make their way to the Heathrow Animal Reception Center. At the HARC, after presenting all their paperwork and receipts, they were finally presented with one surprisingly content feline. Lily waited until they were outside before grilling her pet, having expected to find him in high dudgeon after hours of confinement.

"Well," he said, "I was rather grumpy when the plane arrived—there was a dog in the hold with me, you see, and it would not cease its yapping. But the lovely lady who took care of me was very appreciative of my natural handsomeness and grace. She gave me milk *and* salmon, if you would believe. Couldn't keep her hands off me."

Lily eyed her cat's self-satisfied expression, unable to stop her lips from curling into a smile despite his obvious implication that she was derelict for her inferior food offerings. "Well, I'm glad you're in a good mood, because you'll have to stay in your carrier for now. I'm sure they won't allow loose pets on the bus."

That wiped the smug expression right off his face, and he settled down into a disgruntled ball of fluff inside his carrier, refusing to speak to her further. That was alright. He would perk up once they'd found a hotel and he could roam free again.

They'd decided not to spend the night in London, but rather to go straight to Oxford and book a hotel. They had a meeting with Helen Pemberton at nine on Monday, and so had all of tomorrow to settle in and track down George Dee. It would just be easier to go straight to Oxford and use it as their staging point rather than try to navigate London's crowded streets. Of course, Oxford's labyrinthine alleys wouldn't be much better—Lily had seen the maps and was very glad neither of them had bothered to get an international driver's license. But at least they would only have to book into one hotel.

It took some tricky navigation through various shuttles, but they finally found their way to Heathrow Central Bus Station. By this time it was past midnight, though to Lily it felt about eight o'clock. Even so, she was dead tired from getting up so early, and took a quick nap, leaning against Sebastian's shoulder as they waited for the bus. The bus to Oxford only came about every two hours this late, or early, in the day, so they had quite a wait. By the time it arrived Sebastian had to shake her awake, and she followed him blearily on board, letting him take care of the necessary exchange of monies while she found a seat to accommodate them, their luggage, and their unhappy feline.

The trip took barely an hour and a half, giving Lily plenty of time to be disappointed at missing the beautiful English countryside they were passing through, now cloaked in darkness. She'd been surprised at how balmy things felt when they'd exited the airport—they'd come prepared for any eventuality of weather, something she'd read was a must in England. It was most definitely chilly, requiring a long skirt and light jacket, clothing she would be sweating in at this time of year in Atlanta. But it was a far cry from the blast of freezing rain she'd been led to expect on any given day in England. Well, except perhaps in July. Other than that, all bets were off.

When they finally arrived at Gloucester Green in the center of Oxford City, they were stumbling with weariness and clueless as to where they might find a pet-friendly hotel. It took them nearly twenty minutes to find the taxi rack, which was hidden one street over between a row of shops, rather than directly next to the bus station. It was deserted at this time of night. Well, morning. Fortunately, Lily had possessed the foresight to purchase them both pre-paid phones at the airport and they were able to call a taxi without much delay. Sebastian took the driver's recommendation of a hotel and they were dropped off at the Macdonald Randolph. Had Lily been fully awake, she would have protested the choice, since it was a five-star hotel and entirely more expensive than they needed. But at this point Sebastian was steering the ship and she simply followed along, lugging her oversized suitcase and carrier full of cat. She was awake enough to notice Sebastian's hesitation when the lady at the front desk tried to put them in one room. But it was only for a moment, then he smiled politely and said that, no, they would require separate rooms with a pet-friendly one for the miss.

At last, at long, long last, Lily dragged herself into her hotel room. She had only enough energy to free Sir Kipling from his carrier and set out food and water and a litter pan before collapsing onto the bed, fully clothed and fully unconscious.

Chapter 2

THE MOST HONORABLE
HOUSE OF BARRINGTON

I T WAS WELL PAST NOON ON SUNDAY BEFORE SHE FELT ALIVE ENOUGH TO GET UP.
The first thing she saw was Sir Kipling sitting on the
windowsill, watching the street outside with some
interest.

"What is it?" Lily asked blearily, rubbing sleep from her
eyes.

"We're in England, right?" her cat asked.

"Yes…why?"

"Because it looks like downtown Beijing out there,
there's so many Asians. And they're all waving these strange
sticks around above their heads. I can't tell if they're angry
or if it's some sort of mating ritual. England certainly is an
odd place."

Confused, but curious, Lily stumbled out of bed and

joined Sir Kipling at the window. He hadn't been exaggerating. The street was thronging with life, and yes, most of them appeared to be Asian. She laughed. "Those are tour groups, silly. See all the tour guides waving their umbrellas and shouting? And the sticks are to help the tourists take pictures with their cell phones."

"I see," he muttered, tail twitching thoughtfully. "I suppose I expected there to be more, well, Englishmen in England."

Lily's smile was interrupted by a yawn and she stretched, trying to get the kinks out of her back. "I'm sure it will calm down during the week. But remember, this is Oxford. It's home to one of the most internationally famous universities in the world. I'm sure there are thousands of students and scholars here from every country imaginable. Now, why don't you make yourself useful and go wake Sebastian up. We need to get to Aylesbury as soon as possible."

In response to her request, Sir Kipling lifted a paw and started washing between his toes.

Lily rolled her eyes, looking around for her pre-paid phone. She wanted to call Allen to see how Madam Barrington was doing. The phone was in her hand, number half dialed, before she remembered that Atlanta was five hours behind. She would check in later. Putting the phone down, she headed for the bathroom and a much-needed shower.

When she emerged, wrapped in a towel and ready to get dressed, Sir Kipling was gone. Lily smiled, knowing her cat wasn't unwilling to help, he just had an image to maintain. After all, he was a cat. He couldn't look like he was actually taking orders since, as he would say, "obeying is for dogs."

In short order Lily was freshened, dressed, and ready for

the day. Knowing they were going to meet a very important and powerful wizard, she'd taken extra care with her outfit. According to the weather report, it was supposed to be sunny and in the mid-sixties—an uncommonly beautiful September day by English standards, if a bit chilly to a southerner. Lily had actually seen some people on the street in short sleeves but knew she would freeze if she tried it. So instead, she donned a professional yet stylish grey knit suit with a pale blue blouse and put a bit of glamour on her ward bracelet to make it match her silver pearl-drop earrings. Her hair, as always, was pulled back in a bun, though nothing so severe as Madam Barrington wore. She'd toyed with the idea of hair sticks over the years, but every time she considered trying them out, she imagined falling and stabbing herself in the neck. It would be just like her to die of self-inflicted hair-stick wounds.

It was unfortunate there hadn't been time to come up with a sensible "adventure" outfit, as she had begun to think of it. She'd promised herself she would buy, design, or acquire one somehow at the earliest opportunity. But here she was, already in England and still wearing constrictive skirts and heeled oxfords. Was it too much to ask for something she could run and climb in while still looking fit to meet a noble? Well, there wasn't time now to worry about it, so she shelved the problem and prayed they wouldn't be running or climbing anytime soon.

By the time she had collected her things into a sensible leather handbag, it was almost two o'clock. And they hadn't even had breakfast yet. She went to the next room over and knocked on Sebastian's door. Waiting for an answer, she stared morosely at her leather bag, wishing she had her much larger carpetbag instead. As it was she'd had to fit her eduba, personal effects, and a few casting supplies into something half its size.

The door opened with a click and Lily looked up, expecting to see Sebastian's face. But there was no one there.

"He's just finishing up, you can come in," came a voice at her feet.

Looking down, she saw Sir Kipling sitting in the doorway, looking quite proud of himself.

"What—how did you—" she spluttered. Finally she just threw up her hands and stepped into the room, thoroughly convinced her cat was using magic to open locked doors. That had to be it. There was no other way. Was there?

She was so preoccupied with her cat's mysterious ways that she didn't notice the sound of the bathroom door opening. She looked up just in time to avoid colliding with a dripping Sebastian, clad only in a towel around the waist as he exited the bathroom.

"Oh my—"

"Holy cow—"

They exclaimed in unison, a shocked Sebastian almost losing his grip on the towel as Lily spun away, covering her eyes and blushing beet-red. Mumbling apologies and not waiting for him to speak, she shuffled sideways, eyes tightly shut as she felt for the door handle. Upon finding it, she fled, making a quick escape to her own room where she collapsed on the bed.

That. Bad. Cat. There would be no milk, salmon, or clotted cream for that devious little reprobate anytime soon.

Lying on her back and feeling the heat radiating off her cheeks, she could just hear Sebastian's voice in the other room, no doubt having a talk with her mischievous feline. Whether he was angry or amused, however, she couldn't tell.

"Uuuggg…" she groaned to herself, covering her eyes again. She'd never been so embarrassed in her life. What made it even worse was that, for the split second before she spun around, she'd enjoyed the view...

Desperate for a distraction, she jumped back up and carefully peeked out of the room. With no sign of Sebastian, she hurried down the hall and to the elevators, heading for the hotel restaurant to find some breakfast. Well, lunch, actually.

She was halfway through her Eggs Benedict when Sebastian found her. Sir Kipling was nowhere in sight, no doubt sneaking around since, as far as the hotel was concerned, all pets were supposed to be on a leash or in a carrier.

Unable to meet Sebastian's eyes without blushing furiously, Lily kept her attention on her food. He sat down across from her and a waiter took his order. They sat in silence for several minutes before he finally spoke.

"So, what's the plan for today?"

Relief filled her from crown to toe. If he wasn't going to mention their little, ahem, encounter, neither was she.

"We need to find your grandfather, George Dee, and tell him what's going on," Lily said, finally looking up. Besides there being a bit more twinkle in his eyes than normal, Sebastian looked as he always did, though Lily noticed he'd tucked in his shirt. Come to think of it, the general quality of his button-down top and slacks was much higher than he generally wore and... "Sebastian, did you comb your hair?" Lily asked, flabbergasted.

"Um...yeah?" he said, running a hand through it self-consciously. "Does it look bad?"

"No, it looks great. It's just...you usually don't...that is." She stopped, stymied.

Sebastian grinned at her. "You mean I don't usually make an effort? You know, just because I don't dress "nice" doesn't mean I don't know how. We've got important stuff to do. I told you I was going to help. I keep my word."

"Well…" Lily said slowly, momentarily speechless. "I admit…I'm impressed."

"Are you now?" Sebastian's grin grew wider, and one of his eyebrows tilted in such a way that Lily could tell he was laughing inside.

Rather than let the conversation veer off into dangerous territory, she cleared her throat and got back to business. "Yes, well, anyway. Madam Barrington told me we needed to locate George Dee and ask him for help. I don't suppose you know where he lives?"

Sebastian shook his head, tucking in to the steak sandwich the waiter had just brought him. "I've never met him in my life. Dad didn't want us associating with the 'practicing wizards' in the family, though he made somewhat of an exception where Aunt B. was concerned. No idea why."

"I see. Well, they most likely have a manor in Aylesbury, only about an hour away by bus. I'm sure there'll be a phone book or directory somewhere we can reference. Now, finish up quickly, if you don't mind. I'll go enquire about a bus."

Gloucester Green—the main bus station of Oxford— turned out to be only five minutes from the Macdonald Randolph hotel. They'd actually arrived there last night on the bus from London, but it had been so late they barely remembered it, or the taxi ride to the hotel. Since it was nearby, Lily insisted they walk, not only to save money, which made her feel better, but also so they could see Oxford up close.

Their hotel was on Beaumont Street, directly across

from the Ashmolean Museum, so named for Elias Ashmole, a prominent British politician, antiquary, and astrologer who donated his collection of oddities to help create the museum. Lily itched to get inside. Just the sight of its grand molded and columned façade made her tingle with excitement. She'd read it contained such wonders as the Kish tablet—a limestone tablet of proto-cuneiform signs from the ancient Sumerian city of Kish—and a set of Arab ceremonial robes owned by Lawrence of Arabia himself. She had quite a weakness for Middle Eastern culture and history, from prehistoric Mesopotamia to the Arab revolt of World War I. She just hoped they would have an excuse to visit the museum during their hunt for Morgan le Fay. It wouldn't exactly be responsible to "take time off" from saving the world to do a bit of sightseeing.

As they set off on foot toward the bus station, Sir Kipling mysteriously reappeared to join them. Lily ignored him, still undecided about whether to pretend his little trick had never happened or to punish him severely for it. For now, the cold shoulder of silence would do. Being a cat, of course, he didn't seem to care. He simply trotted alongside them, fluffy tail held high. Many of the tourists pointed, cooing and *aww*ing over him like a bunch of schoolgirls. He lapped up the attention and milked it for all it was worth as he twined between legs, rubbing and purring but staying just out of reach.

In an effort to ignore her cat's successful scorning of her cold shoulder, Lily focused instead on the scenery, absolutely enchanted by the wonder that was Oxford. The first and most pressing detail that filled her senses was the air. England smelled different. Or, perhaps not so much *smelled* as *felt* different. It felt invigorating. Perhaps because it was a cooler, more northerly climate, it lacked the heavy, lazy feeling of the South. Somehow it reminded Lily of spring, the way it smelled of life and awakening. Yet here in England it was September. Maybe it smelled like this all year 'round.

Lily breathed deeply as she walked, happily drawing in the snappy English air as she examined the buildings along the street. It seemed that Oxford was very much a stone city. Nearly everything was made of it: stone walls, stone buildings, cobblestone streets. Most of it was pale grey, but some of it had a yellowish tinge. She vaguely remembered reading somewhere that after the Great Fire of London in 1666, building regulations were changed to ban the use of anything but brick and stone to erect buildings. Perhaps that was why so much of Oxford was made of that cold, durable, majestic material. And majestic it was. Beautifully jointed stone walls broken up by ornate carvings rose into the blue sky on either side of the street, and what little of the skyline she could see was dotted with ornamented spires. Gargoyles carved into the shape of angels, demons, and even a bishop here and there stuck out from the edges of roofs. Tiles were the standard roofing material, some of them mottled with age and speckled with ancient lichen and moss.

Everything she saw around her had a feeling of incredible age. Well, not everything, exactly. There were more modern buildings here and there, and they stuck out like sore thumbs with their concrete and metal façades. To be fair, though, it wasn't just the modern architecture that confused the eye. In fact, she spotted a wide range of architectural styles sitting right next to each other. The Ashmolean museum with its massive columns and clean lines was made in the classic Greek and Roman style. But right across the corner was a memorial to a group of martyred bishops, which, though erected about the same time, was built in a neo-gothic style. Its elaborate scrolling and stone filigree made it look like a massive confectioner's cone. The dichotomy was almost comical, giving the whole city an air of eccentricity.

Even with its wide range of styles, however, the city had a feeling of heavy, solemn age. Not decrepit, like some abandoned places in Atlanta. No, everything was incredibly well maintained, with old buildings carefully restored and repurposed into shops and houses. It just looked as if the buildings had settled down and weren't entirely straight anymore. Not crooked, just…organic. She could tell life in Oxford was built around a space that had been in use for thousands of years. It was tremendously odd where some of the streets and shops were, popping up and twisting around in a strange labyrinth of stone and history. She supposed it was because they were built around ancient buildings and ancient lives. The awkwardness made her lips quirk. She liked it. The English seemed not to shape the space around them to suit their needs—as Americans did—but rather shaped their needs to fit the space around them.

By this time they'd gone several blocks, turning from Beaumont onto Gloucester Street, which eventually spilled into Gloucester Green Town Square. Besides all the tourists crowding the sidewalk—she'd learned it was called the "pavement" in England—she was struck with how varied everything looked. They were in the middle of one of the most prestigious universities in the world, yet it didn't have the "college campus" feel that Agnes Scott did. Oxford University blended into Oxford City seamlessly, with academic buildings interspersed with restaurants, shops, and historic structures. The people thronging the street weren't just students, they were servers, maids, street performers, professors, tourists, and residents out shopping for groceries.

Nothing like a sunny Sunday afternoon during the tourist season to bring out the crowds. Dozens of people on bikes pedaled past in their own marked bike lane, and tiny cars vied with the ubiquitous black taxicabs for room as they tried to navigate the busy streets. Lily was glad when they finally made it to the bus station. The noise and crowds were almost too much, despite how exciting it was to be in Oxford. She was glad Sir Kipling was as intelligent and wily as he was. She couldn't imagine trying to keep track of a normal pet, or even children, in a place like this.

With minimal confusion, they located the correct bus heading to Aylesbury and settled down in the back. Sebastian let Lily have the window seat, and Sir Kipling worked his magic, appearing under her feet where there had been no furry animal before, with the bus driver none the wiser.

Finally, the bus pulled slowly out of the station and into traffic. Lily watched several passing double-decker buses filled with tourists. While it would have been fun to ride in one of those iconic vehicles, she'd learned that they were only used for intra-city transport. All the ones moving from city to city were more like the Greyhound buses back home.

As Sebastian pointed out later in his best teasing voice, her face was as good as glued to the window for the whole trip. She just couldn't get enough of England. Being there gave her a heady feeling, like she'd just drunk a glass of wine too quickly. It was intoxicating, from the stately buildings to the vividly green grass along the roadside.

They left the city quickly enough, but even the countryside was a beauty to behold. While the leaves were starting to yellow, most things were still green. Yet it all looked so different from what she was used to back home. Georgia and Alabama were full of exploding life, from six-foot-tall weeds to carpets of kudzu to the miles and miles of evergreen and coniferous woods. Things grew all over the place and spread out in messy, thriving masses. England was the complete opposite. Everything looked painstakingly manicured, even the fields. It wasn't that there weren't weeds or grass or trees, just that it all seemed to fit in its own little space, with hedgerows everywhere dividing up the countryside. It had a more restrained beauty to it, which Lily liked just fine.

Though it was only twenty-five miles from Oxford to Aylesbury, it felt like it took forever to get there. England might be a thirtieth the size of the United States—roughly as big as Alabama—but that didn't, apparently, mean you could get around faster. The roads weren't very conducive to quick travel, with more small, winding routes and slower speed limits. Of course, compared to Atlanta's massive twelve- to eighteen-lane highways, everything here felt miniscule.

When they finally arrived at the bus station in Aylesbury's town center, Lily felt a bit disappointed at the lack of ancient buildings and stone spires. Unlike the center of Oxford, Aylesbury was a much more modern town. The bus station sat right next to a gigantic shopping center, and the traffic, people, and stores made it feel almost like home.

It took a bit of wandering to find a pub, the place Lily thought most likely to have a phonebook. There were several George Dees, and Lily gratefully handed off the job of investigating which one was which to Sebastian. With a saunter and a smile, he edged up to the bar and started chatting with the barmaid. Lily's lips thinned and she looked away, annoyed that she was annoyed. She decided to go wait outside and joined Sir Kipling in a little alcove by the pub, watching the passersby on the street.

Sebastian emerged a few minutes later with a satisfied

smile on his face. "The third one is the only address outside the city," he told her.

Lily nodded, turning to look up and down the street for a taxi. She hoped not calling ahead was the right decision. While it would be harder to turn them away if they simply showed up on George Dee's doorstep, they had no guarantee he was even home. But they had to try.

The taxi took them about fifteen minutes outside the city, heading northwest. Once they got off the highway, it was only five minutes before they turned down a long drive lined by trees. Orderly fields bordered it on either side, though the one on the left was only a narrow strip that then melted into woodland. Lily was admiring the yellowing hue of the passing foliage when she saw a flash of silver in the underbrush. They were going too fast for her to get a good look, but she could have sworn it was a fox. She glanced down at Sir Kipling to see if he'd seen the same thing, but he was curled up on the seat in full cat-nap mode.

After about a mile, the long drive turned left and went from pavement to sandy-colored gravel. The trees fell away to reveal the grounds of a grand house that looked suspiciously like a French chateau—Highthorne Manor, the cab driver had called it. Lily wondered if whoever had commissioned the house had been French or simply a fan of the style. Either way, it was a massive house, its yellow stone façade nicely offset by the grey of its slate roof rising in peaks and parapets mixed in with the many chimneys. The masterpiece of a house was made all the more impressive by the rows upon rows of perfectly trimmed shrubbery leading up to it, all set in a manicured lawn that shone emerald green in the mid-day sun. These grounds were in turn encircled by sparse woodland, which spilled out into the surrounding meadows and freshly harvested wheat fields.

The taxi driver pulled up to the large open space in front of the house, tires crunching on gravel as he came to a halt.

"You sure this was where you was meanin' to come?" he asked into the silence, obviously wanting either payment or further instructions.

Lily looked at Sebastian and she could see her own apprehension mirrored in his eyes. This was no replica wannabe mansion like her grandparents had built on their little island north of Atlanta. This estate was easily two hundred years old, and the weight of power and authority accompanying such a landholding was intimidating. The LeFay estate felt like a country cottage compared to this, and Lily was terrified to go knock on that grand front door.

"Look, can you just wait here a bit?" Sebastian asked the driver, handing him more than enough to cover the fare. "If they let us inside the house, you can go ahead and leave, got it?" The cab driver nodded and Sebastian got out, moving around the taxi to open Lily's door. Sir Kipling hopped out readily, sniffing the air with interest. Lily meant to get out. She really did. But for some reason her limbs weren't obeying her.

"Come on, Lil. We've got a job to do. You're not going to make me face him alone, are you?"

The pleading in his eyes seemed to unfreeze her body and she took the hand he proffered, using it to haul herself out of the taxicab.

"Right," she said, straightening her blazer. "Let's go see if your great-grandfather is home."

They approached the manor in silence, the only sound being the crunch of gravel under their feet. Mounting the front steps, they passed under a beautifully arched and columned portico and arrived at the intricately carved oak doors. It took a moment for Sebastian to find the button for the bell, recessed as it was into the stone beside the doorframe. A soft clang echoed inside the house, and then there was silence.

While Sebastian shifted and muttered, Lily simply stood, eyes open but mind far away as she felt out her surroundings. She'd been surprised not to detect any wards around the grounds. Perhaps, unlike the LeFays, George Dee had nothing to hide. But if the grounds were *au naturel*, so to speak, the same could not be said of the house. They were subtle, but wards were sunk into every stone of the gigantic manor, as much a part of the building as its walls, floor, and roof. They felt very old and settled, yet not faded. She wondered what had been used to anchor them.

A sudden creak made Lily jump as the front door opened without warning or sound of approaching footsteps. In the opening stood an imposing figure, every inch the quintessential English butler. Tall and thin, dressed in a starched uniform, and with a head of grey hair combed just so, his expression was polite, but aloof.

"Good day, sir, madam. How may I be of service?"

Sebastian, bless his soul, stepped forward and spoke, giving Lily time to block Sir Kipling's attempt to slip past their legs and into the house. "Stay here," she whispered furiously, knowing he would hear her as she tried to focus on what Sebastian was saying.

"Is Mr. George Dee at home?"

"What business do you have with him, sir?"

"Well." Sebastian glanced reflexively at her and swallowed. "I'm, um…his grandson. Well, great-grandson, technically. We, uh, we need to speak to him."

At his words, the butler's left eyebrow arched ever so slightly, but otherwise his face remained impassive. "May I inform Mr. Dee who is calling?"

"I'm Sebastian Blackwell, and this is my, um, friend, Lily Singer."

"Very well, Mr. Blackwell. If you and Ms. Singer would come this way." The butler opened the door wider and bowed, extending an arm into the house. He eyed Sir Kipling as they passed, but said nothing. Closing the massive doors behind them, they were plunged into momentary darkness as their eyes adjusted to the dim lighting after such bright afternoon sun. A single, but very large, chandelier provided light in the foyer, showing dark wood walls hung with fine tapestries. Through the doors to the left and right stretched high-ceilinged galleries, well lit by large windows. The butler, however, led them straight forward into a drawing room decorated with the most beautiful scarlet wallpaper above honey-colored wood paneling, which protected the lower third of the wall. Everything in the room was lavish, from the gilt-framed paintings to the finely molded mantelpiece and richly embroidered chairs and chaise lounge beside dark wood tables inlaid with mother-of-pearl.

"Wait here, if you please," the butler said, and closed the door behind him as he left.

Lily sat while Sebastian and Sir Kipling explored the room. From her seat, she could keep an eye on the door and still examine her surroundings. They took her breath away, and she was scared to even lean back in her chair for fear of breaking something hundreds of years old. Looking opposite the door they'd come in, she could see out the back windows into the manor's extensive gardens. On the furthest edge she even spotted a gardener in brown trousers, white shirt, and flat cap, pruning the shrubbery.

Her examination was interrupted by the sound of raised voices approaching down one of the galleries. The words were unrecognizable for a moment until they drew closer. Then Lily could hear a woman's voice declaring, "Don't tell me to calm down, Father. I have to see if it's true."

An elderly woman hurried into the room, older-looking than Madam Barrington but surprisingly spry despite her age. Her snow-white hair stood out against the evergreen fabric of her simple but elegant dress sporting a fitted skirt and cropped sleeves. Eyes scanning the room, she noted and immediately dismissed Lily as she searched for something else. Spotting Sebastian, the woman covered her mouth in shock. Then, eyes shining, she stepped forward, arms extended.

"Oh, Sebastian. Look how you've grown. Come here, my dear."

"Grandmother? I—I didn't expect to see—" was all Sebastian managed to get out before the woman wrapped him in a warm embrace, kissing him on both cheeks as she exclaimed over him.

"Oh, Sebastian. I thought I'd never see you again." The woman's voice wavered as if holding back tears.

Lily stared at the two in surprise, completely taken aback by the unexpected warmth of their welcome. When she finally glanced around again, she saw an older gentleman in an impeccable tweed suit of brown and grey standing in the doorway. He looked to be about Madam Barrington's age—that is, in his sixties or seventies, which for a wizard meant he could be over a hundred. He had steel-grey hair and eyes of the deepest brown, with pale skin covered in fine wrinkles and a very long nose in a narrow face, ending in a firm and clean-shaven jaw. With one hand in his pocket and the other leaning on a dark wood cane capped in silver, he watched with an inscrutable expression as the woman embraced Sebastian. Then he turned his piercing gaze on

Lily, eyeing her up and down in a thorough but not impolite way.

He looked, in every way, a most proper English gentleman, and she could barely even tell he was a powerful wizard. Unlike her father—who radiated power with unconcerned arrogance—this man kept his presence carefully masked, much like her mentor. She assumed he was powerful, based on his reputation. But he revealed nothing, giving no advantage to the observer. He made no move to come into the room, seeming content to wait and watch until Sebastian's grandmother got herself under control, which she did without much delay.

Lily tore her eyes away from the man she assumed was George Dee as the woman finally released Sebastian and drew him over to sit with her on one of the chaise lounges. "I can't believe you're here. When Thomas asked us to keep our distance, of course we wanted to respect his wishes. He was your father, after all. But it has been so upsetting. And then they passed so suddenly and my Steven disappeared, and Ethel was named guardian. I decided to come back to England to live with Father rather than stay in America, alone. Please, don't be angry with me."

Sebastian, looking rather shell-shocked, mutely shook his head as if to assure her he wasn't upset. But she barely seemed to notice, barreling on past the sad memories to more cheerful conversation. "Well, well, enough about me. How are you, dear? How is Frederick? Are you keeping busy? Goodness, look how tall and handsome you've grown!"

"Calm down, Grandmother, I wasn't *that* short the last time you saw me," Sebastian said. He still looked surprised, but one side of his mouth quirked upward in a fond smile.

"It seems that our guests will be staying for tea," came a

dry voice from the door in an accent so British that Lily felt uncouth simply listening to it. Every gaze in the room turned to the older man.

"Oh, do excuse me," Sebastian's grandmother laughed. It was a pure sound, filled with joy and none of the hauteur Lily remembered from her own grandmother, Ursula. "Father, this is Sebastian, Thomas and Alison's youngest. I'm sure Mother showed you pictures?"

George nodded, face still unreadable.

"Sebastian, this is your great-grandfather, George Dee," she added formally, confirming Lily's assumption, though it was decidedly odd to realize that this woman looked older than her own father. Lily also noticed that her accent was much less pronounced, possibly dulled from her time in America. "And who is your friend you've brought with you?"

"Oh! Yeah, right, um…this is Lily Singer," Sebastian offered, looking awkward.

When he said no more, Lily's manners kicked in, taking over where her brain failed. She rose and stepped forward to shake the old woman's hand. "It's a pleasure to meet you, ma'am. I'm Madam Barrington's student and a friend of Sebastian's."

"Oh? One of Ethel's students? It's a pleasure to meet you, I'm sure. I'm Elizabeth Blackwell. Sebastian's father, Thomas, was my son."

"I'm glad I could finally meet you, Mrs. Blackwell. I never got to meet Sebastian's parents, or any of his family, really, besides Madam Barrington."

"Yes," Elizabeth said, sadness creeping into her voice. "Sebastian's parents—well, the whole Blackwell side of the family, really—had some very…unique opinions about magic. Over the years they sought to have as little to do with the magic users in the family as possible."

Lily raised her eyebrows in question, not wanting to speculate out loud for fear of being impolite.

Elizabeth laughed again. "Oh, no, not me. Steven Blackwell wouldn't have married me if I were a wizard. But my father, you know...well, perhaps you don't," she finished, glancing up at George who still stood in the doorway, leaning on his cane. "Oh, do come sit down, Father, and speak to your great-grandson." She turned back to Lily and Sebastian. "I'll go arrange for some refreshments. It's close to supper, but I'm sure you're thirsty from your journey."

The woman rose and swept out of the room as George moved inside of it to clear a path. He didn't limp as he approached and chose a chair near the mantlepiece, so Lily assumed the cane was for show, unless...yes, there it was. Now that she was looking, she could sense the dimmu runes inlaid into the silver handle that crowned the smooth wood. At the very least, that cane was a potent power anchor, similar to her amulet. Who knew what other enchantments it might possess?

After the older man sat, crossing his legs and laying his cane across his lap, there was a long and awkward silence. Sebastian's charm seemed to have abandoned him in the face of his austere relative, and Lily was hesitant to butt into what felt like a family affair.

"So, you are the witch." George stared at Sebastian, his precise, deliberate voice slicing through the silence like a knife. As with his face, his words held no hint of emotion. He didn't ask, accuse, or berate. He simply stated.

Sebastian bristled at his words anyway, and Lily couldn't blame him. At the same time, however, she couldn't afford to let his pride jeopardize their mission, so she jumped in before he had a chance to say something insulting. "Yes, Mr. Dee, and a very good friend and reliable ally as well. He knows his craft well and has saved both my life and Madam Barrington's, on multiple occasions."

At her words, George turned his gaze upon her, and, though his expression didn't change, she could tell he disapproved, as if she were a schoolgirl who had spoken out of turn. Her courage fled and she shrank back in her chair. After a few seconds more, George returned his gaze to his great-grandson.

"Ethel has spoken of you, and your…profession. Had she not, and were you any other man, I would have cursed you the moment I felt you enter my house."

Lily's blood ran cold. The matter-of-fact way in which George spoke completely belied his words. She couldn't get any sort of read off him—not that she was good at reading people, but still, based on his words, he should be showing some sort of emotion. Anger, contempt, something. She wanted to stand up for her friend but didn't dare say a word. She felt like a complete coward.

"If you're so ashamed to have a witch in the family, then why let us in at all?" Sebastian's voice was low and tight, almost as tight as his fists as they clenched the arms of his chair.

"Who spoke of shame?" The blunt question caught Sebastian off guard and he hesitated, brow furrowed.

"But, you said…"

George waited, silent, one eyebrow arched in such a Madam Barrington–like manner that Lily had to suppress a nervous giggle.

"You forget, Mr. Blackwell, or else have never bothered to discover, that the Dee legacy includes many witches. Most of them died ignoble deaths. Those who survived did so because they knew where to draw the line. Witchcraft on its most fundamental level is the use of borrowed power, and nothing in the world of magic is free, is it, Mr. Blackwell? Power has a price." George gave Sebastian a knowing look, as if he spoke from experience, rather than theory.

"That it does, sir," Sebastian agreed, anger replaced by wariness.

"And yet power, in and of itself, is not evil. I cannot judge you for having power, only for how you obtained it. And what you choose to do with it."

Sebastian was silent, gaze locked with his great-grandfather's. Finally, the older man spoke again. "I allowed you into my house because I can see you have approached the line...and withdrawn. The price you pay is steep, perhaps foolish. But your friend and your estimable aunt are witness to its good use."

Lily let out a breath she hadn't realized she'd been holding, and George's gaze swung back to her. "You, on the other hand, Miss Singer, are an entirely different matter."

"Me?" Lily almost squeaked, fighting a sudden nervousness. It was unnerving how like Madam Barrington this man was. He could make you feel guilty just by looking at you.

"Your price has yet to be paid, I think."

Lily looked away, thinking of the price she had already paid in terms of certain family members and the trouble they'd dragged her into. How much worse could it get?

"Though I must say," George continued, "with such an enterprising cat, I suspect you consider *him* to be price enough." He pointed his cane to the side where Sir Kipling was in the process of pawing at a book on the bottom shelf of a massive bookcase. Caught in the act, her cat froze for several seconds, then reverted to what all cats did when embarrassed: grooming.

"Kip! Get away from there," Lily hissed at him, face flushing. To George, she apologized. "I'm sorry, he does like to nose about."

"No apology needed. I see he was simply interested in my seventeenth-century bestiary. Quite a read, it is, too."

"What?" Lily stared between her innocence-exuding cat and the confusing wizard before her. "But what good would a book do him?"

"Why, to read, I would imagine."

"But—he—Kip can't read."

"Can he not?" George's eyebrows lifted. "While cats do have odd habits, I do not believe staring at book spines is one of them. Logically, then, the past five minutes he has spent riveted to my bookshelf has been in an effort to read my book titles."

Lily slowly turned her gaze back to her cat, who was now practicing his trademark enigmatic stare.

"Kip," she said in a threatening voice.

"Yes?" The affected innocence was so thick in the air Lily could have spread it on a scone and eaten it with tea.

She glared at him. "Is it true?"

"What?"

"That you can read."

"Well, you work at a library. What else did you expect me to do? Take up underwater basket weaving?"

Lily's eyes widened in sudden realization. "It was *you*. You were the one leaving books lying around everywhere!"

"I feel obligated to point out that, as a creature without opposable thumbs, books are much easier to take off the shelf than to put back on. And anyway, what are librarians for if not to clean up the library?"

If they had been alone, or even with just Sebastian, Lily would have scolded her cat to within an inch of his life.

Fortunately for him, they were not alone. Aware of George Dee's gaze upon her, Lily leaned back, smoothing a hand over her skirt and giving Sir Kipling a sideways glare that promised punishment in no uncertain terms should he harm the tiniest molecule of any book.

"As I said, quite a handful in more ways than one. When it comes time for your price to be paid, what will his part be, I wonder…" The old man trailed off, not looking at Sir Kipling but rather past him, lost in thought.

Lily kept quiet, clueless as to what George was talking about. What did he see in her? Did it have anything to do with that strange entity with the voice like bells? It had given her power in the form of her ward bracelet, and she supposed her cat was a form of power as well, though he was turning out to be a positive double-edged sword.

"Tell me, what has happened to my sister-in-law?" George asked abruptly, eyes back on Sir Kipling, who had decided not to tempt fate by pulling a book off the shelf.

"What? How did you know?" Lily said, astonished.

The wizard's gaze turned to her once more. "No explanation was sent ahead of your arrival, and she is not here herself. Therefore, something has befallen her."

Lily had just opened her mouth to reply when Elizabeth came bustling back in, followed by a maid carrying a laden tea tray. As they fussed and arranged the service, Lily wondered why she hadn't yet seen any constructs. The only experience she had with old wizard blood was her father's family. But they were an anomaly. They'd left England— for business reasons, John Faust had claimed, but she was beginning to suspect that wasn't the whole story—and started a new life in America. Was it normal for wizard families to have constructs? Perhaps George Dee preferred to interact with real people as opposed to machines.

Once the maid exited, Elizabeth poured them all tea—Earl Grey, of course, the tea of choice for most people in England—and they sat back with a saucer and biscuit apiece. Lily noticed that Elizabeth and Sebastian were the only ones to take sugar. She had a bit of cream herself, while George drank his plain.

They sipped in silence for a few moments, and Lily wondered why George didn't restart the conversation. Did he not want to talk about it in front of Elizabeth? She exchanged a meaningful glance with Sebastian, warning him to wait and let their hosts initiate the discussion.

Soon enough, Elizabeth started in on her grandson, eager to hear about his life, his brother, and Madam Barrington. He answered everything with extreme circumspection, making no mention of their recent encounters with John Faust or the reason for their trip. In her eagerness for news, his grandmother didn't seem to notice.

After a while she turned to Lily, catching her in mid-bite of another biscuit. "And you, dear, what about you? Who were your parents? I know most of the family lines in your area from when Stephen and I lived in America."

Lily swallowed hastily, taking a sip of tea to wash down the biscuit. Unfortunately, in her haste she managed to inhale some liquid and broke out in a coughing fit. By the time she had herself back under control she was blushing furiously and kept her eyes on the floor as she replied. "Well, my mother is a Silvester and my father is a LeFay."

The sudden silence in the room made her look up, and she saw with growing apprehension that both her hosts were looking at her with varying degrees of disgust. Elizabeth's was the most pronounced. Her brow was drawn in and there was both pain and anger in her eyes. George only showed a tightening of his lips, though he gripped his cane very tightly with his free hand. She was so astonished at their reaction that she was quite speechless, belatedly remembering Madam Barrington's words: George Dee was no friend of the LeFays.

It was Sebastian who swooped in and saved her, his words halting Elizabeth who had started to rise from her chair. "Not to be indelicate, but now seems the right moment to point out that Lily was abused by her father, John Faust LeFay, as a child. Her mother took her and hid, eventually remarrying and sending Lily to study under Madam Barrington. Lily only found out a few weeks ago who her biological father was, and we're actually here to ask for your help in, well, dealing with him, so to speak."

Elizabeth slowly sank back into her chair, face relaxing into confusion, then pity, though her nostrils still flared whenever Sebastian mentioned the LeFay name. "You poor thing. Of course we'd be happy to help. Anything to hurt the LeFays."

"Now, Eliza, do—"

"Don't 'now Eliza' me, Father," she snapped at George. "You know what they did to my husband's family. What they probably did to—to Steven."

"There is no proof," George said, sternly. "And in any event, it was the Blackwoods, not the LeFays, who were to blame."

"What are you talking about?"

"What did my family do?"

Sebastian and Lily both spoke, clamoring with questions, but George raised his hand in a commanding gesture.

"The past is past, and I would not have us become distracted from the reason you came. Eliza, dear, would you go and make sure the staff know we will be having guests for supper? I need to speak to Mr. Blackwell and Miss Singer. Privately." His tone was pleasant, yet brooked no refusal. Elizabeth pursed her lips in displeasure, but rose, giving Sebastian a quick kiss on the cheek before leaving, closing the door behind her.

Glancing at Sebastian, Lily's heart sank. Elizabeth might have bowed to her father's authority, but it didn't look like Sebastian had any intention of doing the same.

"I want to know what happened to my family," Sebastian said, staring his great-grandfather down. "What *really* happened."

George was silent for a long time, but Sebastian held, perfectly capable of infinite stubbornness. Lily thought it more likely that George was choosing what to say, rather than trying to wait Sebastian out. He struck her as a careful and deliberate person.

When George finally spoke, his words were quiet, almost weary. "When your parents died, I received a letter that was sent as part of the settling of their will. They made only two requests. First, that I help you, should you ever come to me for aid. Second, that I not pass on the grievances of the past so that you and your brother could live free from the bitterness that had destroyed…many things. I intend to keep both promises. So, tell me, what has John Faust done to my sister-in-law?"

Sebastian, one hand gripping something in his pocket, seemed to deflate ever so slightly, as if in defeat. Yet he still glared at his great-grandfather.

Ignoring Sebastian's murderous look, Lily leaned forward and told George Dee everything, starting at the very beginning and answering numerous questions along the way. Sebastian eventually got over his bad mood and chipped in, adding what he knew, though considerably less freely than Lily.

It took more than an hour before George was satisfied and leaned back, looking thoughtful as he tapped the crown of his cane in the palm of one hand. "Very interesting. Ethel was right to send you to her contacts in Oxford. I have no particular knowledge of that era of British history, nor of Morgan herself. Historically, my family has been more interested in Merlin's work than Morgan's. I am afraid there is little I can do to help. I am not as young as I once was and doubt I would be useful as a companion on your quest…" He lapsed into silence, not looking at either of them. Sebastian opened his mouth, but Lily shot him a glare and he closed it again. They waited.

"Here it is, then," George spoke again, obviously having come to a decision. "I believe I am needed more in Savannah than I am here. I have made quite a study of curses, ancient Egypt being my particular interest. If there is any possibility I could aid in Ethel's recovery, I must make the attempt. However, I will leave my manservant with you. One of the lads can accompany me to Georgia. Nigel Hawkins is my trusted right-hand man. He is an initiate, trained to recognize and handle both magical and non-magical situations. You can trust him implicitly. Anything you might tell me, you may tell him. If there is great need, he knows how to contact me. It will work out best this way, in any case, as he can also be your driver. Taxi fares can bankrupt a man these days, I dare say." George shook his head sadly. "Are you sure you do not wish to stay here at the manor? You would be my welcome guests."

"No," Lily insisted. "We need to be close to Oxford. I suspect I'll be doing quite a bit of research and collaboration, plus our hotel is in the center of town barely two blocks from the Bodleian Library."

"Ah yes, the Bodleian." George smiled, eyes distant in memory. "One of my very favorite places in all of England, save perhaps the British Museum." He recalled himself, then waved a hand in their general direction. "At least allow me to cover your expenses while you are here in England. The Macdonald Randolph is not inexpensive."

Sebastian spoke up, shaking his head. "We've got it covered. But thank you."

"Ah, the trust, I assume?"

"Yeah," Sebastian said slowly, brow furrowed. "How did you know?"

"When your grandfather disappeared, I became the executor of your parents' will. I oversaw the proper management and investment of those funds until you came of age. While this is certainly a worthy cause, I suspect there will be greater need of those funds in the future. Please, allow me this."

Sebastian clenched his jaw, but finally nodded. While he looked relatively calm on the outside, Lily knew him better. She couldn't imagine how frustrated he was at George, wanting to know the truth but aware it would be disrespectful to his parents' wishes to try and discover it. She'd faced that very same quandary for most of her life and had finally chosen to ignore her mother's warning. And look where that had gotten her.

They were ironing out more details when the door opened to reveal the butler. "Supper has been laid, Mr. Dee."

"Thank you, Hammond. Please tell Elizabeth we will be along shortly."

The butler bowed and exited, white-gloved hands pulling the door shut quietly behind him.

"Before we partake, I do believe there is one

introduction that has been neglected," George said, giving Lily a significant look before flicking his eyes to Sir Kipling. Her errant cat had taken over Elizabeth's seat and stretched out on the chaise lounge, accepting the dutifully offered belly rubs from Sebastian.

"Oh! Yes. Mr. Dee, this is Sir Edgar Allan Kipling. He can understand you, though I'm the only one who can interpret his poor excuse for English." She grinned shyly, pleased to see a flicker of amusement in George's eyes.

"I'll have you know I speak impeccable English," Sir Kipling informed her. His statement wasn't quite as dignified as he surely meant it to be. It was hard to be dignified when all four of your paws were sticking in the air.

Lily just shook her head, continuing to address her host. "You're not missing much. Most of what he says is rubbish anyway."

"Hey, I heard that," Sir Kipling said, rolling over and glaring at her.

"Yeah? And what are you going to do about it?"

He got sulky at that, jumping down off the sofa and making a beeline for the closed door. "Come on, let me out of here. I bet the cook will be much more sympathetic."

Lily laughed and stood, suggesting they relocate to the dining room.

George led the way out of the drawing room and to the right, down the east gallery. Elizabeth, having come looking for them despite already sending the butler, claimed Sebastian's arm and plied him with more questions as they strolled slowly down the gallery. Sebastian looked a bit stiff—it had probably been more than twenty years since he'd seen his grandmother—yet he seemed to appreciate the attention.

Lily found herself walking beside George Dee, brimming

with a hundred questions and too nervous to ask a single one. Fortunately for her, she didn't need to.

"Who else is caring for Madam Barrington besides Allen LeFay?" the older wizard asked.

"My mother is the one actually nursing her while my uncle concentrates on finding a cure."

"Good, good…" George said distractedly, then looked over, giving her a dry smile. "My dear late wife would have my head should anything happen to Ethel."

"Sir?"

He sighed, a wistful look in his eyes. "Day was always very close to her sister. It pained her terribly when their father disowned Ethel and she left England. They corresponded in secret for many years. I didn't even know my wife had a sister until after their father passed away in 1960. I suspect he might not have willed Day the family estate had he known of her continued relationship with Ethel. Though perhaps I am being too harsh. He was the hardest, most rigid man I had ever met, but Day said he regretted disowning his eldest daughter in the end. He was just too proud to admit it. He even considered *me* second-rate. The Dees are not nobility, after all, simply one of the strongest wizard lines left in England, now that the Mathers and Percys are virtually extinct and the LeFays left for America. Oh, and there were the Witherspoons, but they left over a hundred years ago. With such limited options, the Viscount must have decided blood was more important than title. It was a shame his own title could not pass to a female heir and inevitably went to some distant mundane cousin.

"In any case, after Viscount Barrington passed away I began my own correspondence with Ethel, largely to discuss matters of research and magic. My Day was a queen among women and my dearest companion, but a wizard she was not."

He fell silent, cane tapping a muffled counterpoint to their footsteps on the antique rug beneath their feet.

Speaking hesitantly, Lily braved a question. "How long ago did she pass away?"

"Almost fifteen years…fifteen years in which I have contemplated the curse of longevity, and found its rewards unequal to its price."

Lily took an unsteady breath, sobered both by his words and by the look of pain on his face that no amount of control could hide.

They halted, having reached an open pair of double doors leading into a brightly furnished breakfast room. George gestured, inviting Lily to precede him.

"Let us not dwell on our trials. Good food and pleasant company have always been the best stay of sorrow. There is much to be done, but it can wait until after we sup."

Chapter 3
Of Libraries and Legends

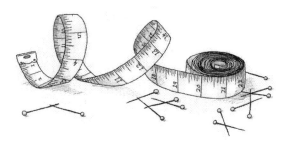

Supper was a delightful affair and afforded both Lily and Sebastian an opportunity to question their hosts on the subtleties of British culture. Lily, on her own, would never have been so forward, but Sebastian was in fine form and led the charge, setting a tone of easy companionship that made them all relax. In the course of the conversation she discovered that, while the English were generally more reserved than their American counterparts, there were always exceptions and plenty of eccentrics who delighted in defying the stereotype. They also learned that the English apologized for everything, whether it was their fault or not, and would often say the exact opposite of what they meant, simply to avoid the appearance of being rude. Lily completely understood. She felt she would fit in quite well here. That is, until she got tired of all the waffling and ambiguity. As loath as her inner introvert was to admit it, she'd inherited too much of her mother's fire—the fault, no doubt, of her French and Italian heritage—to ever be properly British.

All in all, it was a lovely evening, and they prepared to depart feeling much more comfortable now that they had solid allies at their back. Sebastian was happy in his grandmother's presence, but sometimes when there was a lull in the conversation, Lily caught him brooding.

Before they left, George disappeared upstairs to speak with his manservant and explain the situation, Lily assumed. Sebastian volunteered to go to the kitchen to retrieve Sir Kipling, if he could be pried away from the cream and several female cats that were currently occupying his attention. This left Lily alone with Elizabeth, who approached, looking as if she had something to say but wasn't too keen on saying it. The old woman took one of Lily's hands, patting it in a motherly way.

"Are you sure there's nothing more we can do to help? Anything at all? Clothes? Supplies? Food?"

"No, really, Mrs. Blackwell. We have more than enough funds and—" Lily stopped, struck by a sudden thought. "Actually…now that you mention it, I don't suppose you know of any good tailors who can work on short notice? There is something I need but it's highly, um, irregular."

Elizabeth's eyes lit up. "Why of course, dear. My personal tailor, Emmaline Nichols. She's good enough to design for Burberry, or even start her own brand, but she doesn't like the attention. I've told her again and again to get out and rub elbows, but she won't hear of it. In any case, she's not working on anything for me at the moment. I'll give her a ring tonight and see if she is free tomorrow. What is your contact number?"

Lily rummaged in her purse, finding a slip of paper

where she wrote down the information. Elizabeth accepted it gladly, but then hesitated, lips parting to speak without any sound coming from them. Finally, she spit it out.

"You'll...you'll take care of him, won't you? I realize I don't know what you're up against, but anything involving a LeFay will be dangerous." Though her tone held no animosity, Lily couldn't help but notice the double meaning. "He is too like his grandfather," Elizabeth continued, eyes sad. "Steven was never very good at being cautious. I couldn't bear to lose my grandson too, not after..." she paused, sighing. "We all miss Thomas and Alison, but I fear Sebastian never moved past his pain. It has changed him. He was so open and joyful as a child, but now...there are walls everywhere. He is shut so tightly I'm afraid he has forgotten how to let anyone in."

Lily snorted, all too aware of that annoying trait in her friend, but then quieted under Elizabeth's knowing stare.

"But you...the way he looks at you...please, be cautious. You have the power to save him, or utterly destroy him."

Lily looked down, both terrified and elated at the same time. But mostly terrified. The idea that anyone's fate but her own rested in her hands was disconcerting. She swallowed with difficulty, trying to ignore the rapid thump of her heart as she attempted to form an answer.

"I will do everything in my power to...to keep him safe. Though he generally does most of the saving, not the other way around." A nervous giggle escaped her lips, giving her a few seconds of blessed not-talking as she concentrated on suppressing it. Then it was gone, and she had to talk again.

"Sebastian...I...that is—" her voice caught, and she swallowed repeatedly, mouth dry. "I care...deeply"—swallow—"for him. Sebastian, I mean, of course, because there's no one else I could possibly mean—"

Elizabeth laid a hand on her forearm and Lily fell silent, finally daring to look up when the older woman gave her a reassuring squeeze. There was no judgment in Elizabeth's gaze. Her eyes were soft, brows knitted together in concern and, quite possibly, understanding.

"Perhaps you are more British than you imagine. We're altogether horrid at expressing our feelings. Don't take it to heart, dear. I generally find it useful to quote what others have said much more cleverly than I. As a tamed fox once said to a little prince, it is only with the heart that one can see rightly. What is essential is invisible to the eye."

Lily's heart constricted, filling with an aching nostalgia as she remembered lazy summer days of reading that particular book over and over again. But what did Elizabeth mean by it? Was there something specific she was supposed to see?

But she never got the chance to ask, because with a final squeeze, Elizabeth let go, turning to the sound of her approaching grandson as he returned from the kitchen, triumphantly holding a disgruntled Sir Kipling. He set the glowering feline down to give his grandmother a hug and they exchanged a few quiet words. Lily tried not to notice the quick glance Sebastian shot her, much too flustered to do anything but guess wildly at its implications. Soon, though, Elizabeth took her leave, perhaps too full of emotion to stay and watch them depart.

It was then that George returned, followed by a middle-aged man who appeared in every way unremarkable. His height, build, and looks were average. Brown hair adorned a passive face with eyes that looked neither too dull, nor too sharp. He was impeccably dressed in a black suit and tie, and stood at easy attention, giving them each a little bow as George introduced them.

"Hawkins, this is Miss Lily Singer and Mr. Sebastian Blackwell. Miss Singer, Mr. Blackwell, my man Nigel Hawkins. I have informed him of the situation and am putting him at your disposal. He will provide all your transportation and whatever other service you require. Should you have any questions that he cannot answer, he knows how to contact me."

"At your service sir, miss," Hawkins said, giving them another bow. "If you'll wait a moment, I shall bring the car around." With that he turned and glided away down the hall.

Their goodbyes were brief and unemotional. After George shook both their hands, he was silent for a long moment, studying them. "I can see, Miss Singer, that you are already protected by forces far more powerful than I could bring to bear. But you, great-grandson," he eyed Sebastian, seeming to come to a decision. Pulling off a signet ring from a finger on his right hand, he held it out to Sebastian, who slowly took it, looking conflicted.

"You are a Dee, whatever your legal name might be. This ring has protected generations of Dees and will serve you far better than that generic ward you are wearing now. While it grieves my heart that you are not a wizard and I cannot pass on to you the magical knowledge of my ancestors, you have proven yourself willing to take on the responsibilities of the Dee and Blackwell names where Frederick has rejected them. Perhaps one day he will come around, but past are the days when the eldest son is assumed the successor. After Eliza, you and Frederick are my only remaining heirs"—Lily's ears perked at the word 'remaining' and wondered who else there had once been— "and someday soon, decisions will have to be made. Keep this in mind as you go forth. Hold honor and duty as your closest companions and be mindful of the responsibility that accompanies power. If you do not control it, it will control you."

Sebastian nodded solemnly, putting on the ring as George finished. Perhaps she'd been imagining it, but Lily felt like he'd been talking as much to her as he had to his great-grandson.

The door behind them opened, and they turned to see Hawkins standing there, silhouetted by the evening sun. "The car is ready, whenever you have a mind to leave, Mr. Blackwell, Miss Singer."

Sebastian turned to shake George's hand one last time. "Thank you for everything, sir. I think my parents would have approved of you, magic and all."

"Perhaps," George said with the ghost of a smile. "One last thing. If you encounter any wizards from the old families who are, shall we say, reluctant to help, show them my ring. It will clear up any misunderstanding. Though," he hesitated, "perhaps avoid mentioning that you are a witch. My ancestors' inquisitiveness has made our family comparatively open-minded. But wizards distrust witches for good reason, as I am sure you have experienced yourself."

"I could say the same about wizards," Sebastian observed coolly, then sighed. "But I get your drift. I'll be circumspect."

Lily felt a tinge of sadness as they descended the front steps and climbed into Hawkins's awaiting car. She wished they had more time to get to know George and Elizabeth, not to mention their magnificent manor. But perhaps they would have reason to come back someday.

Darkness was falling as they pulled out of the manor's courtyard and onto the long drive. Lily stared out the window lost in thought, and so didn't quite register what she'd seen until they'd already accelerated past the clump of trees marking the entrance to the manor: a silver-grey snout below glittering eyes and perked ears peeking out from the bushes.

Hawkins delivered them safely to the door of their hotel, giving them both his card and instructing them to call him as soon as they needed assistance. Lily let him know they expected to spend most of the next day in Oxford. Depending on what they learned, they might need to travel far and wide in the following days to find Morgan. After a bit of discussion, Hawkins decided to return that night to Highthorne manor to see his master off, then return and install himself at Oxford to be more readily available when the need arose.

After the manservant drove away, Lily and Sebastian decided to make an early night of it. Both still felt jet-lagged, and Lily's meeting with Helen Pemberton was bright and early in the morning. She tried not to blush as they arrived at Sebastian's room and she recalled their encounter earlier that day. His mind must have been elsewhere because he made no comment, simply swiped his room key and wished her goodnight before disappearing inside. She did, however, notice that Sir Kipling had started purring. Drat that cat.

This time Lily changed into her nightclothes before falling into bed. The bed was soft and sleep beckoned, but not so strongly that she didn't notice a certain absence as she reached to switch off the bedside lamp. Where was that cat? He usually slept beside her. She sat up and spotted him sitting by the door, staring at her with yellow eyes. Lily lifted an eyebrow.

"Waiting for me to fall asleep so you can sneak off and

cause more mischief? I haven't forgotten this morning, you know," Lily said darkly.

"If I did my job right, you won't ever forget this morning," he said smugly, showing not a shred of guilt. He even blinked, the universal sign of cat contentment.

Lily considered several heated replies, but discarded each, knowing from experience that she would not come away the victor in such an argument. Finally she settled for, "My personal life is none of your business."

"If it makes you feel better to imagine that, then by all means, keep thinking it."

Lily glowered at him, lips pursed. A price indeed. "Just be careful, okay? We're not in America anymore. There could be wildlife out there you're not used to," she said, thinking of the half-glimpsed silver fox. "Plus I don't know how they treat strays around here."

"Who says I'm going anywhere? Maybe I'm just guarding the door."

"Like a dog? Yeah right," Lily rolled her eyes and turned over, switching off the light and giving up worrying about her cat. Alright, so she tried to give it up, was unsuccessful, and finally pushed it aside to worry about more constructive things, like not embarrassing herself in front of Helen Pemberton tomorrow. Silence settled over the hotel room, broken only by faint sounds from the street below. At no point that she could remember before slipping into sleep's embrace did her door open and close. At least, not that she heard.

The Clarendon building, originally constructed to house the Oxford University Press, had since been given over to the Bodleian Library system for office and meeting space. It was situated on the south side of Broad Street, directly north of the Old Bodleian, the university's oldest library, and the Radcliffe Camera, a more recent but still almost three-century-old building.

Lily looked with longing at the Old Bodleian as she passed, wanting to explore its ancient and heavenly corridors but forcing herself to stay focused. She'd decided to walk the short fifteen-minute distance instead of bothering Hawkins this early in the morning, having left Sir Kipling with strict instructions to keep an eye on Sebastian while she was gone. She realized her cat would just as likely encourage, rather than discourage, her friend's impetuous behavior. But at least it got him out of her hair and away from buildings with a strict no-animal policy.

The woman at the front desk was expecting her and gave her a visitor's badge before directing her several floors up to Mrs. Pemberton's office. Lily tried not to be too jealous of all the people who got to live and work in Oxford. Her job back home was no joke, but this…this was *Oxford*.

Mrs. Pemberton's office door was open, so Lily knocked on the doorframe as she stuck her head in. "Hello? Ms. Pemberton?"

The woman who looked up had a plump and slightly harried-looking face framed by short grey curls. Seeing Lily, however, she smiled in welcome and got up from her desk, coming forward to shake her hand. "Ms. Singer, I presume? A pleasure, of course. Please, sit down. Can I offer you a cup of tea?" She spoke quickly in a businesslike tone, and Lily had a fleeting urge to move to England just to be surrounded by British accents all day.

"It's wonderful to meet you Ms. Pemberton. And no thank you, I just had a cup with breakfast."

"Excellent, then. To business." Mrs. Pemberton sat back

down and bent to shuffle through some drawers, pulling out a sheaf of papers and an official-looking card. Far from making Lily nervous, Mrs. Pemberton's brusqueness actually made her feel much better. This woman was all business and didn't expect any sort of chit-chat or awkward social niceties. It was Lily's favorite kind of interaction.

"Here is your orientation packet with an overview of important rules and regulations, a map of the university and library system, and a list of helpful resources. As we discussed over the phone, I'm giving you visiting researcher status with accompanying ID and library card, which will give you access to all of our libraries, buildings, and research material, excepting of course that of the individual colleges. If you need anything from them you can send a request to be granted special access. Officially, you're here as a professional partner to study our preservation and archive techniques and tour our facilities. Unofficially, of course, I know you have your own research to do, so no one is currently expecting you. If, however, you find time during or after you've completed your research, I'm more than happy to schedule you to work with our archivists for a few days. You have my contact information and I'm generally good at returning calls as long as it's not the beginning or end of term." She gave a strained smile and Lily nodded in sympathy. Agnes Scott had a measly thousand students compared to Oxford's tens of thousands. "But that's not till the beginning of October so you should be fine. Do you have any questions?"

Slightly blown away by the speed at which Mrs. Pemberton imparted all that information, Lily took a moment to think before answering as she rifled through the sheaf of papers. "It looks like most of the information I'll need is here. But if there comes a time when I'm unable to find what I'm looking for in the online database, whom should I ask for help finding material on Morgan le Fay? I don't want to raise any eyebrows. Can I work with the mundane library staff or is there anyone in particular I should speak to?"

"Ah, yes, I'm glad you asked. Dr. Cyril Hawtrey is the one you're looking for. He's a professor of early medieval history from Balliol college. As it happens, he's also our foremost expert on Arthurian legend. I took the liberty of contacting him regarding your visit and he is extremely interested to hear you have records of new primary source material. He is eager to meet you and go over the documents."

Lily was at once relieved and worried. She was relieved that such an expert existed and, even better, was a wizard himself— the very one Madam Barrington had recommended she contact. But she was worried that Cyril's scholarly thirst for knowledge might interfere with their mission. For all she knew, he would want to come with them on their search. And she didn't exactly want to open up about her family's dark secrets to a person whose job it was to preserve the knowledge of things she would rather forget.

Despite her misgivings, she smiled at Mrs. Pemberton and nodded gratefully. "That's wonderful. If you can direct me to his office, I'll stop by as soon as we're done here."

Mrs. Pemberton took out a red pen and marked the spot on Lily's map, writing down the address and office number as well. "Was there anything else?" she asked when she was finished.

"Yes. If it becomes necessary, is there someone who can give me a tour of the main libraries, or at least the Old Bodleian? I'm rather pressed for time and I would hate to waste it getting lost."

"Certainly," Mrs. Pemberton said. "Just ask to see a staff member at whatever building you're visiting and let them know I've specially requested you be given whatever assistance necessary. I doubt any of the librarians themselves will have time, but they'll have an intern or trainee who can show you around."

"Wonderful," Lily said, slipping the papers and card into her bag, then standing to shake Mrs. Pemberton's hand again. "I am beyond indebted to you for arranging everything and making it possible for me to use your university's resources. It may well save a great many lives down the road."

Mrs. Pemberton's eyebrows rose briefly at Lily's rather dramatic statement, but she didn't question it. "Anything for a friend of Ethel's. I only wish she could have come, too. I haven't seen her since before she retired. How is she doing?"

"Um…" Lily swallowed but managed to keep the smile fixed on her face. "A bit under the weather. But I'm sure she'll feel better soon. I'll send her your regards."

"Please do, and good luck with your research."

Lily thanked her again and left the office, heading out of the building and west down Broad Street. She'd actually passed Balliol College on her way to the Clarendon building. It sat on the north side of Broad Street between Trinity College and Magdalen Street, and she admired its yellow stone façade as she passed. She was headed several blocks past Balliol College to the History Faculty building. At Magdalen Street, Broad Street turned into George Street and continued west toward the River Thames.

At the History Faculty building, she showed her new ID and signed in before being directed to Dr. Hawtrey's office. Unlike Mrs. Pemberton's, his door was closed and she knocked, standing nervously in the hall as she waited. It crossed her mind that she hadn't yet seen any signs of magic around her at Oxford and she wondered if that was because wizards had made an effort to keep it out of so public a place, because there were so few wizards left, or because they were better at hiding it than she realized.

The door opened on a much younger man than she'd expected. He appeared to be in his early forties—though of course, with wizards, the older they were, the harder it was to tell—with sandy hair and blue eyes that widened in pleasure at the sight of her. His wide mouth curved in a welcoming smile as he stuck out his hand to shake.

"Ms. Singer, I presume? Welcome, welcome! Please, come in." He opened the door wide and beckoned her into his office. As with most things in England, the space was small. But with the high ceiling, whitewashed walls, and view out onto a green lawn, it didn't feel too cramped. Well, at least it wouldn't have if the other occupant in the room had looked a bit less…picturesque. She'd expected a grey-haired, wrinkled, bespectacled professor with a back bent from thousands of hours studying old manuscripts. What she got instead was entirely too handsome for comfort.

She did her best to hide her unease, however, and sat down in the proffered chair, politely refusing her second cup of tea that morning.

Dr. Hawtrey finally sat as well, leaning forward with his elbows on the desk and hands folded in front of him as he gazed at Lily with contained excitement. "Well, well, this is a pleasure, I must say. I confess I was skeptical when Mrs. Pemberton told me a young wizard wanted help doing research on Morgan le Fay and claimed to have primary source material. But that's honestly just so I wouldn't get my hopes up. We haven't found any new documentation relating to King Arthur in quite some time, especially nothing written during his lifetime. If you'll excuse my forwardness, might I see the material?"

Lily reflexively put a hand on her bag, reluctant to confide in this man. While his demeanor seemed entirely open and innocent, she couldn't help but be reminded of her father's own intense eagerness when talking about the LeFay's history and legacy. The fact that he was good-looking made it even worse. She'd always been terrible at talking to handsome men, and now here was a handsome man with a British accent to boot.

"Um, well, Dr. Hawtrey—"

"Please, call me Cyril. There's no need to stand on ceremony."

Lily swallowed, his friendliness having the opposite effect than he intended. Formality was her only defense. "Right, yes. Cyril…before I, um, show you what I brought, I was hoping I could, um, ask you a few questions?"

"Certainly," he said, looking surprised but still friendly. "Ask away."

"Right, um, first of all, could you tell me a bit more about your relationship with Dr. Grootenboer?"

He leaned back, looking thoughtful. "Well, she was the head of the history department for many years and my supervisor for both my masters and DPhil. So I guess you could say she was my superior as well as my mentor. But she retired about ten years ago. Why? Is there a problem?" he asked, looking genuinely confused.

"No, not at all," Lily hurried to say, still wondering how in the world to know if she could trust this man. As uncomfortable as it made her, she had the feeling she wouldn't know unless she asked. "It's just that, well, I thought maybe you knew…well perhaps not, I know it's a very large university, but would you happen to have met a man named John Faust LeFay at any point? He was a student here in the early eighties I believe."

Cyril's face turned thoughtful once more. "Hmm, LeFay? I'm familiar with the family name, of course, but I don't believe I ever met the man. He would have been a little before my time. I started in the late eighties. But if any of his degree courses had to do with history, he more than likely studied under Dr. Grootenboer at some point. Does he have something to do with the primary source material?" he asked.

It took quite a bit of effort not to sigh in relief. She could detect no hint of deception in Cyril's face or voice. Of course, she hadn't noticed any in her father either, at least not at first. But there had always been a sneaking suspicion that she'd pushed away, and that feeling was completely absent with Cyril. So, at least he wasn't connected to her father. Madam Barrington trusted him, of course, but she'd felt the need to check, just in case. Hopefully, unlike her father, Cyril's interest in Morgan le Fay was completely academic.

"The two are related," Lily said evasively, then moved on to another question. "If you don't mind me asking, I've been wondering about the state of wizards and magic at Oxford. My teacher, Madam Barrington, said you were the one to ask about it. You see, I haven't seen or felt any magic at all within the city, not even in your or Mrs. Pemberton's office. Most wizards I've met so far, though I have to admit I haven't met many, have at least warded their personal spaces and homes."

"Well, that's easy to answer," Cyril laughed, expression clearing. "I certainly ward my home, and I'm sure Mrs. Pemberton and the other wizards at Oxford do as well. But our offices aren't our homes. They are historic buildings many hundreds of years old and we wouldn't dream of defacing them with ward anchors, especially since our offices move around from time to time. In any case, there's really no need. One of us might cast the occasional spell here and there, but on the whole magic isn't as useful as it used to be, not with so much mundane technology. I must admit I even use my archiving spells less and less these days. Every year the internet and online databasing become more advanced. They're just as useful, and certainly less dangerous, than magic."

Lily found herself nodding in agreement, though his words weren't entirely accurate. It was only everyday things that were easily replaced by technology. There were plenty more esoteric, and dangerous, spells that mundane technology couldn't even begin to replicate. Still, his words brought on a strange sadness she couldn't explain.

"Now, I can't say I speak for the majority of wizards. Here at Oxford we take a more open-minded view of mundane research. I suppose we've embraced it in a way. It's all part of the search for knowledge, since it's rather hard to study and experiment with magic in such a public place. I wouldn't say any great advances in magic are happening at Oxford. We certainly do our best to preserve any magical knowledge we have, but it seems more a thing of the past than the future."

Quiet descended, both seemingly preoccupied with their thoughts. Finally, Lily broke the silence. "You mentioned other wizards at Oxford. How many are there, if you don't mind me asking?"

Cyril thought for a moment, as if counting in his head. "Eight—no, seven. Dr. Hughes retired last year."

Interesting, Lily thought. So her father had been

incorrect, or at least uninformed. He'd said there were only two. Perhaps their numbers had grown? That seemed unlikely. It was more plausible that they simply hadn't wanted, or had no reason, to be acquainted with her father. Lily felt relieved at the thought.

"I'm happy to answer your questions," Cyril said, leaning forward again to look at her intently, "but what do they have to do with the documents you brought?"

Lily looked down at her hands, awkward once again and unsure how to explain the situation in a way that didn't sound completely ridiculous. "Well, they…um, relate," she said rather lamely. Where was Sebastian when she needed him? On second thought, considering Cyril's beach-boy hair and blue eyes, Sebastian would not make this situation any easier.

"Ms. Singer, I—"

"Do you believe in legends, Dr. Hawtrey?" Lily asked, cutting him off. For some reason she couldn't bring herself to use his first name, already aware of how silly her objective might sound to a learned scholar. It was rude, she knew, but she needed that distance, that professionalism, to deal with this man.

"Please, call me Cyril, and, yes, I suppose I do to some extent," he said slowly, brows furrowed, no doubt at her odd behavior. "Every historian knows there is a certain amount of truth to every legend, either in reality or in the collective psyche of the culture it came from. Myths were often created to explain natural phenomena that the ancients did not understand, such as lightning, earthquakes, shooting stars, and the like. Why do you ask?"

"Well…" Lily paused again. It was ludicrous how difficult it was to discuss the idea of Morgan le Fay with a *wizard* for goodness' sake. Wizards knew there was more out there than met the eye. Yet she was terrified Cyril wouldn't believe her. He seemed terribly modern and un-wizard-like to her. "Do you believe King Arthur, Merlin, Morgan le Fay and the rest were real people? Real wizards I mean? Well, not King Arthur, but the other two."

Cyril thought about that. "Research possibly points to historical figures from which the legends of King Arthur and Merlin might stem, though the evidence for Morgan le Fay is more sparse. Do I believe it all happened like the legends say? Of course not. Modern stories are based largely on romanticized prose written in the fifteenth century which was only loosely based on a falsely purported "history" written three hundred years after the supposed life of King Arthur."

"Yes, we can agree on that," Lily said. "But do you believe there was an actual wizard named Morgan le Fay? Do you believe there was a place named Avalon? A magical place, I mean, not the Canary Islands."

Now Cyril was giving her a funny look, halfway between hope and disbelief. "I can't really say. It's not impossible, as we both know, but it seems far-fetched. We have no proof, and as a historian I try to stick to the facts." That last part he said almost as a question, as if hoping Lily would contradict him.

For the first time since entering his office, Lily felt a faint smile creep over her face. He wasn't laughing, and the eagerness in his eyes reminded her of her little brother, Jamie. "Don't get too excited," she cautioned as she reached into her bag and pulled out her eduba. "I don't have the originals, only copies, so we can't verify their authenticity by dating the materials. But maybe they'll make more sense to you than they did to me."

His face fell momentarily when she mentioned her lack

of originals, but it lit up again at the sight of her eduba. "That's a beautiful book you have there. An eduba, I assume? My family never had one, at least not one that survived. I made my own of course, for archiving, but it's hard to use regularly since I have to use my computer to interface with the rest of the library system."

He watched with interest as she opened it and called forth the relevant pages: John Faust's translation of Morgan's journal as well as the pictures they'd taken of the tome. She'd kept the original pictures, of course, transferring them onto a computer drive that was regularly backed up. But it was easier to carry around her eduba than a computer. Handing the volume to Cyril and showing him the relevant index, she sat back and let him peruse the material.

She'd read her father's translation herself, of course. She just didn't know what to make of it. The journal was written in very indirect and obscure language, as if Morgan was being obtuse on purpose just to frustrate her reader. Or to keep her secrets hidden, one or the other.

As far as Lily could tell, the journal dealt entirely with the latter part of Morgan's life, after Arthur had ceased being king. According to legend, the king was wounded in a great battle with a rival to the throne and was taken to Avalon by Morgan to be healed. The journal seemed to pick up after Morgan had already been in Avalon for some time. It mostly ranted about some kind of council that kept her from what she claimed was her "birthright." If she truly was King Arthur's half sister, perhaps she considered herself Avalon's rightful ruler? The latter half talked about how the council betrayed her and exiled her from Avalon, but that she would one day return to claim what was hers and put history to right. There were many times when she broke into verse, and Lily was sure these held clues to her whereabouts. Unfortunately, she couldn't make head nor tail of them, probably because she had no context and knew very little about the original legends. She'd brushed up on her general knowledge before leaving for England, but hadn't had time to completely read Geoffrey of Monmouth's *Historia Regum Brittaniae*, and *Vita Merlini*, or Sir Thomas Malory's *Le Morte d'Arthur*.

After about ten minutes of silence in which Lily preoccupied herself with looking out the window and trying not to fidget, Cyril finally put down the eduba with a slow whistle of amazement. His eyes were wide in wonder and his mouth quirked in the way of someone who couldn't believe their luck.

"Well?" Lily asked, anxious.

"I can tell you two things straightaway," he said with a grin.

"Yes?"

"First of all, whoever translated this must have thought they were a lot better at Old Brittonic than they actually were. Second, whoever wrote the original text was most definitely a wizard."

Lily sighed in relief, feeling hope for the first time after several days of intense worry. Her father might have located Morgan le Fay, but if his translation of her journal was flawed, perhaps that meant he wouldn't have all the keys to get *to* her. Her resting place was surely protected by enchantments and probably even physical barriers. A moment later, though, her anxiety returned. What if her father had his own expert in Old Brittonic? Would he trust the translation or seek a second opinion? Did he know about Cyril's expertise? Was he on the way to Oxford at that very moment? Whatever the case, they had no time to lose.

"That's wonderful news. How soon can you get me a corrected translation?" she asked, trying not to sound desperate.

"Well…" he thought about it. "I might be able to work it in before term starts, but it'll be a close thing. It looks like there'll only be about…fourteen pages once it's all typed up on A4 paper. So, maybe three, four weeks?"

Lily's insides twisted and she gulped, forcing herself to ask the question. "Actually, um…could you get it to me by tomorrow?"

Cyril laughed. "That's a good one. You're joking, right?" He stared at her, the mirth slowly melting from his face. "You're not joking, are you?"

Lily shook her head, shrinking in on herself as if by making herself smaller she could minimize the trouble she was causing him.

He laughed again, but this time it was a sort of strained, crazed laugh. "There's no way I could possibly get this done in a day. A week, maybe, if I cancelled all my appointments and put my research on hold. But why in the world do you need it so quickly? Do you have some research deadline?"

"Well, sort of," Lily avoided his gaze, once again wondering how much she could tell him. She supposed that, if she were going to put him through so much trouble, she might as well be up front about why. Here went nothing. "What if I told you that, um, Morgan is definitely real? What if I told you she's my ancestor, and that my father is currently close to finding her resting place and gaining possibly immeasurable power that he will use to hurt a lot of people?" She said all this very quickly, eyes on the floor and words virtually blending together by the time she got to the end. When Cyril didn't immediately respond, she dared a glance upward. As she'd feared, he was looking at her like she was a complete lunatic. So much for that.

"Let me get this straight. You think you're a descendant of Morgan le Fay, and your father is trying to steal magic to hurt people?"

Lily deflated, tense muscles loosening in defeat as she slumped in her chair. She didn't have the energy to be nervous anymore, or embarrassed. As annoying as it was, the feeling was rather freeing. If only she could feel this way all the time. "Remember how I was asking questions about John Faust earlier? Well, he's my father. You know, John Faust *LeFay*?"

Realization dawned on Cyril's face, though it was quickly replaced by more confusion. "Wait, so you're saying the LeFays are the actual blood descendants of Morgan le Fay, or whatever historical figure her legend is based on?"

Sigh. "Yes."

"And you're John Faust's daughter?"

Another sigh. "Unfortunately."

"And he's going to hurt people?" Cyril's voice was becoming increasingly tense.

A very, very large sigh. "He already has."

"Ms. Singer, if you're serious, this sounds like something you should take to the police."

"Yes, I'm serious. And we already tried that. He got away and cursed Madam Barrington in the process. She almost died."

"What!" Cyril shot upright in his chair. "Is she alright?"

"Hopefully she will be. There are...several powerful wizards working on a cure. But I hope you understand how dire the situation is. If it were any less severe, I would be with my teacher, not on the other side of the Atlantic Ocean trying to stop a murderer."

"But, we don't even know if this journal is authentic,

much less whether Morgan le Fay was a real person. Even if she was, who's to say there's anything left after so long?"

Lily massaged her temples. Apparently, despite her youth, she'd seen far more magic than this learned wizard ever had. She supposed such exposure to the wild and wonderful was what happened when your father was an egomaniacal, power-hungry wizard bent on world domination. If only she'd thought to borrow the ring George Dee had given to Sebastian, perhaps it might have helped convince Cyril.

"Dr. Hawtrey, have you ever been in a time loop? Gone through a portal? Seen a demon? Or one of the fae?"

"No, not exactly, but—"

"Well I have. And I can assure you they are all quite real. Please believe me when I say that it is perfectly plausible for Morgan le Fay to still exist, even still be alive, albeit in some sort of suspended animation or time loop. While you are very experienced in historical records, I suspect you cannot claim to have pursued your magical education with as much vigor."

He was silent, observing her with pursed lips. Finally he shook his head. "No, I suppose I can't."

"Very well," Lily said, sitting up and fixing him with a stare. She only felt a slight twinge this time at the sight of that lovely face, and she studiously ignored it. "Let's assume, for a moment, that whatever John Faust is seeking, should he find it, he could, and will, use it to great harm. Further, let's assume that this journal can help me find it first and keep it away from him. If both these things were true, and you knew he already had the item's location and simply needed to figure out how to get to it, how quickly could you re-translate this text?" She tapped her eduba where it lay, open, on Cyril's desk.

The professor sighed and slumped in his chair, rubbing his

face with one hand as he thought. With a snort of exasperation, whether at her or himself she couldn't tell, he sat up, picking up her eduba and waving it at her as he spoke. "Two days. But," he said quickly, forestalling her sigh of relief, "on one condition only."

"Yes?" Lily asked cautiously. She suspected she wasn't going to like it.

"You take me with you. Wherever this leads, whatever happens, you take me with you."

"Absolutely not," Lily said emphatically, trying to imitate her mentor's icy tone. It usually succeeded in shutting up whoever it was directed at. Either she didn't do it right, or else Cyril was immune to icy tones, because he just grinned.

"Take it or leave it. This is an opportunity of a lifetime. Not that I'd ever be able to tell mundanes the truth, of course. But if I could actually meet Morgan le Fay, or even just find her grave? There's no way I'm missing out on that."

Lily had been afraid of that. She groaned, unsure what to do. Perhaps if he realized how dangerous it would be, he might be less enthusiastic.

"Look, I don't think you understand how dangerous my father is. He's already almost killed a wizard much more powerful and experienced than you. Do you know how to battle-cast? Do you know defensive and offensive magic? Can you cast spells without speaking?" That last one was cheating slightly. She was still trying to master silent casting herself and so wasn't exactly the expert at it she implied.

Though her words did dampen the professor's enthusiasm, it did nothing to break his determination. "I'm a quick study. And I don't have to be involved in any fighting. I'm not afraid to run and hide if the situation calls for it. I'm no Indiana Jones."

"No, you certainly aren't," Lily said weakly, thinking exactly the opposite. Though, if she was honest, he looked more like a Lawrence of Arabia than an Indiana Jones. That was film for you.

"So, is that a yes?" he asked, eyes once more alight and eyebrow raised in challenge.

Lily felt trapped. Sebastian was *not* going to be happy about this. While *he* might have no compunction about making a promise with no intention of keeping it, that wasn't her. She was a woman of her word and could not bring herself to accept this man's help without knowing she would honor their agreement. But what choice did she have?

"I...suppose." Lily let all the breath out of her lungs in one big whoosh, knowing as soon as the words left her mouth that they would cause her no end of trouble. The look of boyish glee on Cyril's face did nothing to reassure her.

Chapter 4
BIBLIOPHILE HEAVEN

AFTER COPYING MORGAN'S JOURNAL INTO HIS OWN EDUBA—HE'D HAD TO DIG IT out from under a pile of papers and brush off a layer of dust—Cyril sent her on her way with a list of books and manuscripts to read while he worked on the translation. She needed to get "up to speed," as he put it, on Arthurian lore if they were going to unravel Morgan's journal. The good news was, she was going to get to explore the Old Bodleian, not to mention spend hours reading within its heavenly embrace. The bad news was, it was a very long list.

On her way back up George Street toward the hotel, her phone rang. She had a moment of panic as she scrambled to answer, worried that something had happened to Sebastian. But the number calling was unknown. She answered with a careful "Hello?"

"Yes, hello. Is this Ms. Singer?" said a refined woman's voice in the most perfect Queen's English Lily had ever heard. It was actually rather intimidating.

"It is. May I ask who's calling?"

"This is Emmaline Nichols. Mrs. Blackwell said you were in need of a tailor on short notice."

"Yes! Thank you so much for calling. How soon are you available?"

"As soon as you please, Ms. Singer."

"Oh, good! Um, well I'd like to meet as soon as you can get to Oxford. Or do I need to come to you? I'm sorry, I've never done this before." She laughed nervously, then clamped her mouth shut lest she bungle things even further.

"It's no trouble, Ms. Singer. You're staying at the Macdonald Randolph?"

"Yes. Room 205."

"I can meet you there in an hour."

"Oh, alright. Do I need to bring anything, or, um, have anything ready for you?"

"Nothing at all, Ms. Singer. I'll have everything I need with me."

Lily took a deep breath. "Wonderful. I'll see you in an hour, then."

"Yes. Good day, Ms. Singer."

"Thank you! Um, goodbye." Lily hung up and slid the phone back into her bag, both nervous and excited at the idea of having an outfit tailor-designed. She'd thought idly about it for some time now but had never been able to nail down in her mind what it would look like. Hopefully Emmaline Nichols could help.

It was barely eleven when she got back to the hotel, wanting to check on Sebastian and Sir Kipling before Emmaline arrived. Clouds had come up while she was in Cyril's office, and the sunny fall morning had turned into a dreary, cold day. She was more than happy to reach the warmth of the hotel and only paused to ask the front desk when lunch was being served before heading up to the second floor.

All was quiet in the corridor, so she checked her room first. Finding no life, either four-footed or two, she moved on to Sebastian's room. If no one answered her knock, she would just try calling him.

No one answered, but she thought she heard something inside. Pressing her ear to the door, she listened, finally detecting a soft, rhythmic noise that sounded suspiciously like snoring. Well, at least the world had gone back to normal and Sebastian was acting like his usual, lazy self.

She knocked again, louder this time, and called his name. Nothing. Tentatively, she tried the door handle. The latch must not have caught the last time someone closed it because the door cracked open at her touch. She hesitated before entering, wondering if this was another one of her cat's tricks. It wouldn't hurt to stick her head in and give him a wakeup call, would it?

Eyes tightly shut—just in case—she poked her head into the room and yelled. "Sebastian!"

Nothing.

"Seriously?" she muttered to herself, hand protectively in front of her eyes as she used the pattern on the rug to navigate into the room. Nearing the bed, she stopped and spoke again as loudly as she dared. "Sebastian, wake up!" This time there was a snort, but then the snoring returned to its regular rhythm.

This was ridiculous. Suspecting foul play, she ever so carefully peeked between her fingers, ready to shut her eyes if need be. What she saw made her drop her hand, only to place it firmly on her hip as she gestured with the other in exasperation.

"Kip! Will you get off his chest and let him wake up?

Good grief. I told you to keep an eye on him, not drug him with your magical cat powers of eternal sleep."

Sir Kipling simply stared at her, eyes only slits of yellow beneath hooded lids that looked about to shut again.

"Sir Edgar Allan Kipling, get over here this very minute or I'll—I'll—I'll lock you in your room!"

He yawned, showing exactly what he thought of such a feeble threat.

"Alright, that's it," Lily muttered. "You are in so much trouble. I swear…" Seeing he was still ignoring her, she gave up and steeled herself. Keeping her gaze averted—she had no idea what, if anything, Sebastian had on under the covers—she managed to snag Sir Kipling around the middle and hauled him unceremoniously off Sebastian's chest. The feline attempted to wiggle out of her grip, protesting loudly, but she held on, fueled by righteous anger. Or at least, righteous annoyance.

Turning and hurrying out of the room, she yelled over her shoulder for Sebastian to get up before closing the door behind her with her foot. She was relieved to hear signs of life coming through the door in the form of bleary questions and muttered curses. Now, however, she was stuck. Lily stood in the hotel corridor, hands full of wriggling, whining cat, with no way to swipe her card to get into her own room and discipline said cat.

Performing an act of dexterity she hadn't known she was capable of, she managed to hold onto the squirming ball of fur with one hand long enough to grab him by the scruff of the neck, making sure his weight was fully supported by her hand under his chest. With one last whining mew, he gave up and went limp. She waited a second to make sure he was going to behave, then released his scruff and set him gently on the floor.

"Serves you right," she told him as she unlocked her door and pointed imperiously inside. He slunk in, sulky, like a child caught in a prank. They proceeded to have a frank discussion about a cat's role in matchmaking, namely that they didn't have one. After some pointed interrogation, she discovered he'd been watching reality TV during the day while she was at work. That explained a lot. She resolved to get rid of her TV as soon as they got home. She hardly ever used it anyway.

After extracting a promise that he would stop pulling pranks involving less-than-decent situations, Lily used her room phone to call Sebastian.

He appeared a few minutes later, hair sticking up in directions Lily hadn't even known existed, as he attempted to button his shirt. "Wassit going on?" he asked, giving up on his shirt after two buttons and collapsing into a chair by the window. Lily watched him try to rub the sleep out of his eyes, noting he had his shirt on inside out.

"I thought you'd want to know where we stand before I disappear into the library for the rest of the day."

Sebastian made a noncommittal noise, probably intended to indicate he was still conscious, which was about as much as he could manage at the moment.

"I met with Ms. Pemberton and got all the formal arrangements taken care of."

"Mmm."

"Then I went to meet with Dr. Hawtrey, a wizard in the history department. He's an expert on early medieval history in Britain, specifically Arthurian legend."

"Mm-hm."

Lily pursed her lips. "He was very handsome."

"Wha—what?" Sebastian sat up, managing to look confused and aggressive at the same time.

"I said, he was very solemn," she repeated, trying to hide both a smirk and a blush. She didn't know what had come over her. Was this how Sebastian felt whenever he teased her? "He didn't seem to think it very plausible that Morgan was real, though the copies of the journal got him interested enough to consider translating it properly for us."

"Right…um…consider?" Sebastian asked, not looking entirely convinced, but too groggy to do anything about it. Leaning forward, he scrubbed his face with his hands a few times before giving his head a good shake.

"He was happy enough to translate it but said it would take several weeks. I told him we didn't have time, so he agreed to do it in a few days, but only if, um, well"—she shifted uncomfortably—"only if we let him come with us to find Morgan le Fay."

"What? No, that's ridiculous! He'd slow us down. We can't babysit some bumbling squint whose idea of mortal danger is food and drink in a library."

Lily frowned and crossed her arms. "You mean me?"

"What? No—I meant—you're different, Lily."

She raised an eyebrow.

"Hey, don't look at me like that," Sebastian protested, raising his hands. "You actually do stuff. You get out and combat the forces of evil. We don't know if this guy can even put out a candle, much less pull his weight in a fight against John Faust. This is going to be dangerous. We can't have him tagging along."

"Well, I've already given him my word," she said stiffly. "And food and drink in the library *are* a mortal danger, especially here. This is one of the biggest libraries in all of Britain, and they preserve documents hundreds, even thousands of years old. One misplaced glass of water is all it takes to destroy irreplaceable history."

"Whatever," Sebastian grumbled. "My point is, we can't take him. It would be irresponsible. He might get killed!"

"It'll be fine. We can make him stay behind with Hawkins if there's danger, but he *is* coming. We need his help. Now, go clean up. I have an…appointment and then I'll be in the library the rest of today catching up on research." She didn't know why, but she didn't want to tell Sebastian about her fitting. What if he laughed? Momentarily distracted, she noticed he was staring at her and scrambled to fill the silence. "You, um, you might want to find some…maps! Yes, maps. You know, to get familiar with the lay of the land, or figure out what supplies we'll need or…something. I suspect we'll be traveling into the countryside to old archeological sites, so we'd best be prepared. Alright?"

"Aye, aye, Captain." He gave her a two-finger salute and a roll of the eyes before heaving himself up and exiting the room, muttering grumpily as he went.

Lily let out a sigh, hoping he would be in a better mood after a shower and some food. "Kip, stay with him, alright? Make sure he doesn't, I don't know, annoy a policeman and get arrested or something."

"Who do you think I am? His babysitter?"

"Something like that," Lily said, giving her cat a pointed stare.

With a long-suffering huff, Sir Kipling jumped off the bed and slunk after Sebastian.

Glancing at her watch, she saw she just had time to pop down for a bit of lunch before Emmaline arrived. After hastily enjoying an avocado and prawn sandwich, she headed back upstairs, reaching her room with several minutes to spare. Having nothing else to do, she fidgeted about the room, making sure everything was neatly put away and worrying about what one was supposed to wear to a fitting. She was glad she'd sent Sir Kipling with Sebastian.

She could just imagine him sitting on the bed, making snide comments as he observed the procedure with amused fascination.

A knock on her door interrupted her thoughts, and she hurried to answer it. Lily opened it to reveal a woman who…well…who was very hard to describe. She didn't seem to fit into any normal category you might use to describe a person. She was quite fashionable, but not in a modern sort of way. If anything her tastes had a Goth leaning, but in the most sophisticated, aristocratic way possible. Her face was young and smooth, but her eyes showed age beyond her years. Her hair was a brilliant auburn red that must have been quite long when it was let down. It was currently twisted up into an arrangement of braids so beautifully complex it was a work of art, pure and simple. She looked the picture of refined grace, until you got to her feet, which were clad in a pair of blood-red, calf-high Doc Martens boots.

The overall effect was so surprising that Lily found herself quite speechless and simply stood in the doorway, staring.

After a moment of suitably awkward silence, Emmaline spoke. "That's quite alright, dear. I often have that effect on people."

Completely abashed, Lily moved aside, inviting her guest in with a stream of tumbled apologies and wishing she could offer her a cup of tea.

"Truly, Ms. Singer, it's quite alright. If I wanted to be treated like everyone else, I would dress like everyone else. Now, let's not dally about," she said, setting her shoulder bag on the bed and getting out a tailor's measuring tape. Using motions and a few polite directions, Emmaline positioned her in the middle of the hotel room's open floor space, feet together, back straight, head up, and arms outstretched. With practiced speed, she whipped the tape up, down, and around just about every body part Lily possessed, carefully noting her measurements in a small notebook tucked into a pocket of her skirt.

As she worked, she questioned Lily. "Now, Ms. Singer, what kind of outfit were you wanting?"

"Um, well, I'm not exactly sure. I mean, I know what I want to do in it, but I don't know what it should look like."

"I see. Let's start with what you know, then, shall we?" Emmaline said in a dry voice.

Lily took a deep breath. "Well, I have this…problem. I'm used to dressing quite professionally and fashionably, but of late I've found myself in situations where I need to do rather, um, physical things, and my normal attire gets in the way. Pencil skirts, fitted blouses, and oxford heels aren't exactly conducive to moving around, um, quickly."

"That's understandable. So you need an ensemble suitable for the outdoors?"

"Sort of, but not exactly. I…" Lily hesitated, embarrassed. "I think I need a, well, an adventuring outfit." She bit her lip, ready for the mocking smile or look of incredulity.

But instead Emmaline looked thoughtful. She crossed her arms, one hand lifted to tap her cheek as she examined Lily, though her eyes were distant, as if seeing something else.

Unable to bear the silence, Lily continued, feeling the need to explain herself. "I know it sounds silly. Why can't I just put on a pair of jeans and hiking boots, after all, like a normal person? But I have no idea when I might need to adventure and when I might need to be presentable. I just wish there was a way I could do both, if that makes sense," she finished weakly, looking away.

"It makes perfect sense, Ms. Singer."

Lily looked up, surprised, and saw a wry smile on Emmaline's face.

"You wouldn't believe some of the commissions I receive. I promise you, yours is one of the most reasonable and practical ones I've ever heard. It makes perfect sense to want a wardrobe that is both practical and fashionable. Now, what exactly counts as practical and fashionable varies from person to person, so I'll need you to be a bit more precise."

Turning to her bag, she drew out a sketch pad and took a seat, looking at Lily expectantly.

Put on the spot, Lily sank down onto the bed, thinking. "Well, I prefer wearing pencil skirts, but they restrict movement, so perhaps a pencil skirt with a slit? Or pleats?"

Emmaline nodded thoughtfully, her pencil dancing across the sketchpad.

"The shirt isn't as much the issue. Any loose blouse would do. Though it would probably be best if it had a fitted neck and sleeves, so there weren't any loose bits to get snagged or a low neckline to, um, reveal something at the wrong moment." Lily coughed.

"You know, I once had to give CPR to a man who had collapsed at a dinner party. That was the last time I wore low necklines."

Lily gave a startled laugh, surprised by the sudden remark. "Did you really?"

Emmaline smiled at the memory. "He was extremely overweight, the poor dear. Apparently CPR isn't something many people learn these days. Personally, I like to be prepared."

"I do too," Lily said, smiling. She was liking Emmaline more and more. "Though, I'm not sure I could manage CPR. I'm not very good with people."

"Oh neither am I, dear me. Can't stand the sight of them most of the time."

"Really?" Lily asked, curious. "But you seem so… comfortable. You're not at all, well, um…" she trailed off, realizing it might not be polite to continue that train of thought. But she didn't need to. Emmaline seemed to read her thoughts.

"Awkward? I used to be, but not any more."

"What changed?" Lily asked, now extremely curious. What made this woman so sure of herself? So sure *in* herself?

"Well, I stopped caring what other people thought of me, for a start." Emmaline raised an eyebrow, studying Lily critically as she sketched a few more lines.

Lily couldn't help it, she blushed. How in the world was she supposed to stop caring what other people thought of her? Outward appearance and public decorum were very important. She wanted to always make a good impression. "But…how? Appearances are important."

"Of course they are, Ms. Singer. Now, what about your jacket?"

"Excuse me?" Lily was thrown off by the sudden change in topic.

"You have described your skirt and blouse, but I assume you want some sort of blazer or jacket top to complete the outfit?"

"Oh, yes, um…I'm really not sure. Something elegant. I do enjoy vintage looks, but not old-fashioned. Certainly nothing with shoulder pads. I loathe shoulder pads."

Emmaline chuckled, a soft, musical sound. "An understandable sentiment. Might I suggest something modern with a vintage twist? How do you feel about high collars?"

"That sounds fine," Lily said, though honestly she had no idea. Art and design were not her strong points.

"Good. Now, one last question. Do you love yourself, Ms. Singer?"

Lily recoiled, startled. "What?"

"Exactly what I asked. It is a plain enough question. Do you love yourself?"

About to point out the rudeness of such a question, Lily stopped herself. Emmaline simply looked at her expectantly, expression politely interested. Detecting no hint of avarice or mocking, Lily tried to figure out what this polite, proper, but plainspoken woman wanted from her. She barely knew her and yet felt a strange camaraderie. Lily realized she wanted to be like Emmaline, with her strange sense of fashion and fearless behavior.

"I suppose I love myself," Lily answered slowly, not entirely sure of her answer. "At least, I don't hate myself."

"And yet you are constantly worried what other people think. Generally, that indicates insecurity. And insecurity comes from not loving yourself the way you are. I would be the last to discourage anyone from striving to be the best they can be, but you can't base your standards on other people's opinions. You can't live your life comparing yourself to others. It will leave you quite miserable. You have to be your own person, or you'll never find peace." As she spoke, Emmaline put the last few touches on her sketch, seemingly unbothered by Lily's nervous shifting. "There, that ought to do it," she said, turning her sketchbook around to show Lily what she'd created.

It was bold. It was different. It was strangely exciting. Lily's mouth quirked in a smile as she imagined herself in it. She didn't know if it was "her," but then what, exactly, was *her*? Whatever the answer, she knew the future held hard times, and she would need all the bravery she could muster. This outfit made her feel like she could step into those shoes, be the brave person she needed to be. It was worth a shot.

"It's lovely," Lily said with a smile.

"I thought you might like it." Emmaline mirrored her smile, standing up to tuck her tools back into her bag. "While clothes certainly aren't the whole of one's identity, they can be an important part. They are both an expression, and a shield. And one can't choose one's armor too carefully."

Turning to face her, Emmaline held out a card with contact details on it. "Now, I'll need a few days, but I should have most of the work done near the middle of the week. We can meet then for a second fitting to ensure everything is just as you want it. Is that acceptable?"

"Absolutely," Lily said, taking the card. "The sooner the better. I need this outfit yesterday."

"Then I shall endeavor to proceed with all speed. Thank you for this opportunity, Ms. Singer. I think I shall enjoy the project immensely. After all, it's not every day I get to outfit someone for an adventure." There was a slight sparkle in her eyes as she spoke, and she turned to leave.

At the door, she shook Lily's hand. "One more thing, if I may. Have you considered footwear?"

Lily shook her head. "Not really. I just know I need to be able to run in them, possibly climb things."

"Well, you might consider Doc Martens," Emmaline said, turning her heel slightly to show off her own boots. "They are fabulously comfortable and quite fashionable. It's a tragedy that heeled boots just aren't practical when it comes to real adventure. You might see heroines wearing them in the movies, but the realities of gravity, physics, and the human body guarantee injury if you tried all that in real life. Now, if you'll give me your shoe size, I'd be glad to acquire a pair that complements the outfit."

Grateful for one less thing to worry about, Lily readily agreed. She bade the eccentric tailor farewell, knowing the woman's words of wisdom would follow her for days to come, whether she wanted them to or not.

With only a short delay to check on Sebastian—there was no answer at the door, so she assumed he'd gone out with Sir Kipling—Lily gathered her bag and computer, then headed off to the Old Bodleian. Unlike yesterday's throng of humanity, the streets were lightly populated with backpack-toting students, briefcase-carrying academics, and other "normal" folk as opposed to tourists. There were surprisingly more bicycles in evidence, however, perhaps because they were the transportation of choice for the residents. They were absolutely everywhere, filling up the bike racks found on every block and leaning in rows against the ancient buildings.

Being a weekday, as well as cold and overcast, everyone was hurrying to and from their tasks, not strolling about enjoying the sights. Lily herself was tempted to take her time and examine several interesting buildings that she passed, but the chill wind discouraged such meanderings. It was amazing how different the day felt from yesterday's sunny glory, but then that was England for you.

She was just passing a row of narrow shops when she saw a flash of silver out of the corner of her eye. Turning, she noticed a stone archway leading to a tiny alley that she hadn't noticed before. An ancient-looking oak door stood slightly ajar beneath the arch, and she just saw the tip of a silver tail disappearing through it. Curious, she took a step toward the door, then hesitated. Was the alleyway private property? Looking around and seeing no one nearby, she decided to take a peek. The door was already ajar, so it wouldn't hurt to open it a bit further.

The hinges creaked as she pushed on the ancient wood. It was surprisingly heavy. Having opened it enough to stick her head through, she peered into the alleyway and was surprised to see it full of potted plants. Further down it appeared to open up into a lovely garden between the tall stone buildings. At the end of the alley, she thought she could see eyes peering out at her from the bushes.

She'd already pushed the door fully open and put one foot inside when her brain finally kicked in.

She stopped.

Despite the seeming innocence of the alleyway, something felt off. Lily finally realized it was the plants. They seemed greener, more...intense. As if more fully real than reality itself. Not only that, but they also appeared wild. Unkempt. Untamed. The garden in front of her didn't look at all like the carefully tended and trimmed courtyards and quadrangles that appeared all over Oxford.

Taking a step back, she stood in the doorway, thinking. It was then that the silver fox, perhaps in response to her hesitation, poked its head out of the bush. It examined her, then emerged fully and sat in the middle of the alley, head cocked to the side as if asking why she was taking so long.

Now that was most definitely not right. No matter how curious she was, she knew better than to wander into strange gardens alone with creatures that acted abnormally friendly. That was Wizarding 101. But she couldn't just leave. The alley had appeared for a reason, and it might be important. So, taking out her phone, she started snapping pictures of the alleyway, the garden, the fox, and the location of the archway so she could find it again. When she finished and reached for the door to pull it closed, she noticed that the fox had vanished.

Disappointed, but firm in her decision, she heaved the heavy oak door closed until there was only a crack left between it and the stone frame. Turning away, she headed off down the street as she looked at her phone, checking the pictures she'd just taken. What she saw stopped her in her tracks.

Lily whirled, eyes searching for the archway and alley she'd just left. But they were gone. The two shops on either side of the archway now appeared side-by-side, without the tiniest crack between them. Looking back at her pictures, she held up the phone, comparing them to what was in front of her. Every single picture showed the plain stone of the shops' outer walls, taken at various angles and distances. There was no alley, no garden, and no fox.

Thoroughly unnerved, Lily hurried off down the street, wanting to get inside and away from that alley—or absence of an alley—as quickly as possible. For once, she was desperate to talk to someone, anyone, needing some reassurance that she wasn't dreaming.

She had to swipe her library card at the main doors to get into the Old Bodleian. As she finally entered that ancient refuge of learning, she felt a sense of peace and wonder settle over her that chased away her fleeting paranoia. Stopping, she breathed in deep, instantly put at ease by the smell of old books and the feeling of age that permeated the air. It was refreshingly quiet, and she trod carefully on the flagstone floor as she headed toward a circular desk manned by several people.

The librarian on duty listened politely to her request for a tour, nodding when Lily mentioned Helen Pemberton's name. She asked Lily to wait and disappeared down a side hall, returning less than a minute later with a young woman in somber-colored clothes and thick glasses. She was introduced as Ashley, one of the graduate trainees. Handing Lily a pamphlet containing a handy floor plan of the Old Bodleian—there simply called the Old Library—the librarian returned to her station and left Lily in the expert care of the trainee.

The first thing Ashley did was to ask Lily what type of information she was looking for. Lily showed her the list of books Cyril had given her, and Ashley took a moment to examine it, eyes moving rapidly down the lines of text.

Finally looking up from the sheet of paper, she pushed her glasses further up the bridge of her nose and spoke softly. "It looks like most of the books you'll need will be on the second floor of the Old Library, or in the History Faculty Library over in the Radcliffe Camera. If you like, I can show you how to put a request in and give you a walk around while we wait. I know at least a few of these will come up fairly quickly, and you can get started with your reading. I expect you'll want to read in Duke Humfrey's reading room. It's the most beautiful spot, though the chairs aren't the most comfortable."

Lily agreed with a smile, being no stranger to long hours spent sitting in hard wooden chairs. She was a librarian, archivist, and wizard, after all, though Ashley didn't know about that last one.

Following the trainee, she went up a flight of stairs and around the corner to where a group of photocopying machines and computers nestled in an alcove. To the right, the hall opened up into a long, well-lit reading room, the entrance guarded by what a sign declared to be the main enquiry desk.

Being familiar with the online request system at her own library in Atlanta, Lily followed along easily as Ashley showed her how to put in book requests, explaining that most of the books in the Old Library and the Radcliffe Camera had to be read onsite and could not be checked out. Once they'd requested all the books from Cyril's list, Ashley took her on a tour. The graduate trainee seemed grateful for a chance to get away from her desk, and so the tour was, perhaps, a bit longer and more extensive than strictly necessary. Not that Lily was complaining.

Everything was gorgeous, old, and begging to be touched. Lily couldn't help but run her fingers lightly over the leather-bound spines of shelf after shelf of books as they walked through the Old Library's two upper floors—the ground floor housed the main desk, an exhibition room, gift shop, café, and various offices.

Ashley saved the best for last, finally leading Lily up the south staircase to Duke Humfrey's reading room. Situated above the Divinity School, the reading room was the location of the very first library built by the University, created to house the extensive collection donated by Humfrey, Duke of Gloucester. Later added to and expanded, it was the oldest part of the library and absolutely transcendent in its beauty.

As they exited the staircase and entered the reading room, Lily felt herself shiver with excitement. She gazed with wonder down a long hall filled with rows and rows of freestanding bookshelves, each with its own slanted desk and alcove. This was the Arts End, situated above the entrance hall of the Old Library where she'd originally come in. Moving to the center of this hall and turning left, they had to first check in at the security porter's desk before going further.

Since you couldn't take any bags into Duke Humfrey's, Ashley had already shown her to the lockers where Lily left her bag and personal items. The only things she carried with her were her phone and computer. At the security desk, the porter, a smiling, middle-aged man, checked over her things and sent her on her way with a polite reminder to follow all the library's rules regarding deportment and the handling of books.

Passing the porter's desk, they walked down the oldest section, the medieval hall built directly above the Divinity School. This hall connected the two ends to form a letter *H*. Its walls were one solid mass of shelves, with book spines making a kaleidoscope of color in their massive variety of cloth and leather bindings.

Finally reaching the end of the medieval section, they entered the most magnificent part of Duke Humphrey's reading room: the Selden End. As she stepped inside, Lily's breath caught in her throat and she felt the tingle of goosebumps race up her arms. A momentary break in the clouds filled the long hall with glorious sunlight, which streamed in through massive arched windows at either end of the room. Looking up, she saw that the ceiling opened above them, extending up a floor and a half to a beautifully carved wooden ceiling made up of rows and rows of painted panels depicting the arms of the university. Both walls were covered in books from floor to ceiling, with a landing on either side of the hall allowing access to the upper level of books. The open floor in the middle of the hall was filled with rows of desks with individual reading lights.

Everything around her was dark, smooth, polished wood, and the overwhelming smell of books made her heady, as if she were drunk on wine. Ashley had to say her name several times before Lily heard her and dragged her mind back to earth with painful reluctance. The graduate intern seemed to understand and did not attempt to lead Lily back out of the room, but simply told her to explore while she went to collect Lily's requested reading material.

Lily wandered around in a euphoric daze, wishing with all her heart that she could somehow live in this room for the rest of her life. This was a bibliophile's heaven in every sense of the word. The poets could keep their Elysian fields, for all she cared. If she were in charge of paradise, this was what it would look like. There were few other people in the room and the only noise was the occasional turn of a page. So it was easy for her to imagine that she was alone with the thousands of glorious books around her.

She was up on one of the landings, carefully thumbing through an eighteenth-century book on the Hundred Years' War when Ashley returned with an armful of research material. Taking the books, Lily installed herself at one of the reading desks, got out her computer, and began to read, starting with the books on Cyril's list that he'd marked as most important. Knowing she didn't have time to read through every one of them front to back, she began by scanning the table of contents and index of each, picking out all the sections referencing Avalon or Morgan le Fay. Upon further reading, she added Tintagel Castle—the purported birthplace of King Arthur and therefore possibly Morgan—and several minor characters' names to her list of key words. She took notes on particularly interesting passages using her computer, being a much safer alternative to using her eduba in public, even if there were only four other people in the room, all engrossed in their own reading.

In what felt like no time, closing hour arrived. The sky outside had begun to darken, a surprise to Lily since she'd been too engrossed to notice the changing light. What she did notice, however, was her stiffness and her sore behind when she stood up. She took a few minutes to stretch before closing her computer and gathering her things.

Lily was the last one to leave the reading room. At the entrance to the Selden End she paused, arms full of books and her laptop, and turned to stare longingly at the silent and majestic room. With darkness deepening outside and a subtle chill filling the empty room, Lily felt a sudden longing for her own familiar library at home. It might not be as old or beautiful, but it was always warm and much better lit than this ancient cavern with only desk lamps providing lonely pools of light in the dimness. Even so, Lily was reluctant to leave. She felt safe here. Sure of herself. Nothing seemed too hard or too frightening when she was in a library. It was as if the concentration of books created a bubble of space where time stood still and the world's problems fell away.

With a final sigh, Lily turned, signing out with the security porter and dropping off her armful of books at the staff desk. She stopped by the lockers to collect her belongings and steeled herself for the walk home through cold, empty streets. Though she couldn't sense anyone nearby, magical or otherwise, she couldn't shake the feeling that something was following her. The stone buildings around her, which had seemed so majestic and awe-inspiring in the light of day, now felt ominous and lonely. She was extremely grateful to reach the well-lit, warm interior of the Macdonald Randolph hotel and decided to treat herself to a hot dinner before heading up to her room to do more research on her computer. Her stomach, easily ignored during long hours of reading, was now determined to make its displeasure known as it demanded immediate attention.

A bowl of steaming minestrone soup and a roasted duck leg with a side of poached egg warmed her up considerably, and she polished it all off with gusto. Though it was technically rude to use one's phone at the table, since she was alone Lily decided it didn't matter and finally called her mother to see how things were going at Allen's house. It was still the middle of the afternoon in Savannah, and Freda answered with eager delight, demanding all the details of their trip before Lily could even get out a single question.

After satisfying her mother's curiosity and concern, she finally managed to ask about Madam Barrington. At her question, Freda's voice went from excited to subdued.

"She's not doing too well, the poor thing. The curse is sapping her strength and it's all I can do to keep her warm enough and get her to eat at regular intervals. Allen has tried a few counter-curses, but so far they don't seem to be helping much."

Lily felt her heart sink, but she refused to give in to despair. Madam Barrington was counting on them to stop John Faust, and she knew she couldn't let herself be crippled by worry. Suddenly remembering what George Dee had said about going to Savannah to help, Lily felt a bit of optimism return. If anyone could help Madam Barrington, it was Allen and Mr. Dee. She only hoped they could find a cure in time.

"Oh," Lily said suddenly, realizing she hadn't warned Freda or Allen that Mr. Dee was coming. Keeping her explanation succinct, she told her mother about their visit to Highthorne manor and how its master was coming to aid their efforts to restore Madam Barrington to health. In fact, depending on how early he'd been able to fly out, she warned that he could be arriving at any moment.

Freda was momentarily overjoyed at the news, but then went into a flutter about needing to get an extra guest room ready to receive their honored guest. Lily smiled, wondering how Allen was coping with having a full-fledged "mother" in the house. For that matter, she wondered how Freda and Allen's flock of construct "hand maids" were getting along. Knowing her mother would feel better once she was busy doing something, Lily said goodbye, admonishing her not to forget to pass on a greeting to Madam Barrington amid her frenzy of preparations. After hanging up Lily sat for a moment staring at her plate, now empty but for duck bones and a few sprigs of lettuce. Knowing it did no good to fret about something she couldn't control, she shook herself from her reverie and headed up to her room.

To her surprise, Sebastian was not back yet and so, of course, neither was Sir Kipling. She called Sebastian's number only to get a standard voicemail prompt. Biting her lip, she resisted the urge to head back out and look for him. He was a night owl and an adventurer. It was unrealistic to expect him to be holed up in his room when there was a whole new city to explore.

So instead, she went to her room and unpacked her bag, taking a shower and putting on something more comfortable before settling down at the room's desk with her computer. Several of the books Cyril had listed were available in the Bodleian's digital collection, and she used her new library account to access them.

It was hard to concentrate, however, with anxiety nibbling away at the back of her mind. For the first half hour she kept stopping and listening every time footsteps passed her door. She even called Sebastian several more times, with no luck. Finally, annoyed at herself, she clamped down, put on headphones, and focused on her research.

With a full belly and an exhausting day behind her, it wasn't long before her eyelids began to droop. She struggled mightily, even calling room service to get a cup of strong, black tea in the hopes that caffeine would help perk her up.

Somehow, however, it seemed to do the opposite.

Finally, she could no longer resist laying her head down on her hands, intending to shut her eyes for a just a few minutes. Her awareness became muddled and for a while she drifted, not really asleep, but not awake, either. Though her eyes were closed, she began to see things against the darkness of her eyelids, ethereal lights and shapes taking form in a waking dream. A silver form danced back and forth, leaping and cavorting before her. She couldn't quite see its shape. It could have been a fawn, or a cat, or a fox. The light got brighter and brighter, but the shape was still indistinct, as if seen through a haze.

Lily sat up and rubbed her eyes, trying to see more clearly. Her body felt sluggish and her mind fuzzy like she'd just woken up, but at least she could make out the form now. It was a silver fox, and it sat in front of her, waiting expectantly. She knew it wanted her to follow it, though she wasn't sure how she knew. Pushing back from her desk, which was now fuzzy and indistinct as the fox had once been, she stood up. Her hotel room faded around her, its walls, bed, and chairs barely visible in the dim twilight. But the fox wasn't dim. It glowed a soft silver, so beautiful Lily wished she could stroke its shining fur.

She stepped forward through the desk as if it weren't even there, reaching for the fox. The strange twilight around her must have caused her to misjudge the distance, however, because the creature was no longer directly in front of her, but several yards ahead. So she took another step, and another. It seemed like she was making progress, but as soon as she drew close enough to touch it once again, it sprang away.

"Wait!" Lily called after it.

It stopped and looked over its shoulder at her, and she

felt an insistent desire, even need, to follow it.

"Lily!"

The cry was so faint she barely heard it. She paused, wondering if she'd imagined the sound.

"Lily, stop! Come back!"

There it was again. She was sure she heard it this time. Turning her head to glance behind, she was distracted by a yip. Looking back at the fox, she saw that it had come closer and was looking at her intently. The need to step forward was almost overwhelming, and that beautiful silver light filled her mind. Everything else faded and was swallowed up in the darkness around her.

She stepped forward.

"Lily! Stop right there!"

She tried to turn toward the voice. It was much louder this time, and closer. But she couldn't move. Or perhaps, didn't want to. She hesitated, torn, distracted again by the fox, which had stepped even closer, almost close enough to touch. Lily reached out, eyes and mind filled with silver light. It was so close, so beautiful, so—

Another form, not shining but dull and grey, filled her vision, partially blocking the silver light. The form hissed and yowled, taking a swipe at the fox, who leapt back.

Suddenly there was the sound of footsteps behind her and someone grabbed her wrist, pulling her back with a jerk. Sebastian's voice filled her head even as his tall form slid in front of her, completely blocking her view of the ethereal creature.

"Get behind me and whatever you do, don't let go."

Her first reaction had been to pull away from his sudden and violent hold on her, but his words made her pause, mind working sluggishly. She vaguely remembered rushing through similar darkness, holding fast to someone's hand

and knowing that she mustn't stop, mustn't let go. As the words echoed through her mind she gripped convulsively at Sebastian's hand, his body the only warmth in a suddenly chill darkness. Shivering, Lily laced her fingers through his and held on tight.

"You can't have her," Sebastian was saying, talking to someone Lily couldn't see. "She's not yours to take. She doesn't know, doesn't understand."

The fox growled, a musical yet grating sound that wasn't at all inviting. As if a spell had been broken, Lily felt a terrible fear, wanting nothing more than to be back in her hotel room.

Sebastian, apparently, had the same idea, because he was slowly backing up, nudging her to move as well. She looked behind them and could just barely see a faint light, not silvery, but warm and yellow and reflecting off dim shapes that looked vaguely bed- and chair-like. She headed for it, moving carefully and keeping a firm grip on Sebastian's hand.

"I don't see why you'd want to see her. If you wanted to talk to me you could have just said so."

Sebastian was carrying on some sort of conversation with the fox, though how she had no idea, because the fox made no sound that she could hear.

Apparently satisfied with the increasing distance between Lily and the fox, Sir Kipling retreated, appearing from around Sebastian and trotting past her toward the yellow light with fluffy tail held high like a flag. Somehow it was easier to focus on him than on the dim shape of her hotel room, which kept shifting closer and further away. So she did, keeping her eyes on the white tuft at the end of his tail which showed up strangely bright in the darkness, as if filled with an inner light as pure and white as snow.

The idea of a light bulb strapped to the end of her cat's tail was sufficiently amusing to distract her, causing her to miss the next bit of Sebastian's conversation. When she caught his words again, he sounded less angry, but not at all happy.

"Fine. I get it. But *I'll* bring her, alright? Just give me a few hours to explain things and get ready. Then you can come get us."

They were very close now. Lily could see the shapes of the bed, chair, and desk, and they only looked slightly faded. She tugged on Sebastian's hand, urging him to go faster. She wanted to let go and rush into the room, but her friend's earlier admonition stopped her. Even if she'd tried to let go, though, Sebastian's grip was far too strong. He held on as if she were his lifeline in a raging sea.

"Yes, thank you for your understanding, *melihi'araji*. We'll be ready."

Sebastian's voice sounded oddly deferential, but Lily spared it only a brief thought before focusing wholly on that bright room. A smile touched her lips, seeing Sir Kipling sitting on the bed, waiting for her. And suddenly they were there, standing between the desk and the bed as the twilight receded.

Lily didn't have a chance to collapse onto the bed as she'd intended to because she was swept up into a bone-crushing hug by Sebastian instead.

"Are you *insane*?" he asked after pulling back. His voice was taut and he held her tightly by either shoulder as if he was still worried she would disappear. "You could have been lost forever."

"Will you be needing me further, sir?" asked a very British voice behind her, and Lily almost jumped out of her skin. Looking over her shoulder she saw Hawkins standing in front of the door, looking perfectly at ease despite their sudden appearance out of nowhere.

"No, we're good for now, Hawkins. Thank you. But I'll need to speak to you before…well, we're leaving again soon. Why don't you go get settled in your room and come back in, say, an hour."

"Very good, sir." Hawkins bowed, turned, and left, closing the door softly behind him.

"Wha—what's going on?" Lily asked, her body trying, and failing, to cope with everything that had just happened. Having failed, it decided the next best thing was to go into shock. Her knees suddenly felt very weak, and without warning, Sebastian's hold was the only thing keeping her upright.

Startled by her attempt to collapse, Sebastian half caught, half lowered her onto the bed and helped her sit upright as he took a seat beside her. Sir Kipling crawled into her lap, seeming determined to put things right with a good, solid round of purring. While the medicinal properties of a cat's purr were by no means scientifically proven, at the very least his warmth and comforting weight helped her body cope.

"What just happened?" she asked again, words coming a bit easier now that she was sitting down. Gravitating toward the closest solid object, she leaned against Sebastian's shoulder, feeling dead tired.

"What just happened was that a queen of the fae attempted to lure you into her domain."

"But why?" Lily asked sleepily. She knew this was important and tried her best to keep her eyes open. But she was so tired.

"I'm…not entirely sure. But for whatever reason, you've caught her interest. And what Thiriel wants, Thiriel gets." He heaved a great sigh. "Like it or not, we're taking a trip to the fae realm."

Epilogue

DESPITE HER BEST EFFORTS, LILY'S BODY REBELLED AND DEMANDED SLEEP. But she got only a scant hour before Sebastian shook her awake, telling her she needed to get up and get dressed.

While she put on plain street clothes and a warm jacket, she could hear Sebastian and Hawkins talking in quiet voices out in the hall. It sounded like Sebastian was reassuring the manservant, asking him to stay and look out for their return.

The realization of what they were about to do started to sink in, waking her up more effectively than any amount of shaking. She was frightened. Frightened of that twilight darkness with no clear paths, no way in or out. Was that the fae realm? All darkness and confusion? She hoped not.

More than the darkness, however, was the fear of the unknown. She already struggled to meet and interact with new humans. How would she handle otherworldly beings whose power she didn't understand? What did Thiriel want with her? Sebastian wouldn't lead them into danger if he thought Thiriel meant them harm, would he? What if she got lost or left behind, how would she ever find her way home? These thoughts swirled around in her head, paralyzing her with a fear she didn't want but couldn't overcome.

When Sebastian came back into the room, he found her sitting on the bed, knees drawn up under her chin and arms encircling them protectively. Sir Kipling rubbed and purred in concern, having no lap to jump into as he was used to.

At first Lily didn't hear Sebastian's words, lost as she was in her own internal struggle. But then the sounds filtered through.

"Hey, Lil, you okay? Lily? Lily!"

She jumped, then focused on him. Words tumbled out, seeming as jumbled as her thoughts. "I don't think this is a good idea—I mean we can't afford—there's no time to be messing around—with the fae, that is—and I don't think…I don't know…" she slowed down, then stopped, finishing in a whisper. "I don't think I'm strong enough."

"Don't be ridiculous," Sebastian said with a chuckle that may or may not have been forced. "You know how to take care of yourself. And anyway, I know these creatures. They follow…a higher order, I guess you could say. There are rules, and everyone follows them. As long as we act properly, we have nothing to worry about."

"That's what I'm afraid of," Lily gulped. "How will I know what's proper? You know I'm terrible at social situations."

Sebastian sighed and reached down to pry loose her death grip on her legs. Taking both of her hands in his, he pulled her gently from the bed and into a standing position. "Just stay close and do what I do, alright? I know this might sound weird, but I don't think fae are…allowed to hurt humans. At least, not the way other humans hurt humans. Think of a wild animal. They want to stay as far away from you as they possibly can, and would only attack in self-defense. Well, or if they were hungry. But don't worry, fae don't eat humans." He winked at her, and she let out something that was half laugh, half squeak of terror.

"What about cats?" Sir Kipling asked, very studiously *not* sounding worried.

"Did he just ask if they eat cats?" Sebastian said, looking at Lily with the slightest of grins. The feline's I'm-not-worried-about-this-situation expression was fooling no one.

Lily nodded, not returning the smile.

"Relax, he'll be fine…probably."

Lily groaned. "Do we have to do this?"

Sebastian seemed to shiver, as if a draft had just come through the room. "Yes. It wouldn't do any good to ignore the summons, she'd lure you in some way or another. We just have to use this to our advantage. I…don't know what she wants, but maybe we can bargain for her help with our little 'Mr. Fancypants' problem. After all, Morgan was connected to the fae somehow, and you're her descendant. Maybe they just want to talk to us."

"Or stop us," Lily said darkly.

"Oooor that," Sebastian agreed in a falsely cheery tone, then fell silent. Lily could tell he was far from happy about the situation.

"What's the matter?"

Sebastian didn't answer at first. When he finally looked up, his eyes were haunted. "I promised myself I'd never go back."

Lily shivered. "Was it that bad?"

He shook his head. "No, not in the way you're thinking. Fae are creatures of nature, and nature is beautiful…but they aren't human. They're not even animals. They're…the fae." He was silent for a moment, collecting his thoughts. "When I was there—before—I started to forget…who I was and what was important to me. I went there because I hated who I was, but then, slowly, I became someone I didn't recognize."

"That sounds thoroughly reassuring. But oughtn't we be going? I believe our guide has arrived." Sir Kipling's meow cut off anything Lily might have said, and they both looked around. Where the hotel door should have been sat a silver fox, its fur shining brightly as everything around it dimmed into shadow. It huffed at them, blowing impatiently through its whiskers.

"You got everything you need, Lil?" Sebastian asked, not taking his eyes from the fox.

Grabbing her bag from the bed, Lily slung it across her body. "What about Kip? Do I need to carry him?"

"No. Thiriel is a high fae. If she promises safe passage, it's safe passage we'll get. All of us. Just be sure to stay close, alright, Kip?"

Sir Kipling mewed softly, ears perked and yellow eyes also fixed on the fox.

"If?" Lily asked quietly, trying not to sound nervous.

Sebastian didn't respond, addressing the fox instead. "We're ready. We agree to come of our own free will in exchange for safe passage to *and* from your realm *at the time of our own choosing.* Are we agreed?" His voice was clear and hard.

The fox yipped and, without waiting, turned and trotted off.

Instead of taking off after it, as Lily had expected, Sebastian turned to her. At her look of alarm he grinned, a touch of mischief in his eyes. "Don't worry, he'll come back. I just wanted to…explain a few things first. Because, well, I know I'm usually terrible at it."

For a moment Lily forgot her worries and rolled her eyes, knowing he liked getting a reaction out of her. But far from being annoyed, she felt warm inside, knowing he was going to the trouble. For her.

"The twilight between realms is how the fae get around. I don't know how it works but it's definitely outside the normal laws of space and time. Because we're not fae, we don't have the right, um, senses to find our way through it, which is why we have to have a guide. There's only one rule: don't stop. It's like riding a bike: you have to keep moving or you'll fall down. I don't know where you fall to, but I've heard it's not pleasant. Unlike a certain, conniving mold fae, this fox won't leave us behind. But even if we're going slowly, you can't stop to rest, not even for a second, okay?"

Lily nodded, not feeling especially reassured.

"Oh, and don't touch anything. Don't pick any flowers, or leaves, or fruit. Don't eat anything anyone offers you unless I say it's okay. It may or may not be what it looks like. In fact, most things won't be what they look like, though…" he paused, examining her thoughtfully, "I know you've been able to see through glamour in the past, probably because of the fae magic in your blood you inherited from Morgan. But I don't know how effective it will be in the fae realm. Anyway, you got all that?"

"I—I think so." She didn't, but tried to stand up straight anyway and pretend she wasn't afraid. She thought of Madam Barrington, who was counting on her to succeed; and Emmaline, who didn't care about anyone's opinion; and her mother, who loved her to pieces; and Sebastian, who thought her capable even when she felt small and weak. What she couldn't be for herself, at least she could be for them. She could be strong.

"Let's go," Lily said, gripping her friend's hand tightly.

He smiled. "That's my girl."

INTERLUDE

Twilight's Hour

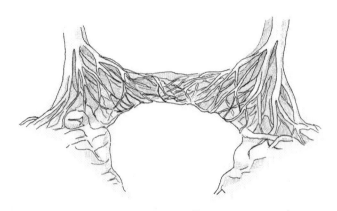

SOMETHING GIVEN, SOMETHING GAINED. THAT WAS THE WITCH'S WAY.

Sometimes it worked out great. Other times it bit you in the butt. It was worth it, though, because you knew it was coming and could plan for it. Then there were the times when you thought you'd made off like a bandit, only to realize you'd been screwed over by the fine print. The fine print you hadn't seen because, well, it wasn't written down and, no matter how many questions you asked, you never knew how much you didn't know until it was too late.

That was the fae in a nutshell. The high fae, at least. The low fae like Pip and Grimmold were simple creatures whose job it was to look after their designated plot of dirt and not cause trouble. Not too much trouble, anyway.

Sebastian.

The whisper in his mind hurt like an old wound: the memory of infliction more painful than any lingering discomfort.

The price of power, indeed.

He'd sworn—*promised* himself—he'd never go back. Not to her. He'd thought that if he laid low, didn't draw attention to himself, she'd forget. Alright, so maybe it had been more of a wistful fancy. She'd given him her duality's staff, for goodness sake. If that didn't say something about her intentions, then not much did.

He'd been running for as long as he could remember. From his parents' death, from his foolish mistakes, from his loneliness. But it looked like this particular problem had finally caught up with him.

Sebastian.

The saving grace of the situation was that she couldn't read minds, though sometimes her uncanny insight made it seem like she could. It was hard to get one up on a being many thousands of years old. Especially since you couldn't lie. Fae could spot lies like a vulture spotted road kill. It came from their being such good liars themselves. Well, not liars, exactly. Fae couldn't speak falsehoods, which unfortunately made his truth coin worthless in the fae realm. But they were masters of the non-answer. Vagueness, avoidance, and the selective sharing of detail were their tools of the trade.

And Lily wondered why he was so bad at opening up.

Sebastian.

He gritted his teeth, refusing to remember. Instead, he gripped Lily's hand more tightly as they ran through the twilight after the bobbing tail of a silver fox.

Lily didn't know it, but between now and whenever they finally returned to reality, she would be the only thing keeping his sanity intact. And, most unfortunately, that would make the whole ordeal ten times worse, since he suspected Lily was not what Thiriel truly wanted. She was simply the bait, which meant he was being a complete fool, and should cut his losses while he could.

If this had been several years ago, he probably would have done just that. But not anymore. Like it or not, Lily Singer had changed him. He hadn't known it then, but from the moment he'd first laid eyes on her, his loner days had been numbered. He still hadn't admitted it, not out loud, at least. But the time had come for him to choose between being with her and being free. He hadn't chosen freedom. The worst part was, he still might lose her. But at least this way, she'd be safe.

The air streaming past his cheeks changed, its cold bite dulling to a damp slap, then a warm caress. It was interesting the similarities between the twilight and outer space. Both were deathly cold and empty, surrounding you with the shadows of possibility while shimmering with pinpricks of light, possibly even life. But there, thankfully, the similarities ended. He was quite fond of not asphyxiating from lack of air, and the changing temperature was a useful guide, inasmuch as anything could be a guide in this treacherous nowhere. Based on the temperature, he knew they were close to arriving.

The idea did not fill him with joy.

He wanted to glance behind, to check on Lily and Kip. But his job was to lead them safely to the other side of nowhere, and so he had to keep his eyes on their guide, Thiriel's messenger. The silver fox was a good choice, considering her range of options. Being the fae queen of decomposition and decay meant she had a wide selection of less-than-delightful choices. Now, granted, it wasn't as disgusting as it sounded. The English language—the whole human psyche, in fact— failed Thiriel when it came to describing her aspect, something that Sebastian had long lamented.

The fox slowed, his silver paws now pattering down on the shadows of grass instead of blank nothingness. Sebastian heard Lily's sigh of relief, probably an indication she'd noticed the changing temperature herself. Perhaps she'd even looked up from her feet long enough to see the faint twinkle of stars that had almost coalesced into reality.

It happened in the space of a breath, that moment of eternity after you'd exhaled, but not yet taken your next lungful of air. In that infinite instant they transitioned, gasping in a relieved breath as they collapsed into the tall grass of an open meadow. Sebastian enjoyed the prickle and scratch of the blades against his skin as he stared up at the now-brilliantly visible canopy of stars above them.

"We made it," Lily puffed between heaving gulps of air. The next gulp came out as a laugh. She seemed euphoric.

Sebastian knew it was just the air. Everything was purer, cleaner, more intense in the fae realm, untouched by humans and their greedy, often corrupting influence. You could get drunk off the air here until your body adjusted. That was fine with him. Lily could use the pick-me-up, and he wasn't feeling too bad himself. Of course, it *had* been a while.

For a moment he tried to let it all go and just enjoy being back, enjoy the beauty, enjoy the purity. "Welcome to Melthalin," he murmured to the open air, "sanctuary of the fae."

Lily rolled over onto her side and propped herself up on an elbow, slinging her other arm across his chest as she grinned widely. She seemed to have gotten her breath back. "It's so beautiful," she whispered in awe, staring into his eyes.

Sebastian swallowed. She was very close. Too close. He wanted so badly to reach up and cup her face in his hand, to run his thumb over her smooth skin, to pull her in…

"Yeah, it's…it's really pretty," he said abruptly, sitting up. "Just wait until you see the forests. Oh, and the streams. Everything here is…perfect." He stared off to the side where the fox had been sitting, but it was nowhere in sight. Playing cat and mouse, then. Yup, definitely not the time, nor the place. Not now, not ever. *She* would make sure of that.

At the sound of spluttering giggles, he turned to find Sir Kipling sitting on Lily's chest, giving her nose a thorough cleaning. He must have been sneaking about in the grass and, having completed his inspection of the immediate area, decided to make himself useful.

"Come on, Kip. Baths can wait. We need to make tracks."

Sebastian got to his feet, reaching down to help Lily to hers. She was still rather giggly, and he wondered how long the effect would last. Not that he minded this happier, more lively version, but he was rather fond of her prickly side. After all, easygoing people weren't much fun to tease.

With a sigh, he looked down and spotted Sir Kipling, head low, fluffy hindquarters skyward, about to pounce on an unsuspecting toad. "Oi!" He snapped his fingers in the cat's direction. The toad, thus alerted, seized the opportunity to make a quick getaway. Lily's feline glared up at him in consternation, but Sebastian wasn't impressed. It was hard to be intimidated by a cat whose belly you rubbed on a regular basis. "I wouldn't hunt anything here if I were you. Not all the animals are as they seem. That toad, for instance, would have singed your whiskers off…or made your tail disappear, depending on how vindictive it was feeling."

Lily giggled again. She put a hand over her mouth to try and suppress it, but it leaked out around the edges, probably on account of the look of abject horror on Sir Kipling's face.

"Humph," the feline huffed. "Laugh all you want. Just wait until you touch the wrong leaf and break out in purple spots or grow a third ear. See if you get any pity from me then." The insulted cat turned away from his mistress, twisting around to clean his tail, as if that would somehow ensure its continued visibility.

Sebastian grinned, then did a double take, eyes widening to saucers and jaw dropping open. Was this place playing tricks on his ears, or had he just heard Sir Kipling talk?

"Uh, Kip. Say something."

"Excuse me?" The cat looked at him archly.

"I heard that!" Sebastian exclaimed, pointing at the cat excitedly. "I heard you talk! I mean I understood you, or whatever. Why can I understand you?" He looked between the cat and Lily, brow creasing. He hadn't really heard words, more like a whining meow, but the memory of meaning shone in his mind as if he'd physically heard the cat speak.

Lily looked as confused as he felt, which was good since it meant she was starting to think straight. She must be adjusting to the air. It would be unwise to go gallivanting off into Melthalin with someone high as a kite who wanted to touch every shiny thing they saw. The shiny things around here tended to bite.

"I don't know. Maybe…" She trailed off, face transforming into that faraway expression she always got whenever she was looking without her eyes. Wizard-y stuff, in other words. There was silence, then a small gasp escaped her lips. "It's so strong," she murmured.

"What? What's strong?" Sebastian asked, sharing a glance of mutual annoyance with Sir Kipling whose tail was flicking back and forth impatiently.

Without replying, Lily cupped her hands in front of her as if catching falling snowflakes. Lips moving soundlessly, eyes staring into nothingness, she looked like she was casting, but he hadn't known she could do it without words. At least, he'd never seen her do it before.

Watching her intently, he saw a flicker like a spark of electricity between her palms, and suddenly the night was lit with a blinding flash of light. Startled, he cried out, hand rising automatically to shield his face. He heard Lily say, "Oops," and the light diminished.

Night vision completely ruined, he lowered his hand to see a small ball of sparking light in Lily's palm.

"Turn that off," he hissed. "Do you want every fae in the area to know we're here?"

The light vanished. "My magic—the Source—it's so strong here. Inside me, around me, everywhere. It's like I've been drinking from a dripping faucet all my life and now I'm standing in a tropical downpour!" She laughed in delight, looking up and raising her hands to the sky as if she could feel the raindrops on her skin.

Alright, so maybe she still had some adjusting to do.

"That's great, really great," he said, reaching out to catch her forearm and towing her in the direction the fox had disappeared. "Now, we'd better get out of here before someone or something comes to investigate your little fireworks show. Not all the fae are as fond of humans as Thiriel. Actually, none of them are, but some are a bit more open about expressing the un-fond feelings in their shriveled little hearts."

By the time they'd reached the edge of the meadow, he'd regained enough of his night vision to see where they were going. The tall grass had been a bit much for Sir Kipling at their hurried pace, so Lily had picked him up and he rode on her shoulders, claws dug into her jacket and fluffy tail waving about as he used it for balance.

Sebastian stopped, holding out a hand to catch Lily as she inevitably ran into him in the dark. Making a shushing noise, he stilled, letting the sounds and smells of the forest surround him. It was unusually quiet, but then it *was* September, and most of the insects had died or gone into hibernation. An owl hooted in the distance, the sound mixing with the normal rustlings and whispers of a forest at night—though normal didn't exactly apply when it came to the fae realm. He smelled pine needles and damp leaves, so he knew they were somewhere in the northern hemisphere. Not that it mattered. Thiriel's court had no geographical location. It wasn't something you found, it was something you were drawn into.

Eyes searching the darkness, he finally spotted what he'd been hoping to see: a faint silver glow reflecting off leaves and undergrowth. It approached slowly, getting brighter and brighter until the silver fox emerged from a nearby bush.

"I figured you'd be back," Sebastian said sarcastically.

You always did like your little games.

Sebastian snorted. That was rich, Thiriel accusing *him* of playing games.

"What?" Lily eyed the fox with suspicion. "What's funny?"

"Nothing," Sebastian said quickly. Feeling defiant, he sought Lily's hand in the shadows and entwined his fingers with hers. It was very dark in the woods, and he didn't want her to get lost. At least that's what he would have said to her if she'd protested, but she seemed to be of the same mind and gripped his hand tightly.

They set off after the fox, forced to move slowly through

the dense wood. Sir Kipling had jumped down from Lily's shoulder, able to move more easily on the forest floor and preferring to make his own way rather than get smacked in the face with tree branches.

"There's usually more light than this," Sebastian whispered as they wove between the trees. "But I think you scared them away with your spell. Give it another fifteen minutes and they'll be back." He didn't elaborate on who "they" were. She would figure it out soon.

Sure enough, after a time spent stumbling around with only a bit of silver glow to illuminate their path, lights did indeed begin to appear. Lights, meaning pixies. Pixie was a general term he used for small fae, and almost all species could glow. He wasn't too firm on the biological details, he just knew that pixies loved playing with light, especially when it meant showing off to each other.

At first they kept their distance, appearing as tiny, multicolored pinpricks of light blinking on and off throughout the wood like fireflies. Then their curiosity kicked in—the eternal bane of all pixies—and the nearer ones started to gather, slowly at first, then in increasing numbers. Their whispered giggles and peeps of interest sounded like a quiet symphony of crickets who'd been drinking too much caffeine.

Lily stopped, watching them with wonder and not a bit of nervousness. Wanting her to maintain a healthy respect for fae in general, he decided not to point out that pixies were, by and large, harmless, though they could be mischievous when grouped in large numbers. They tended to egg each other on.

In fact…he watched carefully as several of the braver ones flitted forward to investigate the newcomer. They were more shy about him, sensing his fae magic and knowing he wasn't just a defenseless human. As soon as the surrounding pixies saw that their fellows were unharmed and having much more fun than they, the swarm converged. Lily yelped in alarm as she was suddenly surrounded by dozens of tiny creatures, most smaller than her pinkie, some even smaller than her fingernail. They inspected her from head to toe, crawling inside her bag—no doubt looking for edible morsels—and playing with the loose strands of her hair.

That was the last straw for Lily. She waved her arms above her head, attempting to ward off the inquisitive swarm. But they just made it into a game, seeing who could get past her defenses to tug at her hair and ears.

"Ack!—Sebastian—get them—off me!" Lily's words were punctuated with more arm waving.

"Aw, be a good sport, Lil. They're just having a little fun. Besides, they'll like you better if you play with them." Sebastian grinned, pausing to enjoy the spectacle.

Then a group of the little troublemakers realized her glasses weren't attached to her face and attempted to make off with them. Lily swore, grabbing for her spectacles and holding them tightly to her face as the rest of the pixies realized there was a new game to play and joined in the tug-of-war.

Sebastian decided it was time to step in before Lily accidentally hurt one of them.

"Alright, alright, break it up." He came closer, waving a hand carefully around Lily's face until the thieves were forced to flee. But as soon as he turned around, they were back, and in greater numbers. The look on Lily's face was no longer annoyed. It was scared. Sebastian knew the pixies weren't malicious, just like little children: focused on the moment and incapable of realizing the consequences of their actions. He wasn't sure why they were so interested in Lily—perhaps they could sense she was a wizard?—but, if he didn't act soon, someone was going to get hurt.

Before he could do a thing, a larger streak of light approached through the trees, moving so fast it was a blur. With a furious war cry—a drawn-out squeak to Sebastian's ears—it whirled about Lily's head, scattering the smaller pixies like bowling pins as they scrambled to get out of the line of fire. It then landed on her head and squeaked a diatribe of threats and insults at the retreating pinpricks of light. The swarm had dispersed, and though a few still hovered at a distance, they seemed to realize it was time to get back to their own business.

"P—Pip? Is that you?" Lily asked, voice only slightly shaky.

The pixie squeaked and hopped from Lily's head to her shoulder, giving her a sympathetic pat on the neck—her ears had already been tugged enough for one night.

Sebastian laughed. "You little pipsqueak! How did you know we were here?"

Pip launched into a complicated explanation that he could barely follow—it had taken years of practice to understand pixies even when they were talking slowly—but he got the general idea. "Wait, you were sent? What do you mean they knew she was coming? Who—"

More squeaking.

"Alright, alright, calm down. Of course you can come with us. I would have asked you anyway, to keep those little buggers off." He gestured around them and several peeps of alarm were heard as lights vanished into the underbrush. "You seem to have taught them a lesson." He winked at Pip, who did a few excited loop-de-loops before coming back to land on Lily's shoulder.

"So, care to fill me in?" Lily raised an eyebrow and Sebastian's smile faded just a little. This was going to be complicated.

"Come on, we'd better keep moving, I'll explain while we walk."

They headed off again after the silver fox, who had stopped to watch in interest as they were mobbed by pixies. The wood was lighter now, faintly lit as far as the eye could see with various fae going about their nightly business. Pip stayed with Lily, throwing a few choice squeaks at any other pixie that got too inquisitive. Sebastian grinned to himself. For a pixie, or even just a fae in general, Pip was unusually affectionate. And it was obvious she had become quite fond of Lily—a sentiment he shared. He only wished he could express it as freely as Pip did.

"So…" Lily's tone was back to normal: businesslike and slightly peeved.

Sebastian sighed, trying to decide how to proceed. If he said too much, it would confuse and worry her. But too little, and she would be unprepared. "I guess the first thing you should know is who's in charge around here. Now, I haven't met any of them except Thiriel, but the fae are ruled by two kings and two queens. Don't think of them like human kings and queens, though. They aren't married, they're more like siblings, or…well two sides of the same coin. They're dualities of the same aspect. All of the fae are ruled by these dual aspects of growth and decay—"

"Like creation and destruction? Life and death?" Lily asked, sounding interested.

Sebastian sighed. "No. Not like that at all. I know the difference seems arbitrary to us, but it's very important. Thiriel is the fae queen of decay, the opposite of growth. Not creation, growth. She is not the aspect of destruction, but decomposition. Creation and destruction are intentional things done by someone to something. They don't happen on their own. Thiriel doesn't destroy things, she simply breaks down things that have already been destroyed. Like how leaves on the forest floor decompose into dirt."

"Okay…I'm following you so far."

"Maybe it'll make more sense when you understand that the fae are stewards, not rulers. Their job is to see order maintained, rules followed. They make sure the wind blows and the rain falls, that plants grow and produce fruit. They aren't the ones who created the order, or the rules, they just make sure nature functions according to its purpose."

"But…mundane science can explain natural phenomena in terms of chemical reactions and the laws of physics. So what do the fae have to do with it?"

Sebastian shrugged, reaching up to hold aside a branch for her to go under. "I don't know that much about science. I'm a witch, not a scholar. But you know, as well as I do, that magic and science aren't contradictory. They're just two ways of looking at the same thing. All I know is that the fae are part of the earth's natural workings. They *are* nature."

"Then why are they all here instead of living among humans?" Lily asked

"Well…" he rubbed the back of his neck, at a loss.

Careful, caretaker. Her eyes have not been opened. She will not understand.

Of course Thiriel was listening in. That's what glowing fox messengers were for, right?

"They're mostly hiding from demons," he finally said. There, that was true. "Demons can't enter the fae realm, at least not without help. From what I understand, fae can do a lot of what they need to do here, and what they can't, well," he shrugged. "It's easy enough to pop back and forth."

"But why would they need to hide?"

Dang it, if she would only stop asking questions.

"You should know that," he shot back. "Didn't they teach it in wizard school?"

"You mean didn't Madam Barrington mention it?" Lily said testily.

"Er, yeah."

"Not exactly. Our focus was on the wizarding arts, the use of Enkinim and dimmu runes."

He threw up his hands. "Okay, okay. I get it. Magical Creatures 101, coming right up. So you know there are four types of beings who use magic: humans, fae, demons, and angels. Well, three if you count demons as just fallen angels, which they are. Anyway, humans are the only ones who, you know, draw power directly from the Source, or whatever it is you call it. The others are literally *made* of magic. They can only use what powers they were created with. That's why there's high fae and low fae, greater demons and lesser demons."

Lily nodded, stepping carefully around a thorn bush.

"So, demons, being demons, always want more power. They can get it two ways: possessing humans or corrupting fae. Poor little guys like Pip would be in real trouble if a demon got hold of them. It doesn't happen often, but it happens. Fae always have to be on their guard in the human realm. Humans are a piece of cake to hide from compared to demons."

Seeming satisfied with the explanation, Lily remained silent, probably mulling it all over. Sebastian was about to continue his general overview of fae society when she asked another question.

"So who makes the rules?"

"What?" Sebastian's train of thought was derailed by the seemingly out-of-the-blue change in topic.

"You said the fae keep the rules, not make them. So who makes the rules? Who's in charge of the fae?"

Sebastian didn't reply. He couldn't, really. He didn't know how.

A yip from the silver fox saved him, drawing their attention to the side. He'd been so absorbed with their conversation he'd forgotten to follow their guide. They'd walked straight past where the glowing creature had stopped.

"Come on, this must be it." He waved Lily over, and Sir Kipling appeared from behind a bush, sticks and leaves tangled in his long fur.

They approached to see the entrance of a low cave in the hillside. It looked dry, at least as far as could be seen by the fox's glow. The smooth floor was covered in a thick layer of leaves and forest debris.

"You're expecting me to go in there?" Lily asked, aghast. "There are probably spiders. I do *not* cope well with spiders."

"Don't worry, I'll eat them for you," Sir Kipling offered gallantly, sidling over to rub on her ankle, then rearing to put his forepaws on her leg in a silent plea to be picked up.

"I feel so much safer," she muttered, though with a tiny smile as she bent to retrieve her cat in shining armor. Or at least a shiny collar.

Pip squeaked encouragingly, flitting into the cave to shed a bit more light and, Sebastian supposed, show that there were no spiders in evidence.

"Come on, let's go," Sebastian said, nudging her gently. "The entrance to Thiriel's court is always different. Just be glad we got a cave this time. One time I had to crawl through a hole underneath a dead tree."

"Wait, we're going underground?" Lily sounded even more nervous at the thought.

"Uh, yeah. She's the queen of decay, remember? Ninety-nine percent of decay happens underground."

Lily wiped her hands on her pants as if the very thought of dirt made her anxious. "Will it be slimy and nasty?"

"No," Sebastian said, exasperated. "Weren't you listening? The things humans find disgusting about decay are mostly the smell and slime of death. You know, that instinct we have that decay means disease? But that's because we never knew the world before, when decay was just decay and there was no such thing as pollution, death, and disease. Dirt isn't disgusting, is it?"

"Um, kinda, yeah." Lily said sheepishly.

Sebastian rolled his eyes. "You grew up on a farm. I figured you'd appreciate it. Ever heard the phrase 'good clean dirt'? Soil is the accumulation of centuries of decayed material, full of healthy minerals and nutrients. And anyway, all fae love the beauty of nature. We're not going to some grubby hole full of worms and beetles. That's Grimmold's home, not Thiriel's. I promise, you'll like it."

Lily took a deep breath. "Alright," she said, sounding hesitant, but willing.

"Why don't you close your eyes, okay? I'll lead you. Trust me, it will make things easier."

She did as he asked, and he took her soft hand in his, feeling an overwhelming surge of affection, followed by a twisting stab of doubt. Her trust in him was thrilling but also a burden. How could he ever live up to her expectations? He shook his head. That was not something to worry about right now, considering where they were going. He needed to be completely calm and focused, the exact opposite of how he felt when standing so close to her slender form...

Snorting in derision at himself, he started forward into

the cave's darkness, bending his tall frame to fit the low ceiling and moving slowly so Lily could find her footing. The fox trotted ahead, no longer waiting for them. It knew there was no more need for a guide. There was only one way to go now that they'd stepped onto the threshold of Thiriel's court. Sebastian knew that, if he looked behind them, the cave entrance would no longer be there, only blank stone and dirt.

Their passage was not like moving through the twilight, but it definitely wasn't a walk in the park, either. At times they seemed to be traversing nothing but air, completely surrounded by absolute blackness, though it was full of drippings and echoes, unlike the total silence of the nowhere between realms.

Pip, her light dimmed to the faintest of glows, had taken refuge in Lily's bag, safely segregated from Sir Kipling, who'd once again latched himself onto Lily's shoulder.

Their journey was not long, or at least it didn't feel like it. Sebastian knew time was a fickle thing in the fae realm. It had normal days, lunar cycles, and seasons just like the human realm, but something about moving through the empty spaces in between threw off the normal workings of time.

When he felt his foot fall once again onto soft earth, he knew they were close. The darkness drew back to reveal a familiar but still breathtaking sight that he would never tire of seeing.

The ceiling above them vaulted upward into a massive cavern that could have easily fit several football fields within its subterranean embrace. On one distant side, a waterfall plunged down from the surface above and filled the cavern with a low thrum. This waterfall fed a large lake which narrowed into a crystal-clear stream, bisecting the room before flowing out a low archway on the other side. The majesty of the room alone was enough to awe any normal person, but the wonders did not end there.

Instead of a purely stone cavern as might have formed naturally, this massive room was equal parts stone, wood, and earth. The reason was easily apparent. Visible at the end of the chamber was a massive taproot that had broken through the stone ceiling and grown downward, following the contours of the walls until it finally plunged into the soft earth of the cavern floor. The root was easily fifteen feet across, hinting at the truly gargantuan majesty of the tree it anchored above. Radiating out from this central root were hundreds of smaller roots of every shape, length, and size. They snaked down the wall and criss-crossed the ceiling, winding between stalactites and even growing down them toward the floor. This created massive pillars of twisting roots throughout the room that, as they reached the floor, had been guided to form beautiful arches, benches, platforms, and chairs, all shaped organically by the living wood.

But even that wasn't the most beautiful part.

Sebastian gently squeezed Lily's hand. "Open your eyes, Lil."

Her gasp of wonder was everything he'd hoped for, and he delighted in the reflection of bioluminescence in her awestruck eyes. All about the gigantic cavern, plants and fungi glowed in a dazzling display of blue, green, purple, red, orange, and gold where they clung to the ceilings, walls, and intricate root system of the tree. If that weren't enough, the waters were also filled with glowing organisms, from plants to fish, and even swarms of minuscule creatures that blinked on and off in pulsing swarms of blue light.

"What do you think?" He asked, unable to keep the grin off his face.

"It's the most beautiful thing I've ever seen in my life," she breathed, eyes wide as if to draw in as much of the magical sight as physically possible.

"Still think the fae queen of decay will be gross?"

"Certainly," Sir Kipling replied for her, "if she's covered in all of these squishy, wet, glowing things. Whose idea was this place anyway? There's entirely too much water down here. I strongly disapprove."

Lily snorted at the same time Sebastian did, and they shared a fond but long-suffering look.

"Just stay on my shoulder and you won't get wet," Lily advised him.

"But then I can't explore," the feline whined in an impressively pitiful tone.

Sebastian grinned. "Good. Maybe that will keep you out of trouble."

The cat glared at him, switching to Lily's other shoulder so that her head was between them.

Pip, having wiggled out of Lily's bag, now zipped over to Sebastian and hid in the front pocket of his shirt. "Hey, calm down, short stock. Nobody's going to bother you here just because you're one of Kaliel's."

The pixie peeped uncertainly.

"Look, why don't you stay in my pocket? You can hear and see well enough, and that's all you were sent for, right?"

A squeak of affirmation came from his pocket, and he smiled.

"Who is Kaliel?" Lily asked, stepping forward carefully with him as they moved into the room. The fox was long gone. Sebastian knew where they were going, having spent…well, a long time here in days past.

"Kaliar and Kaliel are the duality of growth, the opposite of Thiriel. Those aren't their full names, of course, but it's not safe, or polite, to say a fae's full name unless you're carrying on a formal conversation or requesting something."

"Oh…but then who is Thiriel's, um, duality, is it? I thought you said there were four altogether?"

Drat. Sebastian had hoped she wouldn't pick up on that. "It's…complicated."

"Come on, Sebastian. We're in the fae realm, for goodness sake. I know your big secret now and I suspect by the time we leave I'll have learned much more about the fae than I ever wanted to know. When are you going to start being straight with me?"

Your big secret? What a naive child you have brought me.

"Shut up!" Sebastian burst out.

"What?" Lily drew back, hurt written all over her face.

Sebastian ran his free hand through his hair, fingers twitching in frustration. "No, no, not you. I'm sorry, Lily, calm down. I was, um, talking to myself." He drew her back toward him, unwilling to let go of her hand. "Look, I know you're upset, but please believe me when I say I will always tell you everything I can. The fae are masters of secrets. Some of their secrets would put you in great danger, and some of them are not mine to tell. Be patient with me…please?" He couldn't look at her as he said it, knowing he didn't deserve what he asked for, but hoping for it all the same.

He heard her heave a sigh, then felt her hand relax. "Fine. Whatever. But one day I'm going to figure out something that annoys you as much as your secrets annoy me. I'm giving you fair warning now, so you can't complain. Not one—single—peep."

Relief flooded him and he chuckled softly. "I promise I won't say a word."

They'd gone about a third of the way across the cavern, feet sometimes padding over soft earth, sometimes sinking into spongy moss, sometimes echoing over smooth stone. They passed glowing pillars of roots and appreciated clusters of delicate, glowing mushrooms as shadows shifted around them—shadows that Sebastian knew contained the members of Thiriel's court. But as of yet they were not revealing themselves. He heard his name whispered many times over, however, the sound melding into the distant hum and hiss of the waterfall's cascades. It wasn't the name Lily knew him by, of course. Thiriel was the only fae who called him Sebastian, as was her right. No, the name they whispered was a name he hadn't wanted, not once he realized the full weight of responsibility that came with it. Of course, by then it had been too late to give it back.

Qem'nathir, or simply, Nathir. It meant Caretaker in the fae tongue.

Sebastian hated it. He was an orphan, a loner, an outsider, the last person in the world who should be taking care of anything. And yet, without reason, without obligation, the fae had saved him, putting him in their debt. Of course, they'd also manipulated and used him, prompting him to leave in the first place. Now he figured they were even. Not that Thiriel would see it that way.

Lily must have felt some of his inner tension, because she gently squeezed his hand. When he looked at her, her brows were angled in concern. He simply shook his head, unable to give voice to the tumult inside. Her tender care only made it worse, adding guilt on top of guilt.

They'd reached the center of the cavern where the stream cut straight across their path. A bridge of twining roots spanned the gap, arching over the water with surprising elegance. The unearthly glow of bioluminescence shone through the crystal-clear water, painting the underside of the bridge in vibrant blues and greens.

In the middle of the bridge stood a figure, cloaked in shadow. As they neared, the shadows drew back, revealing a humanoid figure that, while familiar to Sebastian's eyes, must have looked totally alien to Lily. The elongated face, bony limbs, and dark brown skin—like rich, freshly turned earth—would throw off anyone who didn't know what to expect. And that wasn't even taking into account the pointed ears and glowing green eyes. Sebastian heard her quiet intake of breath.

"*Elwa Urdi'arak*," he greeted the figure, inclining his head in respect.

"*Elwa Qem'nathir*," the fae replied. There was a long pause before he finally dipped his head, the movement unnaturally jerky for one so elegant and fair. Sebastian knew it galled him to show deference to a human, but kept his smile carefully hidden. The high fae considered it rude to show emotion.

"I come at the behest of Queen Tahiri'elal, and request permission to enter her court." Sebastian spoke in English for Lily's benefit. The fae weren't just stewards of nature, they were also keepers of knowledge. They spoke every language known to man and probably a few that weren't.

Urdiar was silent for a moment, examining them both, but particularly Lily, before he finally stepped aside. "You are expected," was all he said before disappearing back into the shadows.

As Sebastian led them over the bridge, Lily whispered in his ear.

"Who was that?"

"That was the king of the earth. Not the earth as in the planet, but earth like the soil. He's Thiriel's right-hand man, so to speak. He hates my guts."

"Why?" Lily asked, voice slightly muffled since she was looking down to make sure of her footing on the latticework of roots that made up the bridge.

"Um…because I sort of took his place. Not as king of the earth, but as…um…Thiriel's favorite."

"Oh…" Lily sounded thoughtful, which made Sebastian extremely uncomfortable.

Wanting to distract her but having no idea how, he said the first thing that came to mind. "Hey, remember back in Savannah when I told you a certain individual had given me the ability to see through fae glamour? That he thought if I was going to be hanging around the fae, I deserved to know what they really looked like?"

"Yeah," Lily said.

"That was Urdiar."

"I see…so is what I saw back there what they really look like? Or was that glamour? I thought we'd decided I can see through glamour too because of my fae blood from Morgan?"

"Oh yeah, that was his true form. Fae glamour doesn't work on other fae, so they don't use it much in Melthalin."

"So why did Urdiar give you clear sight if you didn't even need it?"

Darn it. There she went again with the uncomfortably shrewd questions.

"Um…there were a few fae who were, um, taking advantage of my human sight to, um…take advantage of me…in various fashions…" he shut his mouth, deciding to cut his losses while he still could and trying not to cringe in horror at his own clumsy words. Only Lily managed to make him this tongue-tied.

"Sounds like there was quite a bit of advantage being taken," Sir Kipling remarked dryly, his tone implying there was much more to be said, but that he wasn't going to say it.

"Oh leave him alone, Kip," Lily whispered, distracted by the shapes that had started to gather, following behind them as they made their way to the giant taproot at the end of the cavern. "I'm sure it was hard being by himself, the only human in this whole place."

Sebastian relaxed, but only slightly. He couldn't figure out if Lily was being subtly sarcastic, or simply nice. At least she'd stopped asking questions, which, while a relief, was only going to last about another sixty seconds. After that, they'd be face-to-face with Thiriel herself and all bets were off.

Sooner than he'd have liked, they'd passed through the last of the root pillars and into a wide, open circle before the massive taproot. Where the root met the floor, a magnificent throne had been carved into the wood. Sebastian, knowing that fae did not use tools and never built things in the traditional sense, knew the throne hadn't actually been carved, but rather etched out by the rapid decay that Thiriel's touch could induce. Inasmuch as fae created anything, Thiriel had created her throne. Around its edges grew beautifully delicate, fluted, and finned fungi in fantastic shapes, all of them glowing with ethereal light. The light shone off a figure on the throne, stately and erect. She was swathed in shadow, its constant shifting like swirling smoke, alternatively revealing and concealing, making it hard to discern exactly what she looked like.

Sebastian didn't need to try, he already knew. All high fae could shape-shift, and Thiriel was one of the few who preferred the human form over animal, plant, or their natural physique. She took the form of a tall, slender woman, retaining some of her natural features in her pointed ears and milky eyes that matched her bone-white hair. More striking, however, was her skin. It was as black as Urdiar's was brown, its smooth surface reflecting the blue and green luminescence around her wherever the shadows parted to reveal skin. Sebastian could easily imagine her inspiring the old Norse legends of *svartalfar,* the black elves, who lived beneath the earth.

Around the edges of the open circle stood other figures, some the tall, elongated forms of fae, some animals, some plants in vaguely humanoid shapes. All were silent, staring. Sebastian could feel Lily trembling beside him as he drew them forward until they stood about ten feet from the throne. There he sank to one knee, head bowed, and nudged Lily to do the same.

"*Elwa melihi'araji,*" he murmured, keeping his eyes on the floor. He could feel Pip shivering in his pocket, understandably nervous in the presence of so many high-ranking fae.

Sir Kipling jumped down off Lily's shoulder and sat beside them, looking around with interest and, being a cat, not showing the slightest hint of deference. In fact, after giving the air a good sniff—probably to confirm that there was no milk, or reasonable possibility of acquiring milk, in his immediate vicinity—he stretched one back paw above his head and proceeded to clean his leg with utter unconcern. Though able to see the feline's rude behavior out of the corner of his eye, Sebastian was helpless to do anything about it without causing a scene. He just hoped Thiriel had a soft spot for cats.

"*Iwat a'elwa Qem'nathir.*" Thiriel's voice was cold and flowing as the stream behind them. "I accept your greeting," she repeated in English.

The required formalities over, Sebastian felt Thiriel rise and step down from her throne, approaching them. His breath seemed to freeze in his throat, lungs refusing to expand, whether from anticipation or fear he couldn't tell. Probably both.

He felt her smooth fingers on his chin, forcing him to look up into her blank eyes. Sebastian could not look away, captivated by the inexorable allure of her presence that demanded the attention of everything around her. It was all he could do not to be overcome by memories, pleasant and unpleasant, both equally painful.

Betrayer. Why did you leave?

Though she showed no outward sign, Sebastian knew she was furious. Dangerously so. But what was he supposed to say? Sorry for running away from something I didn't sign up for?

He swallowed. "I was afraid. I didn't belong." Both very true statements.

She let go, flicking his chin to the side as if tossing him away, obviously unsatisfied by his answer. He returned his eyes to the floor, all too happy to be released from her piercing gaze.

Next, she turned to stare down at Lily. Sebastian watched them out of the corner of his eye, every part of him on edge. After several tense moments, the fae queen spoke, voice as cool as ever. "Your presence is no longer required. My messenger will take you back to your realm. Leave us."

The silver fox appeared out of nowhere, its glow casting silver light on Lily's confused face as she stood. She'd taken several steps backward before realizing he wasn't following her. "Come on, Sebastian. She said we could go."

"Qem'nathir has his own duty to fulfill. Go." The command in Thiriel's voice was unmistakable.

Sebastian's heart sank, despair threatening his carefully constructed façade of confident nonchalance. Usually, in a situation like this, he could charm his way out. That wouldn't be happening this time.

Eyes to the side, he could see Lily hesitating, foot shifting as if to turn and leave. Knowing what was coming yet dreading the cold reality of it, he closed his eyes, unable to watch his best friend—his only friend—leave him.

"No."

The quiet word echoed around the chamber, causing a shocked hush to fall over the assembled fae.

Sebastian's eyes flew open and his head came up. He couldn't believe his ears. Had she just said no to a queen of the fae? To her face? He tried to quash the tiny spark of hope that blossomed in his chest, even opening his mouth to tell her to go and leave him to his fate. It was the right thing to do. But no sound came out.

Thiriel, who had half turned away, slowly turned back. "What did you say, human?" The words sliced through the air like scything blades.

"I said n—no," Lily repeated, voice catching, but then growing stronger. "I'm not leaving without him. If you have something to say, you can say it to both of us."

Being a fae, Thiriel did not show anger, frustration, or contempt. The only perceptible change was that her voice went from cold to arctic. "Beware, human. I have shown great forbearance in allowing you to leave my domain, having seen what you've seen, unchanged and unharmed. I could just as easily banish you into nothingness, or lock you in my dungeons for the rest of eternity."

"But you won't, because you promised us safe passage at the time of our choosing."

Thiriel smiled thinly, a terrifying sight. "Safe is such a

vague word, is it not? And to choose anything at all, you would have to remember that you wanted to..." she let the sentence dangle, pale eyes fixed on Lily.

Sebastian held his breath. He hoped Thiriel was just playing mind games, trying to intimidate Lily into leaving. He'd seen the queen carry out her threats before, and it had not been a pretty sight.

Lips pursed, Lily did not back down, though Sebastian could see that her hands were trembling. Perhaps she thought she was safe because of how strong her magic was here. Or perhaps she was just insane. "I am honored by your majesty's kindness and do not wish to impose on your hospitality. But I am not leaving without my friend."

Well, at least she was smart enough to be polite. Even so, this was not going well. Sebastian tensed, preparing to jump to her defense if need be, even if he paid dearly for it.

Before he could act, however, Thiriel raised her hand, sending forth blackness from the shadows around her to engulf Lily. Yet instead of swallowing her up, the shadows split, cascading around her like a waterfall. They were deflected by a shining, pale bubble that gleamed wherever the shadows touched it.

Thiriel lowered her hand, visibly astonished, which was a first. Sebastian had never seen her so much as bat an eyelid before. He had to hold back a startled chuckle. Normal spells were no match against a fae queen's might. But Lily had that ward bracelet, the one he suspected had been infused with angelic power by the same being who'd inflicted Sir Kipling's sarcastic opinion on them all.

"*Malaaku. Sithqa a'malaaku.*" A rustle of whispers broke out among the encircled fae, a sign of extreme excitement for a race that was generally as expressive as a brick wall. His grasp of the fae tongue had gotten a bit rusty over the years he'd been away, but it sounded like Thiriel's court had come to the same conclusion about the source of Lily's power that he had. What puzzled him was the violence of their reaction.

"What is this wizardry?" Thiriel demanded, voice sharp as if to cut off the mutterings of her subjects. She reached forward with her physical hand this time, but it, too, was halted by the glowing barrier. Lily looked momentarily shocked herself, but then resumed her defiant stance.

As soon as it was clear she could not get past the light surrounding Lily, Thiriel stopped trying. Her composure regained, she loomed threateningly, examining the wizard with inscrutable eyes that stared down at her like pale lamps of impending doom.

After a long moment during which Lily still did not back down, Thiriel spoke a sharp command. "*Yul'ea!*" The fae queen spun, shadows billowing around her like a cloak as she stalked away.

Sebastian rose, disbelieving, and watched as the circle of fae around them dispersed. Lily had just had a showdown with a fae queen, *and won.*

"What did she say?" Lily whispered, eyes darting back and forth between the departing fae.

"She said to come with her," he said, feeling dazed, giddy, and terrified all at the same time. Possibilities whirled through his mind, better than what he'd been expecting five minutes ago, but still with serious drawbacks.

They followed the fae queen through a massive arched doorway and down a series of stone passages which Sebastian knew led to Thiriel's private audience chamber. The room, when they entered it, was just as Sebastian remembered, albeit with a few new roots here and there. It was spacious, with a stone floor covered in places by beds of soft moss. A small stream of water trickled down one wall, cascading over cleverly formed terraces and feeding into a worn trough that guided its flow along the edge of the room and into a corner where it disappeared into a hole. Like all the rest of Thiriel's domain, the only illumination was the natural glow of the surrounding plants, which, now that their eyes had adjusted, provided more than enough light.

"Sit," Thiriel said shortly, waving a hand at the middle of the room. At her gesture, the floor surged and rose, forming two stone seats covered in moss. She turned away from them, moving to the cascade of water where several cups sat on a ledge.

"I thought you said she was the queen of decay. How can she manipulate stone?" Lily whispered at him as they sat.

Sebastian rolled his eyes at his friend, ever the scholar, even in the middle of all this. "The fae kings and queens have power over everything within their domain. Stone, earth, water, these are aspects of decay."

"But water and earth make things grow," Lily pointed out.

"But they also break things down," he countered. "Everything has two sides to it, and both must work together to maintain balance."

Thiriel returned, cutting short his lesson on fae ecology. She handed them each a stone goblet filled to the brim with cool, clear water. Lily looked for his nod of assent before putting it to her lips. Sebastian drank from his own cup, feeling the water's refreshing influence spread from his crown to his toes. The water wasn't exactly magical, just cleaner than any water had been on earth for a very, very long time.

Before sitting down, Thiriel made a shrugging motion

as if taking off a cloak. The swirl of darkness that had been her mantel pooled down over her arms and hands, sinking into the floor and out of sight. Its absence revealed her full raiment: an elaborate gown of sleek grey cloth—probably woven from spider silk—that shimmered iridescent in the luminescent glow. Thousands of tiny black opals were woven into its length in intricate designs, catching and refracting the light as they flowed down her form, following the contours of her body. Black opals glinted at her wrists and neck, and on her head was a crown of pure obsidian. Nothing that she wore looked carved or cut, but rather organically shaped from the elements of the earth.

It was an outfit meant to impress and beguile, and it certainly achieved its goal. Sebastian struggled to tear his eyes away, though it was a bit easier once he noticed Lily's scowl. Averting his gaze, he instead watched Sir Kipling carefully nose about the room, taking experimental nibbles of various plants and rejecting each, one by one, with a betrayed look of disgust.

"Alright," Lily ventured into the oppressive silence. "What's going on? What do you want? Um, Your Majesty," she added belatedly. Though she shifted under Thiriel's stare, she did not back down.

Do you wish to enumerate your misdeeds, Sebastian, or shall I? Or, if you prefer, simply convince her to leave. I swear to you she will come to no harm. It will make all of this much easier.

It had started again. The manipulation. The whispers in his head. The problem wasn't that Thiriel had ever forced him to do anything. The problem was that he usually agreed with her. She spoke to the survivor in him, the person he was but didn't want to be.

No one knew the full story of his past, and here was a

chance to share the burden. Yet it was the last person in the world he wanted knowing his mistakes. *He* already knew he wasn't good enough for her, but did *she* know it yet? What would she do once she realized how irrevocably broken he was? How tainted? How enmeshed in a web of indenture he might never be rid of?

Sebastian looked around the stone room, realizing there was nowhere left to go, no more excuses to make. Lily was not in any danger, so he could send her away with a clear conscience. Well, except for the tiny problem of Mr. Fancypants and his evil schemes for gaining power. But she had Hawkins and Sir Kipling to help her. Did she even need him? Maybe it was best to go back to the way things were. He'd been breaking his cardinal rule of survival for years now, letting himself grow attached to this intelligent, exasperating, beautiful, snobby wizard. Attachments were dangerous. They left you vulnerable and messed with your brain. You made stupid, illogical decisions when you were attached. When you loved someone.

"Sebastian?"

He winced at the sound of Lily's voice. Reluctantly meeting her eyes, he could see the confusion and hurt in them, but also determination. He wanted so badly to tell her everything, even what he felt inside. But one look at the worry lines on her face and the bags under her eyes told him she had enough to deal with already. He wanted her to be safe and happy, and by his side was a distinctly un-safe and un-happy place to be. It was better to break her trust now than risk hurting her even worse down the road.

Sebastian dropped his gaze, insides twisting themselves into guilty knots. But instead of getting to stare at his feet, a Sir Kipling-size mass of fur entered his vision. The cat had jumped up into his lap and was glaring at him. When he tried to look away, the cat dug in his claws.

"Ow!" Sebastian tried to pry him off his lap, but the feline was determined.

"Are you a two-faced coward?" Sir Kipling demanded.

"Of course not," Sebastian replied, but the words were automatic, a knee-jerk reaction. The cat's accusation had come uncomfortably close to the mark, as if he knew exactly what Sebastian was thinking. Sebastian flushed, scowling at the brazen feline whose yellow eyes stared unblinkingly at him without give or mercy.

"Then stop acting like one," the cat said matter-of-factly. Without further ado, he jumped down and sauntered over to the queen's chair. There he delicately sniffed the edge of her gown that was pooled in shimmering folds on the floor. It must have passed his test, because he sat on it, tail curled around his paws and yellow eyes still staring accusingly. Thiriel seemed to find his antics fascinating, peering down at him with the slightest of smiles on her face. Then she returned her gaze to Sebastian.

Now everyone in the room was staring at him. Well, everyone but Pip, who was safely ensconced in her pocket cave, busy listening to every embarrassing word.

Sebastian shivered, hunched over in his chair. Was he going to be a man at the expense of Lily's safety? Or a coward at the expense of her respect? He'd already asked her to trust him, promised he wouldn't let her down. But what was more important, respecting her or keeping her alive? Or was he fooling himself, pretending to be oh-so-noble in his silence when really he was just terrified she would leave him if she knew the truth?

Questions, fears, and doubts chased themselves around inside his head until he was dizzy with them. Even as he begged his mouth to move, to say something, it stayed frozen shut.

"Sebastian? It's alright…I'm not going anywhere."

Her voice was so gentle, her words so unconditional, it stirred something inside him. Something he couldn't walk away from. Even if he might never be with her the way he wanted, she was still his friend, and deserved the truth, consequences be damned.

Clearing his throat, he forced his lips to move, numb though they were. "Aunt B. told you how I tried to, um, resurrect my parents when I was a teenager, right?"

Lily nodded, eyes wide. Thiriel remained impassive. She'd lived this story, so there were no surprises for her.

"Well, what she didn't say, probably because she didn't know, is that for part of the ritual I carved…demonic symbols onto my hand." He held it out, fae tattoo clearly visible. He couldn't hide it here. "It was to help me better channel and control the demon I was after. Yeah, I know. Stupid. Dangerous. Reckless. Moronic. Believe me I've been calling myself those names for years. Even though Aunt B. stopped me from completing the ritual, the marks were still there, and they left me vulnerable to demonic influence." He let out a long sigh, suddenly weary beyond belief. His past felt like a physical burden he'd been chained to for far too long.

"It wasn't too bad at first. I could keep myself closed off, protected. But it got worse. A lot worse. By the time I turned eighteen I knew I had to leave, get far away from everyone so I couldn't hurt them. I was starting to lose control. I thought if I studied more witchcraft, I could find a way to protect myself. There were some wards that helped, but they were all demonic symbols. They might have kept the demons out of my head, but they were like a beacon in the dark. More and more of the buggers kept coming around, poking at my defenses, waiting for me to slip up. So

I started looking for a fix elsewhere. I'd read books about the fae from Aunt B's library when I lived there. Nothing specific, but they were wizard texts, not mundane ones, so they were fairly accurate. They said that fae and demons were arch enemies, so I figured if I could find the fae, they might help me."

He paused, the memories searing painfully across his psyche. "It's funny, I never would have found them if I hadn't been such a demon magnet. Or rather, the fae wouldn't have given me a second glance if I hadn't been swarming with their enemies. I kept poking around, looking for contact, and they probably thought I was some possessed wizard trying to spy on them. Maybe I was, in a way. Anyway, when they finally showed up, they almost took me out along with the demons." He felt an unexpected chuckle bubble up in his chest, remembering the absurdity of that moment, the elation mixed with pure terror.

Thiriel shifted, thinking, perhaps, that she should have just locked him up and been done with it, saving herself a heap of trouble. Maybe she should have. But she hadn't.

"What happened then?" Lily asked, eyes wide.

Sebastian couldn't look at her. Didn't dare. "Thiriel took me in. The rest of the fae weren't too happy about it, but they couldn't exactly argue. Demons couldn't get to me in Melthalin, so as long as I stayed, I was safe. I lived here for…I don't know how long. Time is funny in the fae realm. But it felt like years."

"What did you do all that time?" Lily's soft question made him wince.

"Um…a lot of things," he hedged. "You know, eating, sleeping, exploring, learning about the fae—"

The cat spoke the truth. Thiriel's voice needled him.

Glaring at her, he finished "—and serving Queen Thiriel."

There was a moment of silence. Tortured by not knowing, Sebastian finally looked at his friend but couldn't read her expression. Her face had become closed.

"Serving?" she asked, voice neutral.

"Yes, serving. Paying off my debts." He didn't elaborate further. "But I always missed home. I wanted to go back. I wanted to fix my problem, not just hide from it. So Thiriel offered me a deal. She could tattoo my hand with fae magic that would block the demon symbols. The tattoo was both a ward and a summoning spell for the staff you've seen me use...Tahir, the staff of unmaking. It belonged to...someone else, once. The deal was, she'd give me this power, to protect me wherever I went, if I would use the power to help the fae. And I do," he finished, glaring at Thiriel. "I destroy demons wherever I find them, and I keep your secrets."

"That is like reaping the corner of a field and claiming you have collected the harvest." Thiriel replied, voice cold and flat. "You are the caretaker of Tahir, you owe us more than an afterthought."

"But you didn't say that!" Sebastian snapped, finally losing his temper. He'd never put his anger to words, this feeling that the fae had tricked him into something he hadn't wanted, chained him to a responsibility he'd never be able to fulfill. No, he'd simply left and never come back.

"The weight of power speaks for itself. It was meant to bring balance. *You* were meant to bring balance. Did you think I would give such a weapon to be used as a toy?" She stood up, anger coursing just under the surface. Sebastian knew he was on dangerous ground, but didn't care.

"No! I was just stupid enough to think you actually cared about *me* and wanted to help *me*. But no, all you wanted was a surrogate, a warm body to slot into the empty place beside you and pretend everything was back to normal."

Standing himself, he squared his shoulders and stabbed a furious finger in Thiriel's direction. "Well, I'm not your champion. *I'm not Thiriar.*"

The charged silence stretched into eternity. He desperately wanted to look at Lily, to know what she was thinking, but he kept his gaze fixed on Thiriel's white eyes. He'd finally had the nerve to do what he should have done years ago. Thiriel could snap him like a twig, and maybe she would. But at least it would put an end to things. At least he'd no longer be running.

"Shame on you."

Lily's voice shattered the silence and both he and Thiriel turned to stare at her, astonished. For a split second, he thought she was talking to him, but then she stood and took his hand, putting herself in front of him as if shielding him from Thiriel's anger. To his utter horror, she proceeded to berate the queen. "Shame on you for expecting a human to do the work of a fae. No wonder he left. You don't understand what this place is like for us, do you? You don't understand the effect you have. You take unfair advantage of him and expect him to be grateful? Well, take it back. Take your power back and I'll protect him myself. Don't think I can't, because I can."

Sebastian felt a dazed sense of elation at the ridiculous words coming out of Lily's mouth. Despite everything he'd done, she was defending him. Not just defending him, but trying to save him.

Him.

It wasn't as though he'd expected her to reject him completely—feared perhaps, but not expected. Such a one-eighty wasn't like her. But he'd expected at least *some* semblance of self-preservation when confronted with someone both tainted by demons and beholden to the fae.

She was completely ignorant of both demonology and the subtleties of fae magic, and yet here she was spouting off orders like she expected Thiriel to hop to it. He tensed, waiting for Thiriel to put this "puny human" in her place.

But Thiriel just stared at them, unmoving. It took a moment for Sebastian to notice the pale glow Lily was emitting, white amid all the blue, green, and purple of bioluminescence.

"Uh, Lily, you're glowing." He pointed out weakly.

"Yes, I know." She was surprisingly calm as she stared Thiriel down. "I understand something now that I couldn't see until we came here, where the Source is so much stronger. My gift—the angelic magic, or whatever it is—I can see it now. I can command it. And she knows it." There was the slightest hint of threat in her tone.

Sebastian gaped. It was ridiculous, but so glorious he could no longer concentrate on being upset. She was regal in her confidence, like a queen herself surrounded by angelic glory. And she was doing it for him.

"Ahem." A cat clearing its throat didn't have quite the same air of solemnity as a human doing the same. It sounded more like he was trying to hack up a hairball. But it had the desired effect, and all eyes dropped to Sir Kipling sitting on the floor between them. The cat had that lazy-eyed look he adopted whenever Lily was being particularly obtuse. He, too, was glowing faintly. "Before anyone does anything rash, I've been given a message to convey."

Turning to Thiriel, he spoke, but no longer in his own voice. The voice was deep and resonant, like the reverberating toll of a massive bell. "Remember your purpose. Aid these image-bearers and the prophecy will be fulfilled in due time." He paused, clearing his throat again in a normal, hairball-hacking voice. "Ahem, yes. That is all. Carry on." Tail held high, he sauntered off toward the inner chamber, apparently ready for more poking about.

Inasmuch as Sebastian had ever seen her show emotion, Thiriel looked speechless. Her blank eyes followed the cat as his glow faded and he disappeared into the dimness. Then she looked back at Lily, then at him, then at Lily again.

"Yes, he does that sometimes." Lily offered, as if answering a question. "I promise, it's as annoying to us as it is to you."

Thiriel slowly but gracefully sank back down into her chair. "I believe," she said, voice soft, "that we need to talk."

Sebastian looked at Lily, who returned his gaze with a determined nod, and they both settled back into their stone chairs.

As succinctly as they could manage, they told Thiriel about John Faust and his plans concerning Morgan le Fay. Just as Sebastian had predicted, the fae queen was extremely interested to discover that Lily was a descendant of Morgan. It seemed the fae had been looking for that ancient wizard for a very long time. They *had* given Morgan magic, and they wanted it back. Pretty badly, too, judging by the glow of Thiriel's eyes when she spoke of it.

Sebastian and Lily settled in for what was clearly going to be a lengthy how-to-get-rid-of-Morgan-le-Fay brainstorming session. An attendant brought a platter of fresh fruit and mushrooms along with a bowl brimming with dried nuts for them to munch on. After the other fae had left, Lily gave Sebastian a questioning look. He led by example and popped a chestnut into his mouth, grinning at the flavorful, almost sweet crunch of it between his teeth. Fresh food from the fae realm was nothing to worry about.

It was their prepared dishes you had to watch out for, since you had no idea what was in them.

As they talked, Sebastian started to think that perhaps an alliance with the fae wouldn't be so bad after all. No one had mentioned the elephant in the room yet, though. Well, either of the elephants. He knew Thiriel hadn't forgiven him, even if she seemed willing to let the matter of his "caretaker" duties drop as long as he was helping them get to Morgan. And as for the other elephant, Sebastian knew Lily would be pestering him with questions about this "prophecy" as soon as they were on their own.

The problem was, he didn't know what to tell her. He barely knew any more than she did. Thiriel had made esoteric references to it on several occasions, but all he'd gathered so far was that it had to do with bringing balance, and that the fae took it very seriously. There had been a time back when he'd lived with the fae that Thiriel seemed to think *he* was a part of it. While he certainly wanted to do right by the fae—inasmuch as he was capable—he refused to get roped into some cosmic struggle for "balance," whatever the fae thought that meant. He had more important things to do. Namely, watch Lily's back.

Heart full, not caring what Thiriel thought anymore, Sebastian couldn't help staring at Lily while she listened to the fae queen. This incredible woman was like a burr: prickly and impossible to get rid of. While those might be negatives in the case of a burr, he felt they were Lily's best qualities. Her stubborn refusal to see sense and hightail it for the hills was impossibly endearing. It wasn't that she was besotted with him like some girls had been—in fact, she took every opportunity to point out his faults. As crazy as it sounded, she genuinely seemed to think him worth sticking up for. No one had ever done that before. Not since his parents had died had he felt anyone was solidly, unequivocally on his side.

Just past his friend, Sebastian could see Sir Kipling nestled in a comfortable catloaf position on a bed of soft moss, observing their powwow. The cat's disgustingly self-satisfied expression—as if he had single-handedly brought them all to this point—made Sebastian grin. Perhaps the crafty feline had. He was, after all, one helluva cat.

Tucking his grin away, Sebastian remembered that he'd once thought Lily's friendship was enough—or at least all he'd ever get. Now…he barely dared hope. Yet that tiny bit of hope was all it took to topple his carefully constructed walls and let his heart feel in a way it hadn't for years. It left him completely vulnerable in the most terrifying, yet thrilling way. Now if only he could figure out how to express all that to Lily.

Though distracted by the new flood of feelings coursing through him, he did manage to focus enough to participate in the planning as they took advantage of Thiriel's inside knowledge of Morgan's involvement with the fae. She'd been there, after all.

According to the brief and circumspect explanation they pried out of her, that whole episode in history had been a regrettable mistake. Though perhaps it only seemed that way in hindsight. One of the high fae of Kaliar's court had given some of his magic to a young Morgan as a gesture of faith and goodwill. The hope had been that she could help usher in an era of peace and cooperation between humans and fae during a time when some of the population still believed in such things. But when she had betrayed their trust and used the magic to further her own quest for power, they'd withdrawn completely and given up humanity as a lost cause, focusing instead on their commission to tend the earth.

"If things had progressed naturally," Thiriel said, face as emotionless as ever, "once Morgan le Fay died, the gifted magic would have returned to the earth and, eventually, to its rightful owner."

"Only, she never died," Lily pointed out, busy eating a handful of grapes that must have been rather tart, judging by her puckered lips.

"Correct," Thiriel agreed. "She simply disappeared, and we have not been able to discover her whereabouts in the centuries since."

"Bummer." Sebastian quipped. Both women turned to glare at him, but he just shrugged, feeling remarkably, perhaps even recklessly, carefree. Lily had stood up for him. She wasn't going anywhere—her words—and he was determined to not let any amount of fae drama ruin his good mood.

Choosing to ignore his insensitive humor, Lily pulled out her eduba from her bag and got down to business. Using Thiriel's knowledge, combined with their translation of Morgan's diary—imperfect as it was—they concocted a plan to strip that ancient wizard of her fae magic. It was the first step to defeating her. If they could reduce her power, they might have a chance of neutralizing her *and* stopping John Faust.

Unfortunately for them, Thiriel staunchly refused to help with the actual fighting, insisting that the less fae meddled in human affairs, the better. She carefully did *not* look at him as she said it. Her only concern, she insisted, was returning what had been lost.

Sebastian, of course, knew that was a load of garbage. Thiriel had much more up her sleeve than she would ever share with them. There was *something* the fae were looking for among humankind. Whether it was a specific person, situation, or item, he had no clue. All he knew was that they were obsessed with balance, didn't have it, and wanted it back.

For now, he and Lily needed to focus on the task at hand: stopping a certain Mr. Fancypants and knocking Morgan down a few notches. But as they said their goodbyes and were led out of Thiriel's court toward home, Sebastian knew with absolute certainty that even if they survived this encounter with Morgan, they hadn't seen the last of the fae. Not by a long shot.

Episode 8

THE GOOD FIGHT

Chapter 1
WEST COUNTRY

WHEN LILY WOKE WEDNESDAY MORNING IN HER HOTEL BED, SHE SPENT the first few sleep-muddled seconds trying to figure out where she was and why she felt so empty. Then, when the vague, half-formed memories began to trickle in, she spent the next five minutes trying to decide if the last twenty-four hours had just been an especially vivid dream. It had felt so real, and yet now the memories were faded and distant. Had she really traveled to a subterranean chamber full of living light and told off a fae queen for hurting her friend? She blushed at the mere thought, rather hoping it *had* all been a ridiculous dream.

Sir Kipling interrupted her confused thoughts by jumping up on the bed and giving her a good lick on the nose.

"Ew! Stop it, you ridiculous cat," Lily protested, pushing him away and sitting up. As she did, something small rolled off her chest and fell into her lap. She stared down at the smooth river stone, still glowing the faintest blue. Her memories sharpened. She'd seen the stone on the ground near the twisting root bridge in Thiriel's court and had picked it up on impulse, perhaps to prove to herself that she'd been there.

So, not a dream.

Lily groaned, flopping back down on the bed with the stone in her hand. She couldn't even comfort herself by pretending it was a stray pebble with blue paint on it. Just holding it in her hand she felt the echo of power that had filled her from the moment she'd set foot in Melthalin. Closing her eyes, she savored the exquisite memory. She'd never felt so close, so in tune with her magic. It had leapt excitedly at her least command, responding to thoughts and intentions as easily as it did to words. And that other magic…the angelic magic. She reached out with her mind, suddenly desperate to feel it again. But all she could detect was the barest whisper where before there had been a roar. Well, at least she still could feel something. Before yesterday she hadn't even been consciously aware it was there. Back here in the human realm, her mind felt sluggish: slow to respond and slow to understand. She might have done great things yesterday, but she despaired at ever being able to replicate them here.

Speaking of yesterday, she thought back, trying to fix as much detail in her memory as possible so as not to forget the important things they'd discussed, such as Morgan le Fay and how to separate her from her fae magic. Of course, that brought back other memories, like the mix of terror and anger she'd felt at the thought of losing Sebastian to that— that hussy of a fae queen. She couldn't believe her own audacity. The whole time she'd been filled with a giddy sense of invulnerability, body reacting instinctively to her flared emotions while her mind dithered in terror.

But she'd done it. Sebastian was safe—at least for now. There hadn't been any true resolution, just an unspoken agreement to let the matter drop for the time being.

Not one to dwell on unpleasantries, Lily instead savored the feeling of…the only word she could think to describe it was unity, with Sebastian. A wall had come down, perhaps not his only one, but it was a start. There was a new closeness between them, the unspoken knowledge that they knew each other's dark secrets. Her heart skipped a beat at the thought, even as her insides squirmed. She didn't like change. It was always messy and inconvenient. But then most things in life were.

She sighed. At the very least, now she knew why he'd always been hesitant to talk about the fae. It made her feel better to know she wasn't the only one with a screwed-up past. But seriously, she couldn't believe it had taken him this long to tell her, as if he expected her to hate him for mistakes he'd made years ago. Yes, his vulnerability to demons worried her, but not because she was afraid of associating with him. She wasn't afraid *of* him, she was afraid *for* him. Somehow they had to find a better way to keep him safe than this complicated relationship with the fae. At least, as long as Thiriel thought he belonged by her side in the fae realm instead of here helping Lily.

Lily shook her head. On their own, they were two rather sorry individuals. But working together, maybe—just maybe—they could help solve each other's problems.

"We have a problem," Sir Kipling commented from the end of the bed. After having his attempts at grooming summarily rejected, he'd retreated there to regroup.

"Is that so?" Lily said, sitting up and throwing off the covers.

"Yes, quite."

"And pray tell what is that?"

"Room service forgot the salmon."

It didn't take long to put on some clothes and head over to Sebastian's room, which was suspiciously quiet—she assumed because he was asleep. They'd taken just enough time last night after returning from Melthalin to assure Hawkins they were not, in fact, dead, and give him a brief update before collapsing into bed. Something about moving between realms was particularly draining, and without the invigorating air of the fae realm, sleep hadn't been an option, it had been an inevitability. But day had come and now they had things to do, so it was alarm clock time.

Lily knocked on Sebastian's door, eyebrows rising in surprise when he actually answered it. Still wearing yesterday's clothes and with a bird's nest on his head, he opened the door just enough to peek out. Lily could only see a sliver of his expression, but he looked like a man driven to exasperation.

"What is it?" she asked, wary.

"We have a problem."

Lily threw up her hands. "You and everyone else. Come on, what is it? We might as well get it over with."

He hesitated, but then opened the door wide enough for her and Sir Kipling to slip in after he'd carefully checked the hall for bystanders.

As soon as Sir Kipling entered the room his ears went back and tail went down. "This place smells like dog. If that's a new cologne or something, I'm declaring cat law and confiscating it."

Glad that Sebastian could no longer understand her

ridiculous cat, Lily sniffed the air herself but didn't notice anything out of the ordinary. She was about to ask Sebastian what in the world was wrong when the bed came into view and she stopped in her tracks. "Oh, no. Not again."

Sitting on the bed was Thiriel's fox messenger. At least, she thought that's what it was. It wasn't glowing silver this time and appeared to be a perfectly ordinary grey fox. But she could think of no other reason why a fox would be sitting calmly on Sebastian's bed unless it had been sent by Thiriel. She eyed it suspiciously. "What's going on?"

"That's what I'm trying to figure out," Sebastian said, running a hand through his hair. At least that explained the bird's nest.

Sir Kipling remained by the door, back arched in hostility as he made little growling noises in his throat, tail thrashing back and forth.

"*I already told you, I am here to help.*"

Lily jumped. "It talks!"

"Not exactly," Sebastian said, now rubbing his face. "You can only hear it in your head."

"*Rather convenient, if you ask me. Nobody really wants to know what a fox says, after all.*"

"But how?" Lily asked.

Sebastian shrugged. "A gift from Thiriel, I expect."

"*Quite right.*"

"But, what is it? Or…who are you?" she said, speaking directly to the fox.

"*I, my lady, am fox.*"

"Fox?" Lily glanced at Sebastian, not sure how to react.

"*More specifically, one half of fox, but still. The other half doesn't like how you smell, so I came instead.*"

"Excuse me?" She was too shocked to decide if she should be offended or not.

"*Well, not you personally, just humans in general. I, however, am of the mind that since you cannot help it, it is no use holding it against you.*"

"Sebastian, do you have any idea what he's talking about?" Lily demanded.

Sebastian was currently looking away, trying to hide a smile behind his hand. He turned back, face straight again, and spoke. "Hem—um, right. My best guess is he's one half of the duality of fox. As in, the animal. All plants and animals have dual aspects. They aren't the same as low or high fae. They're more like the magical representation of each species. They help keep their kind in order, so to speak. I hadn't realized Thiriel's messenger was an *actual* fox."

"*Well, what else were you expecting? A fake fox?*"

Sebastian made a face and shrugged, conceding the point.

"But, don't you have, uh, more fox-like things to do? Carrying messages seems more of a bird thing to me," Lily ventured.

"*Do I look like I know what is going on in the queen's head? I am her messenger, not her therapist. Now, do you want my help or not?*"

"Um…" Lily looked at Sebastian, unsure. Was he really there to help? Or just to spy on them for Thiriel?

"We're very grateful for your offer, uh, Mr. Fox. But really, I think we'll be fine on our own."

"*Nonsense. If you are worried about my, ahem, messenger duties, then do not be. The queen did not send me, I came on my own. She would be rather furious if she knew I was here. I am meddling, you see, and she does not approve of that.*"

Lily and Sebastian looked at each other. Sebastian grinned. She shrugged.

"Oooh, no. No, no, no! We are absolutely *not* letting

that mutt tag along. I forbid it." Sir Kipling, the need to protest overcoming his disgust, had entered the room and jumped up on a table as far away from the bed as possible, glaring at the fox.

"*You, cat, are simply jealous of my tail. Come now, admit it.*" The fox swished it across the covers, and Lily had to admit it was quite magnificent—fluffy, soft, and beautifully patterned—though she would never say so in front of her cat.

Sir Kipling, wisely, did not engage in banter but rather gave Lily a doleful look. "He's a dog. Are we really going to trust a dog?"

The fox made a startling noise, halfway between a bark and a laugh. "*Hardly a dog. But better a dog than a cat. Would not you say, oh cunning and mischievous one?*"

Feline and canine stared at each other, the former with slitted yellow eyes, the latter with wide, guileless blue ones.

"Alright, break it up," Sebastian said, chuckling. "We don't have time to argue. For now, yes, we'd be grateful for your, um, help." Sebastian glanced sideways at her, no doubt wondering—as she did—what sort of help the aspect of fox had in mind.

"*Excellent. So, when do we leave?*"

"That depends entirely on your scholar buddy, Lily. Mr. Hootee or whatever his name is."

"It's Hawtrey, and he's a doctor, not a mister." Lily glared at her friend. "You had better be polite. He's been very kind to help us on such short notice. I won't have you snubbing him just because you're jealous."

"Me? Jealous? As if." Sebastian said, making a dismissive sound.

"It doesn't matter, just be polite. Alright? I'll go see him straight away. Can you make sure Hawkins has all our things together? We need to be ready to leave as soon as Cyril gives us a location, which will be today, hopefully."

"Cyril?" Sebastian asked with raised eyebrows and a mocking tone. "I thought you said he was Dr. Hawtrey."

Lily blushed and glared but refused to be pulled into an argument. Turning back to the fox, she smiled politely. "It's very nice to meet you, Mr. Fox. Please ignore any insults or slights from Sir Kipling, I'm sure you realize he doesn't mean them, deep down."

"*Sir? What is he sir of, pray tell? The litter box?*" asked the fox.

"I most certainly do mean them. Every single word!" Sir Kipling spluttered.

Sebastian chortled. "Ooh boy, this is going to be fun."

Lily threw up her hands and left the room.

She phoned ahead, making sure Cyril was in his office and available to meet. She also left a message for Emmaline saying that they would soon be leaving Oxford and wondering what her progress was on the outfit. Lastly, she called her mother, apprehensive but also hopeful.

There was no good news. But there was no bad news either. George had settled in and was working with Allen, but no progress had been made. Madam Barrington's condition was the same. Lily knew she was needed in England, but she still wished with all her heart to be by her mentor's side instead of half a world away. She couldn't even stay angry at her father, who was the cause of it all. The anger was there, but it smoldered under a heavy weight of sadness. Sadness for the decisions he'd made and the person he'd chosen to be.

Hoping that staying busy would ease her worry, Lily

dressed and headed off to meet with Cyril while Sebastian got busy making arrangements with Hawkins. Sir Kipling, absolutely refusing to be anywhere near their new ally, insisted on coming with her. She took pity and acquiesced, though she warned him he'd have to get used to the fox's company sooner or later. Sir Kipling expressed his displeasure through alternating cold silence and grumbling complaints. He even refused to accompany her into the History Faculty building, mumbling about a bit of grass and trees out back that he wanted to explore. Lily supposed he just needed space for a good sulk. He would find her again once her meeting with the history professor was over.

Upon entering Cyril's office, Lily was shocked to find it in complete disarray. Being the workspace of a professor, there was bound to be a plethora of books and papers. But the last time she'd been there, things had been stacked and ordered with plenty of clear space. Now the room looked like it had been attacked by a paper blizzard. Thick, scholarly-looking books lay open on all surfaces, and every square inch not taken up by books or stacks of paper was occupied by one of a half dozen mugs, some empty, some still containing tea long since gone cold.

"My goodness, Dr. Hawtrey, have you even slept since Monday?" Lily commented as she picked up three books and a large stack of papers from the visitor's chair, placing them carefully on an already precariously balanced pile on the desk.

"Not really, no," he muttered absentmindedly, pencil sticking out of one side of his mouth as he used both hands to flip through a massive dictionary. "Close the door, if you don't mind. I'm almost done. Just a minute more."

Lily settled in the chair, trying to occupy herself with peering about the room while Cyril scribbled furiously.

Large maps of England were laid out everywhere. One was affixed to the wall and had several pins stuck through it, all clustered around various locations in the West Country— that southwestern-most tip of England, encompassing the counties of Cornwall, Devon, Somerset, and Dorset.

"What are these pins?" Lily asked, pointing.

"Hmm? Oh, possible locations of Morgan le Fay's tomb."

"Oh." She fell silent, considering. Cornwall was the location of Tintagel Castle, the purported location of King Arthur's birth and so possibly the home of his half sister as well. Rising from her chair and looking closely at the map, she could see a pin sticking out of the "T" of Tintagel village, right on the coast. There were several other pins clustered nearby, and a few more scattered further afield.

"Done!"

Lily jumped at the sharp word and triumphant slap of Cyril's hand on the table. Turning, she surveyed the older man, now leaning back in his chair and rubbing his face wearily.

"Finished translating? Or making sense of it?"

"Good grief, just translating. Though it's starting to come together in my head simply from going over it so many times."

"That's good, because we're leaving this afternoon."

"What? No, that's impossible. I haven't made arrangements…I'd need to pack…all my appointments… surely you could wait a few days?"

"I'm afraid not, Dr. Hawtrey," Lily said, trying to hide her relief that they might get to leave him behind. "There is much at stake and we can't delay a moment longer than necessary. I do apologize you won't be able to accompany us but—"

"No, no. Don't be silly. I'll make it work. Of course I will. This is a once-in-a-lifetime chance. Can you imagine? The opportunity to discover Morgan's tomb, it's simply mind-boggling. Think of the papers I could write—"

"Ahem." Heart sinking, Lily coughed into her hand, interrupting Cyril's excited ranting. "You do remember the part about armed and dangerous adversaries who are not afraid to use deadly magic?"

"Oh…yes…well. I'll stay in the back, then, shall I?"

Lily sighed and told Cyril when to meet them at the Macdonald Randolph hotel. They would discuss Morgan's journal on the drive. At her request, he suggested the area of Tintagel as the best place to start their search. They could widen the net from there if need be.

Plans made, Lily left him to his frantic preparations as he made calls and scrambled to gather what he would need for the journey. Her cell phone rang as she was exiting the building and she was relieved to see it was Emmaline.

"Hello, Emmaline?" she answered the call.

"Indeed. Hello Ms. Singer. I received your message and I am delighted to say that I've finished your outfit, if you'd like me to bring it by today."

"Really? That's wonderful, of course, but…how? It's barely been two days."

"Oh, I have a few tricks up my sleeve," the tailor replied enigmatically. "And besides, I felt inspired and had nothing particularly urgent to get in the way. You'd be surprised what an artist can accomplish when they feel inspired."

"Well…thank you. I can't wait to see it. Can you come right away? I'm free now and we're hoping to leave in the early afternoon."

"Hmm." There was a pause, as if Emmaline were checking the time. "Yes…I believe I can make it. I have a few stops to make, but I'll be there before noon. Same room?"

"Yes. And thank you again, this will be enormously helpful."

"Just doing what I do best, Ms. Singer. No need to thank me."

They said goodbye and Lily put her phone away with a sigh of relief. Casual clothes were all well and good, she supposed. But she just didn't feel *right* in them. If she were going to risk life and limb she wanted to at least feel properly attired while doing so.

With all the plans made and preparations well under way, all she had left to do was return to the hotel, pack her things, and await Emmaline's arrival. Not sure if Sebastian would be in his room when she got back, she went ahead and called to inform him of their destination so he and Hawkins could prepare accordingly.

Sir Kipling showed up again when Lily was halfway back, and he looked in a much better mood. He also seemed rather rounder than normal, and Lily wondered which shopkeeper nearby he had plied with his feline wiles to get a belly full of treats. She shook her head but didn't comment. She'd already warned him that if he were overweight at his annual vet checkup he would be put on a strict diet. He might ignore her warning, but if he could handle human intelligence, she figured he could handle human responsibility, too.

Back at the hotel she made quick work of the packing, then occupied herself reading more of the online source material Cyril had assigned her. Sebastian and Hawkins were off preparing the car, having agreed to meet her in the lobby to check out at one o'clock.

Noon came sooner than she expected, absorbed as she was in her reading material. She was forewarned, however, of Emmaline's arrival: before the woman had even knocked on the door, her cat's head came up from where he'd curled up on the bed. Ears perked, he listened for a moment, then got up and stretched lazily.

"That clothes lady is here," he commented, sitting alert on the bedspread. Lily knew he was looking forward to this, having missed the initial fitting. She only hoped the outfit was sufficiently impressive to give him no fodder for sarcastic commentary.

With such an excellent watch-cat, she was at the door and opening it almost before Emmaline knocked.

"Good afternoon, Ms. Singer," she greeted Lily, coming straight in, holding a large clothing bag and carrying a shoebox under one arm. "If you would please try all this on for me, so I can check and make certain everything fits. We'll have to make do for the time being if anything is off, but I'll make note of it to fix later, since I assume you'll want more such outfits?"

"Well, I hadn't really thought that far yet, but I suppose that would be a good idea." Picking up the clothing bag and shoebox, she took them into the bathroom to change.

Taking it all out, she admired the fine fabric, the clean cut, and the absolutely perfect craftsmanship of each piece. Still, she wouldn't really know how it looked until she tried it out.

When it was all put on and arranged, Lily exited the bathroom to stand in front of the full-length mirror she'd specially requested for the occasion. Apparently making odd but reasonable requests and expecting them to be met was one of the perks of a five-star hotel.

As Lily stepped in front of the mirror, Emmaline smiled broadly, clasping her hands and watching silently as her subject enjoyed the fruit of her labor.

The woman Lily saw in the mirror was impressive. Both elegant and competent, fashionable and capable. She wore a cream blouse sensibly gathered and pleated at the neck and wrists, tucked into a modified pencil skirt of a hardy brown fabric. Instead of a tube of cloth reaching down to the knee, on one side it stopped just below the hip and slashed across her body in a diagonal line to reach its full length on her far side. Underneath the outer skirt were pleats that would allow freedom of movement—a half skirt, half kilt construction that sounded rather ridiculous, but turned out quite dashing. On the side of the outer skirt, which extended to her knees, there was a discreet but handy pocket. Lily was relieved to discover it was not the tiny, useless excuse for a pocket that most female wear inflicted upon women. Rather it was quite deep, big enough for all manner of knick-knacks.

Underneath the skirt, she wore a sensible pair of leggings—because England was cold—and her feet were clad, no armored, in a pair of Doc Martens. These boots were no joke. They felt solid and capable yet looked exquisitely elegant, as their leather form fit her like a glove, lacing all the way up to the knee. With thick, tough soles and little heel, they would be perfect for running, climbing, jumping, or whatever ridiculous situation she might be dragged into. She felt like a superhero just wearing them, and thought she began to understand why Emmaline carried herself the way she did. It was amazing the difference a pair of good boots could make.

Coming up behind her, Emmaline's smiling face appeared in the mirror over Lily's shoulder. In her hands she held the jacket for the outfit, which she helped slip up Lily's arms and settle on her shoulders. Like the skirt, the jacket was asymmetrical, with one side slashing down below the waist in a sort of side-tail while the other side was cut at waist level. It had a cross body zipper and a high collar, its material both smooth and durable.

"How does the fit feel?" Emmaline asked, eyeing her appraisingly.

"It's wonderful. Like a second skin." Lily ran her hands over it, noting that, though the jacket was form-fitting, the sleeves were loose enough to allow easy movement and reach. Admiring what she saw in the mirror she gave a little laugh. "I feel like Joan of Arc being armored up for battle."

"Well, it's not the best of analogies, but it comes closer to the mark than you might think."

"Really? How so?" Lily asked, suddenly apprehensive.

"Oh, nothing too outrageous, just all the normal spells for fire resistance, waterproofing, and non-conductivity. We've been experimenting with bullet resistant wards but I didn't have much time and thought you wouldn't need it. On the more practical side, it's also warded against tearing, staining, and, my very favorite, wrinkling. It *is* hand wash only, unfortunately, but shouldn't need it that often, so I hope it's not too much of an inconvenience." She was fussing with Lily's collar, and so it was a moment before she looked back up at the mirror and noticed Lily's dropped jaw.

"What? Is hand washing a problem? I suppose I could look into—"

"No, no, that's all fine. I mean—I thought—you're a wizard?" Lily was absolutely floored. She'd examined Emmaline with great interest when they'd first met and she was sure she'd detected no magic.

Emmaline laughed. "Oh goodness, no. Not a wizard, just an initiate. I don't do any of the spell work myself. My family has been designing, making, and spelling clothes for wizards for, dear me, hundreds of years. We make use of everyone's skills. The more independent and artistic of us do the design work and sometimes the actual sewing. I'm particularly fond of sewing, so I do much of it myself. Then there are others of us—wizards, obviously—who do the warding. Or, sometimes, it's the other way round, depending on the needs of the client. We do make pre-warded fabric, which is mostly what I used for yours since I was short on time."

"But—but Elizabeth said that you…"

"Ah, yes. Dear Mrs. Blackwell. She's very kind to me. Thinks I'm too good for the family business. Says I should go mainstream and work for one of the big mundane designers. I could, I suppose. But it would be such a bother, don't you think? All that attention and the fashion shows and the networking. Terribly exhausting, if you ask me. No, I'm much happier where I am. The family takes care of the business side of things and all I have to do is create exceptional clothes. I make a good living that keeps me comfortable, and have plenty of space in which to experiment. That's all I ask for in life."

"Well, I suppose if that's what makes you happy…" Lily murmured, still rather speechless. She peered more closely at the clothes, this time looking for magic. It was so subtle, so beautifully woven into the cloth that she could barely see it. But then, Emmaline's family *had* been doing this for hundreds of years.

"How can I ever thank you?" Lily asked, turning around to smile at the tailor.

"You can wear it proudly." She smiled back. "Oh, yes, and don't try to modify the spells yourself. That usually just ruins the whole thing. If you need repairs or customizations, simply contact me and we will take care of it."

"Oh, alright." That was good to know, though rather inconvenient. The suit itself was already going to cost an arm and a leg, she was sure. Lily wondered if it came with a warranty. At least she'd noticed Emmaline had included several identical sets of the cream blouse, which she hoped were *not* hand wash only. "So, um, whom do I speak to about payment for—"

Emmaline held up a hand, cutting her off. "Mrs. Blackwell has already made the necessary arrangements. It is a gift."

Lily nodded and tried not to show her embarrassment. She wasn't used to such generosity. The last time a rich relative had doted on her, it was in an attempt to marry her off to some entitled sycophant. She wondered if poor Daren Vance had ever found someone to look past his appearance and fall in love with his gentlemanly manners. She also wondered if Charles DuPont had found anybody to look past his frighteningly vulgar behavior and fall in love with his money. The ball at her father's estate seemed so long ago, almost another lifetime. She'd been much different then. Innocent. Whole. But also weaker and less sure of herself. Life had taken its toll, yet given back in turn.

"Well," Lily said, breaking the contemplative silence, "I suppose I'm all suited up and ready for adventure. I wouldn't want to keep you from your appointments. Thank you for everything, and I hope to someday work with you again." She held out her hand and Emmaline shook it with a warm smile.

"You're very welcome, Ms. Singer. I wish you the best of luck, and I must say, you're standing a bit taller today, even before you tried on the outfit. I take it you've been thinking about what I said?"

Lily considered for a moment, mind going back to the whirlwind of adventure, terror, and triumph of the past few days. Of course she'd not said anything about it to Sebastian, but she'd been horrifically embarrassed and uncomfortable standing before a gorgeous fae queen in a pair of jeans and sneakers. She'd been almost paralyzed with self-doubt, despite the powerful magic running through her, simply because Thiriel had been so impressive—a virtual goddess of beauty compared to her. When the queen bade her leave, saying she was no longer needed, Lily had considered doing just that. It was obvious she would never compare to the caliber of beings Sebastian preferred to ally with. Perhaps it would have been better to simply get out of the way. Go back to her simple life and leave the world-saving to people who were actually good enough for it.

In that moment of doubt, she had, indeed, remembered Emmaline's words. The realization that she was basing her self-worth on the opinion of a haughty, conniving little…well, it had simply made her mad. She'd decided then and there to love herself and ignore what Thiriel thought. Whether or not she succeeded didn't matter. She was good enough because she was herself, and for no other reason.

That thought, and the haunted look in Sebastian's eyes, had given her enough courage to say the first "no."

Lily smiled back at Emmaline. "Yes. Yes, I have."

"Good. If you ever need reminding, just give me a ring." The woman gave her a firm nod and another smile, then turned and left, closing the door softly behind her.

They gathered in the lobby at one o'clock to meet up with Cyril and be on their way. As Lily descended the stairs she spotted Sebastian talking to Hawkins. Sebastian turned at the sound of her approach, but when he caught sight of her he stared in surprise.

"Wow…uh, Lily. Where did you—I mean, your clothes, they uh…" he trailed off and Lily hid a smile.

"I had them custom made," she said simply, standing a bit taller and giving him a raised eyebrow.

As his eyes met hers, his lips slowly spread into a lopsided smile, and he winked. "Gee, if I'm not careful I'll lose my status as the best-dressed member of this group. Way to raise the bar, Lil." He flashed her a double thumbs up.

Turning to the front doors to hide her smile, she headed off to wait for Cyril, throwing a parting shot over her shoulder. "If you're my only competition, it won't be much of a fight."

Reaching the front doors, Lily peered out and saw Cyril approaching. With a tug at her jacket to make sure it was straight, she greeted him at the door, leading him inside to introduce to the group. Hawkins was professionally polite, as any manservant would be. Sebastian, to her great relief, made an effort. She could tell his smile was strained, but at least he got Cyril's name right.

Gathering their various belongings, they piled into Hawkins's car, which appeared to be an upgraded version of the standard black taxicabs that thronged the streets. There was a brief holdup when the professor tried to bring two gigantic boxes of books with him, claiming that the data coverage wasn't reliable out on the coast and he might need them for reference material. Sebastian vetoed the idea, insisting they go by Cyril's office to drop off the books before heading out of Oxford. Sir Kipling, being Sir Kipling, appeared from wherever he'd been lurking to hop in the open back door and into Lily's lap. Their new fox companion, being of the fae, generally remained invisible to the human eye—at least those susceptible to fae glamour—

and so went unnoticed by the butler and professor as he slunk into the car after the cat.

Once they were safely shut in the car, Lily made introductions all around so that the fox could spend the rest of the ride visible. Sebastian had a good laugh when, upon its appearance literally inches from Cyril's feet, the professor nearly jumped out the window. He did not, it seemed, have much of a fondness for wildlife. Hawkins, of course, didn't bat an eyelid. Lily suspected he'd been around the block a few times, being George Dee's manservant.

The fox insisted they call him Yuki since his full name was virtually unpronounceable—Ya'ilarbuki'arak, or something equally maddening. He explained it was because foxes were such mischief-makers, their aspect had been given a name so difficult to pronounce that only the truly furious would go to the trouble of trying to say it.

To this, of course, Sir Kipling made many derogatory comments, so much so that Lily banished him to the front to sit on Sebastian's lap while Yuki lay at their feet on the floor in the back.

Once the antagonistic cat had been separated from his archenemy, things went a bit more smoothly, though it was still cramped. It didn't take long for Lily to decide that the three-and-a-half-hour drive down to the West Country was going to be extremely taxing. That's what they got for trying to make a cat and fox get along, not to mention stuffing six life forms plus luggage into a vehicle meant for four. Between Sir Kipling's grumbled mutterings, Sebastian's jokes, Yuki's biting remarks, and Cyril's complaints, she was fast developing a headache. Hawkins, ever the professional, remained silent.

Finally, Lily could take it no longer and put a ban on all non-mission-related conversation. The animals mostly ignored her, but at least she was able to shift the focus from bickering to discussing Morgan's journal with Cyril, while Sebastian and Hawkins chipped in as needed.

By the time they'd gotten off the M5 onto the A30, passing Exeter, Lily was feeling much better about their chances for success. Despite his grumblings and dire predictions of failure without access to his reference books, Cyril had done an excellent job of analyzing Morgan's text. Lily could see how her father's sloppier translation would have sent them in completely the wrong direction had they depended on it.

Unfortunately, since John Faust had Morgan's resting place directly from his location spell, they couldn't count on his faulty translation to steer him in the wrong direction. With luck, however, the key details needed to access the tomb would be jumbled enough that Lily and Cyril could decipher them first.

Lily was distracted from her conversation with Cyril by their sudden decrease in speed. When she looked up, it was to the sight of bumper-to-bumper traffic backed up on the motorway in front of them. For a trip that had gone smoothly so far—minus her headache and the cramped quarters—they were all willing to wait. But as minutes dragged into almost an hour with barely any progress, tempers flared and Hawkins decided to follow the steady trickle of other frustrated motorists off a handy exit. Now the problem was navigating the back roads to get around the holdup. Hawkins pulled out a road map, which he and Cyril consulted—Cyril claiming to have traveled these parts on a regular basis for his research—and they picked out an acceptable detour.

But, after nearly thirty minutes crawling down tiny country lanes, some of them without even road signs, there was still no hint of the motorway. Cyril kept insisting it was only a bit further, while Sebastian countered with biting remarks about England's inferior road system. With both a side-seat and a back-seat driver telling him where to go, even Hawkins' mask of civility started cracking.

In the end, Lily put her foot down. Being the only female in their motley crew, she was the sole individual who retained the ability to use rational thought when it came to directions. She insisted the men admit they were lost and pull over for directions.

They pulled off into the drive of a charming country cottage by the road. According to their map they were somewhere in Devon, but no one knew exactly where. Lily, having insisted they stop in the first place, was volunteered to go ring the bell and ask for directions. Grumbling about the pigheadedness of men, Lily climbed out of the car. The tension in her muscles fell away as she took a deep breath of crisp afternoon air and stretched mightily, extremely grateful for a bit of solitude, however brief.

Turning to the cottage, she admired it as she approached. It was small, probably only three or so rooms, with a tiled roof and walls made of reddish stone. While it was nothing impressive in and of itself, it was surrounded by an extensive cottage garden. Even though September was well upon them there were still flowers blooming. Their riot of pinks, purples, yellows, and whites contrasted with the reddish hue of the cottage as plants spilled over pathways and hung off trellises in a sort of organized chaos.

Feeling a bit better about knocking on a stranger's door—nobody who tended such a lovely garden could be very bad, could they?—Lily walked up the cobblestone path and rapped on the heavy oak door. She saw a flutter of curtains in one many-paned window and heard the steps of someone approaching.

The door opened with measured deliberateness, revealing the smiling face of an older woman, perhaps in her fifties. Rather short of stature, her black hair was shot through with threads of silver but her blue eyes were bright with curiosity and kindness as she addressed the stranger on her doorstep. "Afternoon, dearie. What can I do for you?" She spoke in the thick, slow, warm accent of Devonshire. Lily couldn't help but smile.

"I do apologize for bothering you, ma'am, but my friends and I are traveling to Tintagel and we're rather lost. Do you think you could direct us back to the closest, um, motorway?" She had to remember that interstates were called motorways in England.

"Goin' to Tintagel are you? For a spot of tourin', I expect. 'Tis a popular place. You'd be from America then, would you?"

The woman's curiosity was a bit off-putting, but Lily knew she was just being friendly. "Not tourists, ma'am. More, um, researchers. We're coming from Oxford. So, could you give us directions?"

"Ooh! Oxford. 'Ow lovely. But see now," she said, checking her watch, "it's nigh on time for tea an' I was just goin' to put on the kettle. Why don't you invite your friends o'er there to come on in an' 'ave a sit-down? We don't get many visitors out this way."

"Oh, that's very kind of you, but we wouldn't want to impose—"

"Nonsense, nonsense. Now go call your friends inside. I'm sure I 'ave a tin of biscuits 'round 'ere somewhere..." Not waiting for Lily's reply, the woman turned, leaving the door wide open as she headed back into the house.

Lily just stood for a moment, taken aback, listening to the sounds of rummaging and happy mutterings as the woman talked to herself. "Where is it now…oh for 'eavens' sake…such a delight, visitors for tea…where's the cream, they'll be wantin' that…out of the way, now, Petunia…"

There was a meow of protest, the tinkle of a bell, and a cat appeared in the doorway, sitting down to lick her paw and stare lazily up at Lily. It was a Persian, or something related, with a ridiculously fluffy, pure white coat and a face that looked like someone had shut a door on it. Well, that settled it. Sir Kipling would mutiny if she failed to introduce him to such an enchanting lady cat, plus a nice cup of tea after hours stuck in that car sounded delightful.

Trudging back up the drive to where the car sat idling, she signaled Hawkins to roll down the window.

"How do you all feel about a pit stop for tea and biscuits? This nice lady is happy to give us directions but she's just having tea and has invited us to join her."

Cyril made a sound of delight from the back seat. "That would be splendid! I could use a good stretch."

Sebastian snorted. "Don't be silly. We don't have time. We've wasted enough of it as it is. Come, Lil, we need to be going."

Since there was nothing they could get done that evening except check into a hotel, and since she knew he loved to eat absolutely everything any chance he got, Lily felt sure Sebastian was being difficult for the sake of disagreeing with Cyril.

Sir Kipling, curled up in Sebastian's lap, yawned mightily. "I just spent hours grooming and a jaunt through the countryside would muss my fur. I vote we keep going."

"There's a lady cat." Lily said casually, lifting one eyebrow. "And I overheard the owner talking about fresh cream."

Sir Kipling was up and out of the car like a shot, bounding from Sebastian's lap, to Hawkins's, then right out the window past Lily's face. Landing with customary cat-like grace, he paused to give a few unruly patches of fur a good lick, then trotted off toward the cottage door. "What are you waiting for, slowpokes?" he meowed over his shoulder, ears pointed toward the cottage and the faint tinkle of a bell.

The odd sound of a barking chortle came from inside the car, and Cyril gave a startled yelp, scrambling for the door handle. "*For a cat, he sure does think with his stomach,*" Yuki commented as Cyril made a quick exit of the vehicle. "*I'll just nose about then, shall I?*" The silver fox jumped out of the recently opened door and trotted off toward the nearby tree line. Though Lily could see him, there was a slight shimmer around his form, indicating he was using his fae glamour.

"Well, Sebastian, I think you've been overruled." Lily grinned and motioned for Hawkins to pull the car all the way up to the house. Her friend would be grumpy for about two minutes. Then he would eat some cookies and drink some tea and everything would be fine again. It was amusing how much more enthusiastic Sebastian was about "tea and biscuits" once he realized that "biscuit" was British for "cookie."

They filed into the cottage, wiping their feet carefully on the doormat as they went. Upon entering, Lily found her guess about three rooms had been correct. It looked like there was one large living room-cum-kitchen, with two doors leading off to a bedroom and a washroom.

To her utter non-surprise, Sir Kipling was already lapping at a saucer of cream across from Petunia, who had her own bowl on the floor by the refrigerator. The woman was oohing and aahing over his silken coat and peculiar markings, calling him a "right little gentleman."

Lily interrupted her cat's worship session to introduce herself and her companions.

"Dearie me, what a pleasure to meet you all, I'm sure. I'm Mary Falconer. Mr. Falconer passed several years ago an' all the children are grown an' gone, so it's just me now. Me an' Petunia, course, an' the flowers."

There was an awkward pause, and Lily felt a pang of pity for the old woman, all alone out in the country. But by the looks of the house she was far from unhappy. It was bright and cheery, full of floral patterns and beautifully framed pictures. There were dozens of family portraits on every flat surface in the house, with multiple grandchildren in evidence. So perhaps not alone. Just lonely for a bit of company.

The shrill whistle of the kettle broke the silence, and Mrs. Falconer hurried off to prepare the tea. Lily gently inserted herself into the preparations, taking directions to get out the cups and saucers and cut up fruit and cheese to arrange on a little plate. The menfolk sat down awkwardly in the flowery chairs, sinking into their soft, pastel embrace. All except Hawkins, who stood, looking perfectly at ease while his eyes carefully inspected their surroundings.

With the tea ready, Lily and Mrs. Falconer joined the men and passed out cups of Earl Grey—the best tea, Mrs. Falconer declared, as it was the favorite of the Queen. Sebastian took three biscuits and was reaching for a fourth when Lily caught his attention and gave him the stink eye. Cyril and Hawkins were, of course, perfectly polite, being both English and gentlemen, two traits that Sebastian lacked. Though she supposed she couldn't hold the former against him.

For the sake of politeness, she spearheaded the conversation, asking Mrs. Falconer about her interest in flowers. That kept her chatting for a good five minutes, and Sebastian had started to eye the plate of biscuits again when the old woman surprised them all by asking what they were researching at Tintagel.

Lily glanced at Sebastian who took the cue and answered smoothly, cutting off a bright-eyed Cyril who had opened his mouth to inundate them all with scholarly drivel. "Nothing much, Mrs. Falconer. Just some old myths and legends. Why, have you been there?"

"Oh yes, I certainly 'ave. The coast t'was always Mr. Falconer's favorite place to 'oliday, an' Tintagel is quite the spot to visit. We been out to the ruins several times, though it's become a bloody tourist trap these days, I 'ear. Packed to burstin' in the summer months. Things'll be slowin' down, now September's come 'round, course, though it's hit an' miss with the weather. You best be gettin' up early if you want any privacy. Oh, an' be sure an' check the tides afore you go out. The walkways an' such are all above the water, but there's caves an' beaches down below you'll be wantin' to explore. Since you're 'eadin' out that way, the King's Table's the best 'otel o' the lot. We stayed there countless times, never 'ad a single complaint."

Lily thanked Mrs. Falconer for her useful advice, glad the woman's delight in chatting seemed to have distracted her from her question. She made a mental note to see if Hawkins could get them a room at the King's Table.

They finished up their tea and as Sebastian helped their hostess with the dishes, Lily looked around for her cat. Neither he, nor Petunia, were anywhere in sight. She went outside and called for him, muttering quiet curses under her breath. With no reply, nor tinkle of Petunia's bell, she gave up and went back inside, hoping he chose to grace them with his presence soon.

As she went back in the cottage, she heard Mrs. Falconer giving Hawkins detailed directions to the nearest main road, which would get them back on the motorway. Cyril chimed in every now and then, but it was clear he was only doing so because he'd gotten them lost in the first place and probably felt the need to be a part of the solution. Lily, for her part, wasn't at all upset. She'd quite enjoyed tea, had desperately needed the air, and was glad they'd been able to keep a lonely woman company amidst her beautiful gardens.

Once ready to leave, Lily turned to thank Mrs. Falconer for her hospitality. The older woman took Lily's hands in her own, giving them a kindly squeeze. Her hands were dry and leathery, but warm, and her grip strong, given character no doubt by the many hours spent tending her garden. Lily couldn't help but feel a surge of affection for the woman. She reminded Lily of her own hardworking and sun-weathered mother who oversaw the care of all living things within her domain on their Alabama farm. Freda didn't quite have Mrs. Falconer's green thumb, but Lily knew the two would like each other if they could ever meet.

"Thank you very much for the tea, Mrs. Falconer. It was absolutely lovely. And I'm sure your directions will save us hours of wandering around, lost in the countryside. I don't know how we can ever repay you."

"Nonsense, dearie. You did me quite a service, keepin' an old lady company. Though…" she hesitated, looking embarrassed.

"What is it?" Lily asked.

"Well, I'd 'ate to impose, but…you know I live alone, an' me back an' hips been givin' me trouble…"

"Yes. How can we help?" Lily asked, ignoring Sebastian's sigh of impatience behind her.

Mrs. Falconer smiled tentatively. "Seein' as 'ow you 'ave three fine, strappin' lads with you, I thought perhaps you could move a bit o' rock for me."

Lily's smile turned into a full-blown Cheshire grin as Sebastian let out a groan.

It turned out Mrs. Falconer had a pile of large, flat river stones that a friend had collected for her to repair a spot in her garden wall. The gentleman who'd dropped them off had left them in the wrong place, and she didn't feel up to carrying them all by herself over to her garden.

It didn't take more than five minutes between Sebastian, Cyril, and Hawkins, but the way Sebastian grumbled and groaned you'd have thought he'd been sentenced to a prison camp in Siberia. To make matters even better—or worse depending on who you asked—Sir Kipling and Petunia showed up halfway through and perched on the garden wall to observe and comment on the entertainment.

Mrs. Falconer praised the men to the skies, which Lily noticed improved Sebastian's mood considerably, despite his grumpy façade. As the men worked, the widow showed off her flowers to Lily, rattling off name after name in her thick Devonshire accent: cockscomb, lady's teardrops, dinner plate dahlias, bears breeches, Japanese anemone, melancholy gentleman, bottlebrush, yellow tickseed, hibiscus, phlox, rosemary—Lily finally gave up trying to remember them all. She simply nodded and made appreciative noises, distracted by the sight of Sebastian with rolled-up sleeves, shirt taut against his lean muscles as he lugged rocks back and forth. She tried to relish the sight while not appearing to stare.

By the time they'd finished, washed up, and piled into the car, Sebastian seemed to have forgiven Lily for "inflicting" the whole ordeal on them. He even smiled when Yuki, having sidled, invisible, into the back, reappeared at Cyril's feet, making the poor man jump in fright for at least the fourth time that day.

While Cyril and Sir Kipling muttered about bloody foxes, Sebastian and Yuki shared a laugh, and Hawkins started the car. They were on their way again, and, while today had tried her patience, Lily reflected that their eclectic crew of man and beast certainly promised for interesting times ahead.

Chapter 2
LIKE A THIEF IN THE NIGHT

ACCORDING TO MRS. FALCONER, THE KING'S TABLE WAS FURTHER OUT THAN the rest of the hotels, but that suited Lily just fine. She didn't want to advertise their presence and invite preemptive conflict with John Faust. They would have to be very careful when they went to Tintagel Castle tomorrow. Though she thought it unlikely, in theory John Faust could attack at any time if he knew where they were. More realistically, Lily suspected he would wait for them to find and open Morgan's tomb and then swoop in, assuming he hadn't been able to open it himself and was now long gone.

While she knew it would be wise to prepare for a fight, she still hoped to neutralize John Faust and her half siblings through cunning rather than do anything more drastic. The idea of killing anyone, let alone her own flesh and blood, was horrifying.

It was with such grim thoughts swirling through her

brain that they finally reached their destination. As the coast and town of Tintagel grew closer, the landscape changed. Trees became more and more sparse, while the few that remained grew low, almost like bushes rather than proper trees. Livestock and crops were replaced by vast stretches of lonely fields and hedgerows. The sun was sinking rapidly and shone directly in their faces as they drove, giving everything a brief golden glow before darkness finally fell.

The King's Table Inn, when they finally located it, turned out to be more of a manor house converted into a bed and breakfast rather than a traditional hotel. The building was two stories of grey stone with tiled roofs and a few outbuildings. Since Hawkins, as instructed by his master, insisted on footing the bill, Lily let him make the room arrangements while Sebastian and Cyril unloaded the car. It was rather amusing, as well as unnerving, to see Yuki sitting in the middle of the foyer observing their labor, safely invisible to the hotel staff and visitors. Sir Kipling stuck with her, mysteriously unspotted by the desk clerk as if he, too, had powers of invisibility.

Leaving the men to it, Lily found a quiet spot to make a phone call. Before leaving the US, she had promised Richard, the FBI agent, updates on their progress, since they were supposed to be working "together" to apprehend John Faust. With so many things having happened already, she couldn't keep putting it off, and so dialed his number with trepidation. She might have forgiven him for trying to bug her house during their second—and last—date, but it was still extremely awkward talking to him.

Richard answered on the first ring. "Lily? How are things going? Is everything okay?"

"Hello Agent Grant," she responded coolly, silently cursing caller ID. "Everything is fine."

"Oh…great. Um, have you found John Faust?"

"Not yet, but we think we know where he is, um, headed. We're in Tintagel at the moment. Another day or two and hopefully everything will be over. Have you made any progress on your end?"

"Uh—yeah, yeah. All the kids have had psych evals. None of them are talking much, but they all seem healthy. We're notifying their families now. Problem is, there's not, uh, much besides circumstantial evidence to, uh, tie Mr. LeFay to their kidnappings, or even to the facility we found. Everything is, um, owned by corporations hiding behind layers of shell companies, and the lady we picked up at the mental ward isn't saying a word. We're, you know, still working on it, but it may, uh, take a while to get things sorted out…"

"I see." Lily said, wondering at Richard's nervous tone.

"Yup. So, um…how is it in England? You staying somewhere nice?"

"Just a little hotel called the King's Table. It is very beautiful here. I hope I can come back and visit someday when…well, when things are back to normal."

"Yeah…normal," he chuckled, a thin sound that quickly petered off.

There was an awkward silence.

"So, I guess I'll let you know how things turn out," Lily said, wanting desperately to hang up.

"Uh, yeah! Great. I wish there was more I could do to help, but it being England and all…"

"It's alright. Just keep investigating so you have plenty to…to get to the bottom of things," she finished wearily. Should they ever actually subdue John Faust, she doubted a federal prison would be the wisest place to send him. She hoped there was some sort of wizard prison or island of exile she didn't know about where the wizard community sent their bad apples. What else could they do with him? Lily massaged her temples, wishing that Madam Barrington would get better and take over this whole mess. She would know what to do.

"We'll get it done. Everything's going to be alright." Richard said, voice soft and reassuring as if he could sense the weary bend of her shoulders and wanted to provide some amount of comfort despite the thousands of miles between them.

No matter how much she wished for a comforting arm just then, she knew it wouldn't be wise to encourage him. Squaring her shoulders, she finished in a businesslike tone. "I'm sure you will. Thank you, Agent Grant. Goodbye."

He sighed. "Goodbye…Miss Singer."

Lily hung up, not waiting to see if he would say anything else, and went to help Sebastian with the luggage. Her mood was not improved by the news that, due to a booking error and some unexpected renovations, there were only two rooms available rather than the promised three, though one of them did have twin beds.

All five of her male companions, four-footed and two, looked at her, apparently awaiting her say in the matter. Well, the three humans didn't really look *at* her, just in her general direction while avoiding her gaze with varying degrees of awkwardness. The feline and canine of the group, in contrast, stared directly at her in obvious fascination.

Lily deliberated, weighing convention with convenience. They'd already unloaded everything and, though it wasn't terribly late, she was still weary to the bone and just wanted to eat something and go to sleep.

"Sebastian and I will take the room with twin beds," she finally declared, annoyed at the whole situation, not to mention the little thrill she felt at the idea of sharing a room with Sebastian. Grabbing her bags, she stomped off after the nervous desk clerk who hurried to lead them upstairs.

Their room was clean and cozy—almost too cozy, considering with whom she was sharing it. White linen sheets neatly folded down over dark comforters covered the beds, and their second-story window looked out toward the ocean. At the moment, all was cloaked in shadow, but Lily imagined it would be a nice view in the daylight.

She plopped her things down on the bed by the window, deciding to save Sebastian the trouble of coming up with a plausible excuse to claim the bed by the door. It was the more vulnerable spot and therefore the one he would insist on occupying.

"Lily, I was thinking I should have the bed by the—oh." Sebastian entered the room, stopping mid-sentence when he saw her already bending over the far bed. She hid a smile and kept rummaging through her bag as he deposited his own things and went to inspect the bathroom. Sir Kipling trailed after him, tail upraised, the tip twitching in a lazy fashion as he surveyed his new, albeit temporary, domain.

"Where is Yuki?" she asked her cat.

"The mongrel believes himself too high and mighty to associate with the likes of us," he sniffed, tail sinking to lash back and forth near the floor.

"Meaning…?"

"You guys talking about Yuki?" Sebastian's voice came from the bathroom. He might not be able to understand Sir Kipling, but it was pretty hard to mistake the irritation in that meow. "He doesn't make a habit of sleeping in the human realm. Feels safer at home. Don't blame him. He'll find us again in the morning."

"High and mighty, huh?" Lily asked her cat, who

pretended not to hear, instead crouching to slip under Sebastian's bed and out of sight where he could sulk in peace.

Sebastian emerged from the bathroom, looking like he'd splashed water on his face and run wet hands through his hair to freshen up.

"Shall we go grab a bite? I heard the clerk downstairs say that the dining room will be closing soon."

"Sure. I'm starving," Lily said, keeping her voice level. She absolutely refused to show the tiniest hint of her traitorous emotions. Just because she'd admitted to herself that she was rather partial to Sebastian—oh, alright, very partial—didn't mean she had any business distracting him with such information on the eve of a dangerous mission. Not that this resolution made it any easier to quash the heady thrill running through her. Nor did it provide any help in keeping her mind focused when all her brain really wanted was to daydream about a certain rakishly handsome someone. Nope, she was all on her own for that. Yippee.

Dinner was tasty and uneventful—thankfully—and afterwards all retired to their respective rooms. They had an early day tomorrow and plenty to get done. Except, when Lily got to her room she found Sebastian just leaving. He muttered something about wanting fresh air and headed for the stairs. Lily shrugged and went inside, feeling relieved to be able to get ready for bed in peace and quiet. However, by the time she'd changed, brushed her teeth, and was ready to turn out the lights, he still hadn't returned. As she went to lock the door, she found Sir Kipling at her feet, rubbing and meowing.

"Why are you begging me to let you out?" she asked. "I thought you could open doors all by yourself?"

He twitched his tail. "I know you prefer the illusion of control. Now open the door."

Rolling her eyes, she did so, and he disappeared down the hall in the same direction as Sebastian. Closing and locking the door—Sebastian had a key, and Sir Kipling would find his own way, whatever that was—she turned off the lights and crawled into bed. She refused to speculate about what those two were up to. Most likely nothing. Sir Kipling liked to wander, and Sebastian was a night owl. There, problem solved.

Yet, despite her logical reasoning and attempts to relax, every nerve was on hyper alert for Sebastian's return. Not for any particular reason, but then, when did emotions need a reason? They were by their very nature unreasonable. Illogical. Decidedly traitorous. After all, she'd fallen asleep in the same room as Sebastian before—in the same bed even—when he'd helped her home after their last big showdown with John Faust. That had been no big deal. Of course, she'd been drunk with weariness and half asleep on her feet at the time, but still. No big deal. Now it was like she was sixteen again. Back then she'd had an extremely embarrassing crush on her English teacher. Her breath would quicken and her heart thump just thinking about him. She had no desire to go through *that* again.

But what if this wasn't just a crush? What if it didn't go away? And why in the world had she been desperate to throw herself on Richard, but was now fighting tooth and nail to deny her feelings for Sebastian? It didn't make any sense! It wasn't that she didn't respect him. She thought very highly of her friend, and was even coming to terms with his…unconventional way of doing things. So what was the problem?

Lily turned over in the bed, hiding her head underneath

her pillow and groaning. Why did feelings have to be so complicated?

Despite her tossing and turning, however, time and the demands of the body eventually took their hold and pulled her under.

She wasn't sure what woke her, but the room was still dark and she could hear soft snoring coming from the other bed. Rolling onto her back, she extricated herself from the tangle of sheets, noticing as she did the absence of a certain warm, fluffy weight at her feet. She sat up, eyes attempting to adjust to the blackness as she peered about the room. Perhaps he was sleeping on Sebastian's bed, the little traitor.

Unable to determine if her cat was, or was not, on the neighboring bed, she was about to roll over and go back to sleep when something against the far wall caught her eye. A patch of blackness more black than the rest of the room. But it was so dark she couldn't make out what it was. She stared at it for a while, a nameless unease growing inside her as she began to perceive an outline in the shadows. It seemed to be a human outline, but it was so still she couldn't decide if she really saw it or if her mind was simply playing tricks on her.

Then it moved. For some reason Lily didn't scream, simply stared in frozen fascination as a shadowy hand raised one pale finger to a set of lips hardly visible in the darkness.

"Shhhhh."

The sound was barely audible, like the gentle whisper of wind through the leaves of a tree.

For the second time, Lily didn't scream, though an inner voice scolded her for being so foolish. But for whatever reason, she felt no threat from the shadowy figure. It was ominous and unnerving, but not threatening.

An abrupt snort made Lily start, and she looked over at the sleeping Sebastian, oblivious to the third person in the room. Again, she wondered where Sir Kipling was. Shouldn't he have warned her? Or was he out on a nightly prowl about the inn?

Not sure what else to do, Lily slowly, carefully scooted back so that she could lean against the headboard, where she remained, motionless and staring. It felt like she sat there for hours, growing stiff with motionlessness, though probably it was only a few minutes.

Finally, the shadowed figure moved. Slowly, the hand reached up, but this time to grab hold of the blackness which shrouded the figure's head. It was pulled away, and Lily finally saw a face in the dimness.

Trista.

Lily's breath caught, her pulse quickening in a fight or flight response. But she still didn't scream. After all, why would Trista stand there, even baring her face in a show of trust, if she meant them harm? There had to be something else going on. Besides, Lily was fascinated by this young woman, her own half sister, accomplice to John Faust's plans and yet a mundane. Or *was* she an accomplice? Was she more of an unwilling participant? Lily remembered how Trista had tried to help Sir Kipling, or at least had expressed reluctance to kill him. Even if she'd eventually bowed to her father's command, she'd had enough of a conscience to say something. She certainly hadn't seemed as arrogant or eager for battle as her brother had been. Their brother. Good grief, this was going to take some getting used to.

Taking a chance, Lily whispered into the darkness, hoping it wouldn't waken Sebastian. "Hello…sister."

Trista didn't respond. She could have been considering what to say, or deciding how best to kill her, for all Lily knew.

She tried again, speaking as loudly as she dared in case Trista hadn't heard the first time. "Why are you here?"

"Father sent me." Even as quiet as her voice was, Lily still recognized its flat, emotionless tone. "I'm supposed to steal your copies of Morgan's journal."

Lily swallowed. "How did you know where to find us?"

The dark figure shrugged almost imperceptibly. "Father told me. He has eyes and ears everywhere."

Great. Just great. "So...do you intend to do as he asked?"

Silence. "I haven't decided yet."

Well, that wasn't very reassuring. But it did mean there was an opportunity here. If her sister was good enough to get through a locked door without waking either of them, she was good enough to have completed her task without getting caught. Lily wondered, belatedly, why she hadn't thought to set any ward alarms before going to bed. Probably because she'd been so distracted...

Dragging her mind back to the matter at hand, she wondered what Trista wanted badly enough to prompt her to disobey John Faust. Was it simple curiosity? Or did she secretly want out? If so, it was up to Lily to give her a reason to take the leap.

"What has John Faust told you about me?" Lily asked in a whisper. Perhaps if she could get Trista talking, she could figure out how to turn her.

There was a long pause. "That you're disobedient. Willful. Foolish."

Lily cocked her head. Trista's tone wasn't critical or even scornful. It was almost wistful.

"All things you wish you could be?" Lily guessed.

"...perhaps..."

Lily wracked her brain, trying to think what to say next.

Where was Sebastian when she needed him? A snore from nearby answered that question, and she smiled ever so slightly, not begrudging him his sleep. Yes, his grasp on conversation and social interaction was certainly better than hers, but this was *her* sister.

"Did he tell you that my mother took me away when I was small to protect me from him? Did he tell you she gave me a real life and taught me to think for myself?"

"He said you were stolen from him and raised to hate your own flesh and blood, your own kind. Do you?"

Choosing her words carefully, Lily shook her head. "I don't hate anyone. I just want there to be peace."

"Pity." Trista breathed, a bit of scorn finally creeping into her voice.

"Why?"

"Because I thought maybe you hated wizards as much as I do."

Lily had no idea what to say, unable to think of anything that might soothe the anger and bitterness in her sister's voice.

Finally, she ventured, "Are you sure it's wizards you hate? Or just our father?"

Trista seemed to consider that. Lily could just barely see her lips purse in the darkness. "I hate anyone who thinks they're better just because of the genes they were born with."

"Not all wizards are like that," Lily assured her, trying her best to sound sincere while still speaking in a whisper.

"Aren't they?"

The challenge, while not strictly true, did make Lily wince. She didn't *think* she went around consciously considering herself better than anyone else, but she couldn't deny a certain level of pride she felt in her heritage. She also had to admit to sometimes thinking of mundanes as silly and ignorant. It was hard not to, when you knew what she knew and could do what she did. The question was, did she feel and think those things because she was a wizard? Or because she was educated in knowledge that most didn't have? Was it racism or elitism? Or both?

And she couldn't exactly speak for other wizards. Most—if not all—thought of mundanes with either patronizing disinterest or active disdain. While it was no excuse, being a wizard herself, Lily could understand how hard it was to be humble when you had so much power and knowledge at your disposal. Her mother was probably the only wizard she'd ever met who seemed to truly treat mundanes as equals. Perhaps because she'd hidden her abilities and tried to live as one to protect her family.

Troubled by her thoughts, Lily finally responded. "If they are like that, most don't mean any harm by it. It was how they were taught to think. But we can change that, you and I."

Trista did not reply, so Lily continued. "John Faust is the most selfish, misguided, cruel wizard I know. I would hate wizards, too, if I thought they were all like him. But they're not, and we can help teach them how to be more understanding…" She hesitated. "You can help teach me to be more understanding. Will you do that?"

Her sister was silent for so long that Lily started to worry she'd given offense. She tried a different tack. "You're an adult. It's your right to make your own decisions. You don't have to do anything John Faust or I or anyone else tells you to. So, do you want to keep being a part of the problem? Or do you want to help me fix it?"

"I just want to be left alone. I—I want to be free." Her voice was almost too quiet to hear.

"If you leave John Faust, I can find you a safe place to

stay, somewhere they can't find you. You'll be free to do whatever you want," Lily said, hoping like heck she could keep her promise.

There was another long silence.

Lily was about to open her mouth, but Trista interrupted her with one last, quiet sentence. "I'll think about it."

With that, she turned, as silent as the shadows she faded into, and left the room. The only thing Lily heard was the soft click of the door as it closed, though even that noise was almost masked by another snore from Sebastian.

Lily let out a breath and relaxed, her muscles stiff from sitting, tense, for so long. That hadn't turned out quite the way she'd hoped, but it had certainly been a positive development. It had the potential to turn the tide. If Lily could isolate John Faust, she had an even greater chance of preventing bloodshed. Plus, Trista's knowledge and skills would come in handy if they could convince her to join them. She wondered where in the world the girl had learned to be so stealthy. Certainly not from their father. He must have hired a trainer of some sort.

Suddenly nervous that Trista might still carry out her original mission, Lily slipped out of bed and tiptoed to the door. Cracking it, she could see no sign of Trista in the hall, so she slipped out and checked the door to Hawkins and Cyril's room. With an ear pressed flat against the wood, she could hear no noise, and the knob was securely locked. Unless she wanted to wake them all up, there was nothing else she could do to improve the situation, so she went back to bed, still wondering where her errant feline had gotten to.

Lily was up, showered, and dressed before Sebastian even woke. True to Emmaline's promise, her outfit seemed completely impervious to wrinkles and stains, including those of the underarm kind. She looked as fresh as she had yesterday, and went to wake up Sebastian with a spring in her step. Looking down fondly at his snoring form, she wondered if he had always been such a heavy sleeper, and if so, how he'd managed to survive this long, with all the trouble he seemed to attract.

Sebastian mumbled and groaned at her cheery wakeup call, attempting to hide under the covers. Lily leaned forward to grab them and whip them off but stopped herself just in time. Momentarily frozen in shock, she realized she'd been about to drag Sebastian out of bed. And, of course, as soon as she was aware of how perfectly comfortable she'd been with the situation, all such feelings vanished and she blushed furiously. Drat her stupid emotions.

Carefully stepping back and lacing her fingers together in front of her, she told Sebastian that it was late and they were about to stop serving breakfast, so if he wanted anything to eat he'd better get his butt out of bed. At her warning, a tousled head emerged from beneath the covers and stared about with bleary eyes.

She left Sebastian to it and headed downstairs for a breakfast that, contrary to her threat, was just getting started. As she sat enjoying a fresh cup of English Breakfast with a bit of toast and jam, Sir Kipling jumped up into the chair beside her. He settled down, able to see her but not visible to anyone else unless they came and stood directly over the chair.

"Nice of you to join me," Lily commented, sipping her tea.

"As you know, I live to serve."

"Of course. Though I wonder whom you were serving last night. I woke up several times and saw neither hide nor hair of you in our room."

"Just being polite," he said, then yawned enormously, all pink gums and pointy teeth. "The rooms being renovated were sadly lacking in cat hair, so I shared a bit of mine. All in the name of generosity and sacrifice, of course. After all, you two needed your *privacy*, so I occupied myself elsewhere."

Lily choked on her tea, inhaling instead of swallowing. Now occupied with coughing the tea out of her lungs, she was unable to respond to her cat's insinuations with the righteous indignation they deserved. By the time she could breathe again, he'd laid his head down on his paws and appeared to be asleep.

Glaring down at him, she considered whether or not to inform him of Trista's visit. She finally decided that, if he was going to be a pain, he should get a little of his own medicine. He could wait and hear about it when she told Sebastian. She was just glad that Sebastian hadn't been there to hear her cat's embarrassing comment.

Speaking of Sebastian…the sound of hurried footsteps in the hall leading to the dining room reached her ears, and she looked up to see her friend's anxious face. He stopped abruptly, looking around at the room full of busily breakfasting guests with a confused expression. Spotting her, he headed over and sat down at the little square table opposite Sir Kipling's ostensibly slumbering form.

"I thought you said breakfast was almost over."

"I might have, hmm, exaggerated just a tad." She took another sip of tea, gazing out the window and doing her best to look innocent.

Sebastian was inclined to grumble but was quickly mollified by the arrival of a plate heaped with fried eggs, bacon, sausage, mushrooms, grilled tomatoes, baked beans, and hash browns that she'd ordered for him. When asked by the waiter if he preferred coffee or tea, he demanded both, advising his server to just bring out the whole pot. Faced with such a request, the waiter retreated, looking alarmed and muttering about "American tourists."

"Really, Sebastian. You should at least *try* to be couth," Lily admonished, pursing her lips so that they wouldn't curl up into a smile.

Sebastian grunted. "It's too early to be...whatever you just said."

"Couth, dear, couth," she replied absentmindedly, focusing on her own plate of sausage and eggs. "It means cultured. Refined. Well-mann...er...ed..." her words trailed off as she realized with horror that she'd just called Sebastian "dear." Blushing furiously, she ducked her head, hoping he hadn't noticed. But he simply grunted in reply, appearing too focused on glaring at his hash browns—as if they had personally offended him—to notice anything at all, including her wayward term of endearment.

Hurrying onward, Lily brought up something that was sure to distract him. "So, Trista came by for a word last night."

"What?" Sebastian jerked in shock, dropping the grilled tomato he was trying to sandwich between two hash browns. "She did what? When? Where?"

Sir Kipling's head also came up and he watched Lily closely as she set down her cup of tea and daintily wiped her lips.

"Oh, about three or four a.m., I'd guess, in our bedroom."

"In our wh—what?" he spluttered. "She was in the room? Why didn't you wake me up?"

"Hush! Not so loud." Lily hissed, glancing at their approaching waiter who carried a tray supporting a tea and a coffee pot. Stopping at their table, he looked at Sebastian for a moment, mouth set in a disapproving line. Then he set the tray on the empty half of the table and turned stiffly, leaving without a word.

As if the coffee would somehow clean out his ears and change what Lily had said, Sebastian gulped down three cups of it in quick succession, apparently immune to its scalding heat.

Concerned, Lily put out a hand, stopping him from downing a fourth. "Slow down, Sebastian. You're going to kill yourself. And anyway, I didn't know you were a coffee drinker."

"I'm not. This stuff tastes vile, and I usually don't need it. Of course, I'm also *usually* not woken up at the crack of dawn," he said, now glaring at his fried eggs which had leaked yolk all over his baked beans. "Now stop avoiding my question. Why didn't you wake me up?" He finally raised his eyes to meet hers, looking angry and hurt.

With a huff of annoyance, Lily opened her mouth to say something cutting, but then closed it again. Taking a deep breath, she pushed away her defensiveness and thought about the situation. Her mother had once told her that when men were scared or worried about something they couldn't control, they often responded with anger.

As annoying as it was, Sebastian was probably just worried for her safety and upset at sleeping through a situation where he felt he should have been there to protect her. She also kept in mind that he had fought, and been defeated by, Trista before, and might be feeling insecure about it. So instead of cutting him down for being a patronizing worry-wart, she tried to respond a bit more maturely.

"Trista was not in any way threatening and seemed like she only wanted to talk. *To me.* I thought if I woke you she might run off, or become aggressive. Clearly, if she'd wanted to hurt us, she could have done so long before either of us woke up. I'll admit, though, it was foolish of me to not set any alarm wards last night. I'll be sure to do that from now on."

The tension in Sebastian's face eased a little, and he gave a conciliatory grunt, turning back to his plate of food. "So what did she want?"

"I think she wanted out."

He looked at her sharply. "Out of what?"

Lily smiled a grim smile. "Out from under John Faust's thumb."

"Hmmm…interesting-er and interesting-er." Sebastian chewed thoughtfully, showing a surprising level of "couthness" by swallowing before speaking. "So did she give you anything useful? Or just gripe about Mr. Fancypants?"

Lily rolled her eyes at Sebastian's continued use of the irreverent epitaph for her father, but let it slide. "She didn't turn traitor and spill her guts, if that's what you mean. I doubt she knows most of the details herself, anyway. John Faust probably keeps both her and Caden in the dark. But her simple presence tells us a few important things. First, that John Faust is nearby. Second, that he knows where we are and probably has a way of watching what we do. And third, he doesn't have as much control over his followers as he might like to believe. I don't know what story Trista told him once she got back, but she did say she'd been sent here to steal our copies of Morgan's journal. John Faust probably knows, or guesses, that we've gotten a better translation of it and would rather just steal our copy than go to the trouble of finding a proper scholar of Old Brittonic. All of which means that we have the advantage but are in a vulnerable position strategically."

"My, my. An impressive deduction, Mr. Holmes." Sebastian winked at her, his trademark good humor starting to reemerge—no doubt thanks to the hot food and caffeine. "So, what does that mean for our strategy over the next day or two?"

Lily sat back, looking out the window toward the windswept coastline barely half a mile away. "It means we have to assume he's watching our every move. I think Cyril and I have made a lot of progress on understanding Morgan's journal, or at least as much of it as we can without finding and exploring the tomb itself. I'm fairly certain it's close by. Morgan says in her journal that she prepared her resting place in 'my mother's bosom, from whence I was torn by treachery's cruel hand.'"

"Wow. Sounds pretty dramatic."

"Well, you'd be dramatic too if your father had been murdered and your mother seduced and married off to your father's murderer. It's an incident recounted in Geoffrey's *Historia*. It claims Uther Pendragon—King Arthur's father—fell in love with Igraine, the wife of one of his nobles, Gorlois the duke of Cornwall. The story goes that as soon as Gorlois got wind of Uther's interest in his wife, he fled home and locked her up safely in his impenetrable castle at Tintagel. He then went and set up camp about twenty miles away at a different fort to draw Uther away. But, instead of Uther fighting himself, his lieutenants fought and killed Gorlois while Uther got Merlin to disguise him as Gorlois so he could walk right into Tintagel and seduce Igraine, who thought he was her husband. According to Geoffrey, that was the night Arthur was conceived.

"Now, we know from Morgan's writings that she was Arthur's older half sister. So if Geoffrey's account is anywhere close to being true—personally I'm skeptical about the bit where Merlin enchants Uther to look like Gorlois—Morgan had to endure her father's defeat and murder, and her mother's betrayal. As if that wasn't bad enough, she was then sent away, possibly to a convent or some other place to further her education and keep her out of the way. That would agree with her journal and point to Tintagel as her home and therefore resting place."

"Good grief," Sebastian said, subdued. "No wonder she hated Arthur and Merlin and the rest."

"Possibly. Perhaps that's when the seeds of dissension were planted. But Geoffrey's *Vita Merlini* implies at least some cooperation between Morgan, Merlin, and Arthur. It was only the later, romanticized texts from the thirteenth to fifteenth centuries that painted her as an evil enchantress. I'm sure her actions and motivations were much more complex than any of the stories accounted for. Ultimately, we don't really know what happened, and maybe never will. Though, perhaps if we find her alive and she's, well,"—Lily shrugged, making a face—"not too intent on killing us, we can ask her and find out the truth."

"Good luck with that," Sebastian said as he polished off the last bit of food on his plate, finally sated enough to pour himself a leisurely cup of tea. Looking up, he glanced past her and raised a hand to wave someone over. Lily turned to see Hawkins and Cyril winding their way toward them through the tables. "You have somewhere in mind to start looking?" he asked her.

"Yes."

"Good. Let's let these two get fed, then meet upstairs to talk strategy. I assume you have some sort of spell you can cast to ensure we're not overheard?"

Lily rolled her eyes. "I'm sure I can come up with something," she assured him dryly. When Hawkins and

Cyril arrived she gave them a polite 'good morning' and rose to offer her seat. She was done eating and had research to do in preparation for their day, now that she had Internet access again.

"Alright. Meet you up there in, say, half an hour?"

Lily nodded, nudging the "sleeping" Sir Kipling awake and informing him that he would have to come up to their room if he wanted anything for breakfast.

She left the three men to their food and headed upstairs, mind busy with thoughts about tidal tables and coastal geography. They were a grateful distraction from thinking about…other things.

Chapter 3
THE NARROW FORT

L ILY STOOD AT THE TOP OF A LONG FLIGHT OF WOODEN STAIRS. THEY WOUND down the cliff face, which dropped before her over a hundred feet to the crashing waves below. The stairs, of course, leveled out before they reached the ocean, extending to bridge the gap between the mainland and Tintagel Island. There used to be a passable land bridge between the two, but it had eroded away over the centuries and was now just a tumble of rock. Once over the gap, the stairs climbed again to eventually reach the ancient ruins atop that stony height covered in mossy grass.

Though not the most impressive ruins she'd ever seen, Tintagel Castle's claim to fame was more due to its historical significance. Built half on the mainland and half on the jagged island projecting into the Cornish sea, its historical connection to the legends of King Arthur had inspired the imaginations of countless generations.

Gazing down at the long descent in front of her and the subsequent climb, Lily could easily imagine how strategically important the site might have been as a remote and well-protected stronghold for various rulers, starting with the ancient Romans. Its very name, Tintagel—a combination of the Cornish words din and tagell—meant "fort of the constriction," most likely alluding to the narrow and easily defensible land bridge which led up to where the castle's main stronghold would have been.

It was a good thing, Lily concluded, that she was not afraid of heights. Despite the sturdy railings on either side of the walkway, it still looked treacherous. The wind didn't help, picking at her clothes and hair and making them whip back and forth in the constant gusts. She couldn't imagine braving the climb if things were slippery. Since the day was dry, however, and she was wearing her new boots with impressive rubber treads, she felt brave enough to venture down towards the crashing waves.

Behind her trailed Cyril—wide-eyed with child-like glee as he rattled off historical facts about their surroundings—and Sir Kipling, who looked distinctly unhappy with the way the wind was ruining his long hours of laborious grooming.

Hovering a short way ahead and behind like a pair of guard dogs were Sebastian and Hawkins. Lily was certain John Faust wouldn't bother them out in the open, but Sebastian had been adamant. He pointed out that they wouldn't always be out in the open, and that it was better to be safe than sorry. To keep warm from the wind, Sebastian had produced a worn but hardy leather jacket, and Hawkins showed up in a knee-length wool trench coat and the ubiquitous English flat cap. He looked positively British to the core, gazing about with his perpetually serious expression.

Knowing it wasn't going to get any less steep no matter how long she looked at it, Lily finally started down the wooden walkway, holding tightly to the railing as wind gusted about her with frightening strength. The advantage of this overcast, chilly, and windy weather was that they had the site more or less to themselves. Apparently they'd arrived at the tail end of the summer tourist season, and the groups of holiday-goers still around weren't especially keen on traipsing about in such miserable weather. Sir Kipling did not use the walkway. He found it easier to clamber down over the rocks and mounds of springy grass bordering the staircase where his claws had purchase. Yuki was nowhere in sight, having trotted off as soon as they'd arrived with a mental comment about having smelled a rabbit. Lily wasn't worried. The fox knew to stay within calling distance, and he was serving the role of lookout as he roamed about.

On their way down to the land bridge, they passed several instances of stone ruins marked with placards declaring their history and significance. Cyril, walking behind her, educated her on some of the relevant details as they climbed.

"My goodness, look at those arches! Simply gorgeous. Did you know there was most likely an important Roman settlement here before Rome fell and the Romans abandoned Britain? And later, during the fifth to seventh centuries, they believe this was the site of a thriving coastal town. They've found luxury goods here imported all the way from the Mediterranean."

"That's fascinating," Lily called, voice almost carried away by the wind.

"Of course, very little remains from the time of King Arthur. Most of these stone ruins are left from a castle Earl Richard of Cornwall built in the thirteenth century. Though a strategically powerful location from a defense standpoint, this area had very little political value in the overall power structure of England. Historians believe Richard built a castle here because of the powerful legends attached to the island. By aligning himself with King Arthur of legend, he was probably trying to improve his popularity and status among his subjects here in Cornwall. In any case, the castle didn't last long. It fell into disrepair barely a century later. See these stone foundations here?" Cyril pointed to a line of stone barely visible above the spongy grass that covered the cliffside.

Lily turned, having to hold whipping strands of hair out of her face in order to see the spot he indicated. Her hair would be a complete mess when they finally got back to their rooms.

"These could have been supports for the gatehouse," Cyril said loudly, pointing at several other places around them and making a motion with his hands as if outlining a gigantic roof and mighty portcullis. "And down there, where the walkway bridges the gap," he pointed ahead of them. "The original land bridge, which connected the two parts of the castle, here on the mainland and there on the headland, collapsed around the fifteenth century."

Looking forward, Lily could see where the cliff dove down almost into the water. Only the smallest bit of land was still above the tide, and certainly couldn't have been traversed by anything but man or animal clambering down and back up the rocks—thus the walkway bridge. Nothing killed the tourist trade like inaccessibility. Even with the bridge, though, the number and steep incline of the steps before and after it dissuaded any tourist not fond of a good workout.

Continuing their downward climb, Lily and her friends finally reached the bridge. At mid-morning, the tide was coming off its peak, and waves crashed just below them, the wind catching their spray and blowing it across Lily's face. They crossed the bridge quickly, Cyril having fallen silent to avoid getting a mouthful of salty water.

As they began to climb the other side, Lily heard a piteous meow behind her. She turned, looking for its source. There, on the other side of the bridge, stood Sir Kipling, back hunched and legs tucked close in the cold wind. The crashing waves of the high tide had sprinkled the bridge with water, and the distressed feline kept raising and flicking each front paw as if to somehow escape the dampness.

Lily put her hands on her hips. She was not unsympathetic to her cat's predicament but knew it wasn't as bad as it looked. He wasn't actually scared of anything, he just didn't want to get wet. Unfortunately for him, Lily was not of a mind to go back and carry him across, no matter how pitifully he cried. Water wouldn't kill him.

"Come on, scaredy-cat!" She yelled over the noise of the waves and wind. "It's just a bit of water. If you can't take it, maybe you should go back to the hotel."

That did it. He gave one last yowl as if to psych himself up for the task, then dashed across the bridge as fast as his kitty legs could carry him. Not stopping once across, he kept coming at full speed, bounding up the steps until he reached their group and then making a beeline for the closest patch of grass beside the walkway.

"There, that wasn't so bad, now, was it?" Lily asked.

Sir Kipling, busy rolling in the grass to help dry his fur, stopped to glare at her. "Do you have any idea how disgusting it is to lick salt out of my fur?"

Lily shrugged. "Sorry, but there's going to be more where that came from. If Morgan's resting place is on this island, the entrance is most likely hidden in a cave, and most of those flood at high tide." Her cat didn't reply, being too busy licking his fur into submission.

Looking up, Lily spotted Yuki bringing up the rear. He trotted jauntily across the bridge and even stopped to jump up on the railing and put his head to the wind, closing his eyes as if thoroughly enjoying the experience. The whole display was, Lily suspected, a taunt directed at his rival. And its significance was not lost on said rival, who paused his vigorous grooming to glare daggers at the fox.

"Well, that was glorious. Shall we move on?"

Sebastian chuckled and turned, starting back up the last few flights of steps, which would take them to the beginning of the ruins atop the island. Before following, Lily beckoned Yuki over with a gesture.

"Yes, O radiant one?"

She looked at him askance, not sure if he was trying to be funny. "While we're taking a look around the ruins, I want you to circle the island. Get as far down toward the water's edge as you can and look for caves, crevices, any openings. I assume the entrance to Morgan's tomb will be hidden, magically or otherwise. See if you can find any hint of magic, or even anything that looks like human writing or marks in the stone. Just be careful, alright? Some of the cliffs are dangerously steep."

"Fear not, O noble lady. For my feet are swift and my steps are sure. After all, I am no pussy cat." He gave a barking laugh and loped off, ignoring Sir Kipling's hiss as he passed the scowling feline.

"Well, come on, Kip"—Lily reached down to give her cat a sympathetic scratch behind his damp ears—"you've got a reputation to defend."

***

They spent several hours exploring the island, carefully examining all of the stone ruins and earth foundations that had been excavated, looking for any sign of magic or even inactive dimmu runes. Sebastian and Hawkins spent most of that time standing and gazing about, or talking together in hushed tones, even though Lily had invited them to help look. Either they took their duties as lookout very seriously, or else they were just bored of staring at rocks.

Besides the odd tourist, however, they encountered no other living thing on the island. Lily even kept an eye on the sky above her but saw no suspicious-looking black dot that might be Oculus, her father's raven construct. Seagulls winged past, cawing their raucous cries, and one darker shadow soared high above the coastline only to turn and dive, quickly disappearing among the rocks. Probably a falcon after its dinner.

An hour after noon, they stopped to eat a sparse lunch of sandwiches Lily had packed away in her bag. The break enabled them to sit down and rest while discussing their next move in low tones. Having looked up the tidal times earlier that morning, Lily knew low tide would be around five pm, and so their best chance of finding any hidden entrances would be as the ocean sank and revealed the many caves which dotted the coast. At the mention of caves, Cyril piped up that there was one in particular, called Merlin's cave, that they should explore.

"The story goes this cave was where Merlin caught up baby Arthur from the sea and declared him the future king."

"Hm, was that…" Lily racked her brain, trying to remember the books Cyril had assigned her. "Ah, yes, Tennyson! The *Idylls of the King*?"

"Correct!" Cyril exclaimed, seeming delighted. "Written in the latter half of the nineteenth century, some believe as an allegory of society's conflicts in Britain during the Victorian era."

"Wait a minute." Sebastian held up a hand. "I thought Arthur was born from some duke's wife after that Ufer guy pretended to be her dead husband and…you know," he trailed off delicately.

"Uther, Sebastian, not Ufer," Lily corrected him. "And yes, that is the more likely *historical* chain of events. Tennyson was a poet, however, not a historian. *Idylls of the King* was never meant to be a historical account."

"Well, then why are we interested in this Merlin's cave?"

"We're not, exactly," Lily said, cutting off Cyril's heated reply. "We're interested in caves in general, but I suspect the easily accessed caves along the mainland coast where mundanes have been poking around for decades are the least likely to hold a hidden entrance. That's why I sent Yuki around the seaward side of the island, to look for anything more remote and difficult to access. What do you think, Dr. Hawtrey?"

The professor nodded thoughtfully. "Yes, yes. I suppose you're right, though we can't positively rule out any cave until we've examined it. The entrance is surely concealed from mundanes, so it might be in plain sight, so to speak."

"That is possible," Lily conceded, "but based on the paranoia Morgan displays in her journal, I think we should focus our efforts on the more remote spots first."

"Agreed." Cyril finished his sandwich and stuffed the empty bag into his pocket, full of barely contained excitement. He was disgustingly fresh after a morning spent bent double, examining rocks in minute detail. "Shall we, then?"

"Shouldn't we wait till Yuki gets back?" Sebastian said around a mouthful of sandwich. Knowing his appetite, Lily had made him two.

At a polite cough, all eyes turned toward Hawkins. Lily hadn't even seen him eat his sandwich. It had just...disappeared, she assumed into the manservant's stomach, since he held his empty sandwich bag in his hand. "I believe a wait is unnecessary. The fox has returned."

He pointed at Cyril, or rather, behind Cyril, and the professor turned to find the fox almost on top of him. The poor man started in surprise, wobbled precariously, then slid off the rock he'd been perched upon.

Cyril swore—quite colorfully for a simple scholar—and picked himself up. "Will you stop doing that?" he demanded, ignoring Sebastian, who was slapping his knee in mirth.

"*Doing what?*" The fox sat, ears perked and head tilted, the picture of innocence.

"Inflicting your presence on us," Sir Kipling muttered, giving Cyril some much-needed support that, unfortunately, the wizard couldn't take solace in. All *he* heard was a disgruntled meow.

Lily clapped her hands together, diverting everyone's attention from the potential squabble. "Well, I think we've had plenty of time to eat and rest. Why don't you tell us what you found, Yuki?"

"*There are indeed several caverns on the far side of the island down by the water. But most of them do not go very far back and, of the ones that do, I could not enter, as they were flooded by the tide.*"

Lily's heart sank, but Yuki continued.

"*I did, however, find two things of interest. One was an odd marking on a stone outside one of the flooded caverns.*"

"What did it look like?" Lily asked eagerly.

The fox cocked his head. "*Like two moons, side by side.*"

Lily decided to puzzle over that one later. "And the other thing?"

"A cavern upon the island itself, nestled among the ruins. I did not explore it, simply saw the entrance as I passed."

Brow wrinkling, Lily wondered why they hadn't spotted this cave themselves. "Alright. Let's go take a look at that one, first. Maybe by the time we're done with that, the tide will have gone down enough for us to explore the other cave."

Plans made, they all rose and packed away their things.

The "cave" on the top of the island turned out to be more of a small tunnel, which is why Lily had missed it. From the path, it looked like a simple culvert with a ditch cut into the ground leading up to its sunken entrance. They had to climb over a railing to get to it, and everyone, especially Sebastian, had to crouch to enter it. The walls curved inward to form a peaked ceiling, and the stone surface looked worked as if it had been carved out of the stone rather than formed naturally. The tunnel went back about a dozen yards and was both empty and devoid of any sort of ancient mark. After a thorough search they emerged, disappointed, back into the wind that gusted across the high, plateau-like island.

"What do you think it was for?" Lily asked Cyril as Sebastian bent to dust off his knees and Hawkins climbed back over the railing to make sure no tourists stumbled upon them.

"I'm not sure. Possibly a larder or storage room of some kind. Caves are nature's refrigerators, after all."

Lily shook her head. "Well, I doubt we'll find scraps from Morgan le Fay's last lunch in there, so let's move on."

While the island itself was only about a quarter mile

wide, its sides plunged sharply over two hundred feet before finally meeting the crashing waves of the ocean below. Being much larger and less nimble than the fae fox, it took them forever to find a way down the craggy cliffs to the cave Yuki had found. As they neared the ocean, it became especially treacherous because the sinking tide left behind rocks slick with water and seaweed. After much slow and careful navigation, however, they finally reached the cave entrance, which, judging by the watermarks on the rocks, would be completely submerged at high tide. This was not a place to dally.

"*Here.*" Yuki nosed at an outcropping of rock to the side of the cave.

Lily carefully climbed over, mentally blessing Emmaline for her choice in boots. There was no way she could have accomplished the climb without the grip of their rubber soles. Also, because of the unique way her skirt was designed, she could easily take large steps and move freely without constriction or fear of stepping on her hem. In fact, she fared better than Cyril and Hawkins, both of whom wore more loafer-style shoes with little tread. Sebastian, of course, wore hiking boots.

Reaching the fox, she bent close to peer at the worn rock, fearing the worst. Being in the middle of a tidal zone meant the rock was pounded with waves for hours each day, something no simple carving could withstand without wearing away entirely. But to her delight, the engraving was as crisp and clear as if it had been carved yesterday. That could mean only one thing: magic. Indeed, peering closer, she spotted tiny marks within the engraving that could possibly be dimmu runes, though they were cleverly concealed within the pattern of the figure cut into the rock.

Running her fingers over it, she carefully withdrew her

printed copy of Morgan's journal from her leather bag, safely sealed within a clear, watertight sleeve. As she had suspected, the symbol in the rock was identical to the one on the journal: the ouroboros snake twisting in the figure eight of an infinity loop.

"Over here!" she yelled at the others, voice barely audible over the wind and crashing waves. The others climbed carefully down and crowded around. Cyril was especially interested, taking out a collapsible magnifying glass from the inside pocket of his coat and examining the tiny dimmu runes.

"Ingenious. Absolutely brilliant."

Lily, however, wasn't listening. She was attempting to find a way into the cave whose floor was still flooded with water, at least at the entrance. Peering inside, it looked as if the floor sloped slowly upwards, if only she could find a way to it without wading through the freezing Atlantic tide.

In the end it was Sir Kipling who found a path, something he pointed out rather loudly to Yuki. The way was tricky, but they found a place where they could sidle along on a small ledge, at one point having to grip several outcrops of rock at eye level to keep from falling into the water. But they all made it safely inside the cave, feet sinking slightly into the damp sand of its floor.

Sebastian and Hawkins got out flashlights, but she withdrew a small, etched glass orb from her bag. It was a gift Allen had given her during their long afternoon of study together at his townhouse when they'd first met. He'd taught her many things that day, principally the technique of silent casting—an extremely useful skill as it was turning out, if incredibly tricky—but also some more simple, practical spells. Well, not exactly simple. The spell she was about to cast was a combination of a light spell, like the ones used to power the light orbs in the Basement under McCain Library, and a levitation spell Allen had invented to give his construct "helping" hands their power of flight. While she hadn't had time to master it that very day, she'd carefully memorized it and had practiced it several times since. Now, motioning her companions to back up, just in case, she calmed her mind and sharpened her will, using the Enkinim words of power to bring first light, then weightlessness to her small orb covered in etched dimmu runes, to anchor and preserve the spell.

After carefully outlining the spell's parameters, she poured her magic into the orb, reveling for a moment in the exhilarating rush that casting always brought. But only for a moment. As soon as the orb was appropriately charged, she cut off the flow and spoke words of sealing that would prevent the magic from dissipating. She really should have used this opportunity to practice her silent casting, but they were in a hurry and she didn't want to hold everyone up. It might have taken several tries to get it right.

Letting go of the orb, she stepped back to inspect her handiwork. The enchanted ball hovered in the air right above their heads, shining bright, but not blinding, light all around them, illuminating the cavern. Sebastian whistled, twirling his flashlight around his finger before sticking it in his back pocket for future use.

Cyril came over, peering curiously at the ball of light. "Very impressive, Ms. Singer. I can't say I've seen such a spell before. You must teach me sometime."

"Um, thank you. And, sure." Lily ducked her head, trying not to blush at the unexpected praise. "It's really not much."

Wanting to avoid any more awkward conversation, she turned toward the back of the cave and set off. The orb followed her, having been linked to her ward bracelet as part of the spell so that she didn't have to worry about keeping track of it.

Sir Kipling, who had perched on a nearby ledge while she worked, now stretched and yawned before jumping down and sauntering over to lead the charge. "I can think of several excellent cat toy applications for that trick," he meowed over his shoulder, back to his old smug self.

"*You play with toys? How adorable.*" Yuki trotted over to join them and Lily could swear she saw a very Sebastian-like twinkle in the fox's eyes.

"They're hunting simulators," her cat hissed at the interloper, smugness vanishing as he attempted to establish some semblance of dominance. After all, *he* was the one whose job it was to lead the way, poking his nose into all the places where it didn't belong.

"Yuki, could you stand watch outside the cave?" Lily asked diplomatically. "We really wouldn't want to be surprised in here, either by my father or the changing tide."

"*As you wish. I shall leave the spelunking to the mighty toy-hunter.*" With that he trotted off back the way they'd come.

Sir Kipling gave an emphatic sniff of disdain as if to say "good riddance" and turned back to exploring the cave. The humans followed him, Lily's orb giving them plenty of light to see by, though Hawkins's flashlight was still useful for illuminating dark crevices and clefts in the rock. They followed the cavern back as the sand turned to pebbles and then rock. All too soon, however, the cave began to narrow, and then ended, leaving only a tiny crack that not even Sir Kipling could slip into.

"Well, this is rather disappointing," Cyril commented, voice echoing in the enclosed space around them.

"Don't be so quick to cry defeat, Mr. Hawtree," Sebastian

said in a not-quite mocking voice, mispronouncing the professor's name—deliberately, Lily was sure. "We haven't searched the walls thoroughly for marks or hidden cracks yet."

"Ah, yes. Of course."

Sebastian pulled out his flashlight and tossed it to the professor, who actually managed to catch it, though he almost dropped it as he fumbled to turn it on. Hawkins gave Sebastian a third flashlight and all four of them turned to the walls, Lily and Cyril to one side and Hawkins and Sebastian to the other. They started at the very back of the cave and made their way slowly and painstakingly toward the front. As they worked, Lily reflected that it was a shame the entrance to the cave was submerged twice a day, or else they might have found footprints. That was, of course, assuming John Faust's location spell had led him to this cave, and that he'd managed to find his way down without the help of a magical fox.

About halfway back toward the mouth of the cave, Lily stopped. Cyril had already moved on, having checked that section of wall previously. But Lily had noticed something flicker in the corner of her eye as she'd turned away. Now, looking directly at the wall, there was nothing unusual to be seen. Yet when she turned her head, the edges of her vision flickered like they often did when she looked at Grimmold or Pip. It was the telltale sign of fae glamour that, because of her heritage, didn't seem to affect her.

"Sebastian, come look at this. Tell me what you think."

Everyone crowded around, examining the wall while Sir Kipling sniffed suspiciously at the rocks forming its base.

"I don't see anything," Cyril finally said, and Hawkins murmured in agreement.

Lily, however, looked at Sebastian.

"It's definitely fae glamour. The problem is, I don't see

what it's supposed to be hiding. There isn't anything there."

"Or is there?" Lily said, deciding not to trust her eyes. Closing them, she reached forward to touch the cool stone, slowly feeling her way along the cavern wall to the spot where she'd seen the glimmer. Unexpectedly, the wall seemed to fall away and her hand touched only cold air. She heard Cyril gasp beside her. Opening her eyes, she saw that her hand appeared to disappear into the wall. Withdrawing it, Lily grinned. "It's a dual layer, don't you see? Both fae glamour *and* a wizard's glamour spell. Morgan must have been incredibly paranoid. I would have thought the fae glamour would be enough, since her descendants would be the only ones who could see through it. And she wanted *them* to find her."

"You're forgetting something," Sebastian said, reaching forward to feel for himself and grinning when his hand disappeared into the rock.

"And that is?"

"Thiriel."

"Who?" Cyril asked, confused.

"No one you need to worry about," Sebastian assured him in a suppressive tone. Pulling Lily aside, he spoke quietly. "If Morgan wanted to hide from mundanes, other wizards, *and* the fae, that would have been plenty reason to use double spells. Remember, she and the fae weren't exactly bosom buddies after she decided to use their gifted magic for her own schemes."

Lily nodded in agreement. At least now she knew what to look for. Though even when she went back to the wall and examined it for traces of magic, she couldn't detect any. It was perfectly masked, and they wouldn't have found it if Lily hadn't known what the glimmer in her vision implied. They would need to be very careful. Though she knew ancient wizards were said to have been much more powerful and skilled than modern-day ones, it was hard to conceptualize. She only hoped she was up to the challenge. Well, no, she knew she wasn't. But she had her friends, allies, and beloved cat to help her. They would manage somehow.

Now that they knew where the crack was—even if they couldn't see it—they were able to carefully feel their way around the edges and determine that it was just wide enough for a grown man to slip through, though the headspace was cramped. Despite everyone's protest, Lily went first—well, technically second. Sir Kipling had already nosed his way to the lower edge and hopped through, his whiskers telling him what his eyes couldn't. Lily's orb of light followed her, though she had to physically manhandle it through the opening since it hovered a bit too high to fit through on its own. Beyond the crack was a tunnel, completely different from the cavern they'd first entered. Its walls were smooth, with no sign of tool work, which indicated they'd been created by magic. The floor was stone covered in a thick layer of dust.

While Lily examined the walls, the others squeezed into the tunnel. Sebastian almost got stuck, but with a bit of tugging they finally got him through, though he complained about the scratches it left on his leather jacket. Putting a finger to her lips, she warned them all to be quiet as she pointed at the floor.

In the dust at their feet and disappearing down the tunnel were footprints.

Since everything in the tunnel was dry, there was no way to know if the footprints were recent, or if someone else in ages past had found this tunnel and explored it. Lily felt it was safer to assume they belonged to John Faust.

Now on their guard, they started slowly down the

tunnel, their flashlights and orb the only sources of illumination. Though there had been no mention of any such thing in Morgan's journal, Lily kept on the lookout for booby traps and whispered to the others to do the same. She also kept a sharp eye out for more fae glamour or any magic whatsoever that might indicate a spell had been cast. She'd bet…well, something, that John Faust had left them a nasty surprise, or at the very least a conveyance spell to spy on them.

Contrary to her fears, however, they encountered nothing at all but bare tunnel, which turned several times as it wound deeper under the island. After what felt like ages, they rounded one last turn and came face to face with…

A wall.

"Seriously?" Sebastian whispered. But Lily and Cyril looked at each other with a smile. They were finally on familiar ground. This wall blocking the tunnel was described in Morgan's journal, and she'd left an ancient incantation so that her descendants would be able to open the hidden door.

"Would you like to do the honors?" Lily offered Cyril, feeling generous in their moment of triumph. Of course, the reminder of what lay behind that door, and what she was going to have to do, quickly squashed her momentary elation.

The professor looked sorely tempted, but shook his head. "You're her descendant, just like the book says. I think it would be best if you opened it." He stepped back, but took a small notebook out from his pocket and began scribbling, no doubt taking notes on their discovery.

Lily extracted her clear sleeve from her bag and opened it, shuffling through the papers until she found the incantation. It had been written in Enkinim, of course, and so John Faust would no doubt know it as well, assuming he'd been able to figure out what it was for. Judging by the footprints disappearing where the wall met the dusty floor of the tunnel, Lily guessed that he had.

Taking a deep breath, she tried to calm herself in preparation to tap the Source. It wasn't easy. Her mind was awhirl with excitement, apprehension, curiosity, dread, and much more. But she reminded herself that, based on Morgan's instructions, she and Cyril knew what to expect. As long as there were no ancient traps or unexpected barriers, they would be in and out of there in fifteen minutes and safely back at the hotel in a few hours. Then the real work would begin.

Focusing on the task at hand, she readied her magic and slowly, carefully read the spell from her sheet of paper. This was a completely unfamiliar and unpracticed spell, so there was no way she would attempt to silent-cast it. She was nervous even reading it, there being words that neither she nor Cyril recognized, which meant she had to guess at their pronunciation. Yet, as she finished and sealed the spell, forcing her will upon it, she felt the words come to life and the wall respond. It was a very simple response: it disappeared.

Having no idea what to expect, the others jumped in surprise, peering suspiciously down this new tunnel that had been suddenly revealed. With careful steps they advanced in ominous silence, their light illuminating only ten or so feet in front of them. Everything else was swallowed up in inky blackness thick enough to cut with a knife. As they crept forward, Lily's tension mounted and she caught herself holding her breath.

Without warning, the walls on either side of them disappeared. Lily stopped, looking around anxiously before realizing they'd entered a plain stone chamber, its ceiling higher than that of the tunnel and its walls stretching out a good fifteen feet on either side.

Desperate to know, Lily took a few quick steps, hurrying to the middle of the room. She had to see, had to know...but no. With a whoosh of air Lily let out the breath she'd been holding and sagged in relief.

The room was empty.

Turning to her companions, she gave them the thumbs up. Sebastian, who'd looked alarmed when she'd turned around, now relaxed, arms lowering as if they'd been raised in preparation to summon a certain staff.

Making more motions with her hands, she used a series of crude gestures to indicate that they should all stay silent, but split up and search around the edges of the room. The silence was necessary because, as she'd been expecting, she finally spotted a fresh conveyance spell in the corner of the room, no doubt courtesy of John Faust. It didn't look as if he'd even tried to mask it. She would have to take care of it eventually, but first, she needed her father to see them poking about the tomb.

As Lily's companions began to scour the room, she turned around to examine what she'd sagged against: a rectangular stone plinth about waist high and six feet long. The top was bare, as she'd expected, though the sides were decorated with graceful twining knots common to Celtic cultures. Sir Kipling, scorning the others, had joined her instead and now jumped up on top of the stone platform to observe her labors. Giving the stone an experimental sniff, then a lick, he finally plopped down, sprawling across its surface as if he were the king of the jungle and it was his throne.

Ignoring her irreverent cat, Lily thought carefully,

checked off the signs they'd found so far that confirmed her and Cyril's theory. Hidden passage: check. Enchanted door: check. Empty tomb: check. Now there was only one piece missing.

Finding nothing else interesting on the plinth, she did a quick survey of the room, then joined the others at the far end. They were staring at an arch of dimmu runes on the stone wall. Though she didn't recognize all of them, she recognized enough to know what it was: a portal. It was not, however, active. There was no trace of magic, just the dimmu runes etched into the stone. Without knowing where it was meant to lead, there was no way for her to set it up. This was in contrast to the portal in John Faust's old workroom at the LeFay estate which Lily, Sebastian, and Madam Barrington had used to track down his new hideout—had it only been a week ago? It felt like years. In that instance, the portal had already been enchanted and locked onto its counterpart. All they'd had to do was charge it up and "turn it on" so to speak. But this one was stone cold. It wouldn't be taking anyone anywhere unless its creator one day returned.

Satisfied with their examination, Lily motioned them all to follow her out. They did, filing silently out of the room one by one, letting its smooth walls and stone plinth fall once again into deepest blackness.

Back down the tunnel they went, past the enchanted wall and on through all the twists and turns until finally, they came to the crack leading out into the cave. One by one they squeezed through, Sebastian once again needing to be pushed and pulled until he popped out like a cork from a bottle. Lily went last, pausing before she slipped out into the cave. The next time she came to this place, she hoped it would mark the end of this whole mess. She was both terrified and at peace. There was no guarantee what would happen, or who would come out on top. Even if they managed to subdue her father, it would be a miracle if none of them got hurt in the process. Her thoughts sped across the ocean, coming to rest beside Madam Barrington's sickbed and wishing she could turn back time. If only she'd never answered that invitation to come to the LeFay estate, then none of this would have happened.

Or, perhaps, something even worse might have happened.

Sighing, Lily gently plucked her light orb from the air above her head and slipped through the crack into the cave beyond.

On their way back up the cliff, Lily carefully sprinkled drops of magic-infused aluminum paint onto the rocks where they found their foot- and handholds, hoping it wouldn't rain that night. Like Hansel and Gretel's breadcrumbs, the bits of aluminum would help her find her way back down to the cave and hopefully keep her from breaking her neck in the process, since it would be past midnight when she returned.

Once safely back up on the island, they finally relaxed. Sebastian lost his serious expression and broke into a smile, Cyril stopped chewing his lip, and Hawkins...well Hawkins was just Hawkins. Lily had yet to discern any sort of expression on his face other than blank professionalism.

Waving hello to a couple of confused tourists—Lily and her friends had appeared out of nowhere, so the mundanes' confusion was understandable—they regrouped and headed back toward the walkway that would take them to the mainland. Checking her watch, Lily estimated that they'd been in the cavern no more than thirty minutes and had taken about twenty to get back up to the beaten path. They would be even slower at night. Using those figures, she began calculating when they would need to wake up to get down to the cave just before low tide in the wee hours of the morning.

Satisfied with her timetable, she caught up with Yuki and thanked him for keeping watch. "See anything suspicious while you were out there?" she asked.

"*As a matter of fact, yes. A raven landed nearby and seemed to examine the cave. I did not alert it to my presence, simply observed. After a time, it flew away.*"

"I knew it," she muttered. Even though ravens were technically native to the area, the likelihood of one showing up, by itself, at that precise place and time, was next to nothing. No, John Faust was watching them for sure. "Well, thank you for letting me know. I believe that raven was one of my father's, um, servants." She didn't know if the fox would understand what a construct was. "If you see any more ravens, unless they are grouped together, you can assume John Faust is watching us. Now, we're going to need your help even more tonight. Let me explain what I have in mind."

Once she was finished discussing the night's plans with Yuki, she motioned Hawkins over. "I need you to go into Tintagel village this evening and get a few things for me. Can you do that?"

"Certainly, Miss Singer."

"Good. Now, I don't know if John Faust will try and have one of his minions follow you. I doubt it, since he assumes you are a minor player—"

"Am I not, ma'am?"

"Not at all. You're our secret weapon. You're a mundane, and so he'll underestimate you. And we both know, that would be a grave mistake. Am I right?" Lily looked at him appraisingly, wondering if her guess were correct.

"Most assuredly, ma'am," Hawkins agreed, surprising her with a sly smile. "A grave mistake."

"Good. Then just keep in mind that you might be followed, so try to hide what you're doing, or else conceal it with mundane things like buying groceries or going to the drug store."

"I believe I shall be able to manage. What do you need me to acquire, Miss Singer?"

She told him. Her list, while not long, was rather odd. But Hawkins took it all in stride.

Tasks complete, she picked up her pace to join Sebastian and they walked in companionable silence the rest of the way back to the car.

That night after dinner, they finished with a few last-minute preparations, then all headed to bed. They would have to be back up again in a mere five hours, and they needed to be awake and alert for what lay ahead.

As Lily snuggled down under her covers, this time with alarm wards set and Sir Kipling firmly ensconced at her feet, she paused before turning off her bedside lamp. Rolling over, she looked at Sebastian, who had already bedded down and laid his head on the pillow with eyes closed, attempting to go to sleep despite the lights.

Gazing at his face, memorizing every precious detail, she reflected that she was no longer afraid of the thrill she felt at seeing him. Nervous? Definitely. Embarrassed? Inevitably. Self-conscious? Incurably. But not frightened. She no longer felt the need to fight it, and she couldn't for the life of her figure out why. What had changed that day? She'd gone from finally admitting her feelings but fighting them, to being at peace with them. Accepting them even. She wasn't sure what that meant for her future, but at least she wasn't exhausting herself trying to figure everything out anymore. Feelings were feelings. You couldn't always make sense of them, and they certainly weren't logical, reasonable, or reliable. They just were. And for the first time in her life, that was enough.

Perhaps it had been the opening of Morgan's tomb. Even though Lily knew the woman wasn't technically dead, that's still what it was. A place of endings.

Perhaps it had been thinking about her beloved mentor, still near death with no cure in sight. Though everyone was hopeful, there was no guarantee she would ever recover. Another ending.

And tonight, or tomorrow morning, she supposed, anything could happen. Any one of them might find their end. Even if they emerged unscathed, it would still mark the end of their task, their quest. The end of "them." "Us" would turn into "you" and "me," and Lily realized she didn't want that to happen. At least, not between her and Sebastian.

"Are you still awake?" Lily whispered.

"Unfortunately," Sebastian mumbled.

Silence.

"Thank you."

There was a pause, then Sebastian opened his eyes and looked into hers. Even that simple gesture sent her heart thumping in her chest. Though she didn't try to suppress it, or deny it, she did wish her bodily response wasn't quite so…vigorous. She'd never get to sleep at this rate.

"Why?" Sebastian asked, brow developing a wrinkle as he considered her words.

Lily thought about it, not actually sure what to say. The answer was obvious: everything. But that didn't sound right.

"For being my friend," she finally said, voice barely above a whisper. It was a simple statement, but full of much more meaning than she could have expressed otherwise, no matter how many words she used.

Sebastian looked momentarily taken aback. Then he slowly smiled his crooked smile. For the first time since she'd met him, it seemed to have a tender edge to it. "Right back at'cha, Lil," he said softly. "Right back at'cha."

Chapter 4
AWAKENING MORGAN

THEY ROSE AT 3:00 A.M., PREPARING IN SILENCE AND CONTINUING WITHOUT A word out to the car. The drive to Tintagel village was short and they stopped there, about half a mile from the coastline, so as not to give themselves away with headlights and a parked car. Tintagel Castle and Island were closed, so they were wary of security guards as much as they were of John Faust.

Taking a circuitous route, they headed for the coast below Tintagel Island, planning to hike up along the cliff until they reached the wooden stairway, bypassing the normal tourist entrance. They'd brought red filters for their flashlights to make the light less noticeable and prevent their night vision from being ruined, but by a stroke of luck there was a full moon that night. With the bright light above in a clear sky, they hardly needed their flashlights.

They made it safely down to the walkway bridging the

gap between headland and mainland, but, as they climbed the other side, the sky began to grow dark. Looking up, Lily saw a thick fog rolling in, obscuring the moon. The air grew damp, and they moved closer together, walking single file and almost needing to touch each other to stay together in the fog that grew thicker by the minute. Thankfully, they reached the top of the island without mishap, but Lily was deeply uneasy. What was already going to be a dangerous climb down a cliff face in the dark had become nearly impossible, possibly suicidal.

Sebastian, having the best sense of direction, led the group, kept on point by Yuki, who seemed completely unfazed by the fog. As planned, they headed for the small man-made cave on the western edge of the island. Since it went so far back, there was plenty of room for all the members of their party—two-footed and four—to fit inside and keep hidden from prying eyes.

Gathering at the very back of the cave, they sat down to rest before the next leg of their journey. Lily was glad she'd invested in a pair of extra thick leggings to keep out the cold and damp threatening her with their clammy tendrils. As it was, her hair was covered in tiny droplets of condensation from the fog, and poor Sir Kipling was dripping with it. He took the opportunity to shake and roll about, even though he'd just get wet again when they ventured down to the cave.

They rested about five minutes, then Sebastian went to check the fog. As he came back, crouched to keep his head from hitting the ceiling, Lily could see from his face that the news wasn't good.

"It's ridiculous out there. The fog is even thicker, if anything, and there's no sign of it clearing up. I don't like it, Lily." He turned to her, face taut with worry. "You can't go down there. It's too dangerous. Why don't we come back tomorrow night? You said yourself John Faust doesn't know how to get to Morgan. There's no harm in waiting."

Hawkins and Cyril murmured their agreement.

Lily shivered but shook her head. "We can't wait. There's no guarantee he won't figure it out in the next twenty-four hours, and if he gets to her before we do, it will all be over. We can't risk it. And anyway, low tide tomorrow won't be until seven a.m. That's too late in the morning. We'd risk getting caught, or hurting a tourist in the crossfire if the fighting isn't contained. I won't let that happen. It's now or never."

They stared at each other in silence, exchanging tense, worried looks.

Hawkins, having that mysterious sixth sense that all butlers and manservants seemed to possess, drew Cyril away toward the entrance, asking if he remembered the plan and going over contingencies. This left Lily and Sebastian alone at the back with Sir Kipling nearby grooming and Yuki outside keeping watch.

Lily looked down, unwilling to face Sebastian's pleading stare.

"Don't do this, Lily. Please. You're going to get…"—he paused and swallowed—"you're going to get hurt. I just know it." He reached up, barely brushing his fingertips over her cheek. "I couldn't live with that."

"I have to. You know I do."

"Let me go instead. I'll—I'll figure it out. Somehow."

She looked up then, smiling in spite of herself at his gallant ridiculousness. "Don't be silly. You aren't a wizard, and you aren't Morgan's descendant. You can't do it."

"I'd figure out something," he said stubbornly. "Anything is better than this suicidal plan."

"Stop worrying. I'll have Hawkins to take care of me,"

she pointed out, trying to make him feel better.

"But Hawkins is just…Hawkins. He's a mundane. He won't be able to protect you, not like I can. Please, Lily. Let me go with you. I need—I *need*—to be there. I need to protect you," he finished in a whisper, looking down miserably.

Lily's heart constricted, making it hard to breathe. She was terrified of what she had to do, terrified of leaving him. But she couldn't let herself think about that. Duty drove her. To be true to herself, to continue being the person she knew she was and was meant to be, she could not shrink back. Nor could she let someone else take her place. This was a task only she could do, even if it killed her.

Gently, almost timidly, she took Sebastian's large hands in hers. They were warm, bringing relief to her cold fingers. She squeezed them, and he looked up at her, expression tortured.

"You have to let me go," she whispered, absolutely refusing to let that burning behind her eyes form into tears.

He pulled her gently forward. Their bowed foreheads met and they rested against each other, taking what comfort they could from that meager connection.

"But…I only just found you," he whispered, voice full of pain.

Lily shivered, though it wasn't from the cold. She knew she shouldn't be feeling elated at such a dark, serious moment, but she couldn't help it. He'd as much as said he loved her. Maybe that's not how he meant it. Or maybe it was. Either way, it was the first time he'd ever expressed desire for her of any kind. It filled her with hope. "And now that you *have* found me, I have no intention of disappearing. That would be extremely rude, and I hate being rude."

Foreheads still pressed together, she felt him chuckle,

though it sounded a bit wet, as if she weren't the only one fighting back a certain burning behind the eyes.

"I need you to watch my back, Sebastian. You *will* be there protecting me, just from behind instead of at the front. If you don't do your part, we'll all be doomed."

He nodded, fog-damp bangs brushing against her forehead as he finally lifted his head with a deep, steadying breath.

"Of course. You're right. I won't let you down."

"I know you won't." She tried to smile, but he still looked worried, so she gave his hands a reassuring squeeze. "If you know the enemy and know yourself, you need not fear the result of a hundred battles."

At his look of surprise, Lily gave him a cherubic smile. "What? You aren't the only one who reads Sun Tzu."

Sebastian finally grinned, seeming his old self again. "I guess I should have known better than to try and one-up you."

"Yes, yes you should." She squeezed his hands one last time and let go, fingers brushing over the Dee family ring as she did. "I'm so glad Mr. Dee gave you that. It's incredibly strong. I can feel its power from here." Having a sudden thought, she took his ring hand, drawing it close to her face and examining the heirloom. "There are some active aspects you won't be able to harness, of course, but the passive wards are the best I've seen. You should be safe from average battle spells, quick casts, things that don't have too much power behind them. I'm not saying don't dodge, but at least you won't go down the first, or even the second or third time you're hit. Of course, without being able to recharge and channel more magic into it, it will weaken over time. I'll have to talk to Mr. Dee about its upkeep for you."

"Will it last the night?" Sebastian asked.

"Yes, but don't get the wrong idea. Without the active shield spells, this ward isn't a battle suit. It's more like, um....football padding. The pads soften blows and prevent many injuries, but they can only do so much. So stay on your toes, avoid direct blows, and try to keep close to Cyril. Shield spells have a spatial limit so the further away you are the harder it will be for him to keep you safe."

They stared at each other, solemn in the semi-dark as thoughts of battle, danger, and injury sank in.

Gently letting go of his hand, Lily took a deep breath. "So, yes, well...keep a sharp eye out and wait for Yuki's signal. And *be careful* out there. You'll be in just as much danger as I will be going down those cliffs. I shall be extremely vexed if you...if you get hurt." Lily swallowed, voice thick. "Promise me you'll use the rope?"

"I will if you will," he said, flashing her a grin.

Rolling her eyes with a playful smile, she headed toward the entrance to the cave, spirits lifted at least momentarily. Dwelling on the danger ahead didn't help, so she tried not to.

"You lovebirds have a nice chat?" Sir Kipling asked lazily, in a much better mood now that he was almost dry.

"Oh hush," Lily said in a suppressive tone, even as she was unable to hold back a grin. Looking at her watch, she saw it was about three forty-five. They were on schedule. All of them huddled near the entrance of the cave, flashlights on their lowest setting, the red light barely illuminating their faces like some hellish glow from the depths below.

"Alright," Lily said, speaking quietly. "Remember the plan. Cyril, you're on the defensive. Make sure you keep yourself and Sebastian heavily shielded at all times." The professor nodded, looking even more pale than usual in the red light, but determined. Since he knew little or no battle magic and had refused, in the end, to stay behind, Lily would at least feel better knowing there was a wizard protecting Sebastian's back as he jumped into the fray.

"Sebastian, you're the shock troops. Come in hard and fast. If we don't take them by surprise we might not…well, we'll just do the best we can."

Turning to Hawkins, she met his level, cool eyes. "Do you have my list of things?"

He nodded, taking two coils of rope out of his backpack, one of which he handed to Sebastian. He'd taken the initiative of acquiring a bit more than her list had outlined, however, also picking up sturdy hiking boots for himself and Cyril and four pairs of tight-fitting gloves with anti-slip pads on the palm and fingers, as well as four headlamps with elastic straps. Boots already on their feet, he now distributed the gloves and headlamps, all switched onto the red-light setting. He was an uncanny judge of size—Lily supposed he had to be, being a gentleman's gentleman—and everything fit snugly. Flexing her now much warmer fingers, she wondered if she should look into acquiring a butler. Or would that be a maid? She had no idea, but the thought made her smile, feeling much more optimistic about surviving a climb in which she could see where she was going and wouldn't lose her grip.

The rest of the items he left in the backpack for later use, swinging it onto his back and clipping its various straps. He looked slightly less like a butler, covered in gear as he was. But as she had learned well in recent days, looks weren't everything.

"You ready, Kip?" Lily whispered.

The feline looked out at the fog with great distaste, but twitched his tail in acknowledgment. At least it wasn't raining.

Lily went to the entrance of the cave and called softly into the enveloping fog "Yuki?"

The fox appeared moments later, almost completely invisible as his silver fur blended into the grey fog. "*Is everyone prepared?*"

"Yes. Time to go. Is the coast clear?"

"*As clear as I can determine.*"

Lily nodded, understanding his annoyance at the fog. It might be providing valuable cover for their movements, but it still made everything more difficult. The key was that they had Yuki. Lily honestly had no idea how they would manage without him. Though he firmly refused to fight—his kind did not fight humans, he insisted—he would serve as lookout and messenger, enabling them to stay in contact completely undetected. Lily wished she'd had more time to plan and prepare. If so, she might have been able to fabricate a communications system using conveyance spells. Or just bought headsets and used mundane technology. But both methods would require speech, which could be overheard. Yuki had the advantage over both.

With Yuki and Sir Kipling leading the way—they'd called a temporary truce in order to focus on the mission—Lily and Hawkins set out for the cliff, leaving Sebastian and Cyril to crouch in the cave. Lily looked back after a bare handful of steps, eyes seeking out Sebastian's worried face. Their eyes met for a moment, then the air currents shifted and he disappeared, swallowed by the fog.

Worried about visibility, they moved slowly, and Lily fretted about their progress. If they didn't hurry and things took too long down in the cave, they might be trapped by the rising tide. In theory, she could cast a portal to the Basement back in Atlanta. All she needed was a flat surface—she had all her supplies safely tucked away in a small backpack that

Hawkins had gotten her, since her leather handbag would not have survived the trip. But the problem was distance. She had no idea if the spell would be strong enough to reach all the way from England, not having discussed distance parameters with Madam Barrington and having no way to check now. Hoping it wouldn't come to that, she concentrated on the path in front of her.

As soon as the ground started to slope down, they halted so Hawkins could use his length of rope to tie them securely together. It was an old mountain-climbing trick, a way for each of the climbers to help anchor their fellow should the other slip. Once they were ready, they started down. Thankfully, the fog hadn't affected Lily's aluminum "breadcrumb" trail, and she could sense where to put her feet even through the dense fog. Out here on the cliff face there was a breeze. It wasn't strong enough to blow the fog away, only make it swirl in disorienting eddies around them.

Yuki went first, then Sir Kipling, then Lily, and lastly Hawkins. Everything went smoothly—if slowly—until they were about halfway down. At this point there was a tricky spot where you had to bridge a gap from one rock to another. It wasn't so far that Lily had to jump, but she did have to let go of the steadying cliff face for her legs to reach. Bracing herself and carefully judging the distance, she stepped over the gap. Foot safely planted on the other side, she shifted her weight to get all the way over.

That's when it happened.

Her foot must have landed too close to the edge of the ledge, because the rock and dirt under it gave way and she tumbled down into the darkness, hands grabbing uselessly for anything to catch herself. Her scream was cut off abruptly as the rope went taut around her waist and she slammed into the rock face, all breath smashed from her body. For a second or two she simply hung there, dazed. But the frantic meows of Sir Kipling brought her around.

"Lily? Lily! Are you okay?"

Thank heavens Hawkins had braced himself before she'd taken that fatal step, preparing for just such an eventuality. Had he not been prepared, they would have both tumbled down onto the sharp rocks far below. Such a fall would have broken them to bloody pieces.

With the rope pulled taut around her chest by her dangling weight, she could barely wheeze, much less breathe. Scrabbling at the rock face, she searched desperately for a hand- or foothold to take the pressure off her chest.

First, her no-slip gloves found purchase, gripping a bit of rock that jutted out by her face. Then her booted toes found bits of cliff as well, one giving way under her weight but the other holding firm. Finally able to breathe, Lily took a few moments to regain her strength and calm her quivering limbs as the adrenaline pumped through her.

"Miss Singer? Are you alright?" Hawkins called quietly from above, conscious of their vulnerable position.

"Yes," she gasped. "Just—give me a minute—to get my breath back."

After a short while, between her pushing from below and Hawkins pulling from above, she managed to regain the ledge. Shaken, but undeterred, she rejected Hawkins's suggestion that they sit and rest for a while, knowing that time was running out.

Taking extreme care, she tackled the gap again, this time making it safely across, and bracing herself securely in a cleft of rock as Hawkins made his own way across. Mercifully, they had no more mishaps the rest of the way down. By the time they reached the bottom, it was 4:20 and the cave entrance was nearly dry.

Lily sent Yuki back up the cliff to pass word of their safe descent and stand watch for Sebastian and Cyril. Then she set Sir Kipling to keep an eye on the entrance while she hurried to untie the rope from around her waist. She let Hawkins worry about coiling and stowing it as she headed toward the crack. Though in a hurry, she wasn't so rushed as to forget to look carefully for signs of ambush. She could have guessed wrong about what John Faust would do. He might be waiting for her right now, ready to attack and force her to reveal the secret of Morgan's tomb. But, as she put away her headlamp and got out her light orb—which did a much better job of illuminating the cave—she saw no sign of any living thing. Neither did she see any fresh footprints in the sand, which at least meant no one had been there since the last high tide five hours ago.

There might have not been anything *alive* waiting for them, but there were plenty of other things. Conveyance spells to be exact. Lily ignored them all as if they weren't even there. John Faust needed to think he could track and predict her every move. He needed to think he had the upper hand. In fact, he did have the upper hand, with two skilled wizards and a hand-to-hand fighter against their motley crew. But Lily had initiative on her side, as well as powerful allies and a few surprises tucked away. As far as she knew, even if John Faust planned for Sebastian's pixie friends to show up, he had no way of guessing Thiriel's involvement. She was their trump card. Even if the fae queen refused to stay and fight with them, her presence turned their mission from absolute suicide to merely possible suicide.

Having reached the warded crack they'd squeezed through before, Lily began an urgent search. This was the last piece of the puzzle, the one thing she'd been unsure of. If she couldn't find it…but no, her vision did not let her down. Because she was looking for it, she finally managed to find the small spot, barely the size of silver dollar, that shimmered with fae glamour, slightly apart from the hidden crack. Probing with her fingers, she could feel the smooth disk shape set into the stone that was invisible to the naked eye, even hers, owing to the double cloaking glamour. Noticing the slight resistance she felt when touching the seal, she smiled, theory confirmed.

Lily held out her hand to Hawkins, who rummaged in his backpack, withdrawing a large iron nail about four inches long. She examined it skeptically, unsure it would be hefty enough for what she needed. Looking questioningly at Hawkins, he gave the tiniest shrug as if to say, "It was the best I could find." Lily couldn't blame him. Not many things these days were made out of wrought iron. This nail looked to be quite old and had probably been taken from some antique wagon or house.

Grateful she had gloves to protect her from the iron, she gripped the nail firmly in one hand and reminded herself where the seal was. Then she raised her arm and brought it down with all her might to stab at the disk. The wrought iron—magically inert—passed through the barrier-field around the seal and struck the disk full force.

With a snap, the nail broke.

The seal did not.

Stymied, Lily stood for a moment, fighting down a sudden panic. She could still do this. She had to. What were her other options? Why had she not made a plan B? Touching the seal again, she could feel a tiny dip in it, as if the nail had but chipped away a minuscule portion, but not enough to break the spell. Looking at the two halves of the nail, she doubted she could do anything useful with them, even if she used a rock like a hammer.

At a touch on her shoulder, she looked at Hawkins, who was making subtle motions with his hands. It took her a moment, but she finally figured out he wanted to tell her something, but wasn't sure if he should, knowing John Faust was watching them.

Sighing—this was not going the way she'd hoped—Lily tapped into her ward bracelet and used it to cast a temporary circle around them, raising it into a bubble above their heads. The shield was modified to block light and sound, which meant it appeared from the outside as an opaque dome, and would have been dark from the inside were it not for Lily's floating light orb. Casting this shield would tip off John Faust that they knew he was watching. But then, he'd probably guessed anyway, assuming he was smart enough not to underestimate Lily and her companions. They lost a slight advantage, but the sacrifice had to be made.

"What is it?" Lily asked, nodding to Hawkins encouragingly to let him know it was safe to talk

"I take it you need something made of iron to break a warded object?"

"Yes. There is a small seal imbedded in the rock. It's protected by a barrier-field ward that absorbs kinetic energy, preventing anything from striking it with enough force to break it. Except that iron is magically inert. It dampens and repels magic, so the ward can't affect it. But it looks like even without the ward, the seal was stronger than the nail."

"I believe I have a solution."

"You do?" Lily brightened.

"Yes, however…" he paused, hesitating. "It will necessarily put me at your mercy, Miss Singer."

"My mercy? I don't understand."

Unsnapping the backpack's chest strap, he reached inside his trenchcoat and pulled out something short and stubby. It took her a moment to recognize it as a shotgun. She knew what guns looked like, even if she refused to shoot one herself. Her stepfather and oldest brother Dru both enjoyed hunting, and the family owned several guns. What threw her off was the size: it was incredibly stubby, as if both the barrel and stock had been shortened, thus enabling the manservant to secrete the gun inside his coat.

Looking at it nervously, she hazarded a guess. "I don't know much about guns, but I suspect that one isn't legal?"

Hawkins nodded, turning the gun to tuck it comfortably in the crook of his arm like a country squire off to a duck hunt. "I have a shotgun permit, but with the modifications this one is shorter than the legal limit. Were you to mention this to anyone, I could be arrested and face heavy fines as well as jail time."

Lily's insides squirmed. She did not like guns, not the least because she disliked harming living things in general. But guns, in particular, were just so…messy. So indiscriminately destructive. She fervently hoped to subdue her adversaries without permanent harm, and guns had only one purpose: lethal force. She did not like the idea of Hawkins bringing one into this situation. And that wasn't even considering the absurdity of bringing a gun to a wizard's fight. Most personal wards included the same spell that protected the seal: a field that absorbed kinetic energy, defeating things moving at speed such as bullets, arrows, thrown objects, or even punches in some cases. In addition, any wizard worth his magic could cast a temporary shield that would stop physical objects. She'd used one herself, in fact, to prevent Percy the poltergeist from clubbing Sebastian over the head at the Clay Museum. Wizards could be caught off guard of course, but still, it was the equivalent of bringing a knife to a gunfight.

"I have no intention of telling a soul," she finally said, wanting to put the manservant's mind at ease. "However, I don't see how it will help us. Only iron can pierce the ward, and I believe bullets are made out of lead, are they not?"

Hawkins nodded. "Normally. But I...have connections, shall we say. I have been able to acquire shotgun shells packed with iron buckshot, not lead. It should make quick work of that seal of yours."

Lily felt her blood run cold. There existed a gun that could shoot through wards? That was a terrifying prospect. If word got out, no wizard would be safe. "Hawkins," she said in a hushed voice, as if the wall inside their shield dome had ears, "do you have any idea how dangerous that is? You could kill a wizard!"

"Precisely," he said, seeming unfazed. "Though it is not quite as effective as you are imagining. Though not a wizard myself, I do understand some of the subtle differences between spells, having to concern myself with the safety of my employer. An iron object can pass through passive wards where the spell must act on the object to be blocked, as we saw with the nail. However, remember that active shields which block all physical objects do not affect the objects themselves, simply form a wall off which things are repelled."

"Oh," Lily said, suddenly understanding. It was a small comfort, however, as shield spells had to be actively maintained and took much more energy and concentration than passive wards. You'd almost have to anticipate the gun firing to put up a shield in time to stop the bullet. She eyed Hawkins, torn between her instinct for survival and the desperate hope she clung to that, somehow, they could all get out of this alive, friend and foe alike.

"John Faust would kill us all in the blink of an eye if it

served his purpose," Hawkins said quietly, guessing the reason for her reluctance.

"I know," she admitted in a pained whisper, squeezing her eyes shut. The motion dislodged a tear, which rolled slowly down one cheek. Sniffing, she swiped angrily at it with a damp sleeve, hating the position her father had put her in. Hurting her was one thing, but forcing her to hurt other people to protect herself and those she loved? That was ten times worse. As much as she hated to admit it, they needed Hawkins's shotgun. They needed every single advantage, no matter how tiny, to get out of this situation alive. She'd expected Hawkins to have a way to defend himself, but had imagined it to be some sort of artifact given to him by his employer, not a mundane gun. As if killing with magic was somehow easier to stomach than killing with cold steel. Or iron in this case.

"Do it." Lily spoke through gritted teeth, pointing at the spot on the wall. She hated her father. Hated his greed, his twisted ideals, his selfishness. She didn't want to hate anyone, but at that moment, her hatred blazed so strongly she might have grabbed the gun and shot the man herself if his gloating face had appeared before her. The emotion frightened her.

"Plug your ears, Miss. This will be loud."

Lily dutifully stuck her fingers in her ears as Hawkins pushed her behind him and moved them both to the side, aiming carefully at the spot.

"I will have to shoot at an angle to keep the buckshot from ricocheting back at us. But it should be enough to break the seal. Ready?"

Nodding, she squeezed her eyes shut. She felt Hawkins jerk with the recoil and heard the bang as loudly as if her fingers hadn't even been in her ears. The concussion, contained within the sound barrier, had bounced and rebounded on itself, amplifying the sound. Lily shook her head, dazed and wondering if it had worked. She half expected some great rumble or noise or…something when the seal was broken. But there was only silence.

Ears ringing, she peered at the stone wall. The shot hadn't just broken the seal, it had blasted a miniature crater where the seal had once been.

"Well…I don't think Morgan anticipated guns when she created that seal." Lily commented unnecessarily.

Hawkins carefully reloaded the shotgun, then opened his coat and slid it back into its holster. "Indeed. Should we be moving? I understood that time was of the essence."

Jolted back to cold reality, Lily's adrenaline shot up and her breath quickened. Of course. This was it. With the seal broken, the way was clear to locating Morgan's body, and Lily had to make sure they found it with enough time to enact their plan before John Faust arrived.

Dropping the shield she'd been maintaining, she hurried to squeeze through the crack, calling softly for Sir Kipling to join them. He raced over, hopping through to be followed by Hawkins.

"*Glorious leader. I have detected movement near the cliff face. I hesitate to get too close, but I can tell it is three people. I believe they are headed down to the cavern. Sebastian has told me to assure you he and the fox-hating man are in good health. As agreed, they will wait five minutes, then follow.*"

Momentarily distracted by the mental contact, she felt some of her tension ease, though it was odd to be relieved that her enemies were closing in. At least it confirmed her predictions about how John Faust would react, and Sebastian and Cyril were in place to follow and attack from behind when the time was right.

Motioning for Hawkins and Sir Kipling to back up, Lily knelt by the crack and reached into her backpack to withdraw a device she'd prepared for this very purpose. It was engraved with the same runes she had on her ward bracelet and which had been on the seal: the runes for a passive barrier field. Only, the parameters of this ward were much different. Instead of creating a field of medium strength that would allow easy movement but stop high-velocity objects, this device would create a field so powerful that it had almost the same effect as a physical shield spell. It would make getting through the crack extremely difficult and, hopefully, delay John Faust long enough for them to complete their task.

Placing the device on the ground by the crack, she took a deep, calming breath and was about to begin casting when she heard an odd squeaking noise out in the cave. It sounded like a mouse, or perhaps a bat. Then it dawned on her, and she scowled. Sticking a hand out of the crack and waving, she felt a tiny weight alight upon it. Lily drew in her hand to reveal Pip nestled in her palm.

The pixie took to the air, flying excitedly around her several times before landing on her shoulder and tugging affectionately on her ear.

"Oh no you don't," Lily growled. She'd told Sebastian that under no circumstances was he to send his fae friends with her. She had no idea how Morgan, or even Thiriel, might react to their presence. Obviously, he had ignored her. "You go right back to Sebastian and tell him he needs to do a better job of following orders."

Lily couldn't understand the pixie's rapid speech, but she got the gist of it. With a sigh, she tried one last time. "Yes, I'm sure he told you to ignore whatever I say. But you can't be here. Thiriel will be coming soon. You don't like her, right? Why don't you go back to Sebastian?"

The tiny figure squeaked stubbornly, wrapping her minuscule arms as far around Lily's neck as they would go and hugging her tight, as if to proclaim that they would have to drag her off kicking and screaming—or fluttering and squeaking, in her case.

Heart melting despite herself, Lily let out a sigh. "Alright, fine. You can come."

The pixie took off from her shoulder and did a few triumphant loops in the air before diving into Lily's open backpack. The muffled peeps which drifted out of the bag made it clear she had no intention of leaving.

Muttering to herself, Lily zipped the bag mostly closed, leaving an opening through which the pixie could wiggle free if need be. "Just be quiet, okay? Absolutely silent. Got it?"

She heard an affirmative peep.

"And I might be moving fast, so you'll get jostled around in there if you don't hang onto something."

Another peep.

Having done all she could, she turned back to her task and took a moment to carefully cast the appropriate spells onto her blocking ward, activating its field. When it was finally done, she swung on her backpack and took off down the tunnel at a jog, surprising Hawkins and Sir Kipling. They quickly caught up, and all three raced toward Morgan's tomb, the slap and patter of their feet the only sound in the eerie darkness.

Passing the enchanted wall—still open as she'd left it— they slowed their pace, finally coming to a stop just outside the rectangular room. By some unspoken agreement, they all hesitated. Lily guessed her companions felt the same apprehension and awe that she felt, that of stepping into a tomb that was now occupied with an ancient entity. For Lily knew the pedestal would no longer be empty.

Though the language had been cryptic and the clues difficult to put together, she and Cyril had finally figured out Morgan's great plan to preserve herself for her eventual return. The hidden seal Lily had just broken was a lugal-nam, a time-looping device that Morgan had used to shut herself off from the world for over fifteen hundred years—longer, if they hadn't come looking for her. The tomb had appeared empty because, even though it was the right *location*, it hadn't been the right *time*. Just as she and Sebastian had been suddenly pulled back into the normal flow of time when he'd shattered the lugal-nam in Pitts, so Morgan would have been pulled back to normal time as soon as her seal was broken. A seal which had been preserving her in a pristine state for over a thousand years, hidden in a time loop parallel to, but inaccessible from, the normal flow of time.

Lily was the first to start forward, propelled by the knowledge that John Faust was on his way and having no desire to face him with Morgan in possession of her full power. With her light orb following dutifully above her head, the circle of light slowly advanced to reveal the pedestal. Upon it lay a woman.

The wizard's long, wavy hair encircled her head like a halo as its golden red tresses spread out on all sides. Her skin was pale and smooth and her face regal, with high, prominent cheekbones and a long nose above thin lips. Overall, it seemed a rather harsh face to Lily, but beautiful in a proud and sharp kind of way. Approaching carefully, she admired the woman's richly embroidered clothing. Unlike the clinging medieval dress with flared sleeves that she had imagined—another result of modern fantasy images of Morgan le Fay—this woman wore a looser, smock-like dress of deep purple that reached to her ankles, gathered at the waist by a woven belt. At the lower hem, around the loose sleeves, and along the v-neckline the cloth was richly embroidered with gold and silver thread. About her shoulders and entwined around her folded arms was a shawl or cloak of blue and green. She slept deeply, with only the barest rise and fall of her chest to indicate she was alive and not a well-preserved corpse. Lily knew from the woman's own journal that she'd been cast into an enchanted sleep to wait out the long years, and the same pages contained the spell to awaken her.

Recalling herself, Lily carefully pinpointed the conveyance spell John Faust had left in the room. With dimmu runes only faintly scratched into the stone to anchor it, the spell was already fading, but Lily wanted it completely gone. Taking out a small squirt bottle Hawkins had acquired for her the night before, she aimed it at the runes and soaked them thoroughly with the mixture in the bottle: iron salts dissolved in water. She had no idea whether her innovative, if unorthodox idea would work, but she thought it was worth a try. The runes were near the ceiling and so out of easy reach to destroy any other way. In theory, there should be enough iron in the mixture to disrupt an already weak and fading spell…Yes! Lily could feel the magic fade as the spell dissipated. She would have to pass on the trick to Madam Barrington when she got home.

Now that she was ensured her privacy, Lily got to work, sending Hawkins to stand by the door not only to listen for approaching footsteps, but also so as not to alarm a newly wakened Morgan with too many unfamiliar faces.

With hesitant steps, she approached one end of the pedestal and gently laid her hands on either side of Morgan's temples. The woman's skin was cold to the touch, and she made no movement or sign, being too deep in a magically induced coma to react to outside stimulus.

Lily did not dig out her copy of Morgan's journal for this spell. This one she had memorized, since she would need it later in a hurry and would have no time to read it off a piece of paper. She did, however, clear her mind and breathe slowly and rhythmically, trying to reach that almost meditative state that would enable her to use magic without the crutch of speaking. It was crucial she verify her ability to cast this spell without words. Her plan depended on it.

Having ordered Sir Kipling to hide on the other side of the pedestal, warning him to be quiet no matter what, Lily slowly and carefully drew power from the Source. She called it, shaped it, and propelled it forth with her mind as it flowed from her into Morgan, carrying the commands of the spell. As with most magic, the result was not flashy or impressive. Once she completed the spell, Morgan's breath hitched, then began again, now more deep and rapid. Lily removed her hands and stepped around to the side of the pedestal, nervousness growing as the woman's eyes fluttered and she groaned softly, starting to shift. Though Lily had practiced what she was going to say, she was still terrified of what might happen, unsure if she could maintain the ruse. Lying wasn't her forte.

Finally, Morgan's eyes opened. She looked groggy, and Lily remembered how she herself had felt after coming out of the time loop at Pitts. That feeling would be amplified a hundredfold, though Morgan had the advantage of having slept through the last fifteen hundred-plus years of looping time.

Speaking softly, Lily greeted the woman, hoping to make her presence known without startling her. "Hello, Morgan. My name is Lilith Igraine LeFay, one of your inheritance. I found your journal and have come to awaken you."

Morgan's eyes followed the sound, locking onto Lily's face and widening as understanding slowly dawned. She shifted, struggling to sit up, and Lily reached out hesitantly to help her, feeling downright bizarre to be touching clothes—not to mention the human in them—that were over a millennium and a half old.

Once she had helped the wizard shift to a sitting position, feet dangling off the pedestal, Lily tried again.

"My name is Lilith LeFay. Do you remember where you are?"

Looking around haughtily, Morgan spotted Hawkins and eyed him with suspicion as she gathered her shawl-cloak more closely around her. She spoke a commanding word in a language Lily didn't understand, but assumed was Old Brittonic.

"I'm sorry, I don't understand you," Lily said, hoping to appear both unthreatening and confident at the same time. She tried using hand gestures as she spoke, indicating Hawkins was with her. "That is my manservant. He is no threat."

Morgan le Fay eyed her, looking down her long nose at Lily's exceedingly odd getup—odd at least to someone from ancient Britain. Miraculously, Lily's clothes weren't covered with the dirt and scuffs they should have been, thanks to Emmaline's family magic. But still, with no gold or silver in evidence, Morgan probably thought her a lowly peasant.

The proud wizard spoke a sharp word, gesturing to the room's entrance and looking like she was about to get up.

"No, no!" Lily waved her hands, trying to indicate Morgan should stay seated, then holding up a finger, hoping that it was the universal sign for "wait" even back then.

"Wait just one moment. I am bringing a friend who will help us."

Lily slowly backed away, still holding up that finger. Morgan stilled, perhaps deciding to wait and see what happened. Now with some space between her and the pedestal, Lily prepared herself, running over in her mind the words Sebastian had drilled into her the night before.

"*Elwa Tahiri'elal. Ta'il ihki naroom melihi'ara.*" The words rolled off her tongue, perhaps not with the same grace as Sebastian possessed, but still passable. She watched Morgan carefully as she spoke, and noted that the woman's eyes widened in recognition. Having dealt with the fae herself, she probably understood at least some of the words Lily used.

After the echoing ring of her voice faded, there was a moment of tense silence. For a fleeting breath, Lily felt paralyzing doubt clutch at her heart. What if Thiriel didn't come? They would be doomed.

But then the darkness around them began to swirl and coalesce, and suddenly before them stood the fae queen of decay, tall and regal in her dazzling raiment. Compared to her, Morgan looked like a little girl playing at being princess.

"What is it child, that you have called me to this place?" The queen's words were just as cold and flat as they had been in her own domain. Belatedly, Lily remembered to kneel and bow her head. It annoyed her to do so, but it was necessary to pull off this grand charade. She peeked at Morgan from the corner of her eye and saw that the woman had risen from the pedestal looking unsteady, but standing tall, almost as tall as Thiriel herself.

"Oh Queen of Darkness," Lily began, head bowed, "I have found the great wizard of whom we spoke. I beg that you remember our agreement and grant her the power of decay."

Lily assumed Morgan still couldn't understand them at this point, since they were speaking English. But together with Sebastian, they had already worked out a solution to this in Thiriel's subterranean audience chamber several days before.

Stepping forward, Thiriel reached up and gently placed her ebony black hands on either side of Morgan's temple. The wizard flinched back reflexively, but Thiriel said a word that sounded like the same language Morgan had been speaking, calming the woman. After a moment in which Lily caught the brief green glow of fae magic in her mind's eye, Thiriel stepped back and addressed Morgan again.

"Are you the one they call Morgen of Avalon?"

Shock flashed across Morgan's face, obviously not having expected the sudden ability to understand English. But she quickly recovered. Drawing herself up, she spoke in a clear, musical voice. "I am Morgen, rightful ruler of Avalon. What business have you here…Queen Thiriel?"

From her hesitation, Lily could tell it galled the wizard to address the fae as queen. But the woman was no fool. She knew a powerful fae when she saw one. Which made Lily wonder at her use of the word "rightful." Perhaps an attempt to assert her authority in the face of being expelled from Avalon? If the fae had been privy to that event, Morgan's insecurity would make sense.

"That is for your descendant to explain." Thiriel stepped back, putting Lily front and center.

Lily swallowed, mouth as dry as paper. Daring to raise her head, she met Morgan's eyes, though she remained kneeling just for good measure. "My lady, I am your descendant and faithful servant. Your journal was passed down to me through many generations of LeFays, but I was the first to unravel its secrets and seek you out, so that you may reclaim what is rightly yours and the LeFay name may be returned to honor." Lily barely managed to get the words out around her clumsy tongue—possibly the exact words her father might have used, had he been kneeling there instead. Finishing the speech, she shut her mouth, trying to keep her face relaxed and guilt-free.

Morgan took two slow, measured steps toward her. Eyes locked, she ignored Thiriel completely as she reached down with one slender white hand and took Lily's chin in her grip. Her fingers were like ice, and her blue-eyed gaze as piercing as an arrow to the heart. She stared into Lily's eyes and Lily could feel some sort of magic reaching out, touching her. With growing fear, Lily realized Morgan could silent cast with the best of them, and was most likely attempting to ascertain the truth of Lily's words. Lily could only hope that her ward—with its otherworldly power—would protect her from revealing the truth.

Finally, Morgan smiled. It was a thin smile that didn't reach the eyes, yet Lily was so happy to see it she almost forgot herself and sagged in relief. "You are indeed my inheritance, Lilith. You have done well to find me. Now explain why you have brought this fae to me." She gestured dismissively at Thiriel, and Lily thought she could feel the chamber's temperature drop a degree.

"I sought the fae's help in finding your resting place, and they proposed an alliance," Lily hurried to explain. "They have a gift, as a show of good faith."

"Indeed?" Morgan eyed Thiriel, suspicious. "And why would the fae bestow such a gift? If I recall, it is not in their nature to be so…generous." That last word was said with a curl of the lip as Morgan invited a rebuttal.

"Your servant mistakes the situation," Thiriel said, gaze level. "It is no gift, but a trade. Damiar was a fool to think his minor power could enable you to reach your full potential. I know better, and intend that you be equipped with the tools to achieve our goal."

"Which is, exactly?" Morgan asked, seeming more interested.

"The culling of mundanes. In the centuries you have slept they have bred and spread across the land like locusts, destroying the earth and driving wizards almost to extinction. Thus, their…reduction…would benefit both our races, fae and wizardkind."

"Go on," Morgan said, eyes now glinting maliciously. Lily tried not to shiver, both at the obvious lust in Morgan's eyes, but also at how cold and matter-of-fact Thiriel sounded as she discussed slaughtering humans. As if she really wanted to. It was a good thing this next part was up to the fae queen, because there was no way Lily could convincingly pretend she wanted to perpetrate such atrocities. Though Morgan's journal had alluded to such views, Lily had hoped it was simply her interpretation. That she wasn't the bitter, power-hungry individual every source claimed she was. Perhaps she'd been benevolent once, in her youth. But time and circumstance had changed her. The price of her power had been her heart.

"Not all the fae are in agreement," Thiriel continued. "Damiar is the most against such a plan. Therefore, you will return his power to me. I can give you far greater power in its stead. You shall go forth, unstoppable, and I shall have Damiar by the throat."

Morgan seemed to think about this and Lily held her breath. "We may have the same goal, but how can I be sure your power is the greater? Don't think me a fool, to relinquish what I have for something inferior."

"Inferior?" Thiriel's quiet voice cut through the frigid

air and Lily flinched, hoping the fae queen's wrath was for show. She loomed closer to the skeptical wizard, seeming to grow even taller as the darkness she wore like a cloak flared out, dimming Lily's light orb. "I am Tahiri'elal, the Aspect of Decay. I control the ending of all things. I am destruction. I am death." While not technically true, Lily suspected the fluid and malleable nature of the English language enabled Thiriel to get away with such sweeping statements.

They seemed to have their intended effect, in any case. Though the fae queen had not raised her voice, the power and threat behind the words made Morgan shrink back and she averted her eyes. "It may be as you say. However, it should not be unreasonable to request a demonstration."

Lily's stomach clenched. This was not good. What would Thiriel do? What would convince Morgan to give up her fae magic?

"You, slave. Come here." Thiriel's voice called out and Lily's head whipped up, seeing Hawkins hesitate before slowly approaching. He had never seen a fae before, but Lily and Sebastian had prepared him.

"Yes...O queen?" Hawkins, a fast study, knelt before the fae.

Thiriel looked at Morgan, blank eyes disturbingly hard. "Behold, doubter. This is the power of decay."

With a mere gesture, the shadows surrounding her reached out and enveloped Hawkins. He cried out in surprise, but the sound was immediately cut off. When the shadows withdrew, all that was left was a pile of dust on the stone floor of the chamber.

"NO!" Lily yelled, surging to her feet. She couldn't believe what Thiriel had just done. It had to be an illusion. A trick of fae glamour. But she could see through glamour, and Hawkins was nowhere to be found.

Trying to keep her composure, maintain the charade, she glared at the fae queen. Despite the danger of the situation, she could barely hold back the sudden tears that sought to spring from her eyes. She had liked Hawkins. How would she ever explain this to Mr. Dee?

Catching sight of a whiskered nose poking around the corner of the pedestal and yellow eyes gazing at her with concern, she gave a tiny shake of her head, warning Sir Kipling to stay hidden. "He was *mine*, Thiriel," she gritted out to the fae. "*My* servant. You had no right to touch him. There was no need for—"

"On the contrary," Morgan cut her off, eyes alight with desire as they remained fixed on Thiriel. "You are my servant, therefore he was mine as well. And such a demonstration was exactly what was needed. Show me, fae. Show me how to use such power."

Heart burning with anger and grief, Lily remained silent, comforted at least by the knowledge that Morgan had fallen for their trick, hook, line, and sinker. She couldn't think about anything else right now. The next part was up to Thiriel, and Lily needed to prepare her own spell. She would only have one chance to use it.

Crossing her arms, Lily moved to stand by Morgan's side, as if positioning herself in solidarity with her mistress. Really, she just needed to be within arms reach of the wizard when the time came.

"Take my hands," the fae instructed, ignoring Lily. "Now find the fae magic within you, and relinquish it. Push it away, into me, every last drop. Only then can I fill you with my power."

The wizard and the fae stood, silent. To any mundane, it would seem they were doing nothing at all. But Lily could see the truth. She could see, could feel the immense power leaving Morgan and disappearing into the pulsing, glowing darkness that was Thiriel.

Reminding herself to focus, Lily reached into herself, preparing her spell and hoping Morgan would be too focused on her own task to notice. She needed to be ready…any time now…almost there…

With a gasp, Morgan sagged as the last of her fae magic left her. Lily gripped her arm, ostensibly to help hold her up but making sure she positioned her hands so that they touched Morgan's bare skin.

"Now, fae…now. Give me…what you promised," Morgan panted, staying on her feet only with Lily's help.

But Thiriel simply smiled. It was the first time Lily had seen any kind of overt emotion on the fae queen's face. "You are a fool, Morgan le Fay. I promised no such thing, only implied that it was possible. You are a traitor and enemy of my people and shall never touch a drop of our power ever again." With that, her darkness swirled, enveloping her like smoke, then dissipating to reveal nothing but an empty, dusty floor.

As Morgan screamed in incandescent rage, Lily squeezed her eyes shut and concentrated with all her might, thinking what she hoped was the reverse of Morgan's waking spell. She had to put the wizard to sleep. It was the only way she would survive.

Whether her silent casting failed, or whether her reversal of the spell had been incorrect, she would never know. For instead of collapsing on the floor in an unconscious heap, Morgan wrenched her arm away, throwing Lily violently off her as she began to chant. Lily barely had time to raise her own shield before the spell hit her. She had no idea what it was, but it threw her backward like a rag doll and she smashed against the wall, her head hitting the stone with a crack. Stars danced before her eyes as she slid to the floor in a heap.

Dazed, she vaguely heard the yowling war cry of her cat attacking, and a muffled squeak underneath her as Pip no doubt struggled to extricate herself from the backpack. But the yowls went from defiant to frightened, then silent, and the squeaking from the backpack died.

Lily tried to struggle to her feet, to regain awareness of her surroundings. But before she could gather herself, two icy hands gripped her throat and pushed, pinning her against the wall and crushing her windpipe.

"You vile, traitorous little worm. How dare you awaken me only to steal what is rightfully mine!"

Lily could feel drops of spittle hit her face as Morgan shrieked. But it was only a brief sensation before the screaming pain and desperate burning in her chest became all-encompassing. She struggled, hands scrabbling wildly at Morgan's grip. But the woman was surprisingly strong, fueled by a fury beyond measure. Lily's brain didn't even have enough oxygen left for her to cast a spell in her defense. Any thought she tried to grasp slipped away as her mind slowly slipped into blackness.

She wasn't supposed to be alone. Hawkins. Hawkins was supposed to be there. Where had he gone? And Sebastian. Where was he? Where…was…

Even her muddled thoughts went dark as her arms dropped limply to her side.

Chapter 5
DANCING WITH DEATH

WHUMP!!!

Lily felt the jolt as something large and fast hit Morgan from the side, tearing loose her stranglehold. Slumping to the floor, Lily coughed and gasped, vision still swimming as she tried to get her breath back. She heard the crackle of magic and yelling voices—familiar voices—but tried to simply concentrate on breathing.

When she finally became aware of the room again and managed to sit up, she saw it wasn't filled with the people she'd been hoping for. Seeing her movement, John Faust raised his hands, opening his mouth as if to cast a spell and end her.

But before he could, a figure in black filled her vision. Trista stood over her, not exactly shielding her but getting purposefully in the way. "No need, Father. I'll take care of it."

Trista knelt, putting Lily in a headlock and squeezing. Not expecting a renewed attack, Lily struggled only belatedly, terrified of suffocating again after her near-death experience at the hands of Morgan. But then she heard a whisper in her ear as Trista bent close under the guise of choking her out.

"Slowly stop struggling, then lie still as if you're unconscious."

Lily did as instructed once she realized that, while Trista's grip was tight and unyielding, it did not block off her airway. Since she was already feeling weak and woozy, she only needed to half pretend as she gave one last feeble twitch, then went limp in her sister's grip.

The young woman carefully released her and stood. "She'll be out for a good ten minutes." Her words sounded flat and emotionless.

Lily kept her eyes firmly shut but listened with all her might, hoping that Pip—in her backpack—and Sir Kipling—wherever he'd hidden to get away from Morgan—were smart enough to lay low until the time was right. She didn't even try to reach for her magic, afraid John Faust or Morgan might still be scrutinizing her. Better to wait and see how the situation played out. Things might seem bad, but it looked like her wild card had come through.

"She will not need ten minutes. I shall kill her where she lies." Morgan's icy voice sent chills down Lily's spine and she tensed.

"Please, Your Majesty. There is no need for such hastiness. She might still be useful to us." John Faust's tone was surprisingly deferential. Lily had never heard him fawn before, but her father was a master of manipulation. She wouldn't put it past him to suck up to whomever necessary to get his way. Realizing this made him even more dangerous—people blinded by pride and rigid with arrogance were much easier to predict—she listened carefully to every word.

"I do not see how. In fact I am not yet convinced that you yourself are any use. Tell me again why I should not end you where you stand?"

Lily heard a scrape as if John Faust were kneeling. "Because, great queen, we are your true servants. Your true descendants. This girl is but an imposter, one I have been fighting to eliminate for weeks."

"Which obviously implies you are a weak and useless tool if you could not even find me before that worm."

There was more scraping. Perhaps John Faust had made his children kneel as well? "You must understand, Your Majesty, that she has had the fae on her side, as well as a crafty witch with demonic allies."

Well, that was a lie, but it certainly made John Faust seem less incompetent. Of course, she knew the real reason why she hadn't been "eliminated" was that her father was loath to kill one of his own kind. Sebastian he had no compunction about, but another wizard…it was only when faced with overwhelming threat, as with Madam Barrington, that he had fought with deadly force.

Morgan le Fay, it seemed, had no such inhibitions.

"Very well. She may live for now. But what—

"We are…down the cliffs…hold on…coming."

Lily was distracted by a faint voice in her mind. They must be so far under the island that it was affecting Yuki's range, but she heard it all the same. Her heart leapt and she wished she could somehow warn them about Trista's change in loyalties, or at least make them aware of the current situation. As it was, she had to rely on her friend's expertise and Trista's quick thinking to ensure no one was hurt by friendly fire.

Suddenly remembering Hawkins, her euphoria faded

into despair. How would she explain the manservant's death to Sebastian? The two of them had been thick as thieves this past week. The news would be such a blow, not to mention how he would feel toward Thiriel. Lily thought he'd said fae couldn't kill humans, but perhaps he'd been wrong.

"*Stay low. Sebastian says we are coming in fast, as if his pathetic gait is anything compared to the swiftness of a—what?—oh, sorry, you could hear that too.*"

Despite the situation, Lily had to lock her jaw to keep herself from smiling at her friends' ridiculousness. Any moment now they would come bursting through that doorway. She listened carefully for footsteps, only keeping half an ear on the argument between Morgan and John Faust.

"Please, calm yourself, my queen. There is no need for distress."

"No need? What rubbish is this? I have been robbed. Tricked! Wake her and I will *force* her to help me reclaim what is rightfully mine."

"All in good time, Your Majesty. If you would do me the honor, we have a safe place where you can relax and become accustomed to this new era. I warn you, it is quite different from what you are used to and may take some time to—"

"*Almost there.*"

Lily's ears perked, straining to catch the sound of approaching feet as she cracked her eyelids the tiniest fraction, taking in the room in front of her. She saw John Faust and Morgan in the center of the room by the pedestal. John Faust, though no longer kneeling, stood in a bowed, deferential stance. Between them and her but to the side, closer to the entrance, stood Caden. His attention was on his father, but he glanced at her every few seconds, a dirty look on his face. Hoping the young wizard didn't notice her cracked eyelids, she searched for Trista.

Her sister was crouched by the wall next to the entrance, out of the line of sight of anyone coming from the tunnel. She had her head cocked and was listening intently, a sign Caden and John Faust obviously took to mean they had a capable ally ready to warn them of approaching danger.

They were wrong.

Carefully flexing her muscles one by one, Lily tried to prepare herself. She would need to jump up and begin casting on a moment's notice. Surprise was essential. The problem was, which person should she target first? She had a better chance of taking out Caden, since he was closest, but that would leave her group vulnerable to greater threats. Yet, if she went after Morgan or John Faust, Caden could intercept her before she got to them. She could only hope that everyone's attention would be momentarily focused on the entrance when her friends burst in, giving her time to attack Morgan—the greatest threat of all.

Decision made, she tensed, hearing the faintest shuffle echoing from the tunnel, the noise masked by John Faust's deferential persuasion. With both Caden's and John Faust's backs turned and Morgan's attention on her "servant," only Trista was in a position to shout warning.

She did not.

The moment her brother and father turned toward the entrance, looks of surprise on their faces, Lily heaved herself to her feet, already preparing her first spell. The whole room seemed to move in slow motion as she screamed at her muscles, ordering them to work faster.

Out of the corner of her eye she saw movement at the tunnel's entrance, but she couldn't spare it a glance. She heard John Faust's cry of surprise, saw him throw up his hands in the involuntary gesture of casting a shield spell, then—

BOOM!!

The gunshot echoed impossibly loud in the confined space, making her ears ring painfully. Something whistled past her ear and struck the stone behind her with a sharp crack, but she ignored it. She didn't even look down at Caden as she passed—he had somehow fallen to the floor and was struggling to get back up. No, her eyes were fixed on Morgan, and with a grunt of effort she threw her first spell at the shocked woman, still looking dazed from the blast. Lily had sacrificed strength for speed, so the spell was relatively weak. But it struck true all the same, hitting Morgan in the side and causing her to stumble and clutch at the pedestal for support. John Faust didn't even notice, already locked in a furious battle with Sebastian, Sir Kipling, Hawkins and—what?

Lily did a double take, stunned to see the manservant wielding his sawn-off shotgun like a club and belatedly realizing that, of course, the gunshot had to have come from him.

Unfortunately, her distraction cost her precious seconds and by the time she focused back on Morgan, the wizard had regained her footing and was glaring death at her. Having no time for the calm concentration needed for silent casting, Lily's overstimulated brain fell back on her training.

In a furious whirl of battle magic, the two of them cast spell after spell, sometimes taking the brunt on their wards, sometimes dodging. Lily focused on wearing her opponent down, still hoping for a non-lethal victory, even though she heard—and felt—some pretty nasty curses flung her way. Miraculously, her otherworldly ward stopped every one, though Lily could feel it growing hot on her wrist from the amount of energy it was absorbing.

With no spare attention to look around the room, Lily was clueless as to how her friends were faring. She could hear Sir Kipling's yowl and Sebastian's angry shouts, and something else...was that squeaking coming from her backpack?

Knowing she didn't need her hands to cast—they were more of a physical aid than necessity—she barely managed to keep concentration on her spells while struggling to remove her backpack. It finally fell to the ground and she left it where it lay. Now that it was stationary, she hoped Pip could crawl out without getting slung from side to side.

Sure enough, just as she was trying to find another opening to attack, a tiny green light soared over her head and dove at Morgan like a falling star of pixie wrath. Apparently the tiny creature hadn't gotten the memo that "fae don't fight humans." Morgan screamed in anger as the pixie attacked her face, and the shield she'd been maintaining flickered, giving Lily an opening. As the enraged wizard focused her spells on this new assailant, Lily took a deep breath, gathering her remaining strength for one final effort. She tapped her ward's reserves for extra power and flung the stunning spell at Morgan, screaming the words of power as she pushed with all her might.

Dropping to one knee in sudden exhaustion, she watched the spell hit, bowling the woman over as its kinetic force overwhelmed her passive wards and laid her out flat. Lily waited several seconds, did not see her enemy rise, and so turned, stumbling, to assess the rest of the room.

Hawkins was down, probably stunned. Caden still lay where he'd originally fallen, possibly also stunned or perhaps knocked out by the butt of Hawkins' gun. Sebastian, Trista, and Sir Kipling were circling John Faust, dodging in and out, attempting to get past his shields. Sebastian was bleeding from a large gash on his forehead, the blood getting into his eyes as he swung at his enemy's defenses. Each blow of his glowing staff weakened the shields, and Lily could tell John Faust was tiring. Especially since Trista kept him between herself and Sebastian, forcing him to constantly turn and whirl to protect himself from all sides. She spotted Cyril at the tunnel's entrance, attention laser-focused as he kept his defensive wards strong against John Faust's attacks.

Taking another deep breath, Lily drew on that hidden reserve of strength you found only after you thought you could go no further. Standing tall, she moved toward the remaining fighters.

"STOP!" she bellowed, adding a bit of magic to magnify her voice.

All activity in the room ceased, everyone looking stunned that such a noise had come from her.

"Surrender, Father. We have you outnumbered. There is nothing more to be gained by fighting."

John Faust turned to look at her, swaying as he did. But before his eyes met hers, they fell on Caden, to the left and behind Lily.

John Faust screamed. "NO!"

Whirling, Lily peered through the dim light and finally noticed the pool of blood still spreading around her half brother's crumpled form. It came from a small hole in the side of his neck, and Lily realized he must have been hit by a bit of ricocheting buckshot. Because it was iron, it went right through his barrier-field ward.

"No! No, no, NO!" John Faust was wild with grief, lurching toward his son, but then whirling on her, his face a twisted mask of fury.

"You! You killed my son!"

"No! I didn't—I mean, it was an accident! The buckshot—"

But her father paid no heed, screaming over her protests as he advanced, crackling with renewed energy. "Your brother! You murdered your own brother! My SON!"

Lily just stumbled back, mind frozen blank with shock and too weary, so weary of fighting.

But before John Faust could utter a single spell, Sebastian's staff fell, breaking through the weaker rear of John Faust's shield. Though its power was blunted, it continued, hitting the older man solidly in the back of the head.

John Faust dropped like a rock.

Knowing he wouldn't be seriously injured, only knocked out, Lily rushed to Caden's side. Keeling, her hands fluttered in helpless panic. "No, no, no, Caden. What do we do? Help! Sebastian, help me!"

Tears leaked from her eyes as she ripped off her jacket and pressed it to the wound in the side of her brother's neck, heedless of the blood. Its acrid, metallic tang assaulted her nostrils, adding nausea to her already shocked system.

Then Sebastian was there, pulling her away.

"No! We can't—he might still—stop Sebastian!"

"Lily. Lily! Stop it. It's over. There's too much blood. It must have hit an artery. He would have bled out in less than a minute."

"Nooo…no…" Lily's voice faded to an agonized whisper, turning into Sebastian's embrace as he held her tightly, paying no heed to her blood-covered hands or the blood dripping from his temple.

Out of the corner of her eye she could see Trista standing close by, staring down at her dead brother. There was no emotion on her face, no tears, no sadness. Lily wondered briefly what kind of loveless, miserable life she'd been subjected to, to not even mourn her own brother's passing. She also wondered if she had any hope of healing those wounds.

A yowl from Sir Kipling brought all their heads up just in time to see John Faust scramble to his feet—apparently not as unconscious as they had assumed—and stumble toward the back of the cavern where—no!

Slowly, carefully, silently, Morgan le Fay had crept to the far wall where the arch of dimmu runes was carved into the rock. There she had silently enchanted them to open a portal to only she knew where. Somehow she'd managed to signal to John Faust, who was even now scrambling toward it as fast as he could.

Lily pushed off Sebastian's chest, her weary legs stumbling toward them as her mouth opened, mind searching for any spell that might delay their inevitable departure. Or should she aim at the portal? Any spell's energy had a chance to disrupt the portal's magic, but if she timed it wrong and someone tried to go through right as the spell hit and the portal failed, they would be killed.

It was no use. Her mind was agonizingly sluggish, weighed down by intense fatigue. By the time she'd begun her spell, Morgan le Fay had already disappeared through the archway, and John Faust was at her heel.

Unwilling to risk killing her father, Lily let the spell die on her lips just as he dove head first through the portal. By the time she reached the far wall, the magic had dissipated, leaving only blank stone in its wake.

The sudden silence of the room roared in her ears, its stillness a stark contrast to the furious battle not minutes before. Stumbling to a standstill, she turned and leaned against the wall, intending to slide down it and rest her weary legs. But the sight of a tiny form on the cavern floor made her stiffen.

It was right where Morgan had fallen after being stunned.

"Nooo, Pip. Not you, too." The words dropped from her lips as quietly as the tears dripped from her cheeks, making dark splashes on the dusty floor.

Sinking to her knees and crawling over to the little pixie, Lily gently scooped the limp form up into her palm. Pip's glow had been extinguished, the green of magic that had been her life force snuffed out like a candle, leaving a tiny, frail creature with gossamer wings. Lily cradled the pixie against her cheek, rocking back and forth as crushing sorrow tore cruelly at her heart. The violence of it was unexpected. She had barely known Pip, yet the fae had stuck loyally by her, even died protecting her. Overcome by grief, she wept for the brave little pixie.

Somewhere in that storm of sadness, Lily felt a hand on her shoulder. She heard Sebastian's low, comforting voice, then felt him sit down beside her, pulling her close to lean against him. He rocked with her, sharing her grief as they both mourned their fallen friend.

Lily didn't weep just for Pip. She wept for the evil in the world. The hate. The misguided intentions and greed for power that led to good people dying for no reason.

"I—I—f—failed." Lily sobbed into Sebastian's shirt, overcome by despair. "Pip—is—d—dead, and C—Caden, too. And they g—got away."

He gripped her tighter, as if he could somehow squeeze away her pain. "Hush. Don't talk like that. You didn't fail. You stripped Morgan of a large part of her power. You convinced Trista to side with us. You've taken away all of John Faust's allies and he's on the run. We'll catch him. We'll catch them both. It's going to be alright."

"B—but Pip—"

"Don't think about it. Bad things happen. People..."

Sebastian paused, then took a shuddering breath, every word heavy with pain. "People die. You can't stop it. I promise, you'll drive yourself insane if you try to make sense of it. There is no…no *why*. It just happens. And the only way we can go on is to make sure they didn't die in vain."

Lily tried to nod, tears still streaming down her cheeks even though her shuddering sobs had subsided. There was a why, and she knew what it was. Its name was John Faust, and he had to be stopped. How long would she hold back and let her friends get hurt? That man had killed before and he would kill again. He deserved to die. He ought to die. But could she do it herself? Who else had to suffer before she was finally driven to kill her own father?

Those thoughts did nothing to calm her, so she tried to push them away. She would have to face them eventually, but not today.

"W—what are we going to do now?" Lily asked, trying to dry her eyes on her sleeve before realizing it was already soaked.

"I'm going to summon Thiriel. She owes us. Don't worry, we'll get everything straightened out. I promise."

Not having a shred of strength left in her to do anything but believe him, she believed him with all her heart. That belief gave her the strength to take his hand and haul herself to her feet. It gave her the strength to wrap Pip in a handkerchief and carefully stow her body away in a pocket of her backpack. It gave her the strength to help Trista move Caden's body out of the pool of blood and clean him off as best they could as Sir Kipling sat nearby, watching solemnly over the body. Her faithful cat, perhaps knowing that Sebastian was what she'd needed in her moment of grief, had remained to stand guard by Caden's body like a furred and four-footed honor guard until they came to collect him.

Lily was grateful, feeling that Caden shouldn't be left alone.

Cyril was busy rousing Hawkins, who seemed unhurt but for a massive headache. The manservant looked away sadly when he saw what had happened to Caden, but offered no apology. Lily supposed that, having done what he thought was right in a dangerous situation, Hawkins accepted the consequences of his actions and moved on. She wanted to be angry with him but knew she couldn't. Caden would have done his best to help John Faust kill them all if he hadn't been shot. He might have intercepted Lily before she got to Morgan, turning the tide of the battle against them. His youth was no excuse. So instead, Lily turned her anger toward her father, the man who had betrayed his son by teaching him lies and raising him as a tool of his own selfish quest for power.

As she and Trista finished tending to Caden's body, Lily wondered morbidly what they would do with it. They obviously couldn't take it back to Tintagel village and become embroiled in an international murder investigation. But before she could fret too much, Sebastian appeared at her side. He put a reassuring hand on her arm and spoke clearly, calling out Thiriel's name in the fae tongue.

Slowly, as if she were reluctant to come, the shadows coalesced into her tall, lithe form, white hair cascading down her shoulders in picture-perfect contrast to their disheveled states. She gazed about them, eyes taking in the new faces of Cyril and Trista, then lingering on the bloody pool on the floor. She sighed.

Thiriel took Lily and Sebastian, along with Sir Kipling, with her to the fae realm. She refused to admit the other three of their group, but Hawkins assured her they would be fine making their careful way up the cliff face and back to the hotel. They agreed to meet there once business in the fae realm was taken care of.

Journeying with Thiriel to Melthalin wasn't the long, tiring ordeal they'd experienced before. Apparently, being a high fae meant you had greater control over passage through the twilight. She simply gathered them to her—Lily and Sebastian carrying Caden's body between them—and warned them to stay close. Then the cavern walls faded. The cold blackness lasted only a moment before it was slowly replaced by open woodland, its every leaf glittering with frost as the landscape shone in the first light of dawn.

They buried Caden on a hill under a giant hemlock tree. Lily was saddened that they could not return his body to his mother, but it was out of the question. There was no way to convince the authorities they weren't to blame for his death.

There was no grave to dig. Thiriel simply commanded the earth to open. It shifted in waves, gently swallowing Caden's still-warm body until it was gone from sight. In some sort of cat token of respect, Sir Kipling carefully pressed a paw into the dirt over the grave, leaving a perfectly formed print to keep Caden company.

Lily watched dully as a few curious pixies emerged from the surrounding grass, inspecting the grave. They seemed to understand the gravity of the situation, though whether through some unspoken communication with Thiriel or just their own sensitivity to death, she had no idea. One of them flitted forward, dipping again and again to touch the freshly turned earth with her tiny feet. Wherever she touched, little white flowers emerged from the soil, growing at supernatural speed as they blossomed to make a white carpet over her brother's grave. Lily fought back tears as she silently thanked the little pixie for her gift.

Next, Thiriel took them to the outskirts of the court of Kaliar and Kaliel, the dualities of growth. It was a gigantic, fantastically monstrous tree, soaring hundreds of feet into the air, its trunk as thick as a house. With a jolt of understanding, Lily realized that this was the tree whose roots made up the roof of Thiriel's court below. At Sebastian's insistence, they did not enter it, rather waited as Thiriel went to find the high fae in whose charge Pip had been.

"Believe me, the fewer high fae who take notice of us, the better," Sebastian assured her. "They stay out of human affairs for a reason, and we should stay out of theirs."

"Though the occasion is rare, I must say in this instance that I agree with the man," Sir Kipling meowed, as if that settled it.

They spoke quietly while they waited, keeping an eye on the pixies and other small fae who crept out to inspect them, curious but wary. The sight of the pixies made Lily tear up again and, to distract herself, she asked Sebastian where Yuki had gone.

"He stayed to guard the entrance of the cave while we came to help you, though I'm sure he slunk away with his tail between his legs as soon as he got wind Thiriel was going to show up. She would be none too pleased to find him helping us, even if he didn't actually fight. He'll show back up eventually, once the coast is clear. I'm sure of it. He had too much fun teasing Kip to not be back."

Satisfied, Lily asked another question that had been bothering her. "If the fae aren't supposed to meddle in human affairs, why did Pip fight? Why didn't she just stay away like I told her to?"

Sebastian sighed. "The low fae aren't quite like the high fae in many respects. Less intellectual, more instinctual.

More like animals than they are like humans. They also aren't all that good at following certain rules. Whereas the high fae's very purpose is to maintain order, the low fae are a bit less stiff in that regard. They're usually up for anything, as long as…as long as it's fun and there's, um, something in it for them," he finished, glum.

"Oh," Lily said, watching sadly as two pixies chased each other around a tree branch.

Sir Kipling also eyed them, and Lily nudged him with her foot, giving him a warning glare when he looked up at her with an innocent expression.

"I didn't see Jas. Did he ever show up?"

Sebastian shook his head. "Low fae have personalities just like every other creature, and I've noticed it varies with their species. Pixies like Pip who look after the earth and plants tend to be more emotional, more affectionate. Jas is something of an elemental fae. I've not seen a speck of feeling from him beyond his love for mischief. He wasn't interested in helping us this time. Didn't think it would be any fun."

Lily nodded, not really caring but grateful for something to take her mind off her sorrow.

Thiriel finally returned, followed by a fair-skinned fae whose limbs resembled branches and whose hair was a mane of flowers intertwined with each golden thread. Thiriel introduced her as Shariel, one half of the duality of plants.

Once again fighting back tears, Lily gently removed the handkerchief-wrapped pixie from her backpack and handed the whole bundle to Shariel.

The beautiful fae's face showed no emotion, but she crooned a mournful, wordless melody as she carefully peeled back the white cloth to reveal the tiny form within. Handing the handkerchief back, Shariel bowed her head over her cupped hands and murmured words in the fae language, as if saying a prayer over Pip's body. When she raised her head and held out her hands to Sebastian, Lily gasped. Pip's body had been transformed into a wooden ring, intricately carved with minuscule flowers.

The high fae addressed Sebastian. "You who were her companion, take this. She would have wanted you to have it."

"But—but—is that, I mean…is that her?" Lily couldn't help asking as Sebastian reverently took the ring, sliding it onto his right hand so that it rested near his fae tattoo.

"No, child." Shariel's soft eyes, a curious shade of purple, fell on Lily. "Her essence has long since returned to the Source, and from it I will make her anew, for her responsibilities cannot go unattended."

Lily was about to open her mouth to ask another question when Sebastian coughed, an obvious warning that this was not the time for scholarly inquiry.

With a word of farewell to Thiriel, Shariel glided away back toward the majestic tree, and Thiriel turned toward them. "Come. Your task here is complete. It is time to return you to your own realm."

As before, the journey was short. They appeared on a lonely beach pounded by the Atlantic surf. The sun had just risen over the cliffs to the east and was now shimmering off the foaming waves as they beat upon the sand. At first Lily didn't know where they were, but then she recognized the rock formation in the distance as Tintagel Island.

Moving away from Thiriel, Lily looked back when Sebastian didn't follow. She saw Thiriel leaning in to whisper something in his ear. Sebastian nodded, face grim, then stepped away.

With the sun shining down upon them, the high fae didn't so much disappear in a swirl of darkness as she faded like a fog beneath the warm rays of the coming day.

Epilogue

T O LILY'S RELIEF, TRISTA WAS STILL AT THE HOTEL WHEN THEY FINALLY trudged through its doors forty minutes later. She'd half expected her sister to disappear with the dawn like Thiriel had.

Everyone took hot showers and cleaned up. Thiriel had been kind enough to touch them all with a bit of glamour, hiding their bloodied and disheveled states from the villagers and hotel staff, helpful since Lily was too tired and spent to cast any magic.

Lily had just finished her shower when she got the second good news that morning in the form of a call from her mother. If she hadn't already been sitting down when Freda gave her the update, she would have collapsed in relief. With George Dee's help, Allen had found a way to counteract the curse on Madam Barrington. It wasn't as good as unmaking the curse completely, but it was a step in the right direction. Hopefully, with intensive care and a little patience, her mentor should be well enough to go home in a few weeks.

With all the swiftness their weary bodies could muster, they packed their bags and returned to Oxford, dropping Cyril off at his office. As he said goodbye to Lily, he thanked her again for letting him accompany them on their grand adventure. "But," as he said with a sheepish grin, "next time you need something highly dangerous translated, perhaps you should head over to Cambridge. I'm sure they could help you there."

Lily smiled sadly at that. Cyril seemed to have learned

his lesson that adventure wasn't as glamorous as the stories made it seem, even if he now had fabulous material to write about in one of his papers—not that anyone would believe him. But turning her back on adventure for the comfort of an office chair wasn't a luxury Lily possessed. Even when she finally returned to the safety of her own office within McCain Library's quiet embrace, the adventure would follow her, whether she wanted it to or not.

They said their goodbyes to Oxford. Though they could have, in theory, stayed on another week, Lily decided its novelty had faded, or perhaps she was just weighed down by grief. Either way, it seemed much more grey than it had before, and they were all eager to return home. She would come back someday to plumb the depths of its glorious libraries. Someday, but not then.

Hawkins drove them to Aylesbury to stay at Highthorne manor for the night. Elizabeth welcomed them with warmth and sympathy, tending to their wounds—the visible ones, at least—and laundering all their filthy clothes. Curiously, Lily's outfit barely needed a wash, despite the fact that she'd literally knelt in her brother's blood. Elizabeth didn't comment, however, so neither did Lily, simply grateful that, at the very least, she hadn't ruined a good set of clothes.

Elizabeth also didn't comment on how often she seemed to walk in on Lily and Sebastian holding hands. The first time it happened, Lily let go with a guilty look, remembering the old woman's words about Sebastian. But, far from seeming displeased, the lady simply smiled a knowing smile and gave Lily an approving wink. After that, Lily stopped worrying and simply enjoyed Sebastian's comforting presence.

Trista remained quiet throughout. She accepted Elizabeth's

hospitality with polite silence, doing what she was told but isolating herself from everyone as often as possible. Lily worried about her, knowing she should be trying to reach out, establish some sort of relationship. But every time she looked at her sister, she thought of Caden's bloody body and blank, staring eyes.

Hawkins drove them to the airport the next day, and they said their goodbyes. Sebastian clasped his forearm warmly, and Lily, feeling daring, leaned in to give him a brief but grateful hug. She would miss the steadfast manservant, especially so after thinking she'd lost him. In the quiet of Highthorne manor, she'd finally gotten around to asking him what had happened when Thiriel made him disappear. All he could say was that he had been surrounded by blackness for a second, then found himself back at the top of the cliff. He'd caught up with Sebastian and Cyril, and the rest she knew. Lily wasn't quite sure what to think of Thiriel after hearing his story. She wanted to dislike the fae queen but was hard put to do so after the help she'd given them. If her demeanor seemed aloof, that wasn't her fault. She was a high fae, after all.

They had a safe, if exhausting, trip back to Savannah, Trista in tow. Much to everyone's relief, she had a passport and it survived customs' scrutiny, though Lily knew it had to have been forged, either by John Faust's hand or at his order.

Sir Kipling endured his time of imprisonment in the cat carrier with uncharacteristic grace. Lily was quite proud of him until she overheard two little old ladies who'd sat at the very back of the plane talking about how nice the amenities of air travel were these days: They even provided a cat to keep your lap warm during the long flight!

Despite her cat's in-flight shenanigans, they arrived

safely at Allen's house all in one piece. They learned, upon arriving, that they'd just missed George Dee. He had left that very morning to return to his estates in England.

Her uncle's eyes nearly bugged out of his head when he laid eyes on Trista at his doorstep. Lily overrode his sputtered protest, saying that Trista was on their side now and wouldn't cause any trouble, even if she had helped kidnap him barely weeks ago. Despite her assurances, Allen must have sicced some of his hand constructs on her as a precaution, because a handful of them floated after her wherever she went. She reacted to it the same way she reacted to everything: with emotionless silence. Lily thought for sure she would open up once Freda had a crack at her, but her mother came away shaking her head sadly.

They decided to leave her alone for the time being and give her space, instead debating late into the night whether they should try to contact her biological mother, and where she was going to live once Madam Barrington had recovered.

On that front, at least, things were going well. So well, in fact, that after just a week—about the time Lily was due to return to work at McCain Library—Allen declared Madam Barrington strong enough to go home. While she tired easily and needed a cane to get around, the austere woman looked like a new person compared to her grey-skinned, near-death self a mere two weeks ago. She insisted, quite vigorously, on a full report of *everything* that had happened. Lily and Sebastian gave it together, filling in each other's accounts and staying as calm as possible even through the end. Lily might have leaked a tear or two, and possibly sought out Sebastian's hand underneath the table, twining her fingers between his. But other than that, she was very calm.

They decided, for now, that things needed to go back to normal. Despite John Faust and Morgan's escape, the two had done so with nothing but the clothes on their backs. There had been no artifacts or powerful spells hidden away in Morgan's tomb for John Faust to appropriate, and Morgan le Fay was once more a mere wizard. Personally, Lily didn't find that very comforting. She knew she had only barely bested the ancient wizard. Morgan had been weak and disoriented from her long entombment and, in the end, it was only Pip's distraction that had enabled Lily's final spell to do its work.

Knowing both wizards would be stewing with implacable hatred and who knew what nefarious plans, Madam Barrington assured Lily she would reach out to her contacts far and wide, with George Dee to help on the English front, trying to get a hint of their whereabouts. But until there was word, it was best if everyone went back home to their jobs and lives, to recover and prepare for whatever lay ahead.

Freda would go back to the family farm in Alabama, though she threatened to bring Jamie to Atlanta to see Lily and Madam Barrington on a regular basis. It was decided that, for now, Trista could live in the spare bedroom at Madam Barrington's house. The quiet and solitude would suit her, much more, anyway, than the chaos of the Singer farmhouse.

The night before they planned to drive back to Atlanta, they had a meal together in Allen's kitchen, prepared and served by his "helping" hands. The floating constructs seemed decidedly chipper with so many people in the house to care for. Instead of hovering in a sullen flock above Allen's head, they flitted back and forth through the house, cleaning, seeing to people's needs, and giving Sir Kipling plenty of exercise as he followed them through the halls, waiting for his chance to strike. Of course, that wasn't his only exercise. He and Egbert—Allen's crab-like construct—seemed to have settled into a nice routine, chasing each other back and forth down the halls. That was, until Allen nearly tripped over their scrambling forms and yelled at them to cease their childish antics. After that—and a sufficiently long period of sulking—they confined their games of tag to the third floor, where no one ventured except Allen, and he, only when it was time for bed.

With Egbert banned from the kitchen, Sir Kipling managed not to cause a scene during the meal, content with his bowl of milk and salmon that Allen had given him—over Lily's protests. The six of them, four wizards and two mundanes, one of them being a witch, enjoyed good southern food and amiable conversation. Well, five of them talked and Trista listened. She gave one-word answers to any questions directed at her, but other than that offered no conversation. She excused herself early and left the rest of them enjoying dessert while she retired to her room.

Later that night, when everyone was going to bed, Lily knocked on her sister's door, needing to relay a question from Madam Barrington. There was no answer, and at first Lily assumed Trista was asleep. But then she noticed light coming from under the door, so she tried the knob and found it unlocked.

Opening it a crack, she called softly, asking to enter, but there was no answer. Sticking her head in, she looked about the room. It was empty. Apprehension growing in her stomach, Lily entered, checking behind doors and in the attached bath. No one. All of Trista's things were missing, too.

Lily finally found the note on the dresser, addressed to her.

Dear Lily,
Thanks for taking me in, but I don't belong here.
Don't try and find me. I'll find you, when it's time.

Your sister,
Trista

Sebastian found her sitting on Trista's bed some ten minutes later.

"What's up?" he asked, eyeing the note and looking around the room for Trista.

Lily shook her head. "She's gone."

"What? Where? We need to find her!"

"No." Lily caught his hand, stopping him from exiting the room. "Let her be. She's an adult and needs to make her own way. She knows where to find us if she needs help."

Sebastian sat down beside her with a grunt and a sigh. "I suppose you're right. Still, it doesn't feel…well, safe."

"Safe for you or safe for her?" Lily grinned. "You know she did kick your butt. Twice, if I recall."

"Yeah, yeah. Whatever."

They sat in silence for a while as Lily considered the past and the future, not something she enjoyed doing these days.

"Sebastian?" she asked quietly.

"Mmm?"

"Shariel said she would remake Pip from the Source. Does that mean we're going to see her again someday?"

Sebastian heaved a long, slow sigh, fingering his wooden ring. "Not really, no. We might see the same pixie taking care of the same plot of dirt that Pip did, but it won't be Pip, not really. She'll seem the same: same name, same look, possibly even the same personality. But she won't remember us. Not a thing."

Lily felt a tear threaten to drip from her eyelid onto her

cheek, but swiped it away, determined to honor Pip's memory, not wallow in self-pity. "But...we can make new memories with her...can't we?"

"That we can," Sebastian agreed, face breaking into a tentative smile.

Lily's expression turned thoughtful. "I wonder if the new Pip will like the same mixed drinks," she mused.

"Now that, I can't tell you," Sebastian shrugged. "Some things must remain a mystery."

Silence descended again, and Lily could barely hear Allen's reedy voice down on the first floor, complaining about something his constructs had done. Again.

"Speaking of new memories..." Sebastian began, but then trailed off.

Lily looked at him, lifting an eyebrow. "Yes?"

"Um...well...would you like to, um, maybe... getacupofcoffeesometime?" he finished in a rush.

Lily shrugged. "Sure, I guess. But I thought you didn't like coffee?"

"No, that's not, uh, not quite what I, uh, meant." Sebastian gave a frustrated sigh. "I meant, would you like to get a *cup—of—coffee* sometime...with me." This time, he said it slowly, wiggling his eyebrows in a half silly, half suggestive manner.

Realization slowly dawned on Lily, and she felt her face grow hot, though it was nothing to the blaze that blossomed inside her. Her heart beat a traitorous tattoo against her ribs, seeming as loud as thunder in the silence.

"Sebastian...did you just ask me out on a date?" she asked slowly, trying—and failing—to contain her mile-wide grin.

"Um...well..." He rubbed the back of his neck, seeming conflicted, then finally laughed. "Yeah, I guess I did."

Lily rolled her eyes.

"What? Is that bad?" he asked, face falling.

"No! I just thought you'd never ask."

Silence.

"Um, okay. Well…I did."

She gave him a puzzled look.

"Are you going to answer me? You know…yes or no?"

"Oh!" Lily exclaimed, blushing furiously. "Sorry."

She was momentarily distracted by the sight of Sir Kipling sitting in the doorway, looking so disgustingly smug she was surprised there weren't canary feathers sticking to his chin. Lily shot him a glare, for formality's sake.

Turning back to Sebastian, who was waiting in tortured anticipation, she smiled.

"Yes."

GLOSSARY

aluminum - a metal favored by wizards for its usefulness in absorbing large amounts of magic because of its high energy density potential. Safer and more stable than lithium, it is widely used in crafting spell anchors (see dimmu runes) either as a raw material or an inlay. While spells can be cast onto any substance but wrought iron, aluminum better absorbs the magic fueling the spell, thus making the spell more potent and long-lasting (as long as it is cast in conjunction with the proper dimmu runes and sealing spells).

angel - one of the three species of magic users (human, fae, and angel/demon). Spoken of in myth and lore, their origin, powers, and purpose are largely unknown to modern wizards. It is said that they are the stewards of heaven and the most powerful of the three species.

aspect - every fae belongs to an aspect. As the guardians and caretakers of the earth, they don't just live in harmony with nature, they *are* nature. Every fae has its own aspect, the thing from which it draws its power and the thing which it is responsible for tending.

Basement, the - the magical archive beneath the McCain Library containing a private collection of occult books on magic, wizardry, and arcane science, as well as an assortment of artifacts and enchanted items. Created in 1936 during the library's original construction, it is accessed through a secret portal in the broom closet of the library's own basement archive. At any point in time, the Basement has a gatekeeper, the wizard tasked with its maintenance and protection and upon whom rests the control of its magic. This collection of knowledge was bequeathed as a public resource to wizardkind, but, because of the decline of wizards in modern society, has been very little used by anyone but its gatekeeper. Lily Singer is the current gatekeeper, with Madam Barrington as her predecessor.

battle magic - a dangerous form of quick casting requiring an intuitive mastery of Enkinim along with an adroit enough mind to shape magic on the go. To battle cast one must react largely on instinct. Without as much time to carefully control and constrain the magic used, there is much higher risk of accidents or backfires.

construct - a crafted being, usually built in the likeness of a man or animal, enchanted with abilities. Though complex to make, they can be crafted out of almost any material. While they can be built to act and respond in a very lifelike fashion based on the parameters of their controlling spells, they are not alive in the biological sense and can't be killed. Their magic must be broken or altered for them to stop working. Used for everything from manual labor to mobile wards, messengers, guardians, and spies, they can be created to respond only to certain people, commands, or circumstances.

crafting - the art of creating and enchanting objects. Such objects, once made, can exist and operate separate from their creator or even magic in general, as the controlling spells are anchored to dimmu runes carved, inlaid, or otherwise affixed to them. To craft properly, you must not only know the properties of your materials, but also the dimmu runes needed to attain the desired result.

demon - greater - a fallen angel. They are those who rebelled and were cast down from heaven, their magic corrupted. Each has their own unique name by which they can be commanded, if one is brave enough to speak it and powerful enough to master its owner. They are creatures of great power, hate, and thirst for destruction.

demon - lesser - corrupted fae. Demons can not create, only destroy. Therefore, to acquire underlings, greater demons can perform a ritual to force a part of themselves into a minor fae, something small and weak like a water sprite, to take over its immortal body and turn it into a corrupted, ugly, twisted mockery of its former self. This corruption can not be undone. The lesser demon becomes a slave to its master and can not disobey. This is why the fae hate demons so much, and why fae magic is particularly useful in opposing demons.

dimmu - [dim + mu = {dim = to make, fashion, create, build (du = to build, make + im = clay, mud)} + {mu = word, name, line on a tablet}] the Enkinim word for runes of power, the script used to write Enkinim, the language of power. In and of itself, this script is not magical, and a mundane could write it all day without achieving anything. Dimmu runes are used by wizards to anchor their spells. Infused with magic from the Source, these runes enable and guide the carrying out of the desired enchantment and can preserve the enchantment's effect long after the spell is cast.

duality - fae hierarchy is based on aspects, and each aspect has its duality, the pair of opposite, yet complementary, beings that represent it and rule those who belong to it. Ex: Thiriar and Thiriel are the dualities of the aspect of decay.

ebony staff - a fae staff made of twisting ebony wood belonging to Sebastian Blackwell, a gift from Thiriel, the fae queen of decay. It originally belonged to Thiriar, Thiriel's duality and the fae king of decay. Named Tahir in the fae tongue. With the abilities he was given, Sebastian can summon it from the fae realm at will, but as soon as he releases it, it disappears back from whence it came.

eduba - [e + dub + a = {e = house, temple, plot of land} + {dub = clay (tablet), document} + {a = genitive marker}] the Enkinim word for library, used by ancient Sumerians to indicate the houses where their clay writing tablets were kept. To a wizard, however, it describes a book containing their personal archive of knowledge. Similar to the mundane notion of grimoires, edubas are full of much more than simply spells. They accumulate centuries of history, research, and personal notes as they are passed down, usually from parent to child or teacher to student within powerful wizard families. The knowledge in them is magically archived, such that you must summon the desired text to the physical pages before it can be read. This allows for vast stores of information to be carried around in one physical book.

elwa - fae word of greeting. It carries deeper meaning, however, than a simple hello. It is a request to commune with or share the presence of the named fae. The request may be denied or ignored, in which case the supplicant must withdraw. It is considered extremely rude to ask a second time.

Enkinim - [Enki + inim = {Enki = Sumerian god of creation and friend of mankind} + {inim = word; statement; command, order, decree}] words of power, the language of magic by which wizards control and direct the Source. Named after the Sumerian god Enki, who, it was said, taught mankind language, reading, and writing.

fae - one of the three species of magic users (human, fae, and angel/demon). Myth says they were created to help steward the earth, and that long ago they worked side by side with man to nurture it. But they have long since disappeared from sight and memory of mundanes and are now the subject of fairy tales. Wizards know of their existence and have some lore pertaining to their habits and home in the fae realm, but most of it is theory and conjecture.

fae glamour - a type of fae magic by which fae disguise their true shape. They also use it to create illusions or temporarily change the appearance of inanimate objects. While wizards can cast their own type of glamour to achieve a similar effect, their scrying spells can not see through fae glamour. It can be defeated using a seeing stone, something only fae can make. A fae can see through another fae's glamour.

familiar - a companion creature, being, or entity of some sort. Used in different contexts for witches and wizards. A witch familiar is usually some kind of spirit or creature with which they've made a bargain and formed a partnership. Some such beings can take the form of animals to avoid detection, thus the stereotype of witches having black cats. These dealings can be dangerous, however, and often lead to the practitioner changing, knowingly or not, by simple association. "Something given, something gained" is the witch's way. Most wizard familiars, on the other hand, are nothing more than loyal pets wearing enchanted collars. In rare cases, however, a skilled wizard could create their own familiar by crafting a mechanical body and enchanting it with abilities. These construct familiars were used for everything from manual labor to acting as mobile wards, messengers, protectors, spies, and more.

human - one of the three species of magic users (human, fae, and angel/demon), and the only one of the three with a direct connection to the Source. Whereas fae and angels/demons were created with a set amount of magical power proportional to their status, humans have no innate limit. They are limited only by their own will, discipline, and skill, as well as the frailty of their mortal bodies. Also, not all humans can use magic. While all fae and angels/demons are innately magical, only certain humans descended from the wizard lines manifest the ability to access the Source and manipulate magic. It is thought the difference is genetic and inherited, but no one yet knows how or why.

initiate - a term traditionally used to indicate a member of a wizard family who is not a wizard. Because not all children born to wizards or wizard-mundane couples could use magic—yet were still raised within the magical community with knowledge of its secrets—

there arose the need for a distinguishing word for someone not magical, yet not ignorant like a mundane. Because these mundane children of wizards often became the butlers, valets, housekeepers, etc., of wizards, the term initiate has come to mean someone who works for a wizard family, caring for them and keeping their secrets. It is an old-fashioned term, generally used by the very traditional. Most modern wizards simply call all non-magic humans mundanes, whether they know about magic or not. With the decline of wizard families and magic use in general, along with society's general acceptance of, rather than fear of, magic, the existence of initiates in the traditional sense has all but disappeared.

iron: salts - the common name for ferrous sulfate, a range of salts with high iron content used in various industries as well as a health supplement to treat iron deficiency. It has also long been used by wizards as a natural remedy for certain magical maladies, such as magic poisoning. If a wizard is not trained to properly control, channel, and withdraw from the Source when magic is not in use, the body can become overstressed and, in extreme cases, become catatonic. Also useful to counteracting certain magic-based poisons and potions.

iron: wrought - a metal which repels magic. Spells cannot be anchored to it, affect it, or pass through it, and it dulls the effectiveness of any magic in its vicinity. Because fae and angels/demons are beings of pure magic, it is poisonous to them. It will burn them on contact, its presence weakens them, and it will kill them if ingested in large quantities. A wizard wearing iron or standing near iron will be hampered or completely prevented from casting, depending on their strength and skill. Iron does not, however, hurt wizards in any way beyond a slight weakening effect that is a result of blocking their access to the Source. Only wrought iron has this ability. Other mixtures of iron alloy such as steel have little or no effect.

lugal-nam - [lugal + nam = {lugal = king; master (lu = man + gal = big)} + {nam = planning ability; destiny}] literally translated *master of destiny*, it is the name given to a device created long ago by powerful wizards that can loop time by creating alternate timelines that repeat until the magic ends, at which point they rejoin "real" time. Made of clay and about six inches long by an inch and a half wide, it looks like a cylinder made up of rotating dials.

McCain Library - the library of Agnes Scott College, a private liberal arts women's college near downtown Atlanta. Built in 1936 to replace the smaller Andrew Carnegie Library constructed in 1910, it was originally still called the Carnegie Library, then later renamed the McCain Library after the college's second president in 1951. Complete with four main floors, a grand reading room, and three attached floors dedicated to the stacks, this building is Lily Singer's workplace and domain. She is the college's Archives Manager, and her office is located on the library's main floor. The basement floor contains the library's archives as well as the portal to the secret magical archive of which Lily is the gatekeeper.

Melthalin - name of the fae realm in the fae tongue. Translated literally, it means "place of refuge."

mundane - a term used by wizards to denote non-magical humans. Generally, mundanes are ignorant of the existence of magic, the notable exception being witches. Other enlightened mundanes include members of wizard families who were born without the ability to use magic. These non-magical members of the wizard community were traditionally known as initiates. Historically, the term mundane was derogatory and insulting. Accusing a wizard or initiate of being "mundane" was paramount to calling them ignorant fools. The wizard community looked down on mundanes and considered them little more than animals. The fact that mundanes regularly executed anyone they suspected of using magic helped to solidify wizards' negative attitude toward them. That attitude has largely disappeared with the advance of society, though there still exists a lingering feeling of superiority among wizards.

Oculus - Meaning eye or sight in Latin, this is the name of John Faust LeFay's construct familiar crafted in the form of a raven.

Pilanti'ara - a plant fae befriended by Sebastian Blackwell, who calls her Pip. The *'ara* of the name denotes feminine character. As a plant fae, Pip has a certain area she is responsible for. Within that area she cares for all growing things. Like most pixies, she has a weakness for alcohol, which Sebastian often trades her for various services.

pixie - any fae that are small, quick, and flighty. This is purely a human term and has no relation to actual fae taxonomy (naming and classification). However, it is true that most pixies are energetic, fun-loving, and have a weakness for alcohol, which they can metabolize in vast amounts compared to their body mass without getting drunk. Of all the fae, they are the ones most familiar to, and seen by, humans because of their curiosity and lack of fear.

power anchor - a crafted object—usually something small and wearable like an amulet, necklace, or ring—that wizards use to focus and amplify their magic so as to cast more precise and powerful spells. For particularly powerful spells, wizards can create a one-time-use, secondary power anchor which they might draw or carve on the floor to further channel their magic.

runes of power - also known as dimmu runes, these are the symbols used to write Enkinim, the language of power that shapes magic. They are similar in appearance to the cuneiform script used in Mesopotamia during ancient times.

seeing stone - traditionally a triangular stone with a hole through it, though the stone can be any shape and still work. In ancient times these stones were made by the fae and given to certain humans so they could look through the hole and see past fae glamour. Few were preserved and passed down and so are rare today, for the fae have long since withdrawn from contact with humankind and give no more such gifts as they did in times past.

Source, the - the place from which all magic comes. While many creatures and parts of nature are innately magical, filled with the Source's power, wizards are the only beings in the universe born with an innate connection to it and the ability to draw on it at will. The Source is not sentient, only raw power. Magic drawn from the Source has to be shaped and directed by the caster's will using words of power (Enkinim). Incorrect use of Enkinim or poor control over a spell can cause backfires or spell mutations, resulting in a different outcome than intended and sometimes causing the injury or death of the caster. Though many known, reliable spells exist, the power of the Source is, in theory, limited only by the willpower and knowledge of the caster. Though safe to use within limits and with the proper training, many wizards over the years have died from overestimating their own strength or attempting dangerous spells which they did not properly understand. Thus, use of magic by modern wizards is in decline. With the rise of mundane technology, many wizards feel magic use is not worth the trouble or cost.

spell circle - a simple line or mark on the ground providing a visual aid and anchor to the casting of any sort of circle, such as a shield circle or circle of containment. Spell circles can be permanently engraved or carved into a surface accompanied by dimmu runes that add to the stability and effectiveness of whatever casting is being done.

spell: curse - a category of complicated and dangerous spells that are always meant to harm. Curses require an immense amount of magic to cast, but once the initial spell is completed, they are able to self-sustain by virtue of their complex if-then structure. Because of their strength, they are very difficult to break. Either their effect must be counteracted, or they must be unmade by knowing the exact parameters of the if-then structure. The most effective defense when it comes to curses is to not be cursed in the first place.

spell: portal - a risky yet useful means of transportation not completely understood by wizards, but which is assumed to take advantage of whatever space other magical creatures travel through to and from the human realm (such as fae and demons). The origin of the spell is unknown, but its specific formula has been preserved. Historically, any experimentation with or deviation from the formula has resulted in permanent disappearance. At its most basic, portal spells connect two specific, geographical locations. Because the space between realms is outside the dimensions of time and space, travel is instantaneous. A portal cannot be cast without knowledge of the exact location of its counterpart.

spell of: compulsion - used to control another human. Only works with the initial willingness of the subject, usually gained through subtle suggestion or trickery. Once the subject has been compelled for the first time, however, they are particularly susceptible to it again even if they try to resist. Traditionally a type of magic used only on mundanes, as it is social suicide to compel another wizard. If discovered, the offending wizard will be ostracized and mistrusted by his community.

spell of: containment - a kind of spell circle used to contain magic. It is usually cast as a safety measure when doing spell work.

spell of: conveyance - a type of spell that can transmit sensory input, whether audio, visual, or tactile, from one item to another, even over great distances. Variations of this spell class can be used for many things, even a wizard version of the mundane cell phone.

spell of: invisibility/cloaking - a type of glamour spell that helps conceal the subject from sight. Not true invisibility as mundanes understand it, but rather a spell that mimics the surroundings. When perfectly still, a wizard can be nearly invisible; while moving, a visible outline can be detected with careful observation.

spell of: shielding - a kind of spell used to shield the caster from magic. One type—a barrier through which magic cannot enter—is often cast as a spell circle. Another type—a selective spell that blocks only incoming active or targeted magic—is commonly used in personal wards.

Thiriel - the fae who gave Sebastian Blackwell his ebony staff.

truth coin - a silver coin given to Sebastian Blackwell by his father. It is inscribed with dimmu runes and enchanted to grow warm in the presence of lies. The degree of warmth is directly proportional to the degree of the lie.

twilight, the - the space between the fae and human realms, existing outside normal time and space. Known only to the few wizards who have been friends of the fae over the years. Only fae can enter, navigate, and exit it safely, though they can bring other beings with them without harm.

ward - magical protection of some kind, usually cast into an anchor such as a bracelet (personal ward) or into runes set in/around a location (stationary ward). Ward spells can be customized to do a variety of things. Personal wards usually contain a combination of a shield spell along with various minor spells that help protect the bearer from weariness, sickness, or other physical harm. Stationary wards put up around a house or created to protect a certain location or object, can be set to protect against specific things (just wizards, or alternately, just mundanes, for example). They can also be customized to prevent the passage of physical objects, sound, light, etc.

witch - a mundane who, through trades, favors, and alliances with other beings, gains magical power or the service of said beings. "Something given, something gained," is the way of a witch. While uncommon, the other two magical species (fae and angels/demons) have been known to form alliances with humans, mundane and wizard alike. Besides directly gaining other beings' magic, witches also often trade for the services of various supernatural beings. Many witches favor demonic pacts, as demons are the most eager for contact with humans. Such pacts, however, usually end badly for the witch, or else the witch is irrevocably changed, sometimes tricked or forced into subjugation to whatever demon they were trying to control. Spirits in their various forms are one of the other more common partners of witches. But since they are incorporeal and have no need for physical things, they can be hard to bargain with and, by nature, are unstable. Fae, while shy of humans and largely unknown to them, do occasionally form pacts. Historically, witches who allied with the fae were known as druids, but the term has largely fallen out of use because they are now so rare.

wizard - a human with the ability to access the Source and manipulate its power. The ability is thought to be genetic, as it seems to be passed from parent to child. Legend says magic was given to Gilgamesh and so only his descendants inherited it. Like most inherited genes, it can be diluted by mixing with normal human genes. So a wizard marrying a mundane is less likely to produce wizard children than a wizard-wizard union, though even those are not guaranteed to have all wizard children. A wizard's abilities are not instinctive, they are a skill that must be taught and mastered to use effectively.

words of power - the language (Enkinim) used by wizards to control their magical power. Passed down over the centuries, these words help shape and direct a wizard's spells, both activating and limiting their effects. Though many set spells exist, new ones can be discovered and old ones customized. The stronger a wizard's will, the more adroit their mind, and the better their understanding of Enkinim, the more they can do with magic. Magical experimentation can, however, be extremely dangerous.

Thanks so much for picking up this book and joining Lily, Sebastian, and Sir Kipling in their adventures. We hope they brought you laughter and maybe a tear or two. If you enjoyed the story and want to see more published please take a moment to leave an honest review. Book reviews help authors write better and sell more books and are a great way to show your support. Thank you!

If you'd like to stay up to date with Lydia's newest publications, sign up for her newsletter at lydiasherrer.com/subscribe. This is where you can get behind-the-scene sneak peeks, freebies, book giveaways, and chances to get involved in the story-making process.

You can also connect with Lydia online!

Read all about Lydia and her books: lydiasherrer.com/about

Like her page: facebook.com/lydiasherrerauthor

Follow her on Twitter: @LydiaSherrer
twitter.com/lydiasherrer

Follow her on Instagram: lydiasherrer
instagram.com/lydiasherrer

Listen to her ocarina music: youtube.com/c/lydiasherrer

About the Author

Award-winning and USA Today-bestselling author of snark-filled fantasy, Lydia Sherrer thrives on creating characters and worlds you love to love, and hate to leave. She subsists on liberal amounts of dark chocolate and tea, and hates sleep because it keeps her from writing. Due to the tireless efforts of her fire-spinning gamer husband and her two overlords, er cats, she remains sane and even occasionally remembers to leave the house. Though she graduated with a dual BA in Chinese and Arabic, after traveling the world she came home to Louisville, KY and decided to stay there.

Made in the USA
Columbia, SC
24 January 2019